anniversary (6th August) of its creation. The single pine was still on the hilltop at one end of ranks of carefully-tended graves. Mainly Australians were buried here as a result of the Anzac's heroic but costly seizure of the ridge. Of the nine Victoria Crosses awarded on the Peninsula during August, seven were won that afternoon on this spot. I walked along reading ages that made me feel old; 18, 21, 26, 20, 22, 20 . . . The names of familiar Australian towns transported my mind back to that country, to a hill in the south-west near Albany, to the ANZAC memorial overlooking the bay from which the troop ships sailed to take these young men to the battlefields of Europe. That hill I was remembering had once been in the minds of those that lay beneath my feet as their last view of their homeland. My journey around the world was not so disjointed. There were many links and one of them ran from that hill in SW Australia to this almost identical hill on a remote peninsula in Turkey. No logic, nothing but the whims of fashion.

'Their name liveth for evermore,' read the stones, 'Their glory shall not be blotted out . . . Lord thou knowest best . . . To the memory of my dear husband . . . Reached the fartherest objective till the dawn break, and shadows flee . . . He died for God, Right and Liberty, and such a death is immortality . . . Could I just clasp your hand once more and say, Well Done . . . He has changed his faded coat of brown for one of glorious white . . . A mother's thoughts often wander to this sad and lonely grave . . .' The sentiments vacillated from the emotional to the virtuous, expressions of grief and shreds of comfort to take the place of reason. 565,000 dead sons. How many must mourn 565,000?

Five weeks later I visited the battlefield of the Somme, my last stop before returning to Britain. Its graveyards intensified the emotions I had felt at Gallipoli. 1,200,000 lives were taken here during four months of 1916, half of them Allied soldiers who died for a gain of a thousand yards of mud. 19,240 died on the very first day and the majority in the first hour. The scale of death was meaningless until it became tangible, beautifully landscaped into gardens and symmetrical patterns which occupied great tracts of French farmland.

In a Newfoundlanders' cemetery at Beaumont-Hamel, beneath the bronze statue of a caribou with its head thrown back in full bellow, I met a fifty-year-old Canadian who was working with the

NATO forces in Germany. We looked out at the trenches and bomb craters which were now covered in grass and neatly mown. Rain added a fitting sense of gloom to the scene.

'The worst is that we haven't learnt anything from it,' I commented.

'No,' he answered. 'We should have listened to General Paton at the end of the last war. He said then that seeing as all our army and war machinery were over here, we ought to just carry on and finish off the Communists.'

'Do you honestly believe another twenty million dead Russians would have solved today's problems?' His answer angered and depressed me. 'That's exactly the bigoted attitude that caused all this. Why must everyone always think "fight" and "kill" instead of looking for ways of trying to work together?'

He called me a dreamer, an idealist. We argued for some time until eventually I turned and walked away while he was expounding on the *Soviet Threat*. Employees of the war business always stressed it big. I had no will to fight.

My generation had never known war. We had never experienced its power to unite towards a common goal nor its camaraderie, but we had been spared its destruction and horrors. There had to be a turning point, when the world actively worked towards the ideal of peace rather than hoping to achieve it by threatening war.

Yes, I was a dreamer. It was a modest dream . . . that all the world's leaders might be brought here once every year – for our memories are short – to wander alone through the Somme. They would see tens of thousands of white crosses and roses that bloom red and sway in the breeze, knocking against the inscriptions 'A Soldier of the Great War' and at the bottom, 'Known unto God'. Perhaps they would be able to feel the solitude, the sadness, the folly. Perhaps in this panorama of white tombstones a united sense of responsibility would emerge.

Concluding his *History of the Great War*, John Buchan wrote (in 1921–2),

Again, the ground had been cleared for a better ordering of the world, much of the débris of past ages was now estimated at its true worthlessness, ancient inequitable frontiers could be adjusted, old wrongs could be righted. Again, the magnitude and the horrors of the contest had gone far to sicken mankind of strife

and predispose them to find a more rational way of settling differences. Already the conception of a true internationalism was dawning which should add to the patriotism of races and nations a patriotism of humanity.

I left Beaumont-Hamel and carried my dream northwards. The cemeteries of the Somme seemed to go on forever, stretching insignificantly towards the patriotism of humanity.

17 · Under the Holy Shadow of Mount Athos

The Khalkidhiki Peninsula juts out from the north-east coast of Greece like a three-clawed footprint. At the point of the right-hand claw is Mount Athos, a sharp 6670-foot-high peak which gives its name to a state that is unique in the world. It is an autonomous monastic state, independent from the Greek government, with dimensions twenty-five miles long and five to seven miles wide that are occupied largely by a steep range of hills. This leaves little level ground for its one village situated in the centre, its hundreds of cells and hermitages scattered throughout, and its twenty gigantic monasteries which, for the most part, hold their irreplaceable Byzantine treasures close to the sea. Mount Athos is a restricted area. Its land border is closed to traffic, no woman or female animal is allowed to enter the community and access for male visitors is strictly controlled by a limited number of permits. In order to acquire one of these permits I became the personal message-bearer of the British Consulate. It was a distinction that cost me 840 drachmas (£6).

ΖΑΧΑΡΟΠΛΑΣΤΕΙΟΝ ΛΟΚΜΑΔΕΣ

Shortly after entering the country I stared at this sign and admired the magnificent Greek alphabet. A smaller sign beneath it said 'Do'nuts for sale'. Everything looks much more important in Greek and judging from their love of words ten feet long, the Greeks know it. I travelled from Konstantinoupoli to Alexandroupoli, Eleftheroupoli and Thessaloniki, and bought two extra biros for writing my diary. My application for a permit to visit Mount Athos had to be accompanied by a letter of recommendation from the British Consulate. One morning I was waiting outside the Consul's door when he arrived for work. He ushered me into his office for a short interview.

'Of course Mount Athos is not a place for tourists . . .' he began.

'I don't consider myself a tourist, sir.'

This was the right answer. Without delving any deeper into my character he signed a form and passed it to his secretary. She typed

out the date and four words from my passport on a machine that needed a new ribbon. I felt they could have afforded one out of the fee, but I was delighted to have the bit of paper. It was nothing special, not even headed paper but a skeleton photocopy of diplomatic claptrap with my details filling the blanks, and only distinguished by a rubber stamp:

The British Consulate present their compliments to the Ministry of Northern Greece and have the honour to request them to be so good as to grant a permit to visit Mount Athos to the undermentioned British subject. The British Consulate avail themselves of this opportunity to renew to the Ministry of Northern Greece the assurance of their highest consideration.

Written in Greek, the message would have looked devastating.

Clutching this bit of paper I went to the office of the Ministry to pass on the request and renew the Consulate's assurances. The Ministry took the news calmly and one of its officials explained that all permits were booked for the next week. A permit was valid for a five-day visit and only ten such permits were issued each day. I booked the first available place, paid another fee and took the permit to a police station to be stamped. All that remained was to be at the small harbour town of Ouranoupoli, just under 100 miles away, in time for the morning ferry to Mount Athos on the day my permit specified.

Before leaving Thessaloniki (Salonika) I sent a message home asking for my kilt and sporran to be sent out to me. They had travelled with me, around me, for most of the miles between Iceland and Australia and it seemed fitting that we should end the journey together. The impulse to dash for home was growing ever stronger and there were times when it seemed I could smell the damp heather of the Highlands (I had been away too long and hackneyed images were all that were left, but they held an irresistible attraction all the same). I had decided not to rush Greece but once in Italy to cover the remaining distance to Britain without delay.

The Khalkidhiki footprint was a dry mountainous peninsula where tobacco and grapes were grown, Aristotle once lived and hitching was slow. My first lift was at 10 mph with three old men who laughed often enough for me to see they had twelve teeth between them. They wore large cloth caps and off-the-peg jackets,

off the wrong peg mostly. On hearing I came from Scotland they nodded and frowned sympathetically. Their destination was a village church in the hills where a festival was taking place in honour of the Virgin Mary and they invited me to come along. There would be all-night folk dancing, said the one with three of the teeth, adding that dancing must surely be scarce in Scotland under the present circumstances.

This remark puzzled me. 'Are you familiar with Scotland?' I asked.

No, he admitted, but they had all heard about it and its war with El Salvador. The others agreed. I suggested there had to be a misunderstanding. The two countries were thousands of miles apart and had nothing to quarrel over. They remained adamant. It had been in the news recently. Either they were wrong, I reflected, or else it was high time I was back at home. Or maybe it was best to give home a miss and keep travelling? It was the first time the thought had occurred to me.

The church was outside the village on a forested hillside and was thronged with hundreds of people. On a stage set before the main door a chain of schoolchildren were demonstrating dances to the accompaniment of an electric bouzouki. The musician seesawed and bounced his bow over the strings and occasionally *pizzicatoed* to produce scintillating limb-jerking melodies, but the dancers were restrained compared to what a crowd of Trinidadians would have made of the music. Girls in gypsy frocks seemed most concerned with poise and timing while their dark uniformed partners endeavoured to keep control of a yellow pompom at the end of their long drooping nightcaps, and some clearly wished they were in Trinidad.

Beyond them a shantytown of stalls offered religious souvenirs, hydrogen balloons depicting MIKU MAOUS, TAρZAN swinging through jungle and Superman escaping from green KρyπToNITHΣ; hot dogs, teddy bears and books, amongst which was one in English on the Loch Ness Monster.

'This is in Scotland!' I exclaimed, holding out one of the photographs to the three old men, but they showed no sign of interest as if it were something banal like a Scottish submarine off San Salvador.

Informal dances sprang up in the crowd who, fortified by ouzo, carried on all night. Greek dances were ideal social events as they

absorbed everyone, were simple enough for strangers in boots to cope with and supported the shoulders of those unaccustomed to ouzo. The old men danced away their age and were still dancing when I went to get a few hours sleep in the cemetery which doubled as a campsite. By morning the atmosphere was sober in preparation for the day of religious ceremonies.

These culminated in a procession led by four bishops, resplendent in red, white, yellow and purple dalmatics, gold chains and black hats trailing black veils. They all possessed luxuriously bushy Moses beards and a solemn dignity that inspired rather than conveyed God-fearingness. The one leading flicked an incense ball on a chain in a hypnotic motion that made a regular *chink* and emitted a puff of blue vapour. Behind them came an icon of the Virgin in a ponderous sedan chair carried by four men. The effort was visible in their faces and yet they looked proud and unquestioning as to why a small lightweight picture had to be set in half a ton of baroque woodwork.

I was looking at the icon while its bearers rested before reaching the main crowd when I noticed that policemen had roped the other spectators back and formed a tight cordon around this section of the procession and I was caught in the middle. The crowd suddenly swelled around us, the police tightened their circle to prevent anyone breaking through and the procession set off once more amid shouts and wild gesticulations. My position among the dignitaries was acutely embarrassing but at that moment it appeared less disruptive to try and slip submissively along than to struggle out, and the advancing icon forced me to keep a close step behind the bishops. Rows of adoring faces were smiling at us, hundreds of arms were waving and handkerchiefs were fluttered in abundance. My embarrassment was replaced by surprise. The air was charged with emotion and it was impossible not to respond. The mass of smiling faces was inexhaustible. I smiled back and once I got carried away and gave a little wave. Arms flailed the air. Someone threw a cup of scented water at us. A bishop and I had to duck but we still got wet. He was forced to steady his hat and I tried to catch his eye so we could share a laugh. The crowd was growing hysterical and there was a carnival atmosphere. Then I went cold.

People were bowing, kneeling, holding out clasped hands and crossing themselves. Before the bishops? The icon? – suddenly it didn't seem to matter which. Such was fervour to worship that the

objects of worship became confused and assumed fanatical importance. I merely happened to be caught between an excited crowd and
intermediaries of their faith, and the effect was frightening. People
struggled and fought their way through the densely packed bodies,
broke the police line and threw themselves on the ground before the
bishops and the icon. They waited until the holy image had passed
over them, and those who couldn't reach it threw articles of clothing
into the path of its shadow. I found a way out as the bedlam grew
worse. The procession still held together and disappeared into the
church. The police regained control and formed a chain behind the
tail to stop the throng from following. They pushed and jostled and
clamoured around the blockade. I saw an aged woman who was
pitifully frail. She was down on her hands and knees trying to crawl
between the policemen's legs, and getting nowhere. She had missed
the icon's shadow and was crying.

It was the start of a very unusual day. With one of my tent's
guy-ropes tied to a notice that said 'Camping strictly forbidden' in
four languages, I could hardly tell the policeman who woke me early
in the morning that I hadn't seen it. I apologised and explained that I
preferred these sorts of places as they tended to attract the dedicated
camper and keep away the noisy element, and besides, my campsites
were always left in immaculate condition. Fortunately he accepted
this and didn't delay me as it was the day my Mount Athos permit
became valid and I was still twenty miles short of the ferry at
Ouronoupoli. It was a bus full of workmen that took me there. They
all sat on the left-hand side of the bus for the first half of the journey
and then changed to the right-hand side when we crossed an
isthmus, always keeping as close to the sea as possible. Camping by
the road to the holy Mount was usually frowned upon but topless
sunbathing was often admired.

  A group of around fifty men were waiting for the ferry and most
were Greeks who apparently did not require a permit. We set off and
the boat kicked up a powerful wake alongside the wooded peninsula
that rose steeply to its central ridge. Occasionally valleys cut through
the ridge as deep clefts but there were no roads, monasteries or signs
of life to be seen, just dolphins knitting patterns before our bow and
flying fish gliding on transparent fins that glinted in the sun. Small
hermitages began to appear along the coast and then the storehouses

of monasteries reared up as castellated towers, each with its own jetty. These were impressive enough but the monasteries, when they first came into view, were awesome. They were immense constructions, strikingly similar to the monasteries and palaces of Ladakh, rising to five or six storeys but then doubling their height by sitting on massive fortress walls. The upper sections were of wood and too large for their foundations so that they spilled out and were held over long drops by angled supports. Balconies, rooms and even entire annexes had been tacked on and left precariously attached to the solid core. The buildings had towers, spires, hundreds of windows, red, green or yellow walls and red roofs, and yet each monastery had fitted these ingredients into a unique design. Above all, it was their sheer magnitude that made the most forceful impression.

The majority of monasteries on Mount Athos are one thousand years old, the notable exceptions being the oldest with fifth-century foundations and the two youngest dating from the fourteenth century. All have been either partially or totally rebuilt as a result of accidental fire or damage caused by pirates who repeatedly attacked and preyed on the peninsula. At its peak in the fifteenth century there were 40,000 monks to be found here and forty monasteries, of which only half have survived. They are all Eastern Orthodox, and all are Greek except one Serbian, one Bulgarian and one Russian, the largest, Agiou Panteileimonos. We passed it shortly before reaching the main jetty at Dafni. Beneath its onion domes it was still a vast edifice and said to count 3000 cells within its walls. In 1903 there were 1446 monks using its thirty-five chapels, but now its outer buildings were burnt-out shells and each of the thirty resident monks of Panteileimonos could have had a chapel to himself.

A bus met the boat and took us five miles up multiple bends to the top of the hill and then down a few more to Karies, the state capital. It was a strange place, nestling at the foot of another monastery which dwarfed the few streets. The buildings all had an ecclesiastical appearance except the police-administration office which was Corinthian, a straggle of houses which were tumble-down and a few faceless shops where monks sold crucifixes, maps and a narrow range of wares. The monks walking around were equalled in number by plain-clothed workmen. There wasn't a single woman in Mount Athos. A few dogs strolled the streets, large healthy-looking dogs, all wearing a bell. They were wonderfully friendly and

responded to attention by lowering their heads, looking up from the tops of their eyes and wagging their tails feverishly. Except for the tail-wagging it was a pious gesture. They didn't seem to mind that there wasn't a single bitch in Mount Athos.

At the police station my permit was stamped and an additional fee of 500 drachmas was charged to cover hospitality and accommodation. No more money changed hands during a visitor's stay and he was free to visit any monastery where an evening meal and a bed would be provided if available. From Karies I set off downhill towards the east coast on a gravel road. Little hermitages appeared all over the wooded hillsides. Many looked derelict but inhabited; shoes stood on a doorstep, tinned catfood rested on a window ledge and a mule grazed in a garden below a laden fig tree. When the road came to a fork the choice of routes was marked on the arms of a cross, and a cautionary message was given on a square board alongside. 'A forest is a place of calming and God smiling – protect it from fire.' The only person to pass was a monk driving a Ferrari tractor. Even this was done with great dignity though his tall cylindrical hat looked slightly out of place. Then Iviron Monastery loomed up out of the trees ahead with a sense of unblinking permanence.

A monk leaving on a mule directed me to the entrance in the lofty walls, a passage which led between marble pillars, past golden icons and into a courtyard monopolised by a large church in the middle and a chapel in each corner. The walls of the courtyard were lined with corbelled balconies on different levels, the lowest overgrown with vines that threatened their collapse through the weight of red grapes. There were no more than five monks shuffling about on their own. They each looked 110 years old, small bent figures in black, straggly unkempt beards in white. Their manner was one of being tired and dazed but I supposed that was only to be expected at such an age. None spoke English but one led me upstairs to a dormitory at the end of a long corridor and we were followed by the echo of his lugubrious plod. It was a simple room with a bare wooden floor, cracks in the whitewashed walls, a cupboard with one door missing and the other reduced to a riddle by woodworm, four beds and a small window. Through the window the outer gardens were visible. A monk was working there beside a scarecrow, a black cassock draped over a cross, and for most of the time it was impossible to tell which was which. Another direction showed a

wall of the monastery, a sagging roof, broken slates and windows, drooping balconies and chairs holding one leg in the air over warped floorboards. On this side Iviron's permanence was blinking. It was like a visual puzzle that distorted perspective.

Only three monks came for supper that evening and I sat with them at one end of a marble table with a surface area of thirty square feet. There were twenty-eight of these tables in the dining room, all of them empty except ours. We ate in silence; one portion of white rice, a spoonful of tomato sauce, bread, olives and a glass of water. After the meal it became dark quickly. A monk gave me a kerosene lamp and then he disappeared with the others. Shadows from the lamp danced around me as I made my way back to the dormitory, the air smelt of dust, cobwebs wavered from the ceiling and floor-boards squeaked. One of the passage doors swung with such an evocative multi-toned groan that I gave it an extra push just for the pleasure of listening to it. Never has a building appeared more animate.

I woke in the night to the sound of a door banging in the dark with a regularity that suggested someone was doing it on purpose. It was just the wind. No electricity, no switch for magic light. I fumbled for matches but before I could find them the room suddenly lit up for a fraction of a second. I was still bewildered by all these happenings when a crash of thunder sounded close to the roof and made the whole building shake. I went to the window. A fork of lightning stabbed the darkness and cut a bright scar across the night, throwing the tower of the church into silhouette and an eerie silvery glow over the monastery wall and grounds. The image of the monk standing stiffly in the garden was retained for an instant in my mind and it made my spine shiver. I stood in the dark expecting at any moment to hear a banshee wail, but it never came. Banshees were female. There wasn't a single banshee in the whole of Mount Athos.

It was still dark when I left Iviron the next morning at about six, though time was hard to tell as all of the monastery's clocks were wrong. My destination was the Monastery of Simon Petras, ten miles away over the mountain and on the other coast, where the ferryman had said there was a resident English monk. The walk took most of the day because the peacefulness, crops of wild blackberries and the splendid views made destinations seem unimportant. This changed, however, when Simon Petras came into view. It had the

most dramatic setting of all the monasteries and the furthest to fall. The building was six storeys high, painted a dull white and it perched half on a crag and half off, its foundations on three sides dropping 200 feet to the base of the rock. A typical assortment of balconies ran around the upper reaches and on a few of these some monks were visible gazing at the void below their feet. Judging from the angle of their habits, a breeze at sea level was gale force six in the heights of Simon Petras. Below the monastery terraced fields and gardens fell away steeply to the sea.

The community of monks here seemed younger and friendlier, even though I had no right to expect friendliness when I must have been interrupting their spiritual pursuits. A glass of ouzo, a cup of coffee and a piece of Turkish Delight were placed on a table before me, and a few minutes later a tall thin man in his late twenties approached. He was dressed in customary black but his wild beard was unusual for being ginger. He spoke in Greek but quickly switched to English.

'Father Isaiah,' he said, and added with a smile, 'as in the prophet.' We shook hands and he invited me over to some chairs on a parapet. He had joined the Order many years earlier but had only recently given up his job as an underwriter with Lloyds and come to Mount Athos, having applied from his home in the Midlands and been accepted after a probational period. From where we were sitting a monk was visible as a speck far below through a gap in the floorboards.

'Do you feel safe up here?' I asked.

'It does take a little getting used to especially when earth tremors are not uncommon in these parts. We had one lasting twelve seconds a few weeks back, but it is written that earthquakes will never damage us. Fire is our biggest worry. Twice in our history we have been burnt down.' He related that the last fire had occurred in 1821 when the Abbot was in Russia collecting alms. The news reached him while he was returning so he ordered the ship about and went straight back. He collected money for four more years and raised four times the amount needed to rebuild the monastery. Some of the excess had been invested in property in Athens and this was still an important source of revenue. 'Simon Petras is relatively prosperous compared to others on Mount Athos but we are still desperately short of money to do all the necessary repairs.'

He explained that the European Economic Community had immediately recognised the state as a unique cultural and spiritual centre when Greece became a member and had given considerable financial support. As a result of Greek politics and internal wrangling the distribution of the EEC grant had been unequal and this had caused much ill-feeling. Since then a central body had been set up to administer future grants fairly and to allocate the revenue from visitors to the monasteries that incur costs by receiving them. The monasteries were otherwise self-supporting. The Greek government had seldom shown any concern for Mount Athos and what offers of assistance had been given imposed the obligation to open up for tourism.

Tourism had driven the monks away from Meteora, another region of imposing monasteries in central Greece, and Mount Athos was anxious to avoid the same fate. And yet the ease with which he talked and anticipated questions indicated he was used to visitors. I asked if their (really meaning *my*) intrusion was currently a problem.

'Every year we grit our teeth and bear the onslaught as best we can. So far this summer we've had over one thousand visitors to Simon Petras and often our thirty beds have been full. We like receiving those who come for spiritual guidance and who are genuinely interested in our buildings and history, but many use us for a cheap holiday. Some even complain about the service!'

There were 1500 monks on Mount Athos and about 1000 others. Most lived in the monasteries, some in sketes – holy villages – several hundred in hermitages and a few in 'hollow trees and caves'. Father Isaiah said he could live in a tree if he wanted to but he would have to convince his Abbot that it was necessary for his spiritual development. Simon Petras had sixty monks but some were associates and lived abroad. Many monasteries were having trouble finding recruits and an average of only two or three monks entered Mount Athos each year.

I inquired about the 110 year-old monks at Iviron.

'Yes, they are all very old there. Iviron is one of several that are idiorythmic. They don't have an Abbot and all monks have an equal share in running the monastery. They are allocated their own money and jobs, and work independently of each other. The idea is to give an individual greater freedom to find a routine that suits his own particular spiritual needs. We are cenobitic which is the traditional

system and the most common. We have an Abbot and a hierarchy of elders to govern the monastery. It is the better system as we work together and create a closer community. When I go to Iviron I notice at once that their independence makes them colder and no one takes on responsibility for looking after visitors. It's true that everything works but I feel it is a shell without a soul. And young monks are just not attracted to the idiorythmic system. I don't know what will happen with Iviron.'

'Does your routine follow the clock? I haven't seen one yet that shows the correct time.'

His tone was charitable. 'That's because we work on Byzantine time, not that of mainland Greece. We are four hours ahead of the Greek clock.' His day began at midnight (4 a.m. Byzantine) which was regarded as sunset. He got up and spent some time praying and resting. At 3 a.m. (7 a.m. Byz) he went to the main service which lasted four hours. He returned to his cell and continued praying and resting until the first meal at 10.30 a.m. After that he went to work. His job was attending to visitors' accommodation and he would do this for a year until jobs were reallocated by rotation. Some monks kept their jobs if they had a special skill. Monks originally from the country usually made better gardeners and fishermen while city monks tended towards administrative work. At 5 p.m. he attended Vespers for an hour and then came the second and last meal of the day. For the rest of the evening he was free (no talking permitted after 10 p.m.) until 11.30 when there was a final short service.

'But when do you sleep?

'We get about six hours, interrupted and at different times, but it is enough. You get used to it.'

'Can you change to another monastery or leave altogether?'

'Yes, the option is available but generally when you join a monastery, you stay for life.'

'You make it sound like a sentence . . . does it ever seem that way?'

'No, of course not. We see it as our vocation. We all have had the chance to think about ourselves and our lives before coming here. We are all here by choice. Come, I'll show you where I'll end up.' From the balcony he pointed to a small chapel and shed on the slope down to the sea. He explained that they had a small cemetery there with five graves. Because Simon Petras had a high proportion of

young monks there was concern about how they would cope with the expected burial problem in forty or fifty years time when many would be dying. As a result of this pragmatic foresight they were about to extend the cemetery. 'We bury bodies for three years then dig up the bones and lay them in the charnel-house beside the chapel. We don't have much room for graves and besides, we believe this way shows more respect. When the soul leaves the body we have no more use for that body but because it has carried the soul for so long, we believe it deserves respect. So we place the bones together with those of our past brothers. If the soul ever wants to, it can find its own bones amongst them. That's where I'll be put one day.'

'I can't think of a more beautiful place to end up,' I said. 'The view is stunning.

A smile parted his beard. 'Yes, but it's a bit late for views when you've passed on.'

We were interrupted by a monk hammering on a symendra, a wooden plank which he balanced on one shoulder. It was the call to Vespers. Father Isaiah begged to be excused and calmly vanished into the hinterland of stairs and passages.

In common with St Katharine's Monastery in the Sinai, this building was a labyrinth but by chance I came to the chapel just before the service began. An English visitor, who I later learnt was called Harold, was at the doorway talking to a monk. Harold was in his fifties and a devout Anglican.

'Orthodox?' the monk asked.

'Anglican,' Harold replied. The monk frowned and hmmmmed. '*High* Anglican,' Harold added decisively. The monk continued to frown and hmmmmmmmmed for longer. Then he ushered us into a back room with a view through the main door. Harold was obviously affronted but he said nothing and we sat down. The Great Schism in the Church that split Roman Catholicism from Eastern Orthodoxy in 1054 and resulted in both excommunicating the other for 911 years, had not healed. Catholicism was nevertheless tolerated but Protestantism was regarded as degenerate. We could see monks kissing the icons on the walls as they entered the chapel and then sitting down, never crossing their legs at the knees as this was in some way of sacrilegious through association with the posture of crucifixion. Above me were frescos that mixed Tolkien's dragons with the hell of Hieronymus Bosch. Close to my nose was a flying

maiden whose lower half was a scorpion's tail. There was much I didn't understand.

Vespers was followed by the evening meal. Simon Petras enjoyed richer fare than Iviron and delicious vegetable soup, bread, olives, fruit and a glass of red wine were consumed silently while a monk read from the Scriptures. The atmosphere was less solemn the next morning when breakfast was provided for guests at a separate sitting. Harold hadn't appeared and there were only three Greeks talking quietly when I took my place. A fourth Greek entered, an extrovert character who spoke some German-English, and sat down beside me. I was sipping some herbal tea when he turned to me.

'Orthodox?' he asked.

'Non-aligned,' I replied. He took this to mean Protestant.

'Ach!' he scorned. 'Protestants is *nichts. Nichts, nichts, nichts.*' He took out a piece of paper, drew a circle and wrote 'Orthodox' in the centre. Then he drew four arrows like compass points and labelled them Catholics, Protestants and two undecipherables. 'Orthodox is . . .' He raised his hands and eyes to the ceiling and adored. After this he stubbed his finger hard on the other names and repeated '*nichts*'. I took his bit of paper, drew a straight line with Orthodox, Catholics, Protestants and two undecipherables on the level underneath and then ran a line up from each to the single word 'God'. But he waved the paper away. He wasn't interested in discussing, just in preaching – and he'd finished. He leant forward with a smile on his face to attack the food. Soon he was tearing in with both hands. I passed him the water jug and he stopped gorging himself for a moment to accept it. Having breakfast with a bigot makes you feel very holy.

I was sorry when my time on Mount Athos came to an end. The scenery and extraordinary buildings were only a part of this peninsula's powerful charm. More mysterious, and more alluring, was the profound sanctity that made me feel an unwilling outsider. Even for a non-Orthodox it was a place of calming. As Mount Athos faded from view I caught a glimpse of two black figures standing high above their fortress wall on a wilting balcony. Dolphins and flying fish led the boat back to the outer world, and for the first time in five days I thought of home.

18 · Home: A View with a Room

Things were looking black, one of those rare moments when there was a possibility I might not make it after all. At first there seemed little danger, just the discomfort of the cold but as the minutes went by my doubts increased. What a way to end a journey. 191,000 miles down, almost home, only to end up being slowly calcified into a stalagmite. The *drip, drip, drip* on my head was constant no matter which way I leant and each splash redefined the shape of my skull with its seeping coldness. I began to sing but only timidly. An echo would have been entertaining, even reassuring, but the unseen depths of the cavern absorbed my voice into the darkness and this shrank me further into my isolation. My camera case provided an adequate seat but sitting meant that my kilt failed to cover the ends of my knees and the cold drips found them too. My only consolation was the thought that at least I would make an unusual stalagmite.

The cave was only two hours from the Greek port of Igoumenitsa on the west coast, and from there daily ferries left for Italy. My kilt had been waiting poste restante on my return from Mount Athos and had been an invaluable aid for three weeks of hitching around the country. It had taken several days for me to adjust to wearing a kilt again and to lose my initial feelings of self-consciousness (as well as the smell of mothballs). It was back to the standard reactions; nudges, whispered alerts, conversations choked, long stares, bewilderment, embarrassment, scorn, or friendly smiles, waves and calls of ''allo Scotia!' which made all the others bearable. Psychologically humans have suffered a messy evolution but I had forgotten how additionally intriguing and unpredictable they are when seen from inside a kilt. Wearing a kilt abroad certainly prevents one from taking life too seriously for it comes needing a pinch of salt and good humour, whether or not one feels like salting and humouring.

My experiences in the region of Olympia were cases in point. A group of redundant men sitting outside a café had greeted my appearance with a roar of derision. This had hurt me at the time but the only sensible recourse was to nod in a courteous, orthodox way

while walking by and imagine the whole group on pedestals at a coconut shy. Then later the same afternoon a similar incident had happened only it was a woman who shouted the derogatory remarks and raised a laugh from her neighbours. On this occasion a man emerging from a gate in a high wall had come to my defence and spoken to her so sharply that she had blushed and hurried away.

'You must excuse her,' he had said in fluent English. 'She was making fun of you and saying you were wearing a woman's skirt. It is simply ignorance.'

'Thank you for your support. But what did you say to her? She turned bright red.'

'I reminded her that the Greek national costume is almost identical. Had she forgotten that her father had also worn a "skirt"? Had she laughed at him? . . . '

And it was true. I had seen Greek kilts worn by guards outside the Tomb of the Unknown Soldier in Athens. They were pleated all the way round and worn over woolly white tights with black garters criss-crossed up to the knees. The kilts were a little on the brief side and rather plain in self-coloured fawn (and the accompanying red shoes with a huge black pompom over the toes would not have been my choice) but I had nevertheless felt the affinity of our respective costumes and the shared blue and white of our national flags.

'Your hitching is not going too well, is it?' this man had commented after we had been talking on the roadside for thirty minutes.

'No. At least not at the moment.' In this respect *his* appearance had not helped my chances for he was a doctor in white overalls and stood holding a tray of syringes and a full specimen bottle. But my choice of a place to wait had also been at fault, unwittingly, because behind us was the establishment where he worked. Prisons make notoriously poor sites for hitching. Apart from on this one afternoon the reaction to my kilt had generally been very favourable and hitching had run smoothly as far as my present predicament in the cave at Perama.

It was to have been a quick visit. I entered the cave behind a flock of nuns on a guided tour. They made a noisy procession; off-duty nuns show appreciation even for the smallest things of creation, and Perama Cave is enormous. The guide led us into an underground passage half a mile long which periodically expanded into caverns and was a maze of paths winding through floodlit stalagmites. His

discourse was in Greek and not being able to understand, I soon got bored and wandered on alone. Twenty minutes later I was ambling along admiring the weird multitude of limestone daggers held above my head and feeling secure in the knowledge that I was ahead of the group, when all the lights went out. I didn't dare move. The darkness was absolute. The path had no handrail and twisted and turned illogically amongst hunks of rocks, pools of water and chasms. The nuns had disappeared and there was silence except for the *drip, drip, drip* that I had barely noticed before. Now it seemed very loud. Was it a power cut? What if they had closed for the weekend? I would have to spend thirty-six hours down here. I had felt cold right from the start and soon the drips had wet my hair, my knees and were saturating my thin jersey. My pack was hidden in some bushes outside so that wouldn't help to raise the alarm. I began to shiver intentionally to generate some warmth, and sang to raise my spirits but I didn't like the sound of my voice, nor what happened to it.

Alone, lost and made helpless by five useless senses, I tried to count my blessings but couldn't get beyond three: being alive, uninjured and of reasonably sound mind. My reasonably sound mind turned to other things that had become wearisome or objects of longing after five years as an orphan of the road. Some were absurdly trivial but had assumed disproportionate importance. I was looking forward to morning mail, out-of-the-blue visits from friends, a visible product resulting from my daily output of energy, a choice of clothes that would enable me to look my best, just for a while, and I was longing to write my first personal cheque because the thought of satisfying payment with a scrawled signature seemed a remarkable privilege. These were all related in some way to a diminished sense of identity, no easy factor to maintain on a long journey. At times I had to think hard to remember my name. It was of no more use to me than letters on a passport. No one ever called it across a room or a street, though 'Alstjar' had come close, because I lived in a world of anonymous people. Frequent casual acquaintances helped to compensate for the scarcity of deep friendships but there were still periods when my social life appeared overwhelmingly monastic. I was tiring of leading a scrimping existence attached to a backpack, hunting for hostel beds or dry patches of ground, grappling with the basics of languages too numerous to learn and

being confined to the framework of my mother-tongue, stripped of colour and vitality. Lone travel could seem a selfish world of more opportunities to take than give, an abdication of responsibility and diaries excessively filled with first-person pronouns. My travelling had never been intended as an escape but at that moment it seemed to have become one, a bad one, and I wanted to regain the self and security that had been left behind.

And yet things weren't so bad when compared to the alternatives. Most of my longings could be dismissed either because they were of no more substance than novelty value or because they resulted from being jaded and were nothing that a week of change would not cure. Grass-root travel was often both mentally and physically demanding but it had undoubtedly provided me with my deepest insights and most memorable adventures. There was no more representative level for sampling a country and its people. Missing family and friends was an unavoidable part of journeying but absence in itself did not sever the bonds of special relationships, and travel brought many new ones. Travel was not all take, it was constantly giving though not always in physical terms. It was an exchange of views and trust, a widening of vision for all parties and in these respects it entailed responsibility. And gradually, deep in my cave, my perspective reverted to the attitude that had sustained me for five years. I didn't see this period as a block of weeks and months as others would but as a capricious ramble which had crossed six continents and put 1¼ million words in my diary and 17,000 photographs through my camera. The road had not orphaned me, but adopted me. Its frustrations were trivial and no more than those found at fixed addresses. I was happy in this lifestyle. Suddenly it seemed easier to go on travelling. I needed very little. My earnings from jobs along the way had always been sufficient to cover my costs, so why not continue in the same way? I could take a plane and start a new journey in Indonesia tomorrow. The realisation that one didn't have to travel for four years to reach Indonesia at first seemed unfair but then it opened up all sorts of fabulous travel plans . . . I was having cold feet about returning home.

I was cold all over now and shivering involuntarily. It had been at least forty minutes since the cave had been plunged into darkness and I got to my feet to stamp up some warmth. Suddenly the lights went on. I hurried along the paths in case it was only a temporary measure,

through cavern after cavern until a series of arrows guided me to the exit. The nuns must have taken a shorter route and left the cave before the lights had gone out. A side door led me out into the warm sunlight and railings channelled me back to the main entrance where the custodian was surprised to see me. I asked what had happened. He pointed at some notices. I had already read the first two – 'Breaking the stalagmites is Panished', 'Please don't walk out the path' – but the third was in Greek.

He translated it for me. 'Visitors may only enter Perama Cave with a guide. Between guided tours the lights will be turned off.'

I had never come across Italians in such quantities before as on the ferry from Igoumenitsa to Otranto, a loose tack in Italy's heel. Like the Chinese, their preferred elements are noise and bustle. I had thought the wild gesticulations accredited to them as a national characteristic were exaggerated but it transpired they were under-stated. Theirs is the only language to be simultaneously spoken and mimed, and in the ship's canteen it looked a pointless exercise asking for the salt-cellar to be passed along a table-length of talking Italians. No people are more vivacious and the intensity with which they live can only be admired, unsalted tagliatelle notwithstanding.

The next two weeks passed quickly and I covered the remaining 3071 miles to Calais in exactly eighty lifts. One of the longest was with a New Zealand couple originally from Scotland and it lasted several days as our destinations were the same. First came Pompeii and seeing this old town which Vesuvius had suddenly buried in A D 79 fulfilled a modest ambition of mine, but replaced it with dis-appointment. Half the ruins were fenced off and the weeds grew chest high. The last earthquake to shake Pompeii (1980) had left an attitude worse than apathy, that of intended neglect, and the im-pression that in twenty years archaeologists would have to be sent in to rediscover its houses, erotic signs and paved streets rutted by Roman chariots.

Jim put me in charge of map-reading from Pompeii to the capital because Marge, his wife, tended to confuse lefts and rights, but I found it almost impossible to cope with a tagliatelle road system.

'Did you see which way to go?' I asked at one particularly bad tangle.

'Listen, Jimmy,' replied Jim, reverting to his native Glaswegian

and its simplified nomenclature of the species, 'there's nae need tae worry. A' roads lead tae Rome.'

There seemed to be a lot of truth in this. The choice was the length of auto-tagliatelle that took you there and we managed to find a fairly short one although it increased its loops near the end. Rome soon convinced me it was the most beautiful and fascinating city I had seen, and a ruthlessly efficient jay-walkers' abattoir.

It was a marble city. Marble was everywhere, sandwiching the River Tiber and encasing the seven hills. Marble ran throughout the interior of St Peter's, from its necropolis where an empty sarcophagus had already been inscribed with the name of the current Pope and the first of his dates, to the dome but excluding four public lavatories of a man-made material which stood tall like sentry boxes on the roof. (If you peeped through the minute windows in these toelette you could look down on the streets of Rome, their names carved in polished marble, and on the predatory traffic amongst which even the smallest Fiats, reduced by distance to a scale of motorised rice crispies, were rounding corners on two wheels as they hunted for pedestrians.)

Jim hadn't been allowed into St Peter's for wearing shorts and so Marge and I met him outside the Vatican where he was trying to photograph some Swiss guards. A baggy beret sat severely askew on their heads and they wore knickerbockers made of red, blue and yellow ribbons loosely attached top and bottom so that they bulged and contracted each time the guards moved. The risk of indecency seemed sufficient to keep them motionless until their reliefs arrived, and to ensure a quick change-over. They were touchy about having their uniforms photographed and Jim was rudely ordered to go away. I understood how they felt but thought they would have realised how futile it is getting annoyed when you're wearing something unusual, particularly red, blue and yellow striped knickerbockers.

Vatican City (108.7 acres) was similar to most independent states in having its own citizenship, currency, stamps, newspaper, railway station and radio transmitter (Pius XI asked Marconi to instal the first one) but its art galleries were almighty. Outside the state walls we passed street confessionals, nuns with a million plastic crucifixes to sell and lines of beggars whose outstretched arms tried to reach the constant coming and going of the clergy. Everyone wanted a share

in the Vatican's wealth. Along with at least 20,000 others that day we paid our 1750 lira (£1) entry fee and chose a self-guided tour from markers offering from one to five hours, when five days would have been more realistic to appreciate this art collection. The world's richest treasure house held miles of palatial corridors that were in themselves exhibitions of inlaid marble, stucco-work and murals by the thousand. Here were to be found statues by the most celebrated sculptors sometimes rising six rows high along both walls, countless tapestries and paintings of incomparable expertise, artefacts of genius in gold, silver, ivory and everything else that can be studded with percious stones. Such was the concentration of objects that the display had the crush of an overloaded attic and every second step served as a layman's guide to masterpiece. It was overwhelming, and marvellous to find such a wealth of possessions in one place. It just struck me as odd that it should be in the Vatican.

Near the end of our tour we would have fallen into a deep pit had it not been for a grid. We peered down into the hole and watched a priest wading through a pile of lira as he swept up the donations with a broom. Then we paused by a plaque underneath a tapestry which explained that each square meter represented three years labour for four pairs of hands. Jim was suffering from a surfeit of magnificence by this stage. He didn't even look at the tapestry but reread the plaque out aloud.

'Hear that, Jimmy? Jist like the roads back hame, eh?'

Jim and Marge took me to Assisi where our routes diverged, and let me out beside its cathedral which reared up like a three-dimensional zebra crossing. I hitched on by way of Florence and Venice and vowed in each that I had found the world's most beautiful city. Hitching became erratic in a corner of Yugoslavia where the people could be forgiven for not knowing who they were for they had been Austrian up to the First World War and Italian until the Second. The Austrian border also seemed to have cut through a mode of life and my eagerness to speak German with the people south of Klagenfurt was confounded by some Slavonic tongue. It rained during my night in Vienna woods, Munich was under siege by festival-goers who regarded beer-swilling as a holy mission . . . and so soon I found myself at Calais, tired, excited, anxious, slightly stained with Somme battlefield mud and clutching a ferry ticket to the fifty-third country of the trip.

It was a stormy crossing and spray lashed the ship's windows. The White Cliffs were not visible until we docked. I was first to disembark and place my feet in an English puddle being dimpled by rain. The immigration officer examined my passport briefly, smiled and let me pass. My patched and mistreated kilt caught the eye of a customs officer, John De . . . (the rest was hidden under his lapel), on the fringe of the green zone. He beckoned me over.

'Have you anything to declare?' he asked.

'Only that I'm back.'

John De . . . sighed and rephrased the question with painful exactness. He was obviously used to such tedious little quips. ('I have nothing to declare but my genius.' Oscar Wilde.) He gave a quick rummage through my pack.

'Don't you have any duty-free at all?'

'No.' I had got out of the habit of carrying unnecessary luggage except for a universal bathplug which had acquired sentimental value because of its uselessness.

He too let me pass. I was surrounded by English-speakers. The subtleties of speech were open to me again, notices were comprehensible and billboards advertised familiar products. I left the terminal and wanted to dance, to celebrate no longer being an absent person, to mark the end of a self-imposed exile that had lasted exactly one week short of five years. Elation seized my body but my legs refused to dance because they were weighed down with the rest of me, sixty pounds of essentials and one universal bathplug. The pavement tapered into a grass verge and ended abruptly at NO PEDESTRIANS. I ignored the order. No sign was going to ruin my return by telling me I couldn't walk on my own homeland. Quarter of a mile later I paused to jot a few thoughts down on a scrap of paper when an empty bus pulled up beside me.

'Whereyeforemate?'

'London.'

''op in, then.' It was lift number 3154, and I hadn't even been hitching. We drove on the wrong side of the motorway the whole way. The fields were the greenest I had seen since New Zealand. What would a Mexican bull bound for the arena or an Indian cow bound to a lawn-mower give to be an indolent Friesian munching a trail through Britain? Many of the cars looked new and there was no shortage of them at petrol stations now asking £1.65 for the gallon

that had last cost me seventy-four pence. I asked the driver how much a pint of beer cost now.

'Varies. 'bout sixty-eight.'

At the start of my trip one pound would have bought four and half pints and left one penny change.

On the approach to London it came as a surprise to see so many individual houses instead of the blocks of flats that introduce most of the world's cities. My knowledge of London had been gleaned from postcards, Monopoly boards and one day of sole-splitting sight-seeing and so it should have appeared as just another large strange city. Yet I felt a strong sense of belonging in London. I suddenly found myself noticing things not because they were different but because they were indirectly familiar. It was a new sensation to be constantly reminded of my own background. There were all the things I wanted to find, from institutions to eccentricity; red double-decker buses, red letter boxes and phone booths, runaway dog-walkers, Pig and Whistle pubs with a veneer of the past over everything except their prices, the honesty of milk bottles on doorsteps, the *clink* of the milkman putting them there and the curiosity of passersby using them as indicators of who was lying in, an old woman in a park scolding individual ducks for being greedy and upsetting the fair distribution of a crust among the flock, unarmed policemen, orderly bus queues, the stiff upper locks of punks in shrieking colours and the stiff upper lips of those sufficiently aghast to give a sideways glance, one-and-a-half-window shops with their trivial but soul-stroking chitchat; every second pace revealed something homely or masterfully British.

Simply being back provided hours of entertainment and it was late at night when I decided to sleep rough somewhere and hitch up north the following day. At the back of the Grosvenor Hotel there was a suitable spot but it was already occupied by another dosser. I stepped over him and went up some steps to sleep on a landing. A notice by my head read 'Single Rooms £38'. It probably would have read '£10' if this had been the first night of my trip.

On the way north I was enchanted by hedges, winding lanes, village cricket greens, gardens still fussy with colours even though it was autumn and trees were yellowing, and miles of drystane dykes. Nothing could spoil my delight, not even the factory-scapes abandoned as the detritus of revolution, the abundance of litter, the

madder stampede of traffic and service stations where 'medium' had been reclassified as 'gigantic'. Gradually the countryside became more familiar as distance fell away in the company of a long-haul truck driver.

'You can always tell when you're in Scotland,' he observed, 'as the houses are smaller and neater, made of real stone and have a nice solid look about them.'

'I hadn't noticed that before. Towns had grown a bit bigger and some had been bypassed by roads that now ran straighter. Otherwise it was only the different prices that made me feel a stranger.

My pack had never felt lighter than during my walk through the centre of Edinburgh. I hurried round corners merely for the joy of confirming that I knew what lay beyond them. The back street shop that had made my kilt was still in business but it was closed. Just as well. The aged kiltmaker would have been horrified to have seen what had happened to his handiwork. Opposite was a bakery with trays of irresistible pastries and dainties, and I went in before broaching the final 150 miles that would take my journey full circle to the Spey Valley.

Behind the counter was a cheerful and endearing old lady, of the type to scold ducks for the good of others. Her tongs duplicated my finger movements behind the glass showcase and skimmed over chocolate éclairs, coconut snowballs and sickly cubes of pink and green cake. She noticed I was slightly tanned and asked if I had been abroad. I explained briefly. She raised her eyebrows momentarily but was preoccupied with the vanilla slices which were proving elusive. I could picture her in Greenland selling whale, or in Costa Rica over a pile of pineapples, or dressed her in a Mao blue uniform and she would have fitted into China. Guidebooks to the world take hundreds of pages to tell us how each part is different and in what way its culture is unique, which it may be, but behind the disguises its people are none other than ourselves.

'Well, well! Five years!' she mused, grasping a vanilla slice in triumph. 'And have you had a nice time?'

My kilt hangs undisturbed in a cupboard worrying only about moths, and my boots, the same second-hand pair from Australia, stand underneath and slant away from each other at peculiar angles. And I sit at a desk frequently looking up from my writing to gaze at

the mountains that fill the view from my window. Now we are on the west coast, opposite Skye, and my universal bathplug is as valuable as ever because my current abode has no bath. If we travelled hopefully, we were fortunate to arrive content. The Highlands of Scotland and their constantly changing moods can hold someone accustomed to a constantly changing view.

In summer the mountains were mellowed by the greenness that clamours around the dull sweeps of heather. In autumn they pouted their richest and subtlest hues, the heather blooming purple, bracken faltering between green and gold, moorland grasses adding fawn and rowan trees splashing forebodings in red. Now, in winter, the mountains look lean and austere, their colours have darkened and rocks protrude from their sides like ribs. Soon the snows will come and deer will gather on their south-facing slopes to scratch at the less frozen ground.

The surface of the sea changes hourly and its edges never tire of conjuring up rocks, sand banks and islands and making them disappear again, clouds rise and fall as if toying with the idea of creating a new horizon, mist sometimes lingers thoughtfully but seldom for long, and the intensity of light is never the same but varies from the soft glow of evening to the strong beams that interrupt storms and move mysteriously across the land selecting features to spotlight. The vegetation and climate lend my view its inconsistent and abstracting quality but what makes it so alluring to me are its wildness, emptiness and grandeur.

Yes, we are wholly content. My boots and kilt may nevertheless like to know what my atlas is doing on the windowsill. It lies open at page fifty-seven, a place none of us has yet visited.

Suharto eased into power. From its centre of bland highrises and monuments of impious workmanship it sprawls outwards as poor housing, broken streets, ragged pavements and open drains rife with unmentionables. The thunderous chaos of its traffic outstrips that of Denpasar and is one of the city's more interesting sights. I decided, perhaps unfairly, that whatever pleasure existed in Jakarta required diligent hunting or was experienced in retrospect.

To reach Sumatra it was necessary to take a bus west for three hours and make a two-hour sea crossing on another tired ferry purchased from the rest of the world's obsolete fleets. This one made Raja's precarious place of work seem a sensible choice. To reach Lake Toba involved a further sixty-five hours of surface travel including an eight-hour obligatory diversion on the cul-de-sac road to Palembang. I recalled suffering terribly in a bone-shaking bus in Guatemala two years earlier and seeing a German traveller apparently untroubled and enjoying the journey. I asked him for his secret. He gave a condescending smile and explained how the previous year he had ridden the trans-Sumatran buses. Everything since was proving a jaunt in comparison.

And yet the thought of Sumatra's wildness excited me. It possesses the world's largest flower, *Rafflesia*, with a head one yard across, an extremely rare tiger and even rarer one-horned rhinoceros. It is also responsible for over two-thirds of Indonesia's income, producing eighteen per cent of the world's rubber and sixteen per cent of the world's tin, though none of this was said to be apparent from its vast tracts of impenetrable rain forests. What does soon become apparent, however, is that Sumatra exists on rubber time. Minutes bend, hours stretch and days are completely flexible.

The Musi River and its industrial port of Palembang were reached after two sleepless nights and here it was a relief to discover that the trans-Sumatran buses of Lunas Company had improved since the German had made the trip. Now they had the appearance of a luxury Mercedes fleet boasting video entertainment and three complimentary sweets on departure. Nevertheless there was still a disconcerting amount of wood visible around the interior, the seats were fixed (which in itself was something of a distinction), the engine stalled three times in the first street and I suspected the Mercedes emblem had been stolen and falsely stuck on the front. We left thirty minutes before the scheduled time for receiving the three sweets and spent the next two hours driving around Palembang looking for more custom. Asian bus drivers always seemed to believe that the rest of the population had merely forgotten to be at the station on time. The city was poor and sordid, its wide river was muddy and swollen. We passed a cinema billboard with the words 'Super Action Number One' and below them painted figures twelve feet high dwarfed passersby as it executed a flying karate kick and leapt from a background of luminous colours which depicted fully-clad lovers sharing an adhesive kiss, an exploding car and the clinical details of a fight victim losing an eye. We waited beside this and gained three more passengers. Then began what, under good conditions, was described as a journey of thirty hours to the halfway point of Padang.

For the rest of the day the video played continuous violence adulterated only by scooter love. Super Action Number Ones used a standard oriental plot; boys meet girl and compete for her attention, one by fair means, the other by foul. Eventually they fight (both happen to be virtuoso martial artists) for ten minutes of unrelenting blows, each one accompanied by the sound of a substantial plank being slammed on a table top. Had the punches been in proportion to the sound effect both filmstars would have been decapitated. The bad guy, bloody and beaten, goes off to be blown up in a stolen car. The good guy, without a cut or a bruise, rides off into the sunset with the girl on the back of his scooter. A triumph of good over evil – the theme of all Balinese traditional dances – and a touching recommendation for Yamaha.

The driver was unable to see the screen, thank goodness, so he played music cassettes loudly enough to overcome the sound of the video. We passed houses of milled timber which appeared wealthier than those of Palembang, and dense jungle punctuated with clearings of fields squeezed in-between charred tree stumps. When we stopped for a meal that evening amid a wild lightning storm, we heard that another Lunas bus had been following us but had left the road and rolled. No one had been seriously hurt but our bus was to go and collect the passengers. An hour later it returned with fifty bruised and shaken people. A merchant seaman from Palembang said it had been terrifying. 'People screamed and I thought we were dead already,' he added and, understandably, consumed half a bottle of raw alcohol on the spot.

The courier of our bus apologised but said we could not depart until the matter had been sorted out. A replacement bus was on its way and there would be a police enquiry which would delay us 'a few minutes'. The delay lasted twelve hours and there was little sleep for any of us on the restaurant floor with the coming and going. The next morning the replacement bus arrived already half-full and with a puncture. Our bus was loaded to twice its official capacity (the police had gone) and the luggage was stacked on the roof to increase its height by a third. The rolled bus was towed in and it was with dismay and apprehension that I noticed how easily this wreck blended in with what remained of Lunas' luxury fleet.

The road had been sealed in stretches up until this point but hereafter it was a mass of potholes. We nevertheless averaged 30mph at times but were more often reduced to a crawl over severe sections where the road was largely missing. I wondered who maintained it, or under whose responsibility it disintegrated. The crush inside the bus pressed me against the window but this was my saving grace and enabled me to lean out in the cooling breeze. And the splendid scenery took my mind off the discomfort; we went up and down hills with views into valleys of banana and cocoa trees; crossed rickety bridges with sleepers which rippled under our wheels; looked out on chocolate brown rivers where women thrashed rocks with clothes, naked children splashed each other, men punted canoes with long poles and water buffalo lay swishing their tails lazily in the shallows; jungle, real Edgar Rice Burroughs jungle, with wild monkeys and a tree with gigantic leaves – five would make a golfing umbrella; an isolated hill crowned with a natural monolithic spire; a roadmender, dwarfed by his task, crouched breaking rocks with a household hammer; small boys flying homemade kites; a group of womenfolk pounding wooden posts into wooden troughs; a surprising microwave telephone pylon, and a man climbing high into a coconut tree. There were vague notches in the trunk and he hunched his way up like a caterpillar, carrying a machete crossways in his mouth. He must have had nerves and teeth of steel. Vendors came rushing to the bus at each village, bringing coconut sweet-meats, fruit, and spicy fish wrapped in banana leaves. They seasoned an air that was otherwise dusty, humid and smelt of excess Lunas passengers. Each village also had a small guardhouse of soldiers who looked young, delicate and pathetically expendable. Once a large butterfly appeared with wings as large as my hands, black with bold white blotches. It alighted for a moment on the trousers of a dozing soldier and became invisible against the abstract colours of combat. The journey took *exactly* thirty rubber hours, or forty-five normal ones.

After a break to recover four nights of lost sleep another bus took me the remaining twenty hours to Lake Toba. No other foreigners had crossed my path since Jakarta but they began appearing the nearer the bus came to this popular haunt of off-beat travellers. An Austrian couple got on at one stop and unfortunately they took the two spare seats next to mine. I always felt at my grumpiest when cornered by foreigners in a strange land where it was flattering to believe one was unique. The girl was a strapping figure, my vision of a Tyrolean Helga whose yodel sent a shiver up distant goats. The rest of the journey was another squash because the seats were designed to accommodate three Indonesians, two Europeans or, at the most, a Helga and a half.

Lake Toba is the country's largest lake and in appearance it is the tropical paradise one would hope to find after hacking a way through jungle for months or a seventy-hour super action bus journey. It is dominated by the hilly Samosir Island which is made irresistibly romantic by lush vegetation and perpetually blooming flowers, lingering mist and the unusual Batak houses with their arching roofs rising to points at each end as if modelled on the horns of the island's numerous water buffalo. Here are to be found such villages as Siborongborong, Ambarita and Tuk Tuk, and the colourful Batak people. They were once cannibals but now they are Christians in a predominantly Islamic region and they bury their dead under crosses and sometimes under concrete models of buffalo horn houses. Electricity has only recently been installed although Coca-Cola arrived long ago. Mercifully, Yamaha has made no inroads. Accommodation in Batak houses is comfortable but primitive which means that the people have been spared the effects of large scale tourism, and yet small scale tourism has produced minor conflicts of commercial interests which, from all accounts, were not present in the days when visitors were put on the menu. It was only natural that a poorer people should engineer ways of sharing the wealth of richer people who insisted on visiting them. There was negligible crime

except good-natured cons and mischievously inflated prices, ingenious begging, a great deal of pressure sales techniques and, worst of
all, a lot of inter-neighbour rivalry for custom. Lake Toba was
nevertheless well-established on the overland traveller's itinerary for
its beauty and cheap living. Markets sold six avocados for ten pence,
house restaurants offered peppery Padang dishes, pizzas and fruit
crumble with custard and there was often the possibility of finding
an old copy of *Stern* or *Newsweek* beside the hole-in-the-ground loo
with its door largely consumed by termites.

A ferry took me over the lake to Samosir. My neighbour was a
man wearing a fez but most of the other passengers (apart from the
two Austrians) were middle-aged women returning from market.
They lacked the graceful features of the Balinese and chewed betel
nut continuously. The red juice stained their mouths blood red and
this combined with their protruding teeth was a constant reminder
of their unsavoury past. On their heads they wore an ingenious
assortment of loosely bundled cloth in colours which produced a
shocking clash with those of their gaily patterned sarongs. Some
women had babies bound to their back even though they looked past
their years of motherhood and unlikely to attract anyone to prove it.
My neighbour proved me wrong. He dug me in the ribs, nodded at
them and gave a knowing look. I tried to adopt an unknowing look
and smiled pleasantly at him, an even match with bushy eyebrows
and thick pouting lips, but his lewd suggestions continued and
eventually I had to concentrate on the water reflecting smudges of
white clouds to suppress an intruding image of gargoyles making
love. Up at the bow, Helga looked divine.

Samosir was large enough for a grumpy traveller to find his own
secluded corner. I felt more cheerful the moment the boat moored in
a bay fringed with lilac water lilies. Helga and friend turned left and I
cheerfully turned right to Tuk Tuk. Soon I was eating my way
through bananas and avocados in my own Batak house which cost a
standard forty-five pence per night, and looking out over Lake Toba
through a square cut-out in the wooden wall. My days became filled
with catching up on my diary and going for long rambles. The island
was enhancing but the walks were soured by the persistent hustling
of those with rooms to let. 'Where are you staying,' each one would
ask. 'Where? . . . Oh! No good there . . . They'll steal from you . . .
We've got a room, much better . . . '

On one of these walks I stopped to talk to a woman selling wood carvings and learnt that a man had died the previous day. The funeral was to be held that evening and she and her husband were about to set off for it. I expressed an interest in attending, expecting to be dissuaded, but she invited me along without any hesitation, and confirmed it with her husband. He was sitting morosely in the background and nodded in a disinterested way. 'The dead man', she explained, 'is his father.'

Her name was Karya and Iwan was her husband. She wore her hair pulled back into a bun and had a disquieting way of switching from a benign expression to one of reproach. Iwan looked a man more used to the second of these but perhaps his nervous manner resulted from his present bereavement. His skin was dark and he wore a thin moustache which was carefully trimmed and added to the distinguished appearance given by his jacket and trousers. He might have been an office worker but as we walked along and made occasional conversation Karya said her husband was a farmer and woodworker. She did most of the talking as she spoke more English. It was colloquial but remarkably good on the subjects of food, selling and accommodation.

'Where are you staying?' she asked after a while, and the usual dialogue followed. 'You must come to our place. We have a very nice room.' I explained that my present lodgings were fine but she was extremely persuasive and would not let the subject rest until I had at least agreed to have a look at their room. The room was a little untidy at present, she added, but they would soon have it ready for me. Iwan seemed to become a little more cheerful after this.

After walking a mile we came to a house with a crowd outside and entered a room congested with friends and relatives of the deceased. Children played between the legs of the adults and some women carried babies on their backs. It was very much a family affair. A picture of the Virgin and Child and a poster advertising Smirnoff Vodka were the only wall decorations. A small gamelan band sat in one corner, their numbers augmented by a man hitting a Sprite lemonade bottle with a spoon and another playing a snake charmer's flute – mad capers up and down the scales without much melody or apparent forethought, his great cheeks ballooning as he skilfully maintained a continuous sound through a process of circular breathing. The band only played whenever one of the guests slipped the leader some money and there was no shortage of figures willing to step forward and feed the Tuk Tuk jukebox. Most of the mourners were chatting vivaciously and making merry in a gentle dance of hopping, bending at the knee and waving ceremonial sashes. The men wore fringed turbans with western style shirts and trousers while women were more colourful in bright sarongs or unadorned dresses.

Because of all the people in the room, it took me some time to notice that the dead man was in the far corner. He lay propped up in a coffin on the floor, wearing his suit, a hat and spectacles. Without his ghastly colour he might have been surveying the scene and merely feeling poorly. Some young girls were kneeling beside the body and were the only ones to show signs of grief, occasionally crying and looking up at the dancing figures with apparent resentment. Sometimes dancers would approach the coffin and lean over holding out their arms and rippling their hands through the air as if imitating a stormy sea. This would go on all night, I was told, and the body would be buried the following day. Everyone would bring considerable quantities of food as presents for the bereaved family.

The son of the deceased continued to look dispirited until his wife again touched on the subject of accommodation. I shrugged off any more commitment to accept and returned my attention to the surrounding activity.

'You are liking it?' Karya asked. I hesitated, uncertain of how to reply. I never went wild over funerals. Iwan smiled hopefully, so I nodded.

'Good,' she said, and then twitched her head towards the corpse. 'Tomorrow we' – she didn't know the word and went through the motions of digging – 'him, and you can have the room in the evening.'

'Good God! You mean *this* is the room you want to rent?'

Yes, this was the room. Her father-in-law was no longer needing it, she explained. Her husband's smile had grown to Balinese proportions and he was nodding enthusiastically. Candles turned the dancing into a shadow puppet display on the ceiling, the air held a musty smell of old clothes and the flickering lights teased the corpse with motion. From then on I viewed it with increased repugnance and alarm at the thought of having its ghost as a bedfellow, until some time later I managed to slip away unnoticed. By then my host had turned sombre again and every so often was casting dark glances towards the coffin. He was back in mourning, bitterly assessing the years of lost rent caused by the old man having lingered on for so long.

2 · Thai Jinks
and High Hong Kong

The short flight from Medan in Sumatra to Malaysian Penang is unusual in that both endpoints appear in the top five international airports blacklisted by world aviation. Their faults include unsettled and turbulent weather with frequent zero visibility; exceptionally weak runway lights and inefficient radio transmissions which are often blacked out by power failures; inadequate fire-fighting personnel and safety measures; and radio controllers whose English is incompetent and who are not unknown to disappear for refreshments during a landing. This I discovered later and to anyone travelling in ignorance the flight is an agreeable way to spend thirty minutes. The coffee is excellent.

The seat next to mine acted as a clamp on the bulky frame of Brad Roseberry, a balding Texan with a love of cigars and mysteries. He was a marine engineer currently on loan as an oil consultant to the governments of South-East Asia and his summary of the wells he had spudded across the orient was long, regular and latterly indistinguishable from hiccups. Much more interesting were his theories on the Bermuda Triangle, UFOs and Spontaneous Human Combustion. This last phenomenon, apparently occurring suddenly and causing a person to be reduced to ashes, was one which he genuinely feared.

'You ever heard about Jim Thompson?' Brad asked.

I confessed the name meant nothing to me. 'Did he combust?'

'No, I don't reckon he did. Let me tell you about Jim Thompson. That's a real neat mystery.' His fear of Spontaneous Human Combustion seemed temporarily forgotten as he took out, lit and sucked at an adequate fuse. 'He was an American, at various times a soldier, sailor, spy, raconteur, connoisseur of art, and the founder of the Thai silk industry that made him a millionaire. He was sixty-one years old, fit, healthy and strong on the day in 1967 when he disappeared without a trace.' Jim Thompson had evidently first arrived in Asia during the Second World War, dropped by parachute into Thailand by the forerunner of the CIA to counter the Japanese occupation. After the war he made his home in Bangkok and transformed Thailand's silk industry from a small cottage industry into a multi-million international business. He often used to take breaks at the Cameron Highlands, a former colonial hill station in Malaysia, and always stayed at the same guest house. He knew the area well but it was from here that he mysteriously disappeared.

'The area's all jungle but there ain't no way he got lost,' Brad contended. 'On the day of his disappearance they say he told his hosts that it was impossible to get lost in these jungles. All you had to do was find a stream and follow it down, and its water would keep you alive. Besides, he had been trained in guerrilla warfare and jungle survival.' He had acted strangely that day, it was later reported, at first appearing in high spirits and suggesting to his hosts and a friend that they should all go for a picnic. When everything had been prepared he suddenly decided against it. The others had insisted and he reluctantly went with them but the whole time he looked nervous and on edge. When they got back he did not join them for the customary nap but is thought to have gone for a walk. He was never seen again. A huge search by the army and locals with trackers produced nothing. Rumours abounded. Had he suddenly recognised someone or something that made him afraid during the picnic preparation? An unusually high number of Thai registered cars were said to have been seen in the area that day and stories of high level espionage, underhand business deals and political intrigue kept the press speculating for weeks over reasons for his likely abduction and murder. Brad favoured another theory.

'I reckon he was just acting and it was all a stunt to contrive his own disappearance so he could start a new life. His home in Bangkok contained pictures of the Buddhist prince, Vasantara, who did just that to seek a higher spiritual existence. I guess we'll never know the truth. Maybe Jim Thompson's still around somewhere all dressed up in saffron, but in 1974 they officially declared him dead.'

As our plane descended towards Penang and Brad was once more respudding wells in Sarawak, I decided to go to the scene of the mystery. Malaysia was not a large country and the Cameron Highlands could easily be accommodated on a procrastinator's route to Thailand.

THE MAXIMUM PENALTY FOR TRAFFICKING AND ILLICIT

POSSESSION OF DRUGS AND FIREARMS IS DEATH. The words were startling even though the notice bearing them, positioned on a wall in the customs hall, was no larger than another nearby carrying a cryptic message from Thai Airways ('Please have your check-in bags security checked before check-in, thank you!'). I asked the customs officer if the death penalty was ever implemented. Over thirty Asians had been hanged since the ruling came in seven years ago, he explained, and three Australians, two Britons and a French girl were awaiting trial. 'There are seldom any reprieves. They're having to expand the gallows now,' he added severely, and gave my pack a particularly thorough search. There was nothing to find as I had no interest in getting high, in any sense of the word.

There were many signs in Penang and one in the taxi from the airport to the main city requested me not to spit in English, Malay, Tamil and Chinese. These last three represented the principal ethnic groups in the country and while Malaysia's economists were primarily concerned with rubber, tin and *inflasic* (their improved rendering of 'inflation'), her politicians tried to keep a peaceful working arrangement between Malays, Indians, Chinese and sixteen distinct minority groups. The politicians had failed with the largest concentration of Chinese in 1965 with the result that Singapore separated and became independent, and were still struggling to suppress continued guerrilla activity by communist forces which used the country's seventy-five per cent covering of forest as a refuge. Malaysia was nevertheless boldly overseeing the marriage of her various components, having always been used as a relatively amorphous extension to the empires and trading houses of others, with a history that was an extension of theirs and a population that was of their mixing. To a people that were essentially of Chinese extraction came the Siamese, Sumatrans, Javanese, Portuguese, Dutch and finally (excluding the cruel Japanese invasion during the last war) the British who brought over the Indians to work their mines and plantations and resettled 500,000 Chinese. The result of all this foreign interference, as far as the visitor is concerned, is a fascinating diversity of religions, cultures, cuisine and signs.

Brad had let me share his taxi and soon we pulled up in a Georgetown street between the Penang Moral Uplifting Association and the Peking Chinese Chin Woo Athletic Association. Brad was based in Medan when his wife was with him but when she went for her annual six-week vacation to the States, he immediately moved over to Georgetown to stay with his Chinese girlfriend. He waved goodbye and walked off without giving the Penang Moral Uplifting Association so much as a glance. I set off in the other direction to look for a cheap hotel, and soon developed a liking for Georgetown. The standard of living was sufficiently high to have removed the clamouring street hustlers that plagued Indonesia, the atmosphere was more relaxed, *bases, loris* and *motorsikels* were better behaved, and it was pleasant to look at and be an accepted part of Malaysia's cultural hotch-potch. Not even the thunderous downpour which made the water level of the drains rise two feet in as many hours and forced the odd rat out into the flooded streets, dampened my enthusiasm that evening as I studied a map of the country in a down-market hotel off Love Lane. The Tye Ann Hotel had been a natural choice for it was said to serve the best porridge in South-East Asia and have prices that were immune to *inflasic*.

Two days and six helpings of porridge later I took the ferry over to Butterworth on the mainland and set off south. Hitching proved easy and a succession of *loris* took me across a flat landscape of oil palms, rubber trees with cups fixed below slanting grooves tattooed in their bark, and stretches of fence where hundreds of white rectangles the size of bathmats were hanging – latex that had been hardened by adding formic acid and pressed into mats ready for export. My last lift was with a young Indian, Ashok Saxena, who drove a lorry for the Blue Valley Tea company and was returning to the factory at the far end of the Cameron Highlands. The foothills of distant mountains began at Ipoh and Ashok explained that there was a curfew in force here because of the area's guerrilla activity and role as a drug smuggling centre. The side-road to the Cameron Highlands climbed for forty miles in continuous curves and ended in a cool mountainous region of steep tea plantations neatly clipped in comparison to the luxurious tangles of valley jungle. The area was named after a Scottish explorer, William Cameron, who returned from a trip in 1885 to say he had found a high plateau surrounded by mountains. It was never certain if this particular area was the one he had visited but he was given the benefit of the doubt. Ashok let me out at the village of Tanah Rata and left me his address and an invitation to stay with his family. 'Our house is only fifteen miles from here and from it you can easily visit the tea plantation. If you come in two days' time you can attend a wedding ceremony. It's a big occasion.' I assured him I would just have a quick search for Jim Thompson and be there in time.

Tanah Rata was a sleepy village with wooden or concrete houses painted blue, green or white lining its angled streets. On a wall inside one of its cafés was a pitch fork with two prongs whose inner edges were barbed to prevent the release of a victim's neck – an 'Amok-catcher' – and a sketch alongside showed a crowd chasing an unfortunate Indian with such a device. Nowadays Tanah Rata never ran Amok and it seemed to reserve its energy for cooking. Coffee vendors poured condensed milk into each coffee and mixed it by squirting a three-foot long plume of liquid into the air and nimbly caught it in another mug before it hit the ground. At other stalls roti-makers were vigorously twirling expanding pancakes in the air until they were the size of latex bathmats. Asian cuisine was not just a sensual accomplishment but an athletic event.

The village was shared between Malays and Indians but their influence faded a few miles further on and was replaced by the more solid and commodious buildings of a colonial retreat. I walked past the garden and window boxes of the Old Smokehouse Hotel where a profusion of flowers threatened to smother a nostalgic recreation of Tudor England right down to its black and white bird box, past squadrons of bright and beautiful butterflies impaled by pins inside glass cases and for sale at an isolated shop, and found a dormitory bed in the Holiday Chalet for a nightly charge of five ringgit (£1.30). I used this as a base for two days to scour the jungle.

The jungle paths turned out to be much longer than anticipated because the locally sold map of the area was a diabolical piece of cartography and full of gross inaccuracies. Nevertheless this did not subtract from my enjoyment of jungle peregrination – 'walking' is somehow inadequate in the animistic world of jungle. The way was always dark and dank, twisting under hanging creepers and past snares of tangled roots. The canopy of leaves high above glowed translucent green, patterned by highlighted veins or the silhouettes of lower branches, and parted occasionally to allow a shaft of light to reach the ground where pitcher plants held horn-shaped flowers open to the rationed sky, the few Rajah Brooke butterflies that had escaped the collector's pin flashed their large blue wings, a blundering stag beetle walked with pincers open towards a bush covered in white flowers as if silk handkerchiefs had been laid flat, pinched in the centre and now hung delicately like the roofs of pagodas, and millepedes, when touched, curled their orange and black striped bodies into balls so perfectly formed it was impossible to detect any joints. Sometimes a bird trilled or an insect screeched and sometimes there was just silence that made the sound of my breathing seem desperate. It was impossible to forget that the Indians of this region, though friendly, still hunted with blowpipes and darts tipped with a paralysing poison made from the ipoh tree, and that this really was the ideal place to hide a body. Naturally I never found any trace of Jim Thompson but his disappearance no longer came as a surprise to me. If he had merely gone for a walk then he must have taken the local map and followed it faithfully.

The fifteen miles to the Blue Valley Tea plantation, the highest in Malaysia, and Ashok's village of Kampong Raja, were along a tortuous mountain road where jungle frequently gave way to surprising views of cleared hillsides supporting terraced fields of vegetables. Lettuce and cabbages were enormous. So was the Blue Valley Tea receptionist, Mrs Govinda. She was an amiable woman who wore a thick cardigan above an expanse of filled sarong. Despite an initial smile she looked distinctly inflasick. All movement seemed an effort and her size made her surrounds look small. She was finishing a letter which had put her in a bad mood and asked me to wait. Her office *was* small and Mrs Govinda's position in it left no room for secrecy (six mistakes in six lines). When she had finished she kindly offered to give me a tour.

'I'm afraid the machinery is not running today,' she apologised, 'but you'll get an idea of the process,' and she slowly led me to a verandah with a view of the slopes. I realised suddenly how tea was a commodity I had always taken for granted without wondering what happened to it when it left the bush.

From our vantage point the scattered teapickers looked as if they had been buried from their chests downwards in a lawn for the bushes had been trimmed to leave a flat top. Both men and women were employed as pickers and they supported large wicker baskets on their backs by means of a band around their foreheads. They used shears with a square plastic container attached to the upper blade so that by flicking the shears as they snipped at the uppermost growth, the tender new leaves fell into the container and were then emptied into their basket. As if carrying the heavy baskets through the stubborn bushes was not enough, tea always seemed to favour the steepest slopes.

'It looks exhausting work,' I commented. 'How much do they pick in a day?'

'Each worker averages between forty and fifty kilograms in a seven and a half hour shift. They get paid by the weight, ninety cents per kilogram.' By the time we reached the processing sheds I had calculated this was twenty-four pence.

The teabag machine – 120 per minute – was not working but Mrs Govinda described its mechanics in detail. It was obvious that she had a particular fondness for this machine, seeing it not so much with nuts, bolts and miles of gauze tubing in mind but with a slow secretary's envy. She showed me where the newly cut leaves were withered for twenty hours under large fans before passing through choppers and graders which separated three qualities. The poorest grade contained bits of stalks and was sold in bulk as 'menu' quality to cheap restaurants. The tea was still green at this stage but turned black-brown in twenty minutes during 'fermentation', a moisturing process without using chemicals, and was then dried. Within twenty-two hours tea could be picked, processed and boxed. She apologised for the lack of activity but explained that they only had eighty employees and were short-staffed.

'How many would the factory like to employ?'

'About two hundred.' Her grave expression gradually melted into a weak grin. 'Would you like a job?'

'I don't think my neck muscles could cope.' I bought some tea and thanked Mrs Govinda for the tour, retracing my steps and looking around the plantation with a new awareness. Admittedly the cost of living was lower here but the paucity of workers did not seem surprising when a day's back-breaking labour on these steep slopes earned a wage of £12. I wandered on down to Ashok's house hoping that my packet of tea was not a bargain at his expense.

The house was small but comfortable and when I arrived the family were gathered in the living room making balls of sweet dough for the wedding celebration, talking excitedly and ignoring an American comedy on a colour television. I was welcomed by Ashok, his wife, father, mother, step-mother, two children and the spasmodic traffic of eleven brothers, sisters and their respective families. There was also an old woman who hobbled around on an aluminium walking stick with an ebony handle, muttering, and sometimes she would squat on the floor and shuffle along on hands and feet dragging her body like a wounded tarantula. It was impossible to work out who was who but this was unimportant. Asian families, like roti, seemed endlessly elastic and readily extended to accept a new member.

Ashok was in his late thirties. His father had left Madras fifty years earlier and come by sailing boat and bullock cart to find work. A strong bond with India had been preserved and all the family had subsequently paid visits to the country of their origin. I asked Ashok if he felt Malaysian or Indian.

'Physically I feel Malaysian because I was born here and have always lived here but spiritually I feel Indian. A Malaysian identity is not very strong and we lead a life close to Indian traditions.' He spoke Tamil amongst his family but was fluent in English and Malay. On one side of a wall cabinet was a picture of his initiation ceremony. It showed Ashok as a fifteen-year old boy with a metal skewer six inches long that had been pushed through his tongue while it was extended from his mouth. The skewer had stayed there for about an hour until he had completed the customary round of visits to relatives. On the other side of the cabinet was a framed picture of a forest of English oaks embossed with the words 'I sought my soul, but the soul I could not see. I sought my God, but my God eluded me. I sought my brother, and I found all three.' And between these images of peace and penance the television showed an American farce with tedious bursts of laughter as belated clues to humour. A Malaysian identity was far from apparent, unless this was it.

That evening in heavy rain we drove to a temple in another village where the wedding was to take place. The temple was little more than an enclosure with three walls and a roof garden of statues that darkness reduced to an impression of eroded muppets. Inside sat a painted goddess sprouting a confusing assortment of arms and near her was a donation box guarded by an old woman. Her head remained motionless but her eyes darted from the goddess to me in shifty squints and she appraised me mistrustfully, almost fearfully, her tongue poking this way and that in a half-witted, lizard-like gesture. There were few other people in the temple and the atmosphere was quiet because evidently the wedding had not taken place and there had been a tragic accident. The car containing the groom, his mother, brother and a friend had been speeding and all four had been killed when it left the road. The news seemed to have been accepted with calm fatalism. (Ashok later told me that the father of the friend had forbidden his son to go for some reason and when he heard that his son was dead, he said it was better that way – if a son didn't obey his father, he might as well be dead.) Ashok had never met those involved and shrugged off the misfortune as unavoidable karma, the justice of reward or punishment for past deeds.

'That is Indrani, the Goddess of Rain,' he whispered, pointing to the many-armed figure.

'Don't you get enough rain here?' I asked. 'It seems to pour down every day at 5 p.m.'

He laughed. 'Yes, *we* get enough but the significance is more symbolic. In India rain is regarded as the bringer of food and prosperity.'

An old man, dressed in spectral white – white turban, beard, shirt and longhi – who had been attending to the rain goddess and adding to the moat of flowers and offerings around her, came over to give us roasted peanuts and a banana. More people began arriving and he did the same to them. Everyone casually threw their banana skins away so that they hit and got caught on the temple fence. Anxious to fit in, I did the same even though it was impossible to tell whether this ritual was significant to Indrani or one of mere convenience. The fence was soon predominantly yellow and effectively screened the proceedings. The priest then returned with an oil lamp. Each of my companions warmed his hands over the flame, put his hands together in the praying position, repeated this three times, dipped a finger in some dust on the lampholder and smeared a fingermark on his forehead. When it was my turn I forgot to mark my forehead and one of the others did it for me. I asked what it meant.

'When someone dies and is cremated, you get ashes . . . ' I must have frowned while wondering whose ashes had just been stuck to my forehead. Ashok read my thoughts. ' . . . no, these are not real ashes but represent them. They are to remind us that we too will be ashes one day, to remove our arrogance and make us humble.'

The old priest next came along with a brass goblet containing a viscous liquid with lumps submerged in it. This time he approached me first. He indicated I was to cup my hands and when I did so, he filled them with this liquid. It had the colour of a 10,000-mile oil change and I eyed the evil-looking concoction with an image of bad karma, wondering when drops would start seeping between my fingers and how long it would be possible to postpone the inevitable. The others nodded eagerly so I drank it. It turned out to be a palatable but sickly sweet syrup with chunks of fruit. No one else was offered any but my hands were immediately refilled. Ashok said it was an honour for a visitor. Just when it seemed there would be a chance for me to slip into the background the priest gave me half a coconut filled with bananas and flowers and slipped two garlands of gaily coloured petals around my neck. Everyone began to clap. It was a touching gesture but I felt embarrassed and stood there like the first prize in a flower show, and with a horrible suspicion that my garlands had been intended to adorn a bride and her groom.

'Hindus seem to smile a lot,' I commented to Ashok as we drove back.

'Yes, we like to laugh because when you laugh the heart is big. When you don't laugh, it is hard and small.'

To be a Hindu you must be born a Hindu and then you remain one forever. I could not become one and Ashok could not be anything else; but Malaysia, with a vague face and a big heart, didn't seem too concerned with the fixed state of things.

It was at about this time, while travelling south, that elephants began to rouse my interest. They managed to hold it during my disappointment over the island metropolis of Singapore. I had expected it to have preserved the odd den of colonialism and oriental mystique for those who admired Maugham and Conrad but there was nothing besides Raffles Hotel busily dispensing its daily average of 1000 gin slings (3000 when a liner drops by). And I had expected Chinatown to be some heady stramash of vice and loose chickens but President Lee Kuan Yew's tight fist policy and advertised ethics ('It's nice to be polite', 'Work as a team, and make productivity our theme') had created a clean skyscrapered city. It was laudable the way everything ran smoothly, from the economy to spot fines for jay walkers, but this was taken to the extreme. The city's marvellously diverse population appeared restrained by Swiss virtues; neutrality, tidiness and self-righteous efficiency. The sum of Singapore's parts left me with a total that was lacking. So my attention turned to elephants.

The first one to cross my trail had been dead for almost ninety years but it surfaced in a newspaper where it was the subject of an unfair denouncement. In 1894 a bull elephant charged and derailed a Malayan steam engine. It died in the encounter but for years it was regarded as a hero for valiantly defending his herd. The newspaper debunked this with a report by an animal behaviourist who asserted that the elephant had probably just been bad-tempered as bulls rarely associated with herds and left their defence to old aunts or grannies. After reading this hardly a day went by without mention of elephants. While hitching up Malaysia's east coast I met a traveller who had visited a camp of working elephants at Chiang Mai in north Thailand, and then heard several reports of an impending elephant festival which took place each year in Surin, a city 250 miles east of Bangkok. Some said that the Elephant Round-Up was dull but it was hard to believe that a gathering of 200 elephants could fail as a spectacle if for no other reason than the quantities involved. Surin at once became my next destination.

It was late one evening when I reached Hat Yai, the first major town in southern Thailand. At the Thai border I met Peter Shaw, an Englishman working as a teacher for a year in Malaysia and on his way for a holiday in Bangkok. Together we walked the streets looking for a hotel and soon met with a boy who offered to be our guide. He spoke a smattering of English and apart from his extensive knowledge of each hotel's facilities and their prices, he was a keen follower of world strife.

'Beirut,' he said with bright saucerish eyes, 'bang, bang', and he squatted and shook with the butt of an imaginary gun dug into his stomach. A moment later came 'El Salvador,' a thumbs down, 'bang, bang', then 'Mandarin Hotel, sixty baht double, own bathroom'. It was full. We walked on.

'Iran-Iraq . . . bang, bang', preceded 'King's Hotel, eighty baht' but it was also full. By the time we had heard about England–Argentina, Northern Ireland, Indonesia–Holland, America–Russia – all bang, bang or almost bang, bang – the Hua Nam, Yee Kee and Station Hotel had been accurately reviewed but all had been full. The next hotelier also shook his head, and our wee guide seemed despondent after a particularly vigorous re-enactment of Vietnam.

'No good. Weekend. Hotels full of Malays,' explained our ten-year-old acolyte of bedroom prices and war zones, and added gravely, 'people fucking'.

Eventually an unmarked hotel let us sleep on blankets in the main corridor for ten baht and we passed a night disturbed by footsteps, mosquitos and salacious giggles.

'Don't judge Thailand on last night,' Peter said over breakfast the next morning. 'The Thais are justifiably held to be the most beautiful race on earth. Not just in good looks but with a personality to match. They're cheerful and friendly, and the country is much more than its sinful reputation. Mind you, Bangkok is pretty wild in that respect. Malaysia produces one-third of the world's rubber and I bet most of it ends up in Bangkok.'

Peter headed west to spend a few days at a beach resort while I continued north by train to Surin, one thousand miles away. The elephant get-together was due to begin in two days which meant travelling through the night and stopping in Bangkok only long enough to change trains in order to arrive in time. Thailand's railway schedule was kind on its engines but the service worked with Singaporean efficiency and endearing regard for whistle blasts and the shine on the stationmaster's boots. In any other part of the world the girls who regularly passed along the aisle would have modelled cosmetics or relaxed on the bonnets of new cars but in Thailand they carried trays and sold refreshments. As the train slipped slowly, precisely, through a jigsaw landscape of rice-fields, I became absorbed in a booklet on Thailand's working elephants. Although only a few pages in length, it was a factual summary of the species from the forehead to the final four toes.

'An elephant expresses anger with shrill screams and trumpeting' – but – 'flapping of ears and low rumbling noises, punctuated by squeaks, signify contentment.' An elephant has poor eyesight, it was stated, but acute senses of hearing and smell. Its skin is tough but very sensitive. Each mature adult weighs between three and four tons and consumes one thousand pounds of fodder every twenty-four hours. Elephants are still the most effective machinery for extracting timber in rough country, being strong, good hill climbers and excellent swimmers. They are very similar to human beings, apart from weighing sixteen stone at birth; they reach maturity at twenty, work best between the years of twenty-five and forty-five, retire at sixty or seventy and rarely live to one hundred. It concluded by saying they were generally placid creatures except during the mating season when they experience temperamental periods of musth 'and during this time, between March and May, they take their holidays in the jungle'. I frequently looked up hoping to catch a glimpse of at least one of Thailand's 12,000 working elephants but there was none tethered to the houses on stilts or to the colossal Buddhist stupas rearing up as long-handled domes that we frequently passed. It wasn't even the right season for their holidays and the outcrops of jungle contained nothing wilder than water buffalo and, where they flanked a muddy river, children with fishing rods of sticks and string.

Elephants are allowed in the streets of Surin only during the two days of this festival. To reach the main scene of the activities I followed an elephant ambling along a busy thoroughfare amid the usual Asian turmoil, fumes and cacophony of cars, buses, lorries, scooters and daredevil bicycle trishaws. Its mahout was a youth who appeared unconcerned when it frequently stopped to accept an offering of food and once, when none was offered, it paused in front of a stall owner and intimated with a four-ton gesture that the bananas looked good. It was a slow journey as the streets were full of appetising fodder. At one stall the elephant was given a brown stick of sugar cane about two feet long. This was thrown into its mouth and the trunk immediately extended for another. The vendor gave it two more pieces but then waved away the trunk. Standing next to the stall with her back to the elephant was an elderly woman holding a folded umbrella, brown and about two feet long. As the elephant withdrew its trunk from the stall it suddenly caught sight of the umbrella. Up rose the trunk, the tip arched over the woman's head, turned down and then stopped. Elephants have little tact but an acute sense of smell, and very sensitive skin. The mahout drummed his heels on its neck and they resumed their journey up the street.

On the edge of town we came to a sports ground which had been fenced off into a vast arena. Spectators were packed around the edge. I put the longest lens on my camera, hung it around my neck and attempted to look in a hurry as I followed my elephant into the section reserved for participants. The officials stared at my lens and let me pass. In the far corner was an awesome sight. Over 200 elephants were standing beside a long line of green fodder, their trunks swinging like slow pendulums as they picked up leaves and flung them into their mouths without losing rhythm – thousand pound diets left little time for relaxation. Their mahouts were dressing them in dainty parade harnesses. A few baby elephants peeped out from their mothers' legs and some were so small they could have scarcely weighed sixteen stone. Whenever a calf was given a bunch of bananas it ate them one by one after first peeling them. It held the banana in the curl, not the tip, of its trunk, bit off one end and squeezed the fruit out of its skin. When grown-ups were given a bunch they ate the whole lot including the stalk in a single mouthful. There was much ear-flapping in progress, and I listened hard for low rumbling punctuated by squeaks but it is regretfully easy for the novice to confuse elephantine contentment with indigestion. Yet there is something wonderfully reassuring about an elephant, its relaxed manner, latent strength and ponderous, honest bulk.

It took some time to find a mahout who could speak English but eventually I met Throp and Ananda. Throp was a slight youth in his late teens with a grin to match his chunky shell necklace. A length of tartan was knotted around his head and the loose end hung down until it touched Ananda. He was sitting on her forehead.

'Ananda twenty-six years old,' Throp said from a height advantage of eight feet. 'She is good worker but man elephant is stronger and better with teeth.' In Asia only men elephants evidently grew tusks and these were valuable assets for levering logs. A mature bull might stand ten feet at the shoulder and could carry up to half a ton on his back. I asked how he had come by Ananda.

'She come from camp elephants. In Chiang Mai many elephants. My father has three. One he caught wild in the forest.' He described how wild bulls and cows were occasionally captured by luring or driving them into enclosures or by lassoing a back leg while chasing them on domesticated colleagues. They soon became domesticated and could be ridden within a few weeks but it sometimes took them two years to overcome the shock of capture. Only rarely did they become killers and even then they continued to work but the Burmese practice of replacing their wooden bell with one of brass was usually followed.

'What does Ananda do when she is not working?'

'She likes swimming and football.'

Football? It was time for the festival to begin and Throp rode off laughing. Ananda bounced into a lively gait and left me standing with both boots comfortably inside one of her footprints. She was off to play football.

From a trainer's point of view, one of the beauties of working with elephants is that you only need success with a few and you can have a mass gymnastic display. The afternoon's events started with a synchronised demonstration of commands in which a small herd stood on three feet, balanced their mahout on their tusks (those that had them), knelt, lay down and rolled. If Thai elephants were indeed the most intelligent of their species as they were reputed to be, perhaps they were thinking how easily mankind was amused. Lift a leg and humans clap . . . and I clapped as loudly as anyone. Then came a parade of mahouts and their charges dressed in ornate battledress and they came marching forward as a front 400 tons wide. This cleared the way for the largest bull to be brought on wearing a work harness and pulling a long rope. Fifty soldiers took hold of the other end and soon a tug-of-war was under way. It was a fair match but the elephant proved superior. Ten more soldiers were added to the opposition and this time both sides were equal. The elephant lent forwards with his trunk resting on the ground and the skin around his neck stretched taut by the harness while the soldiers dug their heels in and lent back with their shoulders almost touching the dusty pitch. For five minutes there was a stalemate which neither the exhortations of the mahout or sergeant-major could break. Suddenly the elephant threw out his trunk and let out a long quivering bellow. Gradually he inched all sixty soldiers forwards into foot-shuffling defeat.

I hadn't seen Throp up till then but after a break for mammoth snacks he and Ananda appeared in a *jeux-sans-frontières* contest between ten of the herd. Each elephant stood spaced out on the starting line beside a large basket, facing its own row of bottles set up at ten-yard intervals. On the starting command each had to run to collect the first bottle, return and drop it in the basket, and repeat this until all the bottles had been retrieved. Two competitors were disqualified in this event – one for straying to eat a banana leaf and causing an obstruction, and the one to finish first for cheating. When it had been trailing in second place it began throwing the bottles at the basket from a distance and when they failed to go in, it just turned round and carried on as if they had. Ananda did well and came in second. I hoped she was pleased because she hadn't been selected for the football match.

Two goal markers set up fifty yards apart and a pitch of suitable proportions was marked out for a seven-a-side game of soccer. The mahouts wore either yellow or blue strips and it was a normal game in every respect except that the ball was larger than normal, like a beach ball. One side kicked off and for the next twenty minutes the ball flew around the pitch at all heights and all levels of power, being pursued by twelve elephants and watched by two ten-foot goalkeepers. At first the spectacle was pure comedy but this element declined when one realised that the elephants actually understood the rules and purpose of the game. They knew they were not allowed to use their trunks and that the ball was supposed to cross their opponents' goal line. They took corner kicks and made clearances, and humans only interferred as referee and linesmen. All they lacked was skill in directing the ball and the idea of passing it to a teammate. In fairness, though, the pitch was covered in obstacles. (The average elephant dropping would look formidable if fired from a heavy piece of medieval artillery.) The spectators soon ceased to notice anything unusual in the players and became absorbed in the outcome of the match.

One of the goalkeepers was outstanding. She (it was a mixed game) made three dazzling saves for the Blues, two by boldly charging the attacker and the other at full stretch of her trunk. In the closing minute the Yellow striker found himself bearing down on the ball with only the Blue goalkeeper to beat. His body seemed caught in exhausting slow motion but his stumpy legs were a blur and it was all part of his deceptive style. In no time he was upon the ball. The exact sequence of events was then hard to discern but it appeared that he feinted with the front right, missed with the front left, tripped over the ball, struck it with the back left, fouled it somewhere up front and finally, completely out of control, half-volleyed it with the back right. The ball shot out one side and the goal that followed was no fault of the Blue keeper. She was well placed to block the ball but it bounced awkwardly on the edge of a footprint, evaded her reflex grasp, hit one of her legs and trickled over the line. The realisation that it was an own goal made it all the worse for her. The Yellow striker had come to a sudden stop after scoring and the mahout sitting atop was jubilantly punching the air with both fists.

The elephant himself looked fairly overcome with emotion; there must have been squeaks and rumbles for there was certainly a feverish burst of ear-flapping. For a moment I thought he was going to sink to his knees and kiss the turf (though I suppose he could have done that standing up) but he turned and trotted lightly back to the other Yellows. The final whistle went. 1–0. The Blue goalkeeper had not moved. She stood staring at the ground, her head hung low.

Without entering the depths of tragedy, there are, I believe, few more pathetic sights on this planet than the long face of a four-ton goalkeeper who feels she has let her side down.

My impatience to get to China increased and after the Surin festival I returned to Bangkok and took the first available flight to Hong Kong – an open return ticket costing £105. I didn't mind leaving Thailand after such a tantalising glimpse because of my commitment to return after this circular extension to my journey. There was no option other than to fly because Thailand had become isolated by Burma's closed border to the west and the severely restricted relationships with her other two major neighbours, Laos and Cambodia. My departure was sudden and this made the impact of arrival all the more striking, but then nothing can prepare a traveller for the intensity of Hong Kong save perhaps an image of Manhattan impregnated by Las Vegas and their consummate proliferation.

The grey South China Sea was broken by the appearance of a hilly island. The plane banked as it turned a corner and there, without any warning, lay this bulging megatropolis of five million souls. On either side of the channel of sea thousands of skyscrapers filled the scene, so densely packed together their lines and colours formed abstract patterns and became a floor of crazy paving; those of the Kowloon Peninsula on the left housed 653,000 people per square mile, the world's most concentrated patch of humanity; those of The Island on the right managed less because a steep hill forced them to cluster uncertainly around its base, the uppermost layer threatening a complete domino collapse into the sea. Hong Kong – 400 square miles of territory, 235 islands and yet in essence crushed into a small corner where 250,000 cars create a permanent rushhour, where 'park 'n' shop' centres have no parking within two miles, where any building over ten years old is out of date and any under fifteen storeys is a waste of space, where today's technological toy was on sale yesterday, where a queer is one who prefers the opposite sex to making money, and where Red China receives one-third of her foreign exchange earnings – is a monument to commercial hysteria and, like Singapore, a former fishing village besieged by rampant capitalism. Singapore, however, is Hong Kong's dull, prim sister. The plane dropped so low it seemed to skiff the tops of the buildings, then it swung sharply to the right and descended to the sea, landing on the thin strip of precious land that had been created for Kai Tak airport's main runway.

With the help of a map and a bag of brochures thoughtfully provided free at the arrivals counter, I took a bus into the centre of Kowloon. The stampede of traffic was frightening, the pavement bustle relentless and above the street activity hung a continual barrage of signs, some in English, others in Chinese. We passed 'Good Hope Noodle', 'Yum Yum Supplies' (electronics), 'Wah Ming Optical', 'Hop Yick Leather' and 'Tak Fat Tailor'. I found a cheap bed in a hostel at the top of Chungking Mansions. It was a grandiose name for twenty storeys of congestion but the views from the top were compensation. What would have happened in the event of a fire didn't bear thinking about because the only means of escape was in a lift posted with the Chinese Whisper 'The irresponsible for accidents and overloading'. After leaving my pack in the Mansions and descending to ground level in an irresponsible crush, I went to find a back street travel agency which had been recommended to me. It was just beyond Dor Dor Fook Jewelery.

In response to China's recent policy of opening up to independent travellers many small travel agencies had sprung up to cater for the flux of foreigners wanting the cheapest means of entry, and they dealt directly with border officials rather than with those at the Chinese Embassy. It was all legal but low-profile tourism which China accepted without actively promoting, so the hostel grapevines were all abuzz with the latest reports and travel tips. I chose to travel to Guangzhou (Canton) by night boat and was assured by the agent at Phoenix Travel that the rest was a formality requiring a payment of HK$ 270 (£26, which included visa and fare), and a wait of three days to have the papers processed. Then I had to fill out an exhaustive form in duplicate which, amongst other things, asked for my political leanings. I could think of nothing sensible so put 'Upright'.

'Beijing will be cold now . . . ' the agent said as he perused the forms, catching himself as he noticed my home address, ' . . . but of course if you come from Scotland you will feel very much at home.' I thanked him for his help and immediately went and bought a thick anorak.

The noticeboard of Chungking Mansions was a miscellany of information on China, some useful, some merely interesting – it all depended on what was lying in wait beyond the bamboo curtain. Take dragons and phoenixes, for example. 'The Chinese Dragon', one notice explained, 'is said to have the head of a camel, the horns of a deer, the eyes of a rabbit, the ears of a cow, the neck of a snake, the belly of a frog, the scales of a carp, the claws of a hawk and the palm of a tiger. It has whiskers and a beard and is deaf.' 'The Phoenix is said to resemble a swan in front, a unicorn behind, with the throat of a swallow, the bill of a fowl, the neck of a snake, the tail of a peacock, the forehead of a crane, the crown of a Mandarin duck, the stripes of a dragon and the back of a tortoise.' The first sounded like a retired matron but at least recognisable, which could not be said of the second unless one was acquainted with a crane's forehead and both ends of a unicorn.

That evening I went to visit K.C. Huan who was another casual acquaintance I had made while hitchhiking in Australia. He was an accountant with Jardine and Matheson, one of the colony's leading and longest established trading houses. I had hesitantly phoned him as he had given me his address after only a short lift and it was always hard to know how genuine these 'Look me up sometime' invitations were. But K C had remembered me ('One doesn't meet too many people wearing kilts in Australian deserts') and invited me over to his house. He lived on the south side of The Island at the township of Aberdeen, a surprising and comforting name to me. My route took me first by a continuously shuttling Star Ferry and then by bus through the illuminations of the nighttime city, still roaring where it burnt most fiercely and just humming where it glowed faintly. Seen from Victoria Hill it spread out far into the darkness pulsing with radiant energy and making discernible among the streaks and dot matrix patterns the neck of a snake, the eyes of a rabbit, the claws of a hawk and all the other iridescent constituents of an incumbent Chinese dragon.

My neighbour was a middle-aged Hong Konger, a majority businessman, who chatted amenably and pointed out landmarks.

Everything was a landmark. We passed a nightclub which he said was well known for its passé atmosphere and ageing hostesses. 'It's popularly called the "Whores' Graveyard",' he explained and went on to recount the time he and his wife went there with another couple. 'The hostesses were crones done-up to the eyebrows, and they gave our wives such withering looks I thought we were going to be charged corkage for bringing our own women.' As we approached Aberdeen the piercing neon lights of the Jumbo Floating Restaurant suddenly became visible in the darkness off-shore, isolated except for the erratic attention of water taxies which flitted across the obscurity like drunken fireflies.

K C and his wife were native to Hong Kong and charming hosts. She was petite with waved black hair and a doll-like simplicity to her round face. K C was thin, slightly taller, his hair straight and his features more angular. They had married young fifteen years ago and still walked arm in arm out of pleasure rather than habit. It was pleasantly cool and we walked to a nearby restaurant, passing junks lit up in the harbour's floodlighting with their blunt-ended sterns raised high above the water. Many of them had open boxes containing a dog or hens strapped to the underside of the stern! I was equally surprised to see several men strolling about the streets holding bird cages. 'It's quite a common sight,' K C said. 'The Chinese like to take their pet birds for a walk.'

It was an evening of surprises. The restaurant was small and quiet, with a menu offering a wide choice of strangely mutilated creatures. Amongst them were:

Fried Slice Frog with Ham
Slightly Fried Frog
Fried Garoupa Ball
Fried Slice Ophicephalus cooked in Dishes and in Soup
Fried Compoy's Pig's Giblet and Veg
Braised Duck's Web in Oyster Sauce
Birds' Nests with Shredded Chicken
Stewed Shark's Fins with Superior Soup
Fried Sliced Pigeon with Giblet and Bird's Nest
Fried Pig's Brain with Egg
Braised Ventral Wall of Garoupa with O K Sauce
Sausaged
Braised Chicken Blood with Veg

Shark's Lips with Duck Sauce Thick Soup
Soyed Goose Wing and Webs

It read like the recipe for another dragon. I felt sorely for the duck paddling with webless feet and the Jaws without any lips, and dreaded to think what an Ophicephalus might be. I selected a vegetarian dish.

My hosts were able to answer several things that had been puzzling me. How could some of the poor-looking Chinese in the street afford the gold teeth that were revealed when they talked?

'These are probably those who fled from China during one of its many uprisings or purges. They have known oppression and suffering and are terrified that this will return with either a Chinese invasion or when China assumes control of Hong Kong in 1997. Like all refugees they feel insecure and prefer to keep what little wealth they can amass in a readily transportable form. With gold teeth they can turn and run any time.'

K C illustrated this fear of China with a true story about a former Chinese employee who had returned to the office a few years ago and asked for his job back. His records were consulted and it was found that he had walked out on them twenty years earlier – the date coincided with the Cultural Revolution's implementation. They asked where he had been, and he related a tragic story. He had gone by ship to Shanghai to visit relatives and had been seized in the street by revolutionaries. Accused of anti-state beliefs and activities he was sent to a concentration camp in Northern Mongolia, and he had been doing hard labour there for the last twenty years. One day he was handed a note which said the authorities had discovered that he had been wrongfully arrested and he would be released the following day. He was transported to Canton and given the boatfare to Hong Kong. He arrived with only the clothes he was wearing in a strange and shocking city for Hong Kong had scarcely possessed any skyscrapers when he had last seen it. His wife had thought he was dead and had moved to the USA after remarrying. His mother had died and a brother had divided his share of the family belongings amongst other relatives. He had absolutely nothing and so he returned to Jardines as it was the only thing from his past that was left. 'We managed to give him a job and his brother is looking after him. He's now in his fifties and trying to adjust to having lost his wife, mother and twenty years of his life. Understandably, he has little love for China.'

I asked him about the character of the Chinese, something that might prepare me for what lay ahead. He raised his eyebrows and said the Chinese mind was hard for a Westerner to understand. It was as varied as the menu. 'The Chinese suffer from agoraphobia. They love to be restricted by their environment, to be in crowds and amongst noise. Here in Hong Kong lone figures carry ghetto-blasters to their ear or wear Walkmans – we call them "Chinese Life-Support Systems". They are a very superstitious people. Blond hair is considered lucky, and so is any Chinese who can touch it. Bats also symbolise good luck, and oranges and dried mushrooms are popular as wedding presents to bring happiness and prosperity.' Flowers represented death and were the worst present you could give a Chinese. During funerals spirits had to be persuaded that the deceased was wealthy and important. Professional mourners could be hired to create a greater show of grief, and imitation money, paper clothes, houses, cars and, in the case of departing sailors, paper ships would be burnt as the spirits were easily fooled by the ashes of apparent wealth. Even the government employed a *fung shui*, an advisor on such things as the most auspicious day for official events, and the direction that office desks should face.

'Three is an unlucky number,' Mrs Huan added, 'forecasting death. When a power station was designed with three chimneys, the *fung shui* advised them to build a fourth. So they built an extra full-sized identical chimney which remains unused.'

I didn't want to make the evening an interrogation and restrained my urge to ask questions in order to let K C and his wife eat. They had both chosen Slightly Fried Frog. It looked overdone to me and I realised that the only practical preparation for visiting China was a warm anorak, an open mind and an ability to enjoy your frog the way it comes.

Over the remaining days until my visa was ready I filled my diary with endless impressions and bizarre facts. One of Hong Kong's cemeteries made an entry. In accordance with Chinese beliefs cemeteries were always set on a hill with their gravestones shaped like armchairs facing a valley or the sea. What was unique about this one was that, like everything else in Hong Kong, the graves were leased. Such was the shortage of land that the remains were exhumed after seven years, which was sufficient time for a spirit to complete its earthly affairs, and space was cleared for the next deceased tenant.

Chinese scaffolding also merited a few lines. Long bamboo poles were lashed together with plastic ties by men in casual clothes. They worked without safety equipment and built their sagging twisted frameworks forty storeys high. An American survey, however, asserted that it was the world's most efficient type of scaffolding – light, quickly assembled and stripped, cheap and stronger than other conventional materials through its flexibility. I noted markets selling steam-rollered ducks, a rare junk out in the bay with its distinctive ribbed sails and a newspaper report about a plot of land, two-thirds of an acre, which had been leased for £20 million. In an effort to attract more interest, the auctioneers had allocated it the lot number of 6886 which to the Chinese signifies wealth and happiness.

The only respect in which this city failed in a comparison to Singapore was in caring for its citizens. Singapore endeavoured to create minimum living standards and progress towards an integrated unit, but Hong Kong was overwhelmed by the immensity of its differences and the immensely interesting gamble for fortune. Perhaps this was to be expected of 400 square miles which the British thuggishly wrested from their owner and built into a colony with heinous and immoral earnings from opium. But I loved the city.

Hong Kong waited for no one. Its long-term future was ten years, its ambition was to boast the tallest storeys. It was big, flashy and fast. By contrast, the night boat to China was slow.

3 · Slow Boat to a Hospital Bed

Comprising ninety-four per cent of the population, the Han are the overwhelmingly predominant race in the People's Republic of China but fifty-four ethnic minority groups are also to be found there, mainly close to the country's border which it shares with thirteen neighbours. Neither the Han nor any of the others have O Rhesus Negative blood and so this blood group is not stocked by Chinese hospitals. I was unaware of this when I entered the world's third largest country and became one of its billion people. All excitement and exhilaration would have been swept from my thoughts had my mind known that even as I left Hong Kong my O Rhesus Negative blood was already host to incubating paratyphoid bacteria. But it wasn't to know that anything serious was wrong until I was deep inside the country, and so it tried to keep step with a revelry of impressions. The first was that a sojourn of six weeks was not going to be long enough to steal many Chinese words.

The Chinese language is tonal. One word can have as many as five or more meanings depending on the pitch and cadence of your voice. Minor vocal inflexions are therefore all that might distinguish Cantonese ducks from Cantonese whores, ink pots and bicycle wheel ball-bearings – and a different catalogue of Mandarin sundries. Chinese, in any of its eight distinct forms, is not a language to be whispered or even spoken, but must be howled or screamed. Any restaurant or boat queue will show you how. Pitch and cadence bring understanding but volume brings happiness.

However, none of the crowd of Chinese gathered at the Hong Kong docks was screaming at me even though all about were women happily nagging, scolding and arguing as they differentiated between whores, ducks and ball-bearings with incredibly piercing tones. They ignored me because I really wasn't there. In their eyes they were the only true people and the rest of the world contained 'foreign devils'. This popular denial of my existence caused problems in the queue at the customs gate. Chinese queues are not queues as Occidentals know them but are temporarily arrested riots. The gate was closed but the crowd jostled and pushed, and entire families

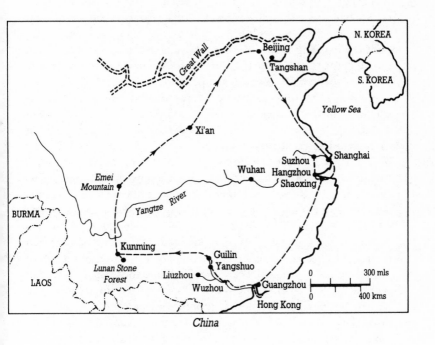

China

weeviled their way through to the front. It made no difference that
many of them carried great parcels strapped across their chests and
held to their waists like sidedrums, and one elderly woman with
bundles fore and aft held by a yoke pivoting on each shoulder
successfully prised me from my place and barged past. When I
tapped her on the shoulder as proof of my existence, she stared right
through me as if I weren't there. When the gates parted and swung
aside the mauling became frantic, the noise hysterical and I realised
the adventure had already begun as the mêlée, having squeezed me to
the rear, sucked me towards its homeland.

A small ferry took us out to a large modern passenger ship at
anchor in the bay. Deck class had been fully booked and my ticket
was for a 'reclining seat'. Naturally I was sceptical but this turned out
to be a bunk bordering a long corridor and not styled on the
Indonesian concept of reclining. We left at 9 p.m., passing naval
ships whose rigging had been gaily strung with coloured lights
either for Christmas or as camouflage against the nocturnal bright-
ness of Hong Kong. My neighbour was an educated man, a weighty
salesman off to Guangzhou to negotiate a contract to build a
catamaran ferry. He was jovial and rotund, with a double chin, red
jowls, red nose and a name that I missed. Even without a hat he
called to mind an oriental Toby-jug. He found the Chinese slow and
cautious in their dealings and was not looking forward to his trip, so
he had bought two bottles of Johnnie Walker and was halfway
through the first. Toby Jug had also bought a bottle of Courvoisier
but only because it came in a presentation pack with two glasses and
he wanted a glass. He said he didn't like brandy and insisted on
giving it to me.

'Why is it', Mr Jug asked, becoming serious when the amber
liquid had sunk to the lower label, 'that the world's oldest cultures
are now its most backward countries? Look at Egypt, Iraq, Turkey,
Crete – and China. Up until five hundred years ago China was the
most advanced country in science, engineering and technology. For
seven thousand years its arts have a continuous record of creativity,
and its written history is three thousand years old.' He interrupted
this impressive recital with a large eructation. 'The Chinese were the
first to develop paper, printing, paper money, books, a navigational
compass and the use of silk. Their calendar is older than the Roman
one and yet today China is a century behind the modern world. The

Chinese produced the first dictionary and yet half the people are illiterate. Why?' He paused to refill our glasses. 'Well I'll tell you why. They've never had enough ferries.'

'What the hell have ferries got to do with it?' I demanded, testing my eyes on the Courvoisier label and failing.

'Exactly! O.K., there's been centuries of corruption and complacency but the root cause is that the masses have been kept immobile. No ferries, no travel, no contact with the rest of the world. They're only just discovering how far behind they are. But now the big time is coming, you mark my words.' Mr Jug was talking himself into his mission. He saw it as the start of the Ferry Dynasty. I said very little as my stomach felt unsettled, and I find it hard to reason after several glasses of brandy.

We docked in Guangzhou at 7 a.m. The other passengers were moving about impatiently searching for an exit. They swarmed down to a lower deck and then rushed up when it proved to be wrong. Their tension and panic gave a non-event the air of an emergency. When the door did open they swept me down a gangway.

'Good morning. You are Mr Scott?'

I was astonished to be greeted at the passport control by a lean Chinese man of student age in a blue boiler suit. He explained that he worked for CITS, China International Tourist Services, and had been sent to meet me. With a copy of my visa application and no other obvious foreigners on the ship, Mr Koo had easily spotted me. It was early days for China's tourist industry and they could spare one officer per tourist. I had been warned to have as little to do with CITS as possible as they generally tried to encourage visitors to fly from one expensive hotel to the next and discouraged interaction with community life. But Mr Koo was polite and helpful.

'What are your travel plans in China, please?' he asked.

I explained my immediate intention of taking a ferry further up the Pearl River to Wuzhou, then travelling west, looping round to Beijing in the north, and returning by the east. Mr Koo nodded but tried to persuade me to spend time in Guangzhou ('You will find it a most modern city') and then to fly to Wuzhou. Eventually he relented and kindly offered to take me to the ferry ticket office which was several miles away. He had not dealt with this request before and had to ask a colleague the way.

He led me to the only car parked in the street. It looked like a new 1950s model from the outside but inside the seats were worn and faded. He instructed the girl driver to do a U-turn and held his arm out to stop the traffic. She waited for a lorry to pass and then edged out into the legions of cyclists who poured past continuously in both directions and paid no attention to the official CITS arm. I had never seen so many bicycles in my life. The car horn sounded and the bicycles parted and sheered around us.

'China manufactures fourteen million bicycles each year,' Mr Koo said, reaping some pride from the inconvenience. A sulphurous tang in the air stung my throat and made my eyes water. The area had all the gloom of old industrial outskirts, neglected and dirty; houses formed shabby tenement blocks, streets were narrow with pavements of ill-fitting concrete slabs and broken edges, and thronged with people. Everyone wore blue collar-less boiler suits though some had different trousers. Men and women were sexlessly identical, no skirts, no fashions, no individual hairstyles but a homogenous race endeavouring to grow into its baggy boiler suits. I commented on the colour. 'Yes, it's a popular colour,' replied my guide. I asked if they had any choice and immediately regretted it. It was a devilish question. Mr Koo smiled and remained quiet.

People, people everywhere. All appeared to be stereotypes, cloned from the same model, factory workers, doing the same thing, leading the same lives. I was struck by the uniformity and lack of individuality but it was refreshing to see workers pushing each other about and joking. Mr Koo noticed my smile and returned it, but his smile referred to the huge stack of cabbages on a trailer that a woman old enough to be his grandmother peddled through the streets behind her bicycle. 'China manufacturers many vegetables,' he explained. The bicycle traffic held us up and we drove alongside her for a while. No one looks older, sadder and more abused than an ancient Chinese woman whose frail legs bow as they peddle a quarter ton of vegetables along a cobbled street. But by the same token few others equal her stamina and grim determination, and these qualities were to show themselves inherent in the Chinese character. Eventually we reached the wharf and, to my surprise, Mr Koo bought me a ticket at the local price rather than at the special tourist one which included a seventy per cent surcharge, and departed after a friendly handshake. Thank you, China. It was a most courteous welcome.

One of several nearby noodle shops enticed me in for a cup of tea before my next voyage. The tea came in a small pot with an equally modest drinking bowl, both exquisite in handpainted flowers. Refills were free. The girls serving shouted into the street for customers and one, a hard sell noodle vendor, pulled people in as they passed the doorway. Then came the problem of knowing which set of squiggly characters on the wall signified 'Ladies' and which 'Gents'. The function is extremely difficult to convey politely in sign language so I risked one but was chased by the hard sell noodle girl, pulled back and directed to the other. The facilities inside were normal except the squats were footprints on either side of a gutter that ran the length of the room, each set of footprints being separated by a waist-high wall but having no front protection. Chinese men seemed skilful at preserving modesty and lowering their trousers no more than the few inches necessary (it's impossible not to notice, and to avoid being noticed). Foreigners soon learnt the technique by necessity for a population of one billion could afford little in the way of privacy.

The ferry left early in the afternoon. Third class (£1.20) was a long orgy of thin mattresses and pillows on a platform which filled a lower deck except for a walkway up the middle. Each berth was separated by a six-inch wooden plank. Gone were Toby Jug's modern ferries – this one was old and wooden but adequately comfortable for the sixteen-hour journey. The realm of antiquity and touches of no-frills modernity had begun. The Pearl River was four hundred yards wide here, sludge brown and hotching with boats. A small motor boat was towing twelve rafts strung out in pairs and making barely measurable progress, sampans scuttled to and fro, their bows covered with an arched tarpaulin and a man at the stern sweeping a single oar through the motions of a fish tail, a junk sailed by and made me think Captain Cook would look out and wave, and there were strange fishing craft supporting a tall metal framework where two men sat high above the water turning a paddle wheel with their feet and this winched in a long line of conical wicker fish traps. The banks showed factory chimneys copiously exhaling smoke and then fields where sickles occasionally flashed in the sun and figures were setting up stooks. With the exception of some water buffalo leisurely becoming silted into the Pearl River, all around was activity and a slow but steady purposefulness.

The canteen opened when it became dark at about 6 p.m. The

cooks were lost in a bank of steam. My phrasebook was essential for trying to translate the menu chalked on a board. Chinese writing is standard across the country but it is complex. Each character expresses an idea and builds into a detailed picture but each must be learnt individually. Some have as many as sixty components, and there are more than 40,000 characters in the language. An educated man might recognize 5,000 but many do not know any of them. Slightly Fried Frog did not appear among the few decipherable dishes so I chose duck, pork, vegetables and rice, I think, but it was all bones, many of them shattered. The poor creatures must have been slaughtered with sledge hammers. I browsed through my book and stared wistfully at 理想片平状至和来片·

Instant porridge oats.

After the meal the passengers retired to the sleeping deck which assumed the appearance of a morgue with open coffins. Everyone seemed wary of me and stared constantly. The mattress next to mine was occupied by a man in his late forties. His face did not grow a beard but he stroked hairs several inches long which sprouted from a mole on his chin. Like most men he smoked whenever he could find a cigarette. I pointed to 'What's your name?' but he just coughed and shook his head. He was unable to read. I smiled understandingly but he turned away. All eyes were fixed on me as they had been all day. Long unyielding stares. Once I stared hard back at a man and counted crocodile seconds. I blinked after ten crocodiles, he blinked after twenty but still stared. I smiled at twenty-five and then his eyes shifted. My smile was returned once in about ten instances. The gulf between us seemed immense, but xenophobia has long been a trait of the Chinese and an understandable one in view of their history. Maybe the children would be different? I held out a bag of sweets to a small girl clinging to her mother's trousers some way down the passage. The passengers came to life and prompted her. She cautiously ventured towards me, ripped the bag from my hand and ran back to her mother. At last everyone laughed and I ended my first day still feeling a misfit but knowing the gulf had been halved. Nevertheless it was going to take a lot of sweets to close it completely.

The boat's creaking timbers lulled me to sleep but it was a quite ghoulish sound which woke me the next morning. A radio was playing Chinese opera. I lay for some time trying to find something enjoyable about it and failing that, something admirable. To its credit, it was consistent in its awfulness. Tinny instruments accompanied the high-pitched wailing of a girl on a rack and a chorus of girls also on racks but at marginally less tension. My body felt in a similar state. My back was painful, my throat and nose had the symptoms of a filthy cold and my head felt delicate as if beginning a headache, something that never normally troubled me. Adding Chinese opera to all this was brutal and aided my disintegration. This is how they slaughter their animals, I thought. This woman sings to them.

We reached Wuzhou at mid-morning. It was a large industrial city and on my route only because buses ran from here to an area of weird rock formations at Yangshuo, 300 miles away. Having worked my way past the line of women porters who were waiting on the jetty with yokes and empty baskets, and found the bus station, I heard that the next bus to Yangshuo was not until 6 a.m. the following morning. Hotels were few in number and hard to find as prominent advertising was unnecessary when only a small number of Chinese had the opportunity to travel. One large hotel per 750,000 head of population was an average ratio. With diligent phrase-book manipulation I managed to find one and a dormitory bed (83p) on its fifth floor. Each floor had a matron behind a desk waiting to receive the empty keyring that guests were given, against a deposit, on entering the building. My matron withdrew a key from her pocket and unlocked the bottom drawer of a slender wooden chest. This revealed another key which opened the next drawer, and a third key which opened the top drawer. Here she kept keyrings complete with keys and she handed me one, kept the empty ring as a tally and then systematically locked up her Chinese box once again. The dormitories were basic but comfortable. Each bed was covered with a ponderous duvet and had a thermos of hot water and a pair of flipflops alongside. Thermos flasks were a welcoming institution throughout the land.

The keyring performance had acted as a tonic and my aches were forgotten as I went for a walk. Before long a teenage boy came running up to me holding an English grammar book. 'I am pleased to meet you,' he said. 'My name is Wang. I am learning English for three years.' Wang offered to show me a street market because he wanted to practice his English. He was so keen to learn that he walked most of the next hundred yards backwards to maintain face-to-face contact. He said that after school he wanted to go to college but it was very hard to find a place. There were only places for six per cent of school-leavers.

'Is English very important in schools?' I asked.

'Very important. In China today more people learn English than speak it in United States!' he laughed. 'One day I like to visit United States.'

'Is there something you particularly want to see there?'

'Yes. I want to see police cars.' He had already seen them on television. Wang was a delightful companion. He helped me buy some tangerines from the only vendor selling fruit and was angry when they turned out to be half-fermented. Shops evidently had fixed prices but street stalls were open to bargaining.

'What's he selling?' I asked, looking towards a man with a washing basin on a counter and a string running from it up to the rafters of his stall. Wang spoke to him and he pulled the string. This hoisted a large perch out of the water and it dangled there helplessly from the end knotted through its dorsal fin.

'It's a bit cruel, isn't it?' I remarked. The word was new to him and needed explanation.

'No. Not cruel. The fish do not think like us,' he argued. I didn't share his conviction when we came to a cage containing a badger with a bone protruding from its broken leg. 'Look over there!' said Wang. 'I don't know the name but it very good to eat.' It was a pangolin, a scaly anteater, and beyond were turtles, snakes and lizards. The latter were cut open like kippers and two were tied 'inside to inside' stretched out across a square frame ready for grilling. But it was the snakes that really turned my stomach. They had been slit in half along their length to reveal their backbone and then coiled into a tight circle and clamped between two sticks. Women stood ready to cook them over glowing charcoals.

Men wore their hair straight and short, middle-aged women seemed to favour single pig-tail and girls displayed variously pony tails, short and straight and some (the richer ones, Wang explained) had waved perms which were astonishing in their rarity and femininity. Cosmetics were on sale but there was no evidence of their use. When we came to a group of women digging a ditch and mixing concrete I asked if they were paid as much as men.

'Yes. In China women do all work and get same money as men.' I asked if he thought they would object to being photographed. He said some might not like it as many older people were still afraid to associate with a foreigner. In Mao's time they would have been punished for it. But he thought it would be worth trying. I took out my camera and the next moment the women had dropped their shovels and fled. 'Yes,' Wang confirmed, 'they have not liked it.'

Wang left shortly after this and I made my way back to the hotel. Every alley in Wuzhou seemed to contain a small factory. Brick works and figures bent over sewing machines or lathes were especially common. One man cranked a miniature foundry at a street corner, rotating a crucible over coals fanned by his bellows, and near him was a merchant recycling rubber and spreading what appeared to be shredded flipflops out to dry on the pavement. Then I came to a small library, a fenced enclosure beside the wall of a house and here people paid a small fee to sit on a wooden bench and read thick booklets of colourful cartoons. Beyond this in a park was a claustrophobic little zoo and a man staring at a fat python in a glass case. I could have sworn he licked his lips. All around the city's flats were dilapidated and old, and yet their roofs were a forest of television aerials. I saw only one cripple, a woman crawling along with one foot and one arm, dragging a stool as she rocked forwards and then fell back on it. She didn't stop to beg. Wuzhou was squalid and the people poor but everyone appeared to have a blue boiler suit and some food.

Diarrhoea and hot-cold shivers kept me awake all night. My diagnosis of flu combined with the unaccustomed diet still convinced me it would all pass soon, but my increasing weakness and apathy were worrying. Interest in my surrounds was rapidly being replaced by resentment at the effort they demanded. I forced myself up at 5 a.m. and set off on the twenty-minute walk to the bus station. Shortly before reaching it I stopped at a dark street corner to take some stomach pills. The bus station was teeming even at this early hour and it was hard to find a seat. Suddenly I noticed something was wrong. My camera case was missing. Panic seized me and my sickness was instantly forgotten. Realising I must have left it at the street corner, I ran back there. No more than ninety seconds had lapsed and the streets were in darkness. Surely it had to be there? My

eyes strained to catch a distant glimpse of the square outline that had
been the principal motivation of my journey for four years and
which now held my fate. But nothing was there. Someone had taken
it and all my possessions of any value. I was sick, 200 miles inside
Red China with £3 of local currency in my pocket.

Then followed my most dejected moments, alternating several
times between the empty street corner and the crowded bus station
where all eyes turned to me with cold curiosity. I checked amongst
the seats in case my mind was playing tricks on me and asked in a
loud voice if anyone had seen a red case. Everyone just stared and
several laughed in embarrassment. I called out for anyone who spoke
English but this met with the same vacant response. The staff behind
the counter also reacted to my appeals with blank expressions and
finally they turned to each other and began to giggle. This was not
meant unkindly but it cut me deeper than anything else and my
helplessness suddenly appeared overwhelming. I felt strangely
naked and very, very much alone. The weight that I had carried from
my right shoulder for so long was suddenly gone. How could I have
let it happen? And the full significance of my loss dawned on me;
over £1000 worth of photographic equipment, £120 in yuan, £600 in
travellers' cheques, an airline ticket, my passport, visa and, what I
then needed most, my only two phrase books.

'So what's next? . . . Now you've thrown everything away, what
other neat little tricks have you learnt on your travels? . . . ' Sarcasm
filled my thoughts and scorned my carelessness. This at least stirred
up a reaction and shook me out of my self-pity. Gradually my mind
turned from the emotional to the practical. The bus was due to leave
in twenty minutes but that was obviously out. There was no
alternative but to return to the hotel where the manager was able to
speak a little English. This sense of purpose helped to reduce my
anxiety but I still felt bitterly disappointed that my travels in China
had ended so abruptly. Approaching the corner for the fifth time,
not in hope but in humiliation, I made out the dim figure of a man
standing there. Maybe he had taken it, I thought, and had come back
to gloat? The contents of the case in monetary terms represented ten
years' income for the average worker. Yet it would be difficult, if not
impossible to dispose of the goods profitably. A poor peasant would
not be able to account for his acquisition honestly or find a secret
buyer, and theft was a serious offence. The man's uniform became

more apparent, the blue jacket and red collar of a policeman, and then my gaze fell to his feet where there was a tatty red case.

My camera case! The initial jolt of relief was electrifying. I couldn't understand what he said but spontaneously hugged him. He stopped speaking in surprise then his features softened and he handed over the case. I could only smile and shake my head in the confusion of gratitude and disbelief and then we made our way to the bus station. Two reversals of my fate in ten minutes had left me exhausted. My stomach felt liquid and forced me to dash off to the footprint loos. The policeman soon appeared before me, unembarrassed, and indicated the bus was about to leave. He helped me scramble aboard in time and waved goodbye. I held my prize possessions close throughout the ten-hour journey, and my spirits temporarily revived.

The bus was a typical long-nosed specimen, very old and with a radio for entertainment. It had been rattled to pieces by years of potholes and opera. A gap of ten inches separated the rear edge of the seat from the lower edge of the backrest and allowed the knees of the passenger behind to poke through. Three people were squashed onto a bench intended for two but luckily I was at the front and was able to stretch my legs. I did so after a while and the bus immediately came to a halt. The driver tinkered about under the dashboard and then sternly indicated a button on the floor which my foot must have pressed. After this we trundled through what might have been a fringe of the Scottish Highlands with its gently undulating hills covered in ferns and a low growth of bushy vegetation. It lacked only pine trees, but they came later. The valley floors were cultivated vegetable plots and bands of fields studded with sheaves of corn. Only eleven per cent of China was cultivated and with so much wasteland in sight, it was hard to believe that China was the world's largest producer of rice, sweet potatoes, kaoling, millet, barley, peanuts and tea. But I had asked Mr Koo to repeat the list and made a note of it. He had also said China ranked third for sheep production. Sheep? Not a single fleece was visible but plenty hens and pigs and a remarkable amount of their offspring. It was also common to see a man with a long stick herding a flock of protesting ducks across the fields. Nothing was left to chance. Every domestic creature had its keeper and was patiently nursed from birth to shattering.

We passed many lawn-mower style tractors, an engine set above two wheels, linked to a trailer where a man sat and steered the skeletal contraption by means of long handlebars; two jeeps and several hundred bicycles per kilometre, but no cars. Later it began to rain. The driver activated a metronome on the dashboard and a small wiper clicked back and forth as it cleared a small peephole of visibility. The rain explained why the peasants in the fields wore great sombreros, even the children who looked especially cute although comically similar to mushrooms. For a time the rain robbed us of the view and made the first roadsign barely legible, to me at least. The sign was mystifying because below the crossbones and grinning skull, the message was in English. 'It's danger – go stow.'

The hills became sharper and more pronounced and then, towards the end of the journey, the scenery had turned into something more bizarre than any Chinese fantasy painting. The valley floor became a checkerboard of fields patterned by furrows and beyond them reared up countless limestone pinnacles, each about 300 feet high with grey walls rising sheer from the flat fields, weathered into irregular shapes and standing like broken gravestones. Yangshuo was situated amongst these remarkable monoliths which erupted at the end of its streets. The Gui River ran past the town and I had come to take a boat trip celebrated for its splendid scenery upstream to Guilin.

Down by the riverside the news was not promising. I was told it was not possible to travel to Guilin by boat. The river was unusually low, the upper half of the trip was impassable and besides, foreigners were only permitted to make the journey in a downstream direction. At that moment a group of tourists arrived by boat from the permitted direction. They drifted towards the blue gaggle of dock-workers like a shower of confetti. The first of them to come ashore confirmed the bad state of the river and appeared anxious to find a glass of whisky. His companion wore a Balmoral complete with a clan badge dangling loosely over his forehead. I asked if he came from Scotland.

'Well sure – at least my ancestors did.' He tapped the badge which was closer to home on the Mississippi. 'MacMirth, related to the MacDonalds.'

I nodded amiably and walked on, moving with difficulty through a herd of ponies that had suddenly materialised with posies of plastic flowers Balmoralling their heads, and made for the town's massive rock garden. The doors of the streets had been closed before the arrival of MacMirth and his party but suddenly they had burgeoned into colourful souvenir stalls. The changing scene. I wondered if it would prove a short evolutionary process from MacMirth to Mac-Donald hamburgers.

Yangshuo's beauty brought me closer to this great unknown country but my health was failing. My appetite had gone and that night I dreaded going to bed for fear of waking up worse. For a week my diary went unwritten.

12 December: What a hellish week – now I'm lying in a hospital in Kunming, 700 miles from Yangshuo, and owe a large debt to two American girls.

I left Yangshuo the day after my arrival and travelled in another ailing bus along the washboard road to Guilin. The driver had short hair which stuck up as if he were in a permanent state of fright. Perhaps it was something to do with the pot-holes. The incredible hill formations continued for hours. We refuelled once near a fire station with a strange fleet of engines including a motorbike with a watertank forming a sidecar, presumably for small quick alarms! We reached Guilin late in the afternoon. Very cold. I hadn't eaten for two days but still had no appetite.

In one street, next to a man with a dozen dead rats strategically placed around a saucer of pink powder to demonstrate the effective-ness of his poison, was a table where two men and two women sat in white overalls, hair covers and surgical masks. [They were street doctors who supplemented the work of 'barefoot doctors'. The latter, an innovation of Mao Zedong, were merely trained in first aid and simple diagnosis.] I went up to them and pointed at 'fever' in my phrase book. A crowd gathered and tried to read my complaint. They needn't have bothered – one of the doctors announced it with an air of triumph. The crowd looked pleased. He handed me a bag of pills. Local pills for local bugs. Two pills, three times daily, twenty-six pence. It took a long time for me to understand. There was a time when Chinese doctors were only paid when they brought about a cure. If that system still operated today, these doctors would have owed me twenty-six pence.

Guilin was freezing. It would be warmer in Kunming, they said. Bananas grew there. I had once heard the same said of Iceland but I left by train that evening even though the thought of a thirty-six-hour journey was horrific. The train had come from Shanghai, a minimum of sixty hours away. That was a good thing about China – whenever you felt alarmed there was always something more alarming to provide a comforting comparison.

The train was packed, a struggle even to get aboard. Some passengers kindly cleared four inches of seat so I could perch on the edge, and there was a small area of table within reach so I could lean over and rest my head. Had a bad cough, a throbbing headache, nausea, and my skin had developed blotches of inflammation. After four hours I went to find an attendant to see if they had any spare sleepers. It took me five minutes to squeeze along the length of two coaches. The attendant was a grumpy woman. There was some misunderstanding and she suddenly started screaming at me and then slammed her cubicle door shut in my face. Returned to my seat and so began my most wretched night.

After twelve sleepless hours, two American girls passed. Deb and Val were students and spoke reasonable Mandarin. Within no time they had found me a spare 'hard sleeper', some fruit and a doctor. The doctor gave me pills. I never realised it was such a pill society. More pills soon arrived, dozens of them, from other passengers who had heard about the sick foreigner. Their kindness was amazing. A man nearby frequently brought me a mug of hot water. Deb and Val brought me some toast. It was hard white bread, too hard for my teeth to penetrate. I glanced out of the window and saw mountains beyond a bleak but lovely heath, like Rannoch Moor, and then fell asleep wishing I were home.

One thousand people must have disembarked with us at Kunming and as many were waiting to board. Val and Deb took me to a hotel and a doctor put me through certain tests. He peered into my throat while holding my tongue down with a spatula and let out a fearful shriek. I thought he had discovered something ghastly but evidently he wanted me to make a similar noise. He gave me pills and a bottle of essence to dab on my temples and nose before sleeping. Had to swallow a tube of ballbearings on the spot and was given five replacement tubes. 'If you do any dancing, you won't need castanets,' said Val, but even laughing was painful.

Later a third doctor came, a charming old man. He spoke French and was seventy-four but still worked a three-day week. He chatted freely and said that during the Cultural Revolution in 1968 he had been dragged from his house one night by Red Guards. They smashed his furniture and took him to prison where he was beaten for being a 'bourgeois intellectual and a French spy'. Because he was such a fine doctor they allowed him to work in a hospital but at night he had to clean the lavatories as a form of routine humiliation. His family thought he was dead during his two-year absence, until he was finally released and, much later, given a full pardon.

On his recommendation I was taken to hospital. The car never arrived so I had to walk one mile, half-supported and half-dragged by two porters. They took me into a large cold stone hall where the sick were huddled in coats and parkas. Up four flights, and then they bundled me into a wheelchair but neither thought to ensure my feet were on the footrail. They pushed me along endless corridors and used my knees to knock open swing doors, and all the time my feet were bent backwards and sweeping the floor. When one at last noticed, they found it very funny. I was not taken with the Chinese sense of humour.

More tests by white-uniformed doctors but not one spoke any English, and my throat was too dry to make a sound. When I indicated my thirst, everyone laughed. Then came the ultimate farce. They wanted a bowel motion sample. One doctor led me to the ward loo – plaster was falling down, the urinal was full of rubble and the footprint gutter was covered in excrement and bits of paper. I asked with signs if he had a recepticle for me to use. He shook his head and waved me to go ahead. Then there was no loo paper. He impatiently indicated for me to get ready but on realising my problem he sighed, went away and returned with a handful of hospital receipts which he thrust at me. I left the room when he seemed uncertain where the sample had gone.

I was put to bed in a single room of bare stone walls and a nurse brought a stand holding five suspended bottles and connected me to it. I watched partly in fascination and partly in fear as the clear liquid dripped slowly into my arm and yet something told me it was what my body was desperately needing. It was a slow process, taking between nineteen and thirty-seven drops before there was a replacement gurgle of air in the bottle. The room was freezing. My arm had to remain above the covers and it soon became so cold it lost all sense of feeling. I had to put up with it for ten hours. A nurse came to change each bottle but there was no sign of her at 2.30 a.m. when the final one was empty. My anxiety mounted as the liquid dropped lower down the tube and the air space neared my open vein. Finally I got out of bed and tried to reach the door but there was insufficient length of tubing, and I had to return and carry the stand closer. After opening the door and calling for help, a nurse appeared. She looked worried and quickly withdrew the needle. But the following day the same thing happened again.

That was three days ago. The intravenous drips have now been replaced with daily injections. These are always painful, like the early throws of a pub darts contest. More zest than accuracy. Odd for a country which practises the precise art of acupuncture. Chinese patients are evidently offered the choice of acupuncture or pharmaceutical cures but foreigners are automatically treated with western medicine. Now I receive pills with each meal and also cough mixture which comes in a curvaceous one-gulp bottle. Every meal is the same; two boiled eggs, cold cabbage, hard white bread with a scraping of jam and a dog bowl of milk, sometimes deliciously hot. Once it was different with rice porridge and scrambled eggs floating in milk. It is quite good and nutritious. Yesterday they moved me to another room and tapped my phrase book at the character for 'hotter'. You wouldn't know it. The whole place is like a morgue with many draughts and no heating whatsoever. There are many discrepancies in their attitudes towards hygiene. They wear pristine white uniforms and face masks but there is no mention of a laundry and my clothes remain unwashed for ten days, and all my luggage is still at the hotel. Yet the staff are friendly, in an official sort of way, and one kindly accepted some money and bought me oranges, tea (not provided) and loo paper – much more effective than hospital receipts. I have no right to complain about anything but it is a relief to now feel well enough to contemplate doing so. My mattress feels like an old rhinoceros hide.

13 December: Must get away from here soon. Every day spent here is a day lost travelling China. This morning, as every morning, several old men gathered at my door to stare. As usual I cheerfully said *Nee haw* – it sounds asinine but means 'hallo' – and, as usual, got no response. Gradually they shuffled away and merged into the distant sound of hawking and coughing. Then a nurse brought a seventy-two-year-old man to see me. He spoke some English and we had a long conversation. He had been an engineer and explained that China works a six-day, forty-eight-hour week with no holidays apart from the three-day spring (harvest) festival and a statutory three days' paid leave every four years. You are given a job wherever there is one and he illustrated the harsh reality of this. A nurse in this hospital is married to a doctor who has been designated a job in a hospital 1000 km away and they have neither the time nor the money to visit each other, except during the annual three-day holiday. If either were to give up their job it would cause them financial hardship and probably mean the end of their career.

With the engineer as a translator I tried to persuade the doctors to release me soon. They smiled benevolently and always repeated 'You must be patient' many times. I don't suppose it works as a pun in Chinese but it does nothing to quell my frustration. The engineer couldn't explain what they were treating me for but said my body was still weak, and to be patient. Eventually they allowed me to go for a short walk inside the building. The doctors rushed off. 'Someone is dying,' explained the old man, and added that his brother had died in this hospital. He himself was in for a short rest and would go home when the weather was warmer. Poor man. He almost sounded convinced.

My walk took me past an open door beyond which a man sat squatting on his bed, his eyes fixed on the floor, his nose and mouth sprouting tubes which held him captive to a machine. It looked grotesque and I hurried on. Everything seemed old, cold and decaying. It was a relief to find a room with a colour TV and a small group of normal people watching it. The news was incomprehensible to me but it showed Reagan and then a London bobby, before moving on to a programme showing factory workers joyfully gathering tins from a conveyor belt and a field labourer laughing as an extra sack of rice was piled onto his wheelbarrow. Then I walked to the main door and looked out on an abandoned garden where some men were building a wall. They didn't look very happy and I wished I could have made them laugh by giving them an extra bag of cement to mix. Two mournful sheep were the gardeners. They stared at me, and for a few moments we shared a mutual gloom.

14 December: 'You must be patient', but I feel much better. Am going to try to leave tomorrow. Val and Deb called in. They have been staying with a family who befriended them but now they've discovered they are expected to return the favour. Apparently the mother and daughter want to leave China and need money. All permits to travel abroad are restricted and issued by the party headquarters. Deb and Val have spent hours petitioning the local representative on their behalf, and the family have asked them to take some sixteenth-century paintings and Ming Dynasty costumes back to the USA to sell for them. They don't know what to do. It sounds too risky.

Went a longer walk today, out into the city. Managed to buy a woolly hat, gloves and long johns but only after a long hunt as most of the shops have empty shelves. A school teacher helped me. He said the Chinese need special coupons to buy anything made of pure cotton as it was rationed, even though it is the country's most valuable cash crop. 'Tourists are exempt,' he explained. It made me feel shamefully privileged.

15 December: My seventh day in hospital, and my last. The old engineer tried repeatedly to persuade me to stay but I was adamant. The doctors looked worried but eventually agreed to let me go with instructions to keep warm, dozens of pills and a warning that my temperature was still high. I paid the bill, 174 ¥ (£58), and shook everyone's hand. I felt quite emotional. How do you thank someone for saving your life? And I was sorry to say goodbye to my old man. It was as warm a day as one could have hoped for.

My luggage was intact at the hotel and the manager had even arranged for my visa to be extended for one month. I still feel a wee bit delicate but also raring to go. *Free!* I'm free again. My first days in China have been traumatic. Now I want to set off and see the country through healthy eyes!

I had been very lucky. If one has to choose a foreign country in which to be ill, China is probably the best as the Chinese know their medicine. On the day of my voluntary discharge from hospital I didn't know my body had lost a stone in weight and that my blood count was still exceptionally high, indicating a dangerously poor level of resistance to disease. A month later a Hong Kong doctor diagnosed bronchitis and paratyphoid. The latter had been cured but the bronchitis was still active and a cough plagued me during the remaining weeks in China, though not obsessively. At that moment my health seemed to have returned and within four days I was climbing a 10,000-foot mountain. Ignorance can be a great blessing.

4 · Forest of Stone and Sacred Mountain

An old Chinese proverb runs, 'If you would be happy for a few hours, get drunk; if you want to be happy for a weekend, get married; if you want to be happy for a week, barbecue a pig; if you want to be happy all your life long, become a gardener.'

There were never any drunks on China's streets and never any obvious purveyors of short-term happiness. Courting couples were often apparent walking the streets (for they had nowhere else to go) hand in hand as they contemplated their partner's eyes and a sublime, legal weekend. Equally as common were those who carted around potential happiness in weekly measures. As I walked through Kunming's streets holding a bus ticket to the Lunan Stone Forest, I came across two men pushing and pulling a killjoy of a pig that had braced its trotters against the cobbles and the direction of their barbecue, a hapless sow bound spreadeagled to a hand cart and a piglet trussed upside-down to a slender carrier above the rear wheel of a pushbike. Judging from the city's lack of gardens, Kunming's citizens were best advised to go for a plentiful supply of pigs if they had ambitions towards lasting contentment.

Gardens of hibiscus trees, pagodas and ornate bridges had been one of my expectations of the country but so far this had appeared misplaced. Kunming was only unusual in that it had less dereliction than other Chinese cities but in every other respect it was typical of the drab urban agglomerations that held the population in concentrated spots and prevented its spill into the country's surprising tracts of wilderness. It was the capital of Unnan Province and because of its strategic position on a fertile plain in the south-west it had been the intersection of important trade routes from the days of silk caravans to the Second World War when it served as a depot on the Burma Road, the country's vital link with the outside during the Japanese invasion. Now Kunming was home to 1.5 million people, a leading industrial city and a tasteless showpiece of modernisation in concrete. With the exception of its very fine hospital and a water park where the air refrained from carrying dust and weeping willows brought life-long happiness to a few, it was easy to understand why the city was considered a 'hardship' posting by the many troops stationed there.

It wasn't the best place for a recuperation and on the evening of my release from hospital I had sat on my hotel bed and replanned my route in view of having lost one week of travelling time. The manager of the hotel had recommended the Stone Forest at Shilin, sixty miles to the south and this appealed to me as a gentle start to travelling again. Of my original objectives, a boat journey through the Yangtze Gorges had now to be deleted and this had left the walk up holy Emei Mountain, the terracotta army of Xi'an – the sight I had wanted to see more than any other ever since news of its discovery reached Edinburgh, Xi'an's twin city – Beijing, and the option of trying to find some offbeat and uncelebrated destination in the east. Further concentration had then become impossible when a woman from the adjacent room wandered along the shared balcony. She was brushing her teeth and practising singing, periodically withdrawing her toothbrush and uttering falsetto shrieks which caused her to foam at the mouth.

At 6.30 a.m. the odd pig was in transit and women were sweeping great brooms in arcs before their feet as they walked in a staggered line which spanned the street. Near the bus station stood dumpling vendors with braziers glowing red and on these sat a wok sending steam through a tower of wooden trays and ultimately into the vendor's face whenever he lifted the cloth cover to serve a customer. The dumplings were either plain or had a filling of meat, vegetable or jam. I bought one but the first bit cloyed in my mouth and after a discreet distance I dropped the remains in a litter bin. Within minutes a woman rummaging along the bins had discovered them and put them in her bag.

Walking on the cobble stones was dangerous because the silent rush hour was beginning and bicycles were never equipped with lights. It was also dangerous to walk on the pavements because of the ghostly army stalking and fighting invisible opponents. Hundreds of figures kicked, leapt and spun in the peripheral glow of weak street lamps, practising the salutory art of *t'ai chi chuan*. Through exercises and controlled breathing they sought to draw in life-giving energy from the air. It made a fascinating spectacle. All ages, shapes and sizes took part. One man stood on his tiptoes as if suspended from his shirt collar, his eyes staring at the ground, his chin resting on his inflated chest and his arms held down stiffly like flippers. An obese woman boxed vigorously with her formidable shadow, two men glided through the darkness with knees bent, their eyes large and lunatic and fixed on their splayed fingers which they held out in the posture of a preying mantis, and an old wrinkled woman unleashed jaw-splintering kicks in a walz of hypnotic slow-motion. Then something in the air made my eyes sting and water. It was inevitably a battle for *t'ai chi chuan* to extract life-giving energy in a land where many cyclists and pedestrians always wore face masks against the appalling level of industrial pollution.

China was never exactly how one imagined it to be and this was true of the Stone Forest. After a four-hour journey the bus deposited me in an understatement of drama where 64,000 acres of intensely packed rock pinnacles formed a natural maze. The similarity to a forest was imaginary for trees played no part in the formation of these limestone shapes, once a ruptured seabed which the receding waves and subsequent rain had eroded into a jagged landscape. The pinnacles were all about sixty feet high and the tangle of paths amongst them sometimes forced visitors to squeeze through tunnels or under perched boulders and frequently ended abruptly in a dark tunnel or precariously on a peak. From such a vantage point the vista resembled a vast hairbrush of grey stone bristle, here and there crowned with a pagoda or hardy tree whose leaves were vibrant clusters of yellow and red. Everyone who entered the Stone Forest became temporarily lost and this was a major attraction. Lost soldiers abounded and I watched one group from the top of a prominent bristle. One soldier had a twin-lens reflex camera and his friends adopted a standard pose for him. One by one they were photographed slouched against a rock, glowering over a shoulder, an unlit cigarette dangling from their lips. Finally the photographer posed and became another picture of disgruntlement. Around them the quiet, private forest also appeared daringly defiant.

At a tea house on the edge of a clearing I stopped for a bowl of roast peanuts. The tables were outside and all occupied by people in heavy coats. I sat next to a strange-looking man reading a book. He had a bald head and wore brown hairy ear muffs which attached individually to each ear. I took out my copy of *China Daily*, a newspaper in English which had been instigated with the help of *The Age* (Melbourne), skipped over the listing of British soccer results and came to a report on agriculture:

> New Farm Techniques; Che Wan, a peasant in Shewan . . . contracted to grow cotton this year on forty *mu* (less than 6.5 acres) of land. Because of new farming techniques and hard work his output was five times higher than that of other peasants. Che's experience reveals; he is willing to learn new farming techniques. Last year he went to a neighbouring farm and found people using an effective new technique. He decided to follow suit. He is bold about investing a large sum of money. He managed to scrape together 3000¥ for new tools, good seeds and chemical fertiliser. Most peasants would consider it too risky to spend that much. He worked hard and knew that chemical fertiliser was good for cotton but bad for soil. Therefore he used 65 tons of manure to 1.2 tons of chemical fertiliser. All peasants should learn from Che Wan and adopt new farming techniques as soon as possible.

My reading was interrupted by the evasive nature of the food. My expertise with chop-sticks was developing well despite my preoccupation with their function as tongs instead of their most common use as a shovel, but my neighbour was still unintentionally receiving the odd peanut and this was how I discovered he spoke English.

'Where are you from?' he asked, tactfully ignoring the nut on his book.

'I'm from Britain. I apologise for disturbing you.'

'Biman . . ?'

'Britain,' I repeated but he still looked blank. The ear muffs were not helping. He moved them slightly to the rear. I tried London.

'Ah! England?' he chimed with such enthusiasm that I nodded. For a Scotsman it was a particularly hard admission. We exchanged backgrounds. Shanghai had been his original home but he had come to Shilin after the war. His father, mother and sister had been killed during a Japanese bombing raid when he was twenty-two and he had spent three years fighting the Japanese. He still hated them but had to put up with those who visited the hotel he managed. He had found it hard to settle here at first as the local people were not Han but a minority group. Their features were less Mongoloid and dominated by rosy cheeks. They wore their own costumes consisting of many layers of brightly coloured and embroidered cloth.

'Are they considered equal to the Han?' I asked.

'They are seen as just different. They live by the same laws but keep their own customs. Mostly they are farmers and weavers.' Two Shilin women passed along the road while we were talking. They carried bulky loads strapped to their torsos and were no more than spindly legs below acutely angled bundles of sticks.

'They work very hard,' I commented, 'but maybe they need to adopt new farming techniques.' I explained about the article. Were these changes happening here too?

'Farming has seen the biggest change in China recently. Now peasants can choose their crop and once they have grown their quota they can sell what's left. Production has risen four times as a result. But no one teaches any changes here, and where can a peasant get 3000 yuan from? It is a lot of money. I earn the average wage of fifty yuan each month.' (3￥ = £1). But in general he saw life in China changing quickly, and for the better. The great strengths of the people, he believed, were their disciplined attitude to work and their ability to endure hardship. He quoted the example of the 1976 earthquake in the north which had flattened the city of Tangshan and killed 242,000 people in twenty-three seconds. Within five years the city had been rebuilt.

Another pot of tea arrived. 'How do you like our tea?' he asked, pouring out the green liquid.

'It's wonderful,' I replied. It was my second white lie. My sense of taste had gradually disappeared as a result of my illness (I couldn't even taste neat brandy) and yet the tea's flavour had been fine in Guangzhou. The problem was the leaves which were as chunky as seaweed and one-third of them always seemed to float. You really needed baleen plates to enjoy the drink.

I changed the subject to the soldiers sitting near us. He pointed to one whose jacket had four pockets and identified him as an officer. 'We only have two ranks in the Chinese army, soldiers and officers. The uniform of soldiers has two pockets, less buttons and sometimes a different lining.' There was evidently no conscription and entry requirements for those wishing to enlist were strict because of the demand. The army was still regarded as a privileged career and a safe one as much time was spent working on community projects.

Our tea went cold and was replaced again and finally he got up to go. He readjusted his ear muffs and we shook hands. 'It has been a pleasure talking to you,' he said bowing slightly, 'but if you will excuse me, my friend, I think you need to adopt a new technique with your chopsticks.'

The following morning I left him my half bottle of Courvoisier in the hope that it might bring a few hours' happiness. The Stone Forest had done as much for me and leaving wasn't easy. It looked the ideal place to become a gardener. But by all accounts Emei Mountain was even better.

To reach Emei Shan (*shan* means mountain) it was necessary to return to Kunming and travel 300 miles north by train. Buying a train ticket in China was an arduous task and a dreaded chore in which success represented a major achievement of the day. If there were any Hong Kong Chinese in sight (easily recognisable by their fashionable clothes and obvious affluence) it was best to solicit their help, but English-speakers usually seemed to disappear when assistance was needed. I would work out the relevant train details from a timetable and write them into a simple ticket request with characters faithfully copied from my guidebook. Queuing sometimes took hours, only to result in the ticketseller closing her window for the day just as you reached it, or being told that you were in the wrong queue, or simple refusals to sell you a ticket. Then you had to try to jam a large phrase book through an absurdly small grille and point to 'What is the problem?' and flick over several more pages to 'Please write it down for me.' This preceded a lengthy hunt to find someone who could translate the problem into English and write a corresponding answer, enabling you to start the process once more at the back of a long queue. The problems were usually translated as 'These tickets are not on sale until after 6 p.m.,' or 'This train has been cancelled. Another leaves in ten minutes via Chongqing, or would you prefer to wait an hour for the one via Changsha?'. The struggle to buy an ordinary seat at Kunming lasted one hour and forty minutes.

Near the ticket office some men sat in a huddle smoking tabacco in tall water bongs which bubbled with each inhalation. Then they lent over and spat on the ground. Everyone spat. It was a national habit and streets, pavements, buses, trains and hotels were generally flecked with vile splotches of slime. The government was trying to control the habit and television showed films on correct behaviour in which a smiling citizen with bulging cheeks walked an extra hundred yards to decorously empty his mouth into the official spitoon provided in some cities. This seemed to be having little effect and some diligent footwork was required to find a clear approach to my seat.

The train left on time – the system was particular about this. The coaches were full but not excessively crowded and I managed to get a window seat which was ideal because it provided a view and a choice of either the wall or the table as a head support for dozing through the night. Departure was the signal for the female attendant of each coach to give a short welcoming address and wish passengers an enjoyable trip. Everyone always listened quietly and then clapped. A few minutes earlier there might have been bedlam in the general effort to board the train but the attendant's welcome had the sobering effect of a call to prayer. She would then check that all luggage was secure on the overhead rack. Nothing was allowed to protrude even an inch over the edge of the rail and yards of baggage usually had to be laboriously rearranged in accordance with this stricture, even though the final result was less stable than before. The act was more perfunctory than practical as the attendant felt the need to make a show of concern in case anyone complained that she had neglected her responsibility. But it was a pleasant service with a buffet car and a self-service urn of continuously boiling water at the end of each coach for making tea. In addition to this the attendant regularly brought round a kettle of hot water because every passenger travelled with a mug resembling a jamjar and a pocketful of seaweed.

One of the advantages of being a lone foreigner amongst strangers was that those who could speak English were usually more willing to approach and open a conversation. The journey had barely been under way when a careworn oldish man with a frail physique came and sat down beside me and introduced himself as Lu. It was hard to put ages to the Chinese because up to about forty they generally looked a decade younger than they actually were and after fifty-five the opposite was true. Lu must have been approaching the latter category and was wearing a blue suit and a furry tea cosy hat which splayed out the tops of his ears. Tortoise-shell glasses and a long wispy moustache which outgrew the grey hairs on his chin gave him an academic, sagacious air. He was curious about my background and wanted to know my father's occupation. I said he worked for a large whisky company, and asked about his father. 'He is a peasant,' he replied. The reference to small farmers as peasants had startled me at first until it was explained that here the term had no disrespectful connotations. Lu was an industrial engineer and had learnt English in order to read foreign manuals and technical works. He had married late and had two children (before the one-child ruling was introduced) but he saw little of his wife and family because nine months of every year were spent away form home on work projects.

'This is a big worry for me,' he explained. 'How can I educate my children properly when I see so little of them? Children must attend school from the ages of seven to eighteen but I want to give my girl and boy special help in science subjects so they will get into college. It is very serious for their future if they fail. At best they will become labourers and never progress, at worst they will find no work and I will have to support them.' China did not *officially* have any unemployment but there was nevertheless a lengthening list of people 'waiting for employment'.

Lu earned seventy yuan a month (£23), slightly more than average because he was qualified. He had not received a single pay rise in the last ten years. Engineers had recently been promised one of ten to twenty yuan per month as a measure to offset the fall in student applications in this profession but he shrugged this off because China had zero inflation. Prices of all essentials remained the same, he paid no tax, he would receive seventy per cent of his final wage as a pension and, he gave a slight smile, his employer would pay for his funeral. This would be a cremation as there was no land available for burials except in remote regions with no access to a crematorium.

'Few Chinese own a house and I rent a company flat with a kitchen, bathroom and two living rooms for only three yuan per month.' He spoke with self-assurance but his manner was defensive as if he felt bound to dwell only on China's good points and avoid questions on Britain that might yield an unfavourable comparison. Nevertheless he was surprisingly frank because of the dramatic improvements in his standard of living. Ten years ago, he said, there wasn't even talk of television sets but now he would soon own a colour model. They cost 500¥ and he was able to lay aside 100¥ a year from his income, this purchase represented five years of saving.

(He could have bought a black and white set for 350¥.) The cheapest tape recorder he had been able to buy to learn English had cost 300¥. Luxury goods were not cheap and a private car was still out of the question as even if he could have afforded the lowest price of 10,000¥, fuel was too scarce and expensive to make it worthwhile.

'What about the one-child law? Does it apply to everyone?' I asked.

'Yes, and it is very hard on our people because we love children, but it is necessary. China's population is rising by fourteen million every year and this is too much for our future welfare.' If a second pregnancy occurred the authorities would try to gain the mother's consent to a free abortion. Couples who refused were disgraced and suffered high financial penalties. The mother would lose her job and five years' pay, and the second child would receive no allowance, no free medical care and no help in finding work later on in life. His son would be encouraged to wait until he was twenty-five before marrying although legally he would be able to at twenty-two, and his daughter at twenty. The 'encouragement' was effective as it became almost impossible to acquire a dwelling until the recommended age.

'What happens if you protest? Can you openly criticise the government?'

'Yes, but nothing will come of it. If you do it too often, our leaders may have to *re-educate* you.'

'And what if you kill someone?'

'I will be shot by firing squad.' Lesser crimes would result in a prison sentence but he believed the food was reasonable and the conditions fair although the days were usually spent labouring or being realigned to Party attitudes. Lu had never suffered from the authorities except during the terrifying years of Mao's Cultural Revolution which started in 1966 and lasted for over a decade. During this time Red Guards rode freely on trains, slept in schools and toured the country to instruct new ethics – the love of physical labour, the prestige of being a peasant and the eradication of class, privilege, wealth, education and any foreign influence. Many works of art and ancient monuments were destroyed as representative of old ideas, old culture, old customs and old habits. Students 'more Red than gifted' were selected by their fellow workers after two years of manual labour according to their enthusiasm for Maoist theory and selflessness in serving the proletariat. Lu frequently had to appear in the street saluting and singing songs in praise of Mao. Not to have done so would have branded him a traitor.

'Mao set himself up as God and now he is criticised for that as it is bad for a country. He is still respected as a great man but he had man's weaknesses, and he made mistakes.'

When I asked about the attitude to religion he replied that all faiths were tolerated. There were temples for Buddhists, Taoists, Confucianists and others, but all these were minorities. 'Most Chinese do not follow a religion. We have The Party.'

I wondered how deep was this faith in The Party. Clearly some form of totalitarian socialism was essential in China for any system of free market forces would not care for such a vast and poor population. But could one billion people really believe these leaders would be different from those of the long violent struggle that had dominated living memory, when their labours were as hard as they had been a century earlier? They appeared to have so little to defend or fight for – did they really care whether they were under dynastic rulers, warlords or The Party? I asked Lu how strong was the sense of national pride.

'We are very proud of China,' he stressed, 'at least those of us who have the intelligence to realise we are progressing. But many of the younger people have too much regard for foreigners. They want to have long hair and dress like them. Have you seen any like this?' – he gave a mocking laugh – 'Oh! They look ridiculous! But they think everything is perfect abroad and that we are so poor and backward. This is bad because they become ashamed of their country and deny their culture. Of course we can learn many good things from abroad but we must not lose our pride in China and think that foreign countries are without problems. Your country, for example, has many people without work and homes, people who are hungry and die from cold. We hear reports.'

By then it was hard to tell what was his personal belief and what was the Party line. I admitted that my country had those who suffered but pointed out that it was a small percentage (and he was amazed to hear that the unemployed were paid by the government). He smiled and seemed comforted. How much should I tell him? I wanted to say, 'But my God! We have individuality and free expression. We can hope to own cars and houses before middle-age,

we can take holidays, go abroad, get promotion, read any book
. . . ' But what was the point? If he realised the differentials, he had
closed his mind to them. If he didn't realise them there was nothing
to be gained by upsetting his balanced view of a situation he was
powerless to alter or exchange. Yet through his command of English
and reading he must have known how poorly off he was in comparison to engineers in other parts of the world. Our conversation
waned and he drifted off to sleep. He had taken out his false teeth.
Hospital and dental treatment were free but false teeth were considered more cosmetic than necessary and so had to be paid for with
hard-earned cash. I admired Lu for the courage behind his pride. I
also wondered what he dreamt about.

I made my way to the buffet car where the breakfast menu of rice
topped with mince was being repeated for lunch. Other diners were
busily holding bowls to their mouths and shovelling in rice with
their chopsticks. By following their example I committed no nui-
sance and made no new acquaintances. On tight bends the old steam
puffer was visible up front belching dark smoke as it pulled us
through a mountainous region. We moved across a hillside high
above a valley littered with glacial moraine and divided by a deep
gorge whose side occasionally fell away to reveal the muddied
waters of the Dadu River and sometimes an odd Kon Tiki raft with a
square sail. On the far side tall buttresses of hills rose in regular
sequences to prop up the large mountain range at the back whose top
was patchy with snow and partially concealed by mist. And everywhere the land appeared wrinkled beyond age, thousands of terraced
fields ran in parallel lines and followed the irregular contours of
every bump and hollow as if the surface had been scoured with a
gigantic comb. Some fields were flooded and a stray beam of
sunlight caused them to shine and add a sparkle to the otherwise dull
colours, desaturated greys and browns, and again I was struck by the
similarity to a dreich winter day in the Highlands. There were never
any lonely habitations – that was an anomaly characteristic of the
view – but infrequent towns which too seemed as drab and lifeless as
adobe ghost towns. I found the effect strangely alluring and wished it
were possible to stop the train and get out. Had I tried to do so, there
would have been a policeman waiting to usher me firmly back into
the coach for this area was closed to foreigners. There was said to be a
large missile testing range near here. It looked as if something might

have backfired. But 155 miles of tunnels restricted our view and more than half the journey passed in darkness.

Two other Europeans disembarked when our train came to a halt at Emei and let out a final wail of steam: a tall lean figure from Sheffield called John and a squat red-bearded Swiss called Bruno who had lived for several years in Canada. The former was an unemployed graduate of sociology and the latter, in Chinese terms, was a peasant. It was already evening and we took a bus past trees used as pig-proof storehouses, their upper branches laden with haystacks and massive yellow bundles of corncobs, and soon reached Fu Hu Monastery. Emei Shan was sacred to Buddhists and interspersed along the paths to its summit were numerous monasteries which also served as hostels. Fu Hu was at the start of one of the longer routes; two days up, one day down and a round trip of twenty-nine miles. We climbed the long flight of steps and entered a collection of wooden buildings with pagoda roofs and were confronted by an enormous Buddha and four horror-stricken warriors each twenty feet tall.

'Do you think they know something about the climb that we don't?' John asked.

A short Chinese man of indeterminable width because of many layers of coats appeared from behind a warrior's knees and asked for our special permits to visit the area. None of us had realised these were required. We pretended not to understand and eventually he grew tired and pretended he hadn't asked. We went to bed early because the monastery fell silent after 8 p.m. save for squeaking floorboards which marked the progress of feet from one end of the building to the other, and because Fu Hu's lightbulbs were too dim for comfortable reading. The dormitory beds each provided a parka (which must have been civilian designs for none had any buttons) and were fitted with mosquito nets but all sensible mosquitos were hibernating in the near-freezing temperature.

For half an hour the next morning only steam issued from the kitchen hatch while we waited for breakfast, eager to be on our way. Then a rat emerged from the hatch, walked across the floor, up a chair, over a table, up a wall and disappeared into a hole between two rafters. We watched its progress in silence. Bruno was the first to speak.

'Well, I guess that's blown the menu.'

John nodded. 'I don't care what we eat but I wish it'd hurry up. If that cook works any slower rigor mortis'll set in.' Presently we were spooning into unfilled dumplings, rice porridge, a plate of ginger so strong it left us panting and sour bean curd in brine.

Bruno had the only map and this was a highly stylised one which showed the main path leapfrogging over precipitous foothills, rising sharply into a belt of swirling mist, running along Immortality Terrace and then shooting up to the summit at the angle desired on all The Party's productivity charts. Emei was only half a mountain at its 10,167 foot summit, the other half had gone and left cliffs falling sheer into the swirling mist. All the sketch lacked was a few deaf Chinese dragons, but we were to encounter creatures equally as ferocious. For the first few hours the track undulated past men ploughing stony fields with buffalo, women hoeing and stone markers whose figures were confusing. Possibly they were indicating the distance in Chinese miles (*li*). These were about one-third of ours but ingenious in concept and variable according to the terrain. Uphill or rugged country *li* were shorter than flat or easy *li* so that in theory they served as a more accurate estimate of travelling time. A few *li* after our path had begun to climb steeply we met a travelling band who stopped to give us a recital. We clapped when it was finished and they went off laughing.

'Do you think they're part of a bigger band?' I asked.

'I don't know,' Bruno answered, 'but they made a good noise.' This was a compliment for three drums and a dozen pairs of cymbals.

The path developed into a continuous stone staircase which struck up heaven-wards with relentless severity.

'It's incredible!' exclaimed John at one point, examining a typical step one yard in length and six inches square. 'These steps have been hand-carved, carried here and then laid one above the other to the top of a 10,000-foot mountain! And there are several of these paths. How many labourers and how many years did it all take?' We carried on in silence, each trying to put figures against this Herculean labour.

'I've just noticed something strange,' I said some time later, partly as an excuse for a rest on a section that had become as steep and monotonous as a spiral staircase. 'There's no birdsong. We've hardly seen a single bird.'

This didn't win a rest or even any reaction from the others. My mind seized on this as if they hadn't heard or had deliberately ignored me. As we trudged on the absence of birds grew oppressive as a result of a thought being spoken and going unacknowledged. For an hour my head was court to one endless bouncing question, '*Why aren't there any birds here? . . . Why aren't there any birds . . .* ' Back and forth it went until the words had lost all meaning but become something of great importance for a tiring mind to shout about. We were all tiring and it was a relief to come to a small hut where a man sold rice and noodle soup. He asked us for food coupons as even rice was rationed. We had none so the price went up by a small amount.

'That's what's happened to your birds,' Bruno said between mouthfuls. He pointed through a back door to a basket trap poised over a handful of rice. I stirred my soup into whirlpools and was glad to see it contained no meat.

At mid-afternoon we met a party of Chinese walkers descending the path. They seemed agitated and shook reprimanding fingers at us, and several snarled, grunted and swiped the air. Whatever they were warning us about was given a hard act to follow. 'Tiger?' suggested Bruno after they had gone, but we had to round a few more corners before it all became clear. Two wild apes were sitting on the edge of the track where it squeezed between a steep drop and a thicket of bushes. The rest of the troop appeared in the branches to our right and some dropped down to the track behind and trapped us. They began closing in. John and I picked up some stones and Bruno found a stick which he brandished at them. This excited them and they began to leap around, darting close and baring evil yellow teeth. They kept out of range of the stick and avoided my first stone but there were so many leaping about that it was impossible to guard all sides and some came close enough to claw our clothing. We only managed to escape when the apes noticed a small group of Chinese walkers approaching down the path. The incident had shaken us and left John with a ripped jacket pocket but we felt lucky not to have been bitten. These walkers also shook fingers at us and showed us their way of getting past the marauding animals. They threw food into the bushes before reaching the apes and dashed past when the way was clear. 'If everyone feeds them, no wonder they've become so precocious,' John retorted.

We were weary when we reached the halfway monastery at dusk.

It was a sprawling building, two storeys high, made of wood but built on a stone base. The area had a light covering of snow and the monastery looked welcoming behind its fringe of long icicles. An old monk wearing two habits, one black over one white, greeted us warmly and led us past more monstrous effigies of warriors to a dormitory. If there were other monks they were indistinguisable from the lay workers and packed in the same bulk of clothing. After their chores the workers listened to a radio and played cards while huddled around a coal brazier which provided the only source of heat in the building. Nothing can break a Chinaman's concentration when it comes to playing cards, not even opera. One youth spoke a little English and between hands he said he was on a government course studying tourism. Part of the course was to spend six months on this mountain. There was no electricity here and the candles were low, so we were in bed by 7 p.m.

Before breakfast the next morning I went for a stroll among the lion statues in the monastery's garden. Chinese lions were peculiar creatures with square jaws and this was because the first craftsmen to sculpture them had never seen a real lion but had to base their image on the descriptions related by travellers. An approaching sound caught my attention and suddenly a group of fearsome people came round a corner and up the steps towards me. The men were all over six feet tall, broad-shouldered and carried long knives in scabbards decorated with crudely worked silver, coral and turquoise. Their skin was weathered brown but their cheeks remained ruddy and in their features they were akin to North American Red Indians. Pigtails, large dangling earrings and several finger rings were common to both men and women, and below green parkas secured around the neck as a cape, they wore sheepskin coats and high leather boots with studs that crunched on the stone path. They gave me an expressionless glance on passing, looking tough and war-like and smelling strongly of rancid butter-fat. They stopped in turn before each statue, touched their heads three times to the cold stone and entered the monastery.

'They're Tibetans,' Bruno whispered when they entered the barn that served as a dining room. We were waiting at the counter but when the food appeared they barged us out of the way and took all the meat dumplings. The only ones left were a few filled with raw sugar. We waited for the next batch but just as I took hold of one plate a Tibetan appeared and grabbed the other end. With the possible exception of a drunk Greenlander and some of the faces seen the previous day, there can be few sights more menacing than the one which confronted me then. I held on defiantly but the Tibetan pulled harder, gave a fierce growl and his face screwed up into a snarl that dissolved my side of the argument. Discretion being the delight of every coward, I let go. He had a square jaw and evil yellow teeth.

The rest of the day was a long haul up the eternal steps. The spiral staircase continued for four hours and then the path levelled and took us through a sparkling winterscape of trees, bamboo thickets and rhododendron bushes under a thick layer of snow. Once we came across a small pagoda perched on a rock and overlooking a breathtaking drop to a monastery far below with mist curling lovingly around like an ermine stole. We had a noodle lunch at a modest hermitage and bought some sweets from a hatch below the sign 'XIth Xi'an Pool Short Store'.

'I think it's called "short" because of its opening hours,' John noted as the proprietor locked it again after conducting two minutes' worth of business.

We reached the Golden Summit Monastery late in the afternoon and found the Tibetans were already there. They were praying before a little Buddha laughing heartily despite the loss of both nipples and a mutilated belly button. The Tibetan women were shy but the men were suspiciously curious by now and touched our clothes to test the material. We let them have the first serving of a greasy soup, and watched as the drops they spilt instantly solidified like wax. My hands felt like ice and I went to warm them in some steam flowing through a vent but I found it was just a hole in the wall and cloud drifting in. It was a cold night, well below freezing, and under my bed the washbasin remained full of dirty ice after the last person to wash in it before the advent of winter.

Emei Shan was famous for its sunrises. We got up at seven, an hour before dawn, and joined the Tibetans already waiting on the summit beside a wall which protected us from the bitter wind. The sun appeared as a fireball rising gently above the expanse of cloud on the horizon and cast a pink glow over our group and the great buttress of rock that fell away at our feet. Below us hands of mist were grasping at black peaks, ridges poked through the main body of whiteness to show their fringe of pine trees as silhouettes, and eternity seemed a chilling drop just a few feet away. In the opposite direction, beyond the modern intrusion of a radio antenna, blue ranges of mountains fell away with diminishing clarity into the haze.

'Your map was pretty accurate after all, Bruno,' I said, and this time I didn't need my response. We were shivering with the cold but it was the sort of view that amply rewarded 10,000 steps. It was also the view that had inspired innumerable pilgrims to leap to their death in ecstasy.

We took a slower way and completed the descent in one day by a different path. The constant pounding left my legs shaking and feeling weak by the time we reached Quing Yin Monastery at the bottom. A herbal medicine man at a stall indicated he had just the thing. He rummaged around amongst fungus, roots, squirrel skins and other desiccated parts of animals, and produced *Musk and Tiger Bone Plaster, Bovine Calculus Pills* and a bottle with a label which stated in English 'Aromatic stimulant for opening up one's mind or regaining consciousness and promotes physiological function, too'. I bought some of the latter as a gesture of goodwill, and then we went off to see a twenty-two-foot Buddha on a bronze elephant which had been painted white. I sniffed my stimulant and opened up my mind to the attendant's assurance that the elephant weighed sixty-two tons and was one thousand and two years old.

China seemed just the place to be.

5 · Down the Edge of the Chinese Dragon

China's first emperor, Qin Shihuang, was born 259 years before Christ and was eleven years old when he started arranging his own funeral. He conscripted a workforce of 700,000 men to build his tomb, a task which kept them busy for the remaining thirty-eight years of his life, and turned his attention to administering a brutal regime. Through warfare, a strict penal code, the burning of all books and records in case they incited opposition, and the standardisation of currency, writing and measures, his regime brought about the successful unification of China. He implemented high rates of taxation to finance his massive scale of construction projects such as an advanced network of roads and canals, and being an absolute ruler he had no difficulty in finding a spare 500,000 labourers to start building the 'world's longest graveyard', the only man-made construction visible to astronauts on the moon – the 3160 mile-long Great Wall. But despite his success and power, his concubines and lavish palaces, Qin Shihuang was discontent. He was afraid of death. He craved immortality with a passion that turned his tomb into an obsessive fantasy.

Near the city of Xi'an he planned a vast chamber containing a world in miniature which he would rule for eternity; imitation buildings in gold and silver, oceans fed by rivers of flowing mercury and heavens studded with jewels. The tomb would be deep underground, protected against intruders by an assortment of engineered traps – pit falls, false corridors and primed crossbows triggered by tripwires. It would be protected against evil spirits on three sides by propitious landmarks and on the fourth by a replica of his own elite bodyguard, a terracotta army of 8000 lifesize warriors.

The 700,000 who were forced to turn this dream into reality comprised criminals, peasants, dissenting scholars, thieves whose faces had been tattooed as a mark of disgrace, potters, metal workers, architects, overseers and perhaps 100 master sculptors. The bulk of the workforce was engaged in excavating foundations, constructing buildings, transporting clay and preparing moulds for the torsos of the terracotta warriors and horses. It was left to the master sculptors to create heads for the clay army, each one bearing individual characteristics. The 8000 figures were then fired in kilns, painted in the full colours of their uniforms and set up in battle formation in their subterranean chamber. Many labourers were forced to wear leg irons or were chained to the spot, and ended their days in mass graves. The punishment for idleness was death by being buried up to the neck in sand and decapitated, and the reward for those whose designs and hard work brought about the completion of their Emperor's tomb was the compulsory honour of sharing it with him. Architects, masons, childless concubines and even 100 horses were interred alive within.

The terracotta army was discovered in 1974 by peasants digging a well. Terrified that they had unearthed evil spirits, they hanged the first clay figures from trees to ensure they were dead. Archaeologists began excavating the chamber two years later and work is still going on for it will take longer to uncover this find than was originally required for its creation. Xi'an's archaeological treasure, one of the world's most important and exciting discoveries, was situated half-way along the railway line to my next main destination of Beijing and made a convenient point to break the journey.

The trip up Emei Shan had been a welcome escape from China's intensive bustle but the eighteen-hour journey to Xi'an showed it was over. John and Bruno had headed south and so when the train arrived shortly before dawn, I was alone as a foreigner among the hundreds of passengers to alight at the main station. Police and officials, who always enjoyed using loudhailers, were bawling restraint at the crowds with little effect, ten fluorescent light tubes in the national symbol of a star were glowing brightly and uselessly in the centre of the roof, leaving the ticket counters in darkness, and women were waiting to offer us hot flannels for a small fee. Xi'an, once the largest city in the world and capital of the nation for eleven dynasties, now had to content itself with a dim station and an industrial designation; textiles, fertilisers, plastics and boilers.

A local tour bus bound for the Chin Army Vaults was waiting outside the station. The Vaults were some distance from the city and my excitement mounted during the journey. When the bus stopped, I followed the direction indicated by the driver and rushed up an

unassuming hill expecting to see the clay army but being disappointed to find nothing but slopes of pomegranate trees. I was
unaware until later that the hill, 120 feet high and almost four miles
in circumference at its base, was man-made and contained the tomb
and underground world of Qin Shihuang where, supposedly, rivers
of mercury were eternally flowing. No one could know what
treasures lay within that hill as archaeologists had not begun to
excavate it, but initial soil tests *had* shown an unusually high
concentration of mercury.

The clay army was situated one and a half miles further on under a
large protective roof. Inside the sight was truly astonishing. The
army had been looted just four years after the emperor's death but
many of the figures so far uncovered were either intact or had been
meticulously repaired. They stood below the level of the entrance
hall, and we looked out over the ranks drawn up in battle formation
seventy figures across and 150 deep. First were the infantrymen and
kneeling crossbowmen and then came the charioteers with stable
boys tending their horses, and beyond them other footsoldiers with
their hair knotted in buns and officers wearing headdresses. Their
faces were all slightly different but most were smiling gently, and
some still displayed the faint colours of their uniforms. The front
lines stood clear of the mud embankment that had buried them for
two thousand years but the columns behind were positioned in
trenches running back to the final figures still engulfed. They were in
disarray and stuck out of the yellow-brown mud at angles, some
headless, some buried up to their chests, some no more than hands or
arms poking through. The presentation was spectacular and gave the
impression that this ghostly army was slowly marching out of the
ground.

The sight left me mesmerised for some time and I was oblivious of
the many other visitors, both nationals and foreigners, who were
walking around the viewing platform and of the notices that stated
photography was forbidden. Taking out my camera was a reflex
action but in an instant a guard was at my side speaking angrily and
making it clear that he wanted the film out of my camera. He already
held several films as a tangle in one hand. My protestations of
innocence were getting nowhere when a foreign girl intervened. She
spoke fluent Chinese and managed to convince the guard that no
photograph had been taken. He remained suspicious but went away.

'Whew . . !' I breathed, ' . . . thanks a lot.'

'No problem,' she replied. 'They're a little bit touchy about cameras here.' Her name was Lynn, a slim attractive girl in her mid-twenties with a wild ball of frizzy hair. She was American but of half-Chinese parentage, and a teacher working an exchange year in Shaoxing.

'Have you ever been to Shaoxing?' she asked.

'I've never heard of it.'

'No one ever has. It's near Shanghai but it's not on the tourist route. It's easy to remember . . . "She sells seashells on Shaoshing's seashore". I get all my students to say that.' She scribbled a number on a piece of paper. 'If you ever make it, get in touch. I'll show you around.' She smiled and sauntered off.

I put the piece of paper carefully away, having just found my offbeat destination and turned back towards the clay army. Two bald Chinese men next to me were looking the opposite way and beyond them a crowd of at least thirty Chinese had also turned their backs on the greatest artistic creation in their 7000-year history and were lost in awe at the sight of a retreating American hairstyle.

Most Chinese cities seem to have sprung out of the ground for they are the same sullied colour as the dull winter earth on which they sit. The capital, Beijing, 'Northern Peace' (synthetic fibres, petrochemicals, machinery, electronics and advanced weapons) is no exception. It is situated close to the latitudes of Madrid and New York and is a flat city apart from fifteen-storey blocks of flats and a Ming hill created from the excavations of a Ming moat. Beijing's individuality is confined to its centre which contains wide streets, an absence of traffic that is a surprising delight in a city of eight million and the beautiful, monumental buildings surrounding Tiananmen Square, the world's largest at ninety-eight acres. Only one side of the square is not fronted by a modern temple of polished stone and colossal pillars and here a gate leads to the Imperial Palace, a fourteenth-century pagoda city with 9000 rooms. At its peak each room had a lady-in-waiting in addition to the palace's permanent staff of 100,000 eunuchs. In the gardens grazed a unique herd of strange creatures which had been extinct in the wilds for over two thousand years called four-in-one. They were described as having 'the antlers of deer, necks of camels, tails of donkeys and hooves of oxen' and yet were a long way short of being dragons. When European collectors heard a report about them from the French missionary Père Armand in 1865, they petitioned to have specimens sent to them. Fortunately the Chinese agreed because the remainder of the Imperial Palace's herd either drowned in floods or were eaten by starving soldiers during the Boxer Rebellion. Recently a small herd had been returned to China, only now the animals live under the name of Père David's Deer.

A chill wind was blowing through Beijing on the evening of my arrival. I suddenly realised that the date was 25 December. Christmas Day, my fifth away from home. Here it was no more than another work day. No cards, decorations, trees. My family were far away and it saddened me to realise Christmas had all but passed and I hadn't even spared them a special thought. But twenty-one hours in a train made it hard to muster any festive spirit.

The journey had left me hungry and after booking in at a hotel I went to the nearest noodle shop, a café-style eating house. It was miserably cold inside and snowflakes were falling through a hole in the roof and landing in my bowl of something similar to Irish Stew. The table was square and I shared it with three men whose bowls were raised to their lips. None of them spoke because eating was always a serious matter and food was bolted down in silence as if time and quantity played on their minds. They shovelled in food until it spilled from their lips, and chewed with their mouths open to reveal a swirling washing-machine action of semi-masticated rice. Meal-times in noodle shops were visually as exciting as waiting in a busy launderette. I was just wondering whether my neighbours were swallowing the many small bones that seemed to infest my meal when something bounced in the centre of the table and hit the side of my bowl with a loud *ping*. The man opposite had spat a bone at me. I looked up but he showed no signs of being aware of what he had done and he was already shovelling in more food, his eyes cast down. Before long bones were being spat across the table by both neighbours and then the man opposite spat a second which hit my elbow. I immediately guddled around in my stew until my chopsticks located a sizeable bone, put it in my mouth and spat it nonchalantly towards my opposing number. It hit his tumbler of water and spun on the spot for a short while. He looked up but his eyes were unfocused and shifted to the distance. Bones were soon piling up on the table. Our stew must have been the result of a particularly messy slaughter. No Christmas turkey for us, just badly shattered duck. After several more experiments I discovered that hits to my opponent's bowl, hand and lap evinced no perceptible response. Bone spitting was not intended as either a competition or a test of skill but was merely a socially acceptable habit. And this was my Christmas dinner!...*on earth peace, and good will toward men.* All the same, it was annoying to run out of bones when the score was 8 – 4 in his favour.

The following morning a long queue of several thousand people stood before the Chairman Mao Memorial Hall on the last day before it closed for the winter. Little if any expense had been spared on the workmanship of this elaborate stone mausoleum, a single-storey square building with a high roof, tall windows on two sides and a surround of forty-eight columns. There was plenty of time to count them while standing at the rear of the queue that followed a ropeway around most of Tiananmen's acres. The queue kept moving slowly forwards as no one was allowed to stop inside the building. No hand luggage was allowed either so I had to leave my camera case with an official controlling the crowd – or more exactly, with a plain-clothed stranger amongst Beijing's thousands who made out that he was an official. (An hour later he was still guarding it on the same spot.) Pressure from behind pushed us up the steps four abreast and then were split left and right into two lines, entering the Hall by different doors and filing past the preserved body on both sides.

Chairman Mao Zedong (1893–1976) was lying within a crystal sarcophagus dressed in his uniform and covered up to his chest with blankets. Few men in history have commanded such an influence or imprinted their character on a nation as decisively as this man. His life spanned close to half a century of turmoil and suffering in China. In 1912 centuries of imperialism ended with the abdication of the Manchu Dynasty, and the Nationalists (Kuomintang) came to the fore. Then followed fifteen years of civil war in which the Nationalists fought the warlords; a further ten as the Nationalists tried to annihilate their former allies, the youthful Communist Party and its Red Army; a famine which took between five and ten million lives; the Japanese invasion of Manchuria, resulting in the occupation of one-fifth of Chinese territory; eight years of bloody fighting against the Japanese; and four years of internecine strife ending in the supremacy of Mao Zedong's Communist Party. He was not a padded-leather Chairman but a foot-slogging general who once led a 6000-mile march across eighteen mountain ranges and twenty-four major rivers whilst under daily enemy attack. From his beginnings as the mildly rebellious son of a 'rich' peasant who had to work his father's land at the age of six, self-motivated and self-financed student, humble librarian, poet, author, revolutionary soldier whose sister and first wife were executed by the Nationalists, 'number one Red bandit' with a bounty of 250,000 silver dollars offered for his capture, dead or alive, Mao Zedong progressed to become the man who promulgated the People's Republic of China in 1949, and who founded, fashioned and led a nation of one billion. But, like any human, he made mistakes. One, in particular, destroyed an entire generation. It is estimated that 20 million people died as a result of Mao's Great Proletarian Cultural Revolution. Despite this catastrophic policy he did eradicate a top heavy and often corrupt system of administration. His exhibited body adds little to his eloquent legend. In 1966 at the age of seventy-three he swam the Yangtze at Wuhan where it is nine miles wide as a public demonstration of physical health. Regrettably, he still looks a little blue from the experience.

I decided I did not like the sight of bodies extended beyond their normal durability, and made my way to the Summer Palace where no one had thought of preserving the remains of the Dowager Empress Tzu Hsi. She had been the complete opposite of Mao Zedong. The palace was ten miles away and to reach it I took one of the city's double-length buses which wiggled round corners like dislocated vertebrates. At one stop a crowd poured in and delayed departure for several minutes until the attendant got rid of the hangers-on by compressing them in the hydraulic door until they volunteered to leave. At the entrance to a nearby park a street photographer was at work, cashing in on the rarity value of cars. He had parked his vehicle on a pavement and behind him stretched a long queue of people waiting to sit in the driving seat. One by one they posed, leaning out of the window, smiling and resting a hand on the steering wheel of the car they would never own. For many in Beijing a rush hour was the unobtainable dream.

After passing through wooden hills the bus reached the Summer

Palace and stopped in a scene more reminiscent of Holland in winter. Hundreds of people were skating on the frozen lake below a magnificent conglomeration of pagodas which was built to replace the original palace burnt in 1860 by British foreign devils as an inducement for the imperial court to see things their way. It was here that the hen-pecking Tzu Hsi ended forty-seven years as effective ruler, having domineered her husband for most of his life until the turn of the century when she tired of the charade and usurped his power. The Summer Palace was where she imprisoned him and where she liked to be offered 128 courses each day for lunch. Here also was her small but life-size paddle steamer made of marble, never intended to float but pretending to on the edge of the lake. This delightful folly helped to squander funds ironically set aside to create China's first modern navy and the cause had to be temporarily abandoned.

While walking across the lake to the marble boat I was approached by a thin wiry Chinese man in his early forties, wearing a raincoat, jacket, frayed shirt and tie, round glasses which gave him a studious look, and the strangest hat – a white, wide-brimmed topi.

'Are you Scott from Britain?' he asked.

I was completely taken aback. 'How do you know my name?'

He ignored this and said he was glad to make my acquaintance, adding that he worked for an English radio station and wanted to ask me about my impressions of China. He wouldn't name the radio station, his English was broken and he spoke without conviction.

'Before I answer any questions, would you mind explaining how you got my name and how you found me?' He said he went each day to my hotel and asked if there were any British visitors, and had been given my name. This didn't explain how he had recognised one particular foreigner from a name in a hotel register, and managed to find him several miles away and several hours later.

'Have you been following me since this morning?' He smiled weakly and continued with his story about the radio company. It was full of contradictions and clearly contained little truth. Why had he waited all day until this place or moment to approach me? The only possible motives to spring to mind were espionage or smuggling and both seemed far-fetched. I asked him bluntly what he wanted from me. He wouldn't answer directly and it was only after several minutes of hard questioning that he presented another incomplete picture. He said he was a graduate in English but had never had a job since university. He wanted to go to Britain but the authorities refused to give him a passport. Why? Because he was 'too important'. He spoke English and might say bad things about China. Was he a political dissident? No. He justed wanted to leave China. And how did he think I could help him? He thought a foreigner might be able to petition the authorities more effectively on his behalf. He conveyed a feeling of genuine desperation but his reasoning seemed full of half-truths intended to conceal some more important issue. I offered to help if he told me everything and explained exactly what he wanted me to do, but when he returned to the radio interview story I lost interest and walked away. He followed me for some time and then disappeared. The whole incident was mystifying.

'Did the Japanese man find you?' the hotel receptionist asked on my return.

'Japanese? You mean the man with the white hat? But he was Chinese?'

'No, he is certainly *not* Chinese. He is Japanese,' she replied but she was unable to shed any light on the affair beyond affirming that he frequently came looking for foreign visitors. It was not until much later that a possible explanation for some of the details was given to me. If the man was about forty years old then his birth coincided with, and probably would have been a result of, the Japanese invasion. Japan was still the hated enemy and even though his mother might have been Chinese, the slightest Japanese blood was recognised and despised. If this were the case, he would receive no help in getting a job, would not be allowed to leave and would be shunned by those around him. Perhaps he had been hoping for the remote chance that a foreigner might be able to offer him a way into the stories that were his only escape. It must be hard enough being born in a poor country, but how much worse to be born one of its outcasts?

I left Beijing in the direction of Shaoxing's seashells feeling haunted by the gaunt face of Mao Zedong and a white hat following me, always following me, bobbing through crowds of blue figures waiting to buy a picture of a motor car.

Shaoxing was south of Beijing, separated by 750 flat miles of farm plots, and it was as far again to Guangzhou where my route would complete its circle. I arrived in Shaoxing after midnight, too late to contact Lynn, and was walking through the streets looking for a place to sleep when there was a power cut and everything was plunged into darkness. There were too many canals running through the streets to risk fumbling my way in obscurity so I sat on my camera case and waited. Ten minutes later the current was restored but only at half-power and the street lights remained dim. They were nevertheless sufficient for spotting a hotel sign within a few minutes. My proficiency at recognising such signs had become a source of pride. The character resembled the unsimplified mathematical equation $1\frac{1}{1\frac{1}{2}}$ and usually this was the only way of recognising a hotel. I knocked heavily on the door. Nothing happened until my third assault when candlelight flickered at a window and a man in night clothes opened the door. He stared at me with a look of surprise and indignation. I pointed at the statement in my phrase book 'I would like to sleep here tonight, please.' He rubbed his eyes, held the candle closer to the page and reread it. Then he turned to me, scowling, and his answer was a gruff '*Mao!*' (No!) I was used to hotels being reluctant to deal with foreigners and the need for persistence. I showed him the question 'Do you have a . . . ' and was flicking through the subsequent pages of toiletry and linen, looking for 'bed' when I looked up to smile reassurance at the stony countenance. On doing so my eyes caught sight of shelves of books in the background and I suddenly realised my mistake. The next moment the door was slammed shut. After a tiring journey it is easy to confuse the characters for hotels and bookshops. At 1 a.m. I realised I wasn't doing Anglo-Sino relations any good.

A hotel did take me in that night but only as a result of a youth whose kindness was remarkable. He read my phrase book and beckoned me to follow. We visited $1\frac{1}{1\frac{1}{2}}$ after $1\frac{1}{1\frac{1}{2}}$ and walked as many miles before finding an obscure hostelry which had a spare bed. He refused to take any reward for his trouble and walked cheerfully off into the night.

I phoned Lynn the next morning and we arranged to meet at the bus station after her morning class and visit a monastery outside the city. Shaoxing – rice wine, silk, paper, handicrafts – like most Chinese cities measured its population in hundreds of thousands, of which it had 250, and its importance in factory chimneys. A thick cloud of smoke, dark and heavy with soot, hung permanently overhead. Despite the prestige of so many chimneys it was not an affluent city. Dead finches and rats were for sale in its meat markets. And yet Shaoxing had great charm with its whitewashed houses, tree-lined streets and a varied flotilla of crafts splashing through its network of canals. The inhabitants showed a bewildered fascination for foreigners but blended this with an unusual degree of friendliness.

Lynn's hair was slightly wilder than my recollection of it but even if it had been normal, her sparkle and smile would have been equally as arresting. Her students were going to be disappointed with Westerners if they modelled their expectations on her. A mere handshake felt like the renewal of an old friendship. We boarded the bus for Tien Dong Tzur.

'Do you get used to everyone staring at your hair?'

'Yes. Well, at least I thought I had until a recent visit to the zoo. I got a bit uptight when everyone just gawped at me and ignored the gibbons.' She came from San Francisco and had studied Chinese at college there. Her mother was Chinese but born in the USA, and Lynn's oriental features were so soft they were scarcely apparent. She was beginning to want to return home after almost a year of teaching here. Each week she divided her time between a language school and a special commune for artists, musicians, singers and writers. Anyone who showed special talent was sent to such a commune to have their skills cultivated and here they would be paid to perform and create. She was well treated and enjoyed her job because her students were eager to learn and deeply curious about the West, but she felt that many of her friendships were superficial, based more on envy of the material society she represented rather than on human qualities. 'It's now the in-thing to be associated with a foreigner and everyone wants to go to the States. The young are becoming increasingly cynical and disillusioned with The Party. It goes right across the board from peasants who buy calendars showing pictures of homes with television sets to China's 400 million television viewers who every evening see other things they haven't got. I think this is going to be a big problem in future. They tend to forget the great progress that has been made and want faster change.'

'How do the young react to the one-child policy?'

'I think most accept that it's necessary but they may feel differently when they get married. One of the saddest aspects of the policy is the fear that infanticide is on the increase because the Chinese still crave having a son. If the first child is a daughter then she may not remain the "one surviving child" they are allowed.' She saw my look of alarm. 'It can't be *that* common but there have been enough instances in rural areas to cause concern.'

People were hawking and coughing on the bus and I commented on how so many looked in poor health. Lynn said the country was still plagued by diseases the rest of the world had eradicated thirty years ago – tuberculosis, rheumatic fever, strep-throat – and malaria was rife in South China. She found the air pollution so bad that she developed cold symptoms every fortnight and yet many of her students shared the general fetish for opening windows 'to let in fresh air'. Apart from the effects of the pollution, this resulted in many suffering from chilblains and cold sores.

It made a welcome change having a companion to explain the many sights that were new to me. In a small village on the edge of a heath we saw a woman walking along ringing a handbell. 'You're not going to believe this,' Lynn smiled, 'but she neuters cocks. She is a cock-neuterer by trade.' I didn't believe it but she assured me this was true. 'A virile cock is considered bad luck, and neutered ones grow big and fat. Neuterers are always in demand.'

'Good God! It makes the one-child policy seem very lenient.'

Lynn sparkled for a moment. 'One of the things I've learnt here is that you have to take the Chinese seriously, even in their strangest behaviour. Have you seen the wonderful abacus they use in shops and banks, straight out of a playpen? I used to laugh at them but they are extremely complex to use *and* can be faster than electronic calculators. This country always likes to find its own way of doing things and there's generally a good reason for their funny habits.'

The monastery at Tien Dong Tzur was like any on Emei Shan, but I didn't tell Lynn this. We wandered around for a while and then she fell into conversation with a monk whose face, round and ploughed with wrinkles, resembled one of the old caricature etchings on a courtyard wall. I left them and wandered off for a short walk through plots of farmland where peasants with buckets were ladling water over individual vegetables. After a while the road began to climb and passed above a squat stone building at the base of a steep slope. A woman at the doorway spotted me and shouted something inside. The next moment over twenty factory girls came running up the hill with their foreman yelling in pursuit. They crowded round me, stared and giggled nervously while a few bolder ones felt the material of my clothes. I took out my phrase book but got no chance to use it as it was soon being passed from hand to hand amid much hilarity. They ignored the foreman's spirited speech. For five minutes we could do no more than exchange amused and curious smiles, and eventually they all ran back to work. My smile lasted for most of the walk back to the monastery, until I saw a security policeman come striding towards me.

He began shouting angrily and immediately grabbed me by the wrist and led me back to a room in the monastery. Lynn was nowhere to be seen. My passport had to be produced but this was the limit of our communication. My inability to understand Chinese seemed of no consequence to him and he lectured to me for twenty minutes. Sometimes he tapped my passport, raised his voice and banged his fist on the table. I tried to look suitably humble but it felt ridiculous when all his words were gibberish. The gist of my offence was nevertheless obvious. Foreigners were permitted to visit the monastery and only the monastery. One hundred yards beyond was closed territory. Eventually he considered me repentant or incorrigible and let me go.

'Where on earth were you?' Lynn asked when we found each other again. 'I've been looking everywhere for you.'

'I was hoping you'd come along and rescue me again.' I explained what had happened.

'You were lucky he didn't make you write a confession. That's the normal penalty for wayward foreigners. Do you always get into trouble . . ?'

We returned to the rice wine city for some happier hours.

Over the next week Lynn managed to rearrange some of her classes and we made several long excursions. One of these was to Hangzhou (heavy industry and parasols) which was renowned for its lake, islands and pavilions with wonderful names. This nation loved grandiloquent titles where even the smallest details had to be capitalised. None was finer than Lotus in the Breeze at Crooked Courtyard Corner Pavilion. And we went to Suzhou where many trees had been ripped up during the Cultural Revolution ('Cultural Suicide,' Lynn called it) because they represented the workers' money squandered on beautifying the city for the pleasure of lazy aristocracy and intellectuals. Suzhou was given a good airing in most Chinese sayings ('An argument in Suzhou is more pleasing than flattery in Guangzhou') but was best known for its gardens. At last I had found my gardens.

'Chinese gardens must have replica mountains, water, plants and pagodas,' Lynn explained as she tiptoed along a wall in the Humble Administrator's Garden. We crossed Small Flying Rainbow Bridge and reached the Hall of Distant Fragrance. 'They are an escape, places to contemplate philosophy and poetry.' We were now at the Pavilion of Expecting Frost and agreed to contemplate poetry. For two minutes we sat in silence on a stone bench.

'Well? What did you think of?' Lynn asked.

' "I met a traveller from an antique land, who said . . . " That was all. I couldn't remember any more. After that I began thinking – that I'm going to have to move on fairly soon . . . ' We sat in silence for a little longer. 'And you?'

She seemed to have lost her sparkle. ' . . . that this seat is hellish cold.'

Two days later, in Shaoxing, the crowing of a cock roused me. I would have gladly paid a bellringer to fix it and gone back to sleep, but it was my early morning call. I went to the Pavilion for Reluctantly Thinking About Moving On for a ticket to Guangzhou.

'The happy man should be born in Hangzhou, the beautiful willow-pattern city; should marry in Suzhou where the beautiful girls come from; should die in Liuzhou where the trees make good coffins; and should eat in Guangzhou.'

Consciously staying well clear of Liuzhou, my route completed the course of this last saying. Six weeks in China should have made a traveller immune to surprises but Guangzhou had one in store for me. It was not a typical city but in part a showpiece designed to reflect some of the glitter of nearby Hong Kong. The bright lights made hotels simple to spot but finding a bed in one proved to be a three-hour hunt. I first went to one of the top hotels, the Liahua, because paradoxically the most expensive hotels often had the cheapest beds in a dormitory at the back. The receptionists told me the dormitory was full but they kindly rang around other hotels and eventually found one with a spare bed. By the time I got there the bed had been taken. A trail of other possibilities yielded nothing.

Wearily I returned to the Liahua, intent on sitting up all night in a chair in the foyer. The receptionists watched me for an hour and then one of them came over to me.

'How many are you?' she enquired.

'One.'

'In that case we do have a spare bed.' She led me to the dormitory where my bed was the only one out of seven to be occupied that night.

The surprise came after breakfast. A large group of foreign tourists were milling around the postcard racks and showcases of jade frogs when the main door opened and two meat delivery boys entered. They pushed a large wire trolly across the foyer of one of Guangzhou's most prestigious international hotels, wove in and out of the guests, across the plush carpet leading to the dining room, and disappeared through the kitchen door at the far end of the corridor. The trolly had contained five domestic dogs, skinned, deep-frozen, their legs sticking out at unnatural angles, their necks twisted and jaws fixed open in a frenzied snarl. *The happy man should . . . eat in Guangzhou.* That morning in the foyer of the Liahua Hotel many of Guangzhou's diners looked sick.

The 6000 miles in China came to an end on a train heading for Hong Kong and my return flight to Thailand. My last impressions were of vegetables being cultivated on the graves of a terraced cemetery, a six-week absence of sports grounds and a man with brown hairy werewolf ears telling me about flies. ' . . . We used to have so many but we killed them during Chairman Mao's Public Health Campaign. Every day each of us had to hand in ten dead flies at a collection point. We killed our flies, ten billion every day.' An instrumental version of the Beatles' song *Ob-la-dee, ob-la-da* was playing over the train's loudspeakers and a small boy looked over the seat in front and stared at me. He wore a small blue suit and a blue cap with a red five-pointed star above the peak. I smiled at him and winked. I had done this before and children usually shied away or gazed blankly. But this boy broke into a grin and winked back. It was a sign of the times.

The woman sitting beside me had a smaller child whose trousers had the common feature of the opening on the rear side. These ones had no fastenings and as the child crawled over her the split parted to reveal his bare bottom. When he began crying she made him squat on the floor and without removing his trousers, he deposited the cause of his discontent a short distance from my foot. From all around came the regular sounds of gargling coughs, hawking and spitting. I tried to think of something pleasant, of 10,000 steps up a majestic mountain, of Chinese sitting on the toenails of a Buddha 234 feet high carved out of a cliff at Leshan, but the floor was covered in a mosaic of reminders. And so at times it was easy to get annoyed with the Chinese for their senselessness, their lack of hygiene, their prolonged stares, for jumping queues you had been waiting in for an hour and for telling you their sincere lies. At other times they treated you with overwhelming kindness and left you with an insight of great beauty and profound admiration. The diversity of China's character evoked the complete range of human emotions within a few hours, and every few hours. The Chinese have a different mentality, a different set of values and it is unjust to judge by other standards those things we cannot understand. And yet it is hard not to. One person in five in the world is Chinese. What must it be like to be born here where the Middle Ages and television sets meet? One in a billion are frightening odds. I wished the country, for all its material poverty, had shown a higher level of spiritual contentment but maybe it is simply that foreign devils are short-sighted.

'The Chinese are a very good nation,' Lu had said, 'but they are not rebellious by nature. They have a slave spirit.'

Now that spirit seemed to be changing. The Great Dragon was stirring. I might live to be an old devil but it is doubtful whether I would fully understand China's diverse nature. This, of course, is why the country holds such fascination and why I long to return.

6 · Twenty-Five Years and One Hour in Bangkok

Bangkok, a city of three million inhabitants, a mixture of modest high rises, haughty palaces, temples and squalor, an expanse of congested streets that are dirty, noisy and full of choking fumes, has a personality which I find irresistible and which makes its faults seem minor blemishes. It sprawls on flat ground beside the Chao Phraya river and when it crosses over, it becomes Thon-buri, a water-logged extremity on stilts and embankments with an extensive network of canals. Long canoes with cargo or rows of passengers two abreast roar across the river and through these waterways, throwing up wings of spray from their bows and shaving splinters from their gunwales as they cut corners. Their gunwales are worn. Passenger canoes stop at individual houses to pick up and deliver (one short hop between boat and front door), and then rocket off, steered by a frail man who has to lean with all his weight to pivot a heavy outboard engine with a long propeller shaft whose tip reluctantly enters the water as far behind the stern as possible.

Perpetual bustle on the water, non-stop frenzy in the streets. In Singapore jay-walking is illegal, in Bangkok it is impossible. Through its blue haze run hordes of cars, the ubiquitous trishaws and battered buses whose capacity is measured in pounds of human flesh per cubic foot. They are never full until five passengers with a fingernail hold are hanging out of the door and it is not uncommon to see schoolchildren inside – wearing uniforms of starched white shirts, grey shorts or skirts – apparently locked in half-nelsons under the arms of adults and yet bravely enduring the crushed journey with a smile.

Early each morning, before the sun's reflection is fragmented by the Grand Palace which has been severely hit by a storm of sequins, lines of monks in vibrant orange robes walk the streets. They carry a begging bowl for their only meal of the day and stop at *khow phat* stalls (this dish is a national favourite and, contrary to its sound, consists of spicy fried rice topped with cucumber and a fried egg).

And somewhere 'Ha, ha, hee, ho, ho, hee, hee . . . ' will be chanted by a squad of recruits never looking as happy as they sound, their utterances cutting across the rhythm of a forced pace as they jog through the humid streets in full uniform. Then the city gives itself over to hours of furor, tiring after dark and at this time it is possible to chance upon a group of nocturnal street dancers, bewitchingly beautiful and wearing costumes to match, performing elegant movements with disciplined eyes and backward-pointing fingers and toes. Every now and then one will burst into a spontaneous smile, inexplicable unless prompted by pleasure or the recollection of a good joke. Both are abundant in the country. The Thais are a friendly, handsome race, the world's most handsome in fact, and they like to laugh. Some of them are human enough to want to pick a pocket or leave a fellow without any pockets but until this is suffered personally, the impression remains of a people endowed with exceptional grace, charm and kindness.

However, not everyone shared my enthusiasm for Bangkok and not everyone stayed there by choice. In an area of cheap *khow phat* stalls in the west of the city, a hostel noticeboard carried the following message. 'There is an Australian girl in prison here serving twenty-five years – she would love visitors, *any* visitors. Please take her some cigarettes. Her name is Kay——— . Take bus number . . . ' I asked the owners of the hostel if they knew any more but they had only heard that she had been caught in possession of heroin. One afternoon near the end of my stay I went to visit her.

By then it was ten days since my arrival in Bangkok. This was the first stage of my triple-bounce across closed borders; from Hong Kong to Thailand, to Burma, and then to India. During the previous days I had been north to Chiang Mai where the country's elephants work, take their holidays and play home matches. (There had been no sign of Throp or Ananda, but plenty of others carrying bits of the forest about.) It felt reassuring to be back in Bangkok once more because it was becoming familiar, and that was unusual on a long one-way journey. It brought me a sense of belonging and homeliness to be able to look out of the bus window, when the crush of my fellow passengers allowed, and recognise streets. We passed close to the museum-house of vanished Thai Silk millionaire Jim Thompson – actually a collection of wooden houses he picked up on his travels and had fitted together, one having been re-erected inside-out so he could admire the exterior workmanship in comfort. We passed a minor suburb of Buddhas for sale, gently smiling through wrinkled clingfilm and imitating the one in Wat Trimitr – it had been regarded as an ordinary stucco for over a century until a crane accidently dropped it during removals and shattered the disguise of a solid gold statue weighing five tons. Then we were into unknown suburbs which remained featureless until the appearance of a long fence of barbed wire.

To a prisoner arriving on the scene, the prospects of escape looked grim. The prison was designed as an impregnable fortress under constant surveillance and set in a wide expanse of obstacles where any movement was visible for a mile. The buildings were hidden within a tall wall surmounted by five strands of electric fence and overlooked by a high watch tower. Around the outside of the wall ran a first moat with all crossings guarded, then an empty belt of land, a second guarded moat and finally the barbed wire perimeter fence. A prisoner serving life would find the sentence too short for digging a tunnel and so some form of deception appeared to be the only feasible means of escape.

The guards at the main gate let me pass without any checks and a gathering of scooter taxis offered a pillion lift along the road between the moats to the women's block which was at the far end. (To my surprise local men were fishing the inner moat with cast nets.) I entered the main arched gate of heavy bars, opened and shut by a woman guard. All the guards and wardens here were Thai women, many being slight and pretty, and in hotching abundance. I was questioned briefly and taken over to a Dutch couple, Niels and Johanna, who had also seen the notice and arrived shortly before me. We were led to one end of the hall where there was a wall up to waist height and then bars, spaced three inches apart, which ran to the ceiling. Beyond this was a no-man's land, a gap five feet wide to separate 'us' from 'them', and then a similar wall and bars, only the prisoners' side had bare brick divisions to afford one inmate some privacy from the next. While we waited here Niels and Johanna told me what little they had heard about Kay, although they didn't know her exact crime. Mere possession of heroin carried a twenty-five year sentence in Thailand. Traffickers went before a firing squad.

They said she had been inside for three years and until the previous month had only received two visitors. One of her friends had recently been released and had posted the notice in the hostel. Since then a regular flow of visitors had appeared. Her parents had not been to visit her. To me this seemed hard to understand, until I thought more about it. What good would it do either party? Her parents could travel from Australia to spend ten minutes with their daughter each day. At best there could only be tears on both sides and at worst, tears on one side and bitter recriminations on the other. The parents could only ask the unanswerable 'why?' that must have tormented every idle moment of their daughter's mind, and gaze at the child they could not touch or see in freedom for twenty-five years. The full significance of this suddenly hit me. *Twenty-five years out of a person's life . . .* And Kay? She could only feel more acutely regret and a sense of failure or else resentment at their intrusion into a private world where emotion had to be denied. She had been twenty-two when sentenced and would be forty-seven when her release came due. Would her parents live that long? A meeting would just leave memories to make the pain cut deeper. Best to write. The words of a letter can be gentler and less personal. They can hide a lot of hurt.

All around heavy gates were constantly being opened and shut, a continuous noise of jingling keys, of sliding and clanging metal that sent resonant echoes rippling along the boundaries of this enclosed world. They pervaded every sense as a persistent reminder of being locked inside. Then two Thai prisoners were led across the hall wearing dark orange uniforms of a shapeless blouse and knee-length skirt. One whispered to her companion while staring in the direction of Niels and myself, swung her hips and tossed up the back of her skirt. She looked back over her shoulder with a sly grin until the wardens rebuked her. The gesture looked one of defiance to irritate them but perhaps it was also a mild flirt to bolster a sagging sense of femininity, a wistful stimulant later to be embraced in a quiet moment of fantasy.

Kay suddenly appeared in one of the brick cubicles beyond the bars. I had to swallow and force a smile to hide my feelings of sadness and indignation which suddenly surged within me. Here was a young girl trapped in a cage. What would be in the next one? . . . The bears or the monkeys, maybe? The image of a zoo came as a hideous parody and strengthened an overwhelming sense of cruelty and injustice. It was an emotional shock I was not prepared for even though the person before me was a stranger. The Dutch couple obviously felt it too and it was left to me to open the conversation. I thought she would be tired of sympathy and of explaining what she had done, and so I was ready to talk about myself in the hope of finding areas of common interest, or about current affairs in the world or to follow whatever lead she offered. It turned out that Kay did most of the talking, speaking freely and at length once a question had been asked. She never once asked anything about our own lives. At the time this struck me as being odd but in retrospect I realised that our answers could have done nothing positive for her. She had once been a traveller too. It was a heavy enough penalty for someone who had once wandered freely to be locked within concrete, bricks and steel bars for the next third of their life, without having to listen to the exotic tales and ambitions of others.

I found myself looking at a girl with long blonde hair falling to below her shoulders, of medium height and with a slender figure, though this was only suggested through her loose orange uniform. She was pretty but must have once been more so. Her face was drawn, her cheekbones protruded slightly and her complexion was bad, pale and with a surfeit of spots not normal for her age. Her eyes looked sunken and without vitality. A natural downwards turn seemed to pull at her mouth and it was only through a conscious effort that she overcame it and managed the odd smile. Her features and manner were hard and undoubtedly I was looking at a brave face fighting off her true feelings. At times it looked as if she might cry but then her expression would stiffen. No tears would come, she would not release them. In prison this was a discipline that had to be learnt. If you didn't harden against your emotions, how could you last twenty-five years of daily breakdowns?

Kay said that she had five close friends here, two French, one German, one Italian and one Portuguese, and that there were forty foreigners inside, mainly Hong Kong Chinese. There had to be as many or more foreigners in the male block. In general they were well treated. Several wardens were touchy but most were nice as long as prisoners behaved. She found the most oppressive aspect of prison life was the bitchiness over trivial things.

'It's hard to maintain a wide outlook and perspective in such a closed and constrained environment. You might put your mug down on a table one day but when you do it the next, all hell breaks loose because it's "someone else's place".' Her voice was strong but flat in tone and only a few words managed to excite an Australian accent.

The prison evidently contained many small factories but the foreigners were unaccustomed to heavy machine work and had found it too hard. They had protested and been locked in their rooms for a week but eventually the authorities had relented and now allowed them other work. Two girls ran a kitchen and cooked food specially for the foreigners. Kay's job was to cut the grass. 'There's miles of grass here. I like the job as it keeps me outside and takes my mind off everything. Time goes by quickly and often I'm so tired at night I just go straight to sleep. Our whole day is taken up with work except for meals and recreation in the evening. The grass will remain my job for as long as I want.'

'Is there anything we can bring you?' Johanna asked.

'The food we get here is all right but we have to buy fruit and yoghurt from a small shop. It also sells toiletry odds and ends such as shampoo and talc, but it's always nice to get any of these things. And books, any books but preferably educational ones or something that will exercise our minds; religion, philosophy, science, anything a bit heavier. We've masses of fiction and stupid love stories.'

(By chance I had brought a book on Darwin called *The Origin*. Niels and Johanna, somewhat tactlessly I felt, had brought a novel entitled *The Right to Die*.)

A foreign girl had recently been released with a King's Pardon. She explained that this act of clemency was occasionally granted by the King but obviously he could not be expected to pardon every foreigner.

'Will you be able to get one?' I asked.

'Maybe but I'll have to wait some time yet. The longer the portion of your sentence you've served, the more weight your petition carries. I'll apply in four or five years. It helps if your parents and embassy campaign strongly for you.' An exchange of prisoners between Thailand and Australia might also result in an early release, and she listed other possibilities of a technical nature which I've forgotten, but all her legal appeals had been turned down and repatriation was only a slim hope. Her offence was classed as a federal offence and most prisons in Australia were for state offenders. Her state did not officially have a prison suitable for her, and besides, it didn't want to know heroin offenders. The King's Pardon was her lowest priority hope.

As we talked she gripped the cell bars with her hands, one at shoulder height, the other at her waist. At times she slid them up or down and at times she gripped them tightly. She often spoke with her head held slightly at an angle, the exact angle a photographer tries to elicit for a pleasing attitude – and it struck me again how pretty she was. But the bars were positioned the same distance apart as our eyes and to look through the spaces meant that one bar always divided our faces into halves. This had a dehumanising effect and made the opposite party seem distorted and alien. She often pressed her nose subconsciously against the bars; they were obviously such a part of her life. When she laughed (once, at the thought of how she would one day be an expert on lawnmowers) a black gap showed where an eye tooth had once been, and I imagined how much her parents would see that she was a shadow of the girl they had known.

Our ten minutes were up. A guard called out in Thai and Kay answered in Thai. She talked on for a while before saying she would have to go. She thanked us for coming. It was always lovely to have visitors. We said goodbye and she walked off, turning after a few paces and calling back, 'Have a good trip.' She disappeared and then came a jingle and the sound of sliding metal. That last remark, meant with all sincerity, hit forcefully. I felt wretched. 'Have a good trip.' Have the good trip that she had not had. For us it was over. Through the gates to freedom and adventure. For her it was back to the world of bitchiness, hollow clangs and the chink of keys. What on earth possessed her to touch heroin? Would she have done so if she had known this might happen? We were ushered out of the prison and took a bus back to the centre of town. At one stop a girl got on wearing a T-shirt splashed with the words YOU'RE ONLY YOUNG ONCE!!

Yes, I thought, and for some it can be a terrible burden.

After talking to someone who had no freedom, it seemed somewhat treacherous to immediately exercise one of the ultimate extremes of free society. But life must go on, my time in Bangkok was limited and there were still other experiences to collect. At least this made a convenient excuse. I went to visit Phatphong Road, Sin City's most infamous street. Prostitution was officially illegal in the country and, officially, Bangkok was anxious to clean up its image. In practice the red lights were allowed to glow brightly as long as taxes were paid, and the pretence at illegality merely shirked official responsibility for ensuring hygienic standards. Bangkok's notoriety in this trade developed apace with its role as a Rest and Recuperation centre for unloved American forces temporarily relieved of their part in dropping seven million tons of bombs on Indo-China. Extremes tend to foster extremes.

'Pretty Girl Escort Services', 'Manpower Centre', 'Sterilisation Clinic', read an ascending series of signs in Phatphong Road. A walk here was not in any sense shocking. Sex was not as ostentatiously for sale as, for example, in the sleazy streets of Amsterdam. However the nature of this area's business was obvious from the predominance of signs advertising massage parlours and bars with live entertainment, and from the many pimps who approached whispering 'You want massage? Beautiful girls? Look, I show you . . . ' They opened a wallet of surprisingly unrevealing photographs which were usually identical to the set produced by the last pimp because they all worked for the same establishment. Ancillary industries were also flourishing, in particular an uncommon number of VD clinics whose signs encouraged temperance and brought a harsh touch of reality to the scene.

Walking the street several times revealed that the average price of a body massage was 400 baht (£11.30) and a hand massage 160 baht. Eventually I entered a parlour that looked reasonably respectable. The door opened into a large reception room, carpeted and comfortably furnished, with a bar running along one wall on the left, and on the right a yellow expanse of one-way mirror which allowed a view into a side room. The Madame was a shapely woman, approaching middle-age but still attractive – small, luxurious black hair and full breasts being squeezed to advantage from a tight black dress of twinkling lamé and minimum length. She beckoned me over to the bar where a shrimpish barman was polishing and repolishing already polished glasses, and indicated the stool next to hers. She sat with a cigarette held high in delicate fingers, snug within an aura of smoke and oozed charm. Every expression, mannerism and movement of hand and eye was intentional and designed to produce a cumulative appeal. If seduction was written between the lines, it occupied the best part of the page. She raised the edge of her dress in a casual gesture of flicking off some ash and revealed an expanse of thigh as she uncrossed her legs.

'What took you so long?' she chided. Her voice was low and undulating but uncomfortably gritty and this felt reassuring, as if I had found a flaw that made her resistible. 'I saw you pass earlier?'

'I needed about five passes to find enough courage to come in.'

'Courage? Why?'

'I didn't know what to expect . . . so many people hassle you in the street.'

'Well now you're here, have a drink.'

My remark to the effect that *because* I was here I no longer needed one evinced a laugh that seemed spontaneous and the first break from a rehearsed routine. 'You don't look the shy type,' she cajoled. She was a professional and through my mind flashed a sudden realisation. Hell, she was going to win.

Conversation gradually turned to business. She nodded towards the yellow tinted glass wall and from where we sat was a clear view of a stunning assembly of faces. Each girl wore an identical smock which was pink and stylish. Some talked, others just sat and one girl read a newspaper. The Madame tried to persuade me to have a body massage but I didn't want to admit my ignorance of the jargon and recalled the temperance signs outside in the street. Her manner became less effusive when she was unable to dissuade me from the hand massage. We were approached by an even older hostess, long-legged and seemingly misused.

'Here you are,' said the Madame, 'I recommend this one. Andrea is one of the best.' It was second-hand sales talk. My moment of defiance came and I declined in preference to one beyond the looking glass.

Staring at the rows of faultlessly beautiful girls before me was not one of my proudest moments. I felt the same sense of injustice as at the prison. If that had been shameful as a human zoo then this was little better as its lending library. Only here I was an active part of it.

'How about the one reading the newspaper?' I suggested. There was nothing to choose between their looks but this girl was obviously literate and at the back of my mind was the vague reasoning that if her massage was lousy, perhaps her conversation might make up for it.

'You mean number seven,' said the Madame curtly as if they were all reading newspapers. I hadn't even noticed the small number tags each girl wore at the shoulder. (Who looks at shoulders?) The girl was called and after neatly folding her paper, she came out. Number Seven took my hand and led me upstairs.

We walked along a plush carpet in a long corridor whose walls were newly painted, and entered one of dozens of doors. The room was small and to the standard of a good hotel with a double bed and bath, though scarcely any room to stand between them. She ran a deep foamy bath and then we lay on the bed talking. Her name was Saita and she came from Thailand's second city, the elephant city of Chiang Mai. She had married at the age of sixteen and lived for three years in Singapore where her husband was working, but then their marriage broke down and after their divorce she returned to Thailand with her son. She was now twenty-nine and her son was eleven. I was surprised to find that not only did she speak fluent English but she had a deep and enquiring mind.

She wanted to know my impressions of Thailand. I spoke enthusiastically (and honestly) about the hospitality I had received, the beauty of Ko Samui Island and her native Chiang Mai, the intrigue of the elephant football match and the ruins of Sukhothai, but complained that *khow phats* were often too spicy. Saita smiled and said it saddened her to think that so many tourists came to Thailand for Phatphong Road and never tried to learn about its people and culture.

'And yet you are a part of this Phatphong scene?'

She said she didn't like her work, but had no alternative. There was no work in Chiang Mai. She spoke English but couldn't write it which was essential for most of the job opportunities in this line. 'Many girls come here,' she explained, 'but there is no work for them, except prostitution. It sickens me to see young girls of thirteen or fourteen coming here and being taken in to work. Once you are in, it's so hard to leave.'

She worked from 5 p.m. to 1.30 a.m. and was only paid if a client selected her. Of the 160 baht fee for a hand massage, she received 25 baht (70 pence) and 45 baht if she administered a body massage. I challenged her on this because an irregular income of such a pittance was scarcely viable in Thailand – the cost of living was not that low. She assured me it was true but that this was not the only place she worked. Her father had died a few years ago and she was the only earner in the family. She would only work for two or three years more ('That's all I may have left. I'm not so young for this business any more') but by then her two brothers would have left university and would be able to support her and her son.

At that I got up to go, realising it was a mistake to have come here, and told her that I would just give her the fee plus a present of more and be on my way. She looked hurt and then apologised, saying she didn't normally talk so much about herself or so openly, and wouldn't have told me these things if she thought I would react this way. I tried to see flattery and connivance in everything about her, but could only see sincerity and tenderness. 'You'd better have your bath,' she said. 'It's getting cold.'

Some time later – it is possible to gauge passing time in massage parlours as the minutes spent with your limbs being bent the wrong way seem exceedingly long and all others frustratingly short – I was lying on my stomach with Saita walking along my legs and up my spine. Conversation was difficult but still possible.

'What do you look forward to in the future?' I asked, wondering if the only thing going for me would be an ambulance.

'I don't know. I'd love to have another child.'

'Surely in this profession you have ample opportunity?' My words were not intended unkindly but they received a sharp response.

'That's where you're wrong. I could only have a child by a man I really cared for. It's hard to meet such a man when I work here. And anyhow, that would mean marrying again. A child without a father has it very hard at school. I don't want another marriage.'

In the immediate future she would carry on here. It wasn't too bad. The worst part to her mind was the long wait in the room with the one-way mirror. They called it the 'fish tank'. There was a television they could watch but programmes stopped for two hours after 6 p.m. They could glimpse clients arriving by means of a gap at the top of the tinted glass and could see much more through it than was imagined, but she preferred to pass the time reading. The Madame got very angry if any girl became drowsy and closed her eyes, but this was still one of the better establishments as it catered for tourists. There were only four such parlours for locals, some housing up to 200 girls, but she would never work there. Tourists were generally much better behaved although she had been involved in some fights when a client became a bit heavy. Sometimes couples came in together and even single girls but they were always lesbians. She hated dealing with drunks. Arabs and Indians were loathsome and she disliked Germans. Best were the Japanese. They were kind, grateful and polite.

'You must know every nationality and their characteristics!' I joked. She smiled, and remarked that my accent didn't sound very Scottish.

A buzzer on the wall sounded. My hour was up. Saita returned to the fish tank and became number seven again while I went out into the street. I felt relaxed and pleasantly collapsible after what had been little more than an enjoyable but expensive hot bath followed by muscle stretching, spine cracking and skin-pummelling. What more there may be in these parlours depends primarily on the willingness of the masseuse and then accordingly on a surcharge . . . or else on the bather's imagination.

I walked to the end of Phatphong Road and stopped to look back, realising how naive I had been a little over an hour earlier. Naive, not so much in carnal matters but more in my failing to see those who practise them for a living as people no different from myself with private lives, problems and emotions of their own.

It was a warm evening at the end of January and on the telephone and electricity wires suspended high above the glare of the street illuminations were thousands upon thousands of swallows. There was scarcely a gap on any wire where another bird might have found room to perch. Most of them appeared to be sleeping, their heads tucked against their chests, their forked tails almost closed; just other migrants finding Rest and Recuperation.

To anyone capable of looking beyond the bright signs of Phatphong Road and fortunate enough not to be confined behind bars, Thailand revealed a multitude of surprises, and not least among them a gold image dressed cheaply.

7 · An Enchanting Ration of Burma

Bing, bong, ding, dong
Ping, pong, bing, bong
Dong, ding, ping, 'bop'
'bop', bing, ding, dong

In Rangoon, clockbells were ringing.

Sadly, and yet often in delightful little ways, Burma is dilapidated. Devastated by the Second World War and then retarded by economic turmoil following independence, the country has never recovered. Until 1964 it was the world's greatest exporter of rice (now it lags behind the USA and Thailand) and although still a major producer of rice and teak, its world firsts are confined to a virtual monopoly on rubies and the highest mortality rate from snakebites. 'The Burmese way to socialism', led by Ne Win for nineteen years after his successful political coup in 1962, has proved long, downhill and disastrous. Severe monetary policies and trade restrictions have caused economic apoplexy and a heavy reliance on the country's black market. Marxism has failed to dominate the oft conflicting doctrines of Buddhism and to unite what has always been a country of diverse peoples. Marx would not have approved of 100,000 men begging and being revered as monks, nor of the attitudes that more merit is acquired by building monasteries and pagodas than hospitals. Of the sixty-seven ethnic groups found in the country some, such as the former head-hunting Wais and those in the opium belt of the Golden Triangle, have remained outside governmental control.

Burma's earlier rulers had not found unification any easier despite even harsher measures. Opium users were once punished by having molten lead poured down their throats, trial by immersion was practised – the winner being the one to stay under water the longest – and execution by impalement was common as a Portuguese adventurer called De Brito discovered in 1613. After thirteen years of usurped power (during which he stole and lost a forty-ton bell from the capital city) and relentless persecution of Buddhism, he suffered this agonising fate. He took three days to die. The next two hundred years saw the war between the Burmese and the Mons in the south, the latter eventually being suppressed and the capital, Dagon, being renamed Rangoon ('war over') in commemoration. The gesture was premature for there followed two wars with Britain, resulting in Burma falling under British control in 1885. Britain's campaigns were costly in terms of lives and immoral in terms of mercenary interests but British rule did result in the longest period of peace Burma had known for centuries, ending with the arrival of the Japanese and the deaths of hundreds of thousands of Burmese.

In Bangkok my visa application to visit the country had been refused when I put down 'photographer' as my profession ('We don't issue visas to members of the media') and it took some persuasion to convince them I had no links with the media, and to be allowed to choose a less suspicious profession. It was a short flight from Bangkok to Burma's international airport, an old worn building that would have suggested a winter home for cattle had it not been for a neon sign stating 'Rangoon Airport'. Passengers' luggage was left dumped on the tarmac outside the building. As I took hold of my pack and wrested it from the heap a porter came rushing up and begged to be allowed to take it.

'You sell whisky? Cigarettes? I give you three hundred chats for them . . . ' (Burmese kyats were pronounced this way), he said with a grin. When I politely declined he simply dropped my pack and went off to find someone else who might want relieved of the weight of their duty free. Inside the terminus, beyond the doors with creaking hinges and amongst a confusion of wooden desks and baggage, the immigration officers were at work. 'Passport,' they demanded and then paused before stamping it. 'Any whisky or cigarettes to sell? Three hundred chats, O.K?' I refused, suspecting it might be a trap but others accepted. It was no trap and 300 kyats changed hands and the officers quickly put a bottle of Johnnie Walker and a carton of 555 cigarettes under the counter. The black market was illegal but ignored. Lead was out. Offenders had the option of whisky being poured down their throats.

It took one and a half hours to pass through immigration and customs although the checks were minimal and the delays were caused by the lengthy procedure of currency declarations and completing forms in six-fold. This, believe it or not, was aimed at restricting foreigners changing their money to kyats on the black market, five yards away, which offered three times the official rate. Most foreigners, myself included, changed the minimum amount officially and sold their duty free on the street where the better price of 370 kyats (equal to £27.80 at the official rate) could be obtained and this was almost sufficient to cover a week of cheap travel in the country. The unfortunate but understandable side of this was that every Rangoon citizen pestered foreigners for these imports which were otherwise unobtainable. 'How much for your Red Label and 555?' asked my Indian taxi driver. On hearing my price he gave a cynical laugh. When this failed to adjust the price he stopped the taxi to discuss it further. I threatened to drink and smoke the lot there and then if he didn't drive on, and reluctantly he gave way. 'If you sell them for three hundred and seventy,' he threatened as we resumed the journey, 'I'll cut my throat.' In order to avoid messing up one adequate taxi I hope he never came across the restaurateur who found the price quite acceptable an hour later.

My image of Burma ('the first inhabitants of the world') led me to expect a timeless land of teak forest and jungle, great sluggish rivers, pagodas and an unsophisticated, unhurried lifestyle for its people. Timelessness had always been the prerogative of the Burmese and the bane of Europeans anxious to get things done without delay. Perhaps this difference appealed to the post-independent rulers of a country which enjoys a joke for today the foreigner is forced to count minutes more carefully and less willingly than ever before. Burma had closed its borders to all surface travellers and only granted a maximum stay of one week to those who arrived by air. This meant a rush similar to that endured by Phileas Fogg in *Around the World in Eighty Days*, battling against a stopwatch and a schedule tightened by the disintegration of the country's transport system. My chief destination was the fabled city of Pagan, situated north of Rangoon, twenty-one hours and five minutes away (on a good day) by train, horsecart, minibus, horsecart, truck, truck and horsecart. Pagan was a ruined city, and I had expected this, but it was a surprise to find Rangoon going the same way.

Dusk was already falling when the taxi dropped me off in the city centre. The buildings formed long blocks three storeys high on either side of wide thoroughfares. The street lights came on without any enthusiasm but were nevertheless bright enough to enhance the city's neglect by stretching paint peeling from houses into long shadows, emboldening the dents of crumbling plaster façades, and illuminating broken window frames, rickety doors, broken pavements, manholes without covers and bumpy streets of potholes. These hazards were testing the suspension of the few cars to be seen and most looked as if they had already completed nineteen years on Ne Win's road. Some were museum pieces, though not as fine a selection or as well preserved as those in Uruguay. Rangoon's buses were strange, shorter than normal, rusty, windowless contraptions built on the chassis of Canadian trucks left over from the Second World War, and their similarity to 1930s bread vans made Bangkok's clattercans seem futuristic in comparison. The air was warm and humid, the whine of mosquitoes pierced the lulls of quiet, and the redolence of cheroot smoke lingered behind the passing figures, men in longyis indistinguishable in the distance from women. Burma intuitively felt welcoming. The Burmese appeared to have done for grinning what the Balinese had done for smiling. They looked content in their crumbling city.

In the bar of the Strand Hotel whose former colonial glory was now in tatters, I fell into conversation with an elderly Scotsman who stood out in a room of young shoestringers. Jim Lennox was a sturdy thick-set man despite being in his late seventies, with a narrow blunt-ended moustache and thin white hair making an island of his bald crown. He wore a jacket and club tie and his presence restored some of the standards once expected of The Strand. He had first come to Burma in the early 1920s and spent most of his working life in the Burma oilfields. Now he had returned for a week to see the country after a long absence.

'It was a beautiful country then, and we were all Burmaphiles – loved the place. Rangoon was clean and well-kept and this used to be *the* hotel.' His eyes wandered nostalgically round the room. 'During the cool season from November to January it was always full of up-country British who came for the horse-racing, one of the highlights of the social calendar. The "fishing fleet" arrived at this time too – at least that's what we called the young ladies shipped out from Britain ostensibly to visit their relatives but mainly in the hope that the unmarried ones would find a husband!'

'Everything in Burma must be very different from the way you remember it?'

'The south has changed the most with everything becoming so

run down but the north was never developed to the same extent. There are more roads in the country now, and they've done daft little things like change to driving on the right when all the cars are right-hand drive and all their neighbours drive on the left. I didn't manage to get back to the oilfield area I knew best but Upper Burma seemed to have changed very little. The Burmese themselves are still the same.' He saw them as wonderful people, always laughing and friendly, as the 'Irishmen of the East' because they never worried. With a full moon for their spiritual well-being and a full belly of rice, they were happy. He had found them astute and yet indolent, to the European's way of thinking, but this was just the way of the tropics. Their hospitality was limitless and often two or three full cups of tea would be placed before a guest at the same time. This put him in mind of an incident which took place around 1926.

Some of the oilfields north of Prome, on the road to Mandalay, were close to the Irrawaddy river on both banks. They were served by paddle-steamers which towed the oil away in two tank barges. There were no jetties there and the steamers simply ran their bows into the riverbank in order to load and offload. In April-May, just before the monsoon broke, the river would be at its lowest and small patrol boats had to mark the safest course by placing bamboo poles around the sandbanks. Kerosene cans dangled from the poles and caught the sunlight to form an avenue of flashing reflectors. It was an extremely effective method.' At this time Jim was working close to the Irrawaddy. On one occasion while on his way to meet a steamer at one of the riverbank ghats, he was approached from a jungle path by an odd-looking man. The figure had hair down to his shoulders, wore a khaki shirt, shorts and sandals, and carried a small haversack. He was in his mid-twenties and had striking blue eyes, skin burnt almost African black, and a mouthful of gold teeth. In the conversation that followed the stranger explained that he came from America. He had been a factory worker until he fell ill and a doctor advised him to take up walking for exercise. He began walking in the evening, then also at weekends, then on holidays until walking became an obsession. Eventually he decided to give up his job and walk around the world, and *Worldwide Magazine* had agreed to pay his expenses in exchange for his story. A large part of the journey had been completed by then; in Turkey he had been beaten up by bandits and his back still bore the scars but in Burma he had fared best of all.

'He said the Burmese were so hospitable that often they couldn't find enough cups of tea to fill and place before him!'

'Do you know what happened to him?' I asked.

'Not for certain. He was a strange character. Carried next to nothing, no food or medicine, little more than a toothbrush. He had already walked thirty miles that day and only eaten a banana, some sweet corn and rice. I managed to get him a free passage upriver and then months later I heard – it might have been in the *Rangoon Gazette* – that this traveller had got as far as China and had disappeared. Rumour had it that he had been killed and eaten as China was suffering a severe famine at that time.'

Jim had been one of the last to walk out of Burma after the organised demolition of the oilfields in 1942, shortly before the arrival of the Japanese. He had *walked* 150 miles and escaped to India through jungle rife with leeches and the danger of encountering an enemy patrol. Before leaving, some evacuees buried valuables in tin trunks in the hope of recovery after the war. 'One asked a Burmese friend to keep an eye on his two buried trunks,' Jim recalled. 'This Burman thought he would stay in the area but when he heard of the Japanese atrocities he decided to leave. He dug up the trunks and took them with him, burying them each time he found a safe place but having to move on several times. Eventually he was caught and the Japs somehow learnt of these two trunks. He was tortured but did not reveal where he had hidden them. After the war the owner duly returned and was given all his goods back. Such is the Burmese heart.' Jim had also returned and was surprised to see the Japanese had decorated the pagodas with millions of their own worthless banknotes. After the declaration of independence for Burma in 1948, Jim left the country, realising his happy Burmese days could never be repeated.'

'You should visit Pagan,' he recommended as I got up to go. 'It's a remarkable place. Inle Lake is very pretty too.' We shook hands and I left Jim sitting in a chair that must have supported a legion of Burmaphiles and collected their loose kyats under its cushions since the earliest years of the fishing fleet.

The Strand was full and so were the next three hotels. I stopped at a stall selling rice, a pungent relish called *ngapi* and some fried delicacies that tasted like burnt crisps. A group of women crouched frog-like beside another counter selling massive cheroots. One wizened old smoker had difficulty in keeping hers going and she frequently reached for the stallowner's lighter, a length of smoulder- ing rope hanging from the wall like a cow's tail. Her face was covered in deep wrinkles which expanded and contracted with each puff and inhalation. From a distant open window could be heard a gathering of children practising a song for the approaching Union of Burma Festival (12th February) and if the words were the same as the English version they were singing, 'Those were the days, my friend, we thought they'd never end, we'd sing and dance forever . . . ' I wondered which days they referred to? The Raj? Or those of the Shwe Dagon Pagoda? Rangoon's most celebrated sight was visible from the stall. It stood floodlit, bright gold on a hill about one mile away, resembling a colossal handbell 326 feet tall. Eight hairs from the Buddha's head and a duplicate of one of his teeth (the one in Kandy, Sri Lanka, which has the magical ability to duplicate itself to accommodate an expanding religion) were said to be enshrined within. Crowning a city which struggled to retain even a plain coat of paint, the pagoda was magnificent, a monumental whoopee plated with 8688 slabs of pure gold and encrusted with almost as many diamonds, rubies, sapphires, topazes and one large emerald at the top. I would have admired it for longer but my *ngapi*, fermented fish, was too strong for enjoyment and my fried grasshoppers were finished.

The YMCA was also full but the manager let me sleep on the wooden stage of its assembly hall. Sleep eluded me for a long time as my mind toyed with compromise routes in a beautiful country rationed to only a week. Nearby on a YMCA Roll of Honour were the names Elizer Grofit Fao, Saw Say Plah Shein, Michael Mg Mg Chu, and others; it would have been no surprise to have seen Phileas Fogg amongst them. Mosquitoes hummed outside my loose- ly propped-up net and the only salvageable amusement from my insomnia was, paradoxically, the plaintiff sound of passing time. *Dong, ding, ping,* 'bop'.

I decided to make a triangular route; north to Inle Lake, west to Pagan and then returning south to Rangoon, but if this was to be completed in the allotted time one stage of the journey had to be flown. The flight to Inle Lake cost me the equivalent of a bottle of Johnnie Walker and 150 cigarettes. In the plane I sat next to a fifty-year old Italian called Antonio Fluvio and it wasn't long before his constant grousing made me wish he could be ejected into the scene below. He would have landed on flat brown farmland where he could have waited for the monsoon to transform faint outlines of plots into brightly coloured crops, or perhaps he would have landed on the white roads that cut striking geometric patterns across the plain and there he might have been run over by a 1930s bread van. That would have been something to complain about but instead he went on about how depressing he had found Rangoon and how his hotel handbasin had been attached to the wall *outside* his window, forcing him to open it and lean out each time he brushed his teeth. I found this hilarious and he sulked until we had passed over low green hills. Inle Lake stretched out at their base as a blue oval surrounded by a fringe of swampland, canals and houses on stilts.

'The Indians here are famous for leg-paddling their canoes,' I remarked, trying to cheer him up.

'I know,' he replied. 'I have a good guide book.'

'I bet it doesn't mention their floating gardens?' I challenged.

'It says they can grow vegetables all year on them.' This victory made him gloat.

I preferred him looking miserable and tried dropping him in the middle of the lake even though he wouldn't have made much of a splash. It was only eight feet deep.

The leg-paddling fishermen were intriguing. With one leg wrapped around the paddle shaft (held in place by hooking the heel over the blade) and one hand gripping the top, each fisherman stood balancing on one leg on the flat bow of his canoe and gently paddled across the surface scanning the shallow lake for fish. In his other hand he held a fish trap, a basket in the shape of an elongated bell. Whenever he saw a fish taking cover in the lakebed weeds, or sometimes just at random, he plunged the basket to the bottom and held it there – the basket was always tall enough to protrude above the surface. Then he poked a pole through the top of the trap to scare the fish into the gill net covering the sides of the basket. This performance looked uncomfortable but it was practical to the Intha Indians who had learnt to adapt a fishing technique which ideally required one and a half pairs of hands.

At the lakeside village of Yawng-hwe there were canoe taxis for hire but the jetty was deserted and the only notice was in Burmese.

This was a fascinating script of circles and their segments and gave the impression that everything was written in spaghetti and noodles. Unfortunately this was of no advantage to an Italian and the message remained indecipherable. Shortly after Antonio had wandered off to look for help one of the boatmen came along and I took the opportunity to escape from my companion. The canoe's outboard powered us across the lake towards the far side where the surface merged with the blue haze of distance and a straggle of fishing canoes with conical baskets resting on their bows hovered in the mirage like huge dragonflies.

The far shore was a maze of canals half-choked with water hyacinths and frequently bordered by the Inthas' amazing floating gardens. Reeds were lashed together to form mats about one hundred yards long by two yards wide. These were taken to Yawng-hwe, loaded with soil and towed back to the Inthas' end of the lake. Then they were anchored with enough space between each for a floating gardener to manoeuvre a canoe while tending to them. Occasionally mud from the lake was added to top up their levels. The gardens were said to be extremely fertile. Cauliflowers, cabbages, tomatoes, cucumbers and a surprising amount of flowers undulated in our wake as we passed.

When I met Antonio later that afternoon in Yawng-hwe he seemed in a good mood as he had also found a boatman and been round the lake, but he had been irritated by the local children. 'They are so noisy,' he complained, 'and always they ask me for peas. Why do they want peas?' This had me bewildered but we walked on and the answer was not long in coming.

'Peas,' said the first child we met. The next one child did the same but gave a two-fingered victory salute at the same time.

The answer suddenly dawned on me. 'It's *peace* they're saying!' I couldn't think who or what had inspired this touching gesture in ones so young but it happened continuously. Even a wee mite of a toddler wobbled up and offered a courageous but insipid 'psssss'. As we travelled by bus to the nearest town of Taung-gyi to find a hotel children stood waving by the roadside. Whenever anyone waved back they gave shrieks of delight and bounced with excitement. A girl perched on the rump of a water buffalo waved so vigorously she almost fell off. It seemed a game that never failed to amuse.

Day Three had to be spent travelling to Pagan. Antonio was going the same way. He reached the bus station shortly before me at 4 a.m., boarded the wrong bus and would have gone to Mandalay if the engine had started but Taung-gyi's mountain air was cold and the driver had to light a bonfire under the diesel engine before it would come to life. This gave Antonio time to realise his mistake. Our 'minibus' was a small Toyota pick-up which carried nineteen people – three in the cab, three standing on the near flap with a handhold on the roofrack, and thirteen in-between. The crush and the long delay before leaving were Antonio's themes in a soliloquy that lasted two hours.

No jungle appeared on our long downhill journey, just flat savannah made poorly by the dry season. Sporadic villages of brick houses provided mud water holes and the only gaps in the scrub. The road surface was sealed and this preserved potholes and bumps that frequently jolted nineteen pairs of feet into the air. Early in the afternoon we slowed for a funeral taking place on the verge. The body lay under a shelter decked with flowers. Antonio was fond of funerals and he looked up *funerali* in his guide book. It did appear to be an extremely good book. After a while he turned to me.

'It says here that often a coin is placed in the body's mouth. This is so the soul can pay the ferryman for the journey to the next world.'

'Really? It'll be a slow journey if the ferryman's a leg-paddler!' I quipped. This produced no response and I vowed I'd go my own way in Pagan. His sourness made me vindictive. 'I don't suppose your book mentions anything about a letter of discharge?'

He wisely ignored my question and prevented me from passing on a snippet about a strange custom that Jim Lennox had said was practised in his day. When a worker died his colleagues and relatives would evidently get the employer to write a formal letter to the deceased to say that his services were no longer required, otherwise they believed the spirit would turn up for work as usual and haunt them. The fear was most acute amongst those working in the teak forests where malicious spirits were more prevalent and might easily add to the many occupational hazards. Although the Burmese were Buddhists there were strong animistic elements in their rituals.

Our fellow passengers were largely women on short journeys and most of them had painted their cheeks with powdered thanaka bark, a fawn paste applied in large daubs or spiralling circles as protection against the sun. Several monks boarded when we stopped by a pagoda where hundreds of their kind were sitting cross-legged chanting mantras, and in their robes of reds and yellows, bright and faded, they covered the ground like a layer of autumn leaves. Antonio fumbled in his index. (*Buddismo; monaci.*) He was becoming an interesting companion.

'A monk's life is governed by two hundred and twenty-seven rules,' he summarised, 'and he is only allowed to own nine things; four pieces of clothing, a bowl, a filter for water, razor, sewing needle and' – he didn't know the English word and fanned his face – '*un ventaglio.*' He turned to the monk in the next seat and stared at him as if counting. Then he continued. 'To be a monk a man must be twenty years old and not have physical deformities. He must not have any debts or owe service to others . . . ' The monk looked towards me and I smiled in case he understood English and resented this analysis. He grinned and revealed a mouthful of gold teeth. For a moment I thought he might be Jim's lost American walker but only a Burman could have grinned so broadly. It was an enjoyable journey.

On some maps Pagan is represented by a dot whose size would indicate it is Burma's third largest city but in reality it is a village of around two hundred houses lying within sight of the Irrawaddy River. The discrepancy is accounted for by the awesome collection of ruins which surrounds this village; over 2200 temples and pagodas still stand on a flat area of five square miles. At the peak of its glorious period in the mid-thirteenth century this former capital covered three times its present area and contained 13,000 religious structures, but many have been destroyed by centuries of war, one-third of the city has been washed away by the Irrawaddy's floods and the remainder suffered serious damage during an earthquake in 1975. Pagan was already well established by the mid-eleventh century when King Anawrathta sent a request to the King of Thaton in Siam for copies of the Buddhist Scriptures. His request received a discourteous refusal and so Anawrathta promptly dispatched his army to go and fetch the originals. Thirty sets of Scriptures were brought back to Pagan on thirty-two sacred white elephants along with religious relics and 30,000 prisoners. Amongst these were craftsmen, engineers and artists and their arrival heralded a new cultural era for Pagan and the expansion of the city into a splendour rivalled only by Angkor Wat in Cambodia.

The sun was beginning to set when we arrived. I left Antonio and raced the sun, scrambling up the stone steps to the top of Gawdaw-palin Temple, an ornate edifice like a cathedral with a stunted spire, to catch the last rays before they sank below the horizon. The view extended for miles over the plain and except for its darker tones of ploughed fields, it glowed a mild yellow as the soft light touched its covering of scrub and parched grass. Rising up in every direction throughout this vista as far as the distant hills tinted blue and pink, were the pointed domes of hundreds upon hundreds of pagodas. Most were plain but some were adorned with short rounded spires made of brick and they studded the barren panorama as tall red nipples. Scattered among them and reaching several times higher were sculpture-laden temples, some white, some a wind-blasted earthen brown. At first the sun was no match for this breathtaking array of labour and creativity and it set gently, poising for long enough to lay a slender span of blood orange across the Irrawaddy before quickly slipping from view. A half-moon rose. No sounds reached the top of my temple, not even those of eight ox-carts in convoy cutting across the scene and raising a low cloud of dust as they moved through the darkening ruins of this astonishing city, and for the first and only time in Burma I was allowed to feel time stand still.

Day Four was a horse and cart day. Pagan had fifty-two horsecart taxis and the one I hired was owned by a youth in his mid-twenties who gave his name and address as Maung Ye Tint, Horsecart No. 12, Pagan, Burma. His English was excellent. He had learnt it from tourists and for some reason he began many of his explanations with the words 'Perhaps I am going to tell you . . . ' As the horse ambled through the ruins and we creaked along behind, Maung said his father had been rich and once owned six cars but he had left all his money to the family of his first wife. Maung was one of the second wife's six children and they had been left little beside a house which they had sold. With the proceeds they had bought a smaller house and this taxi.

'Is a taxi very expensive?' I asked.

'Perhaps I am going to tell you it cost nine thousand chat two years ago.' In practical terms this was £225. It was now worth 15,000 kyats, he said, and a good investment. He only had to feed his horse and care for his wheels. A carefully driven cartwheel could squeak for ten years. 'I make enough money for my wife and two children.

And you? You have a wife?' he asked. 'Or are you a lonely man?'

The question was delightfully phrased and made me pause to think. 'No. I don't have a wife but I'm not particularly lonely,' and we passed a pleasant mile discussing the difference between being single, alone and lonely.

This took us to a group of temples near a crowd of men and women digging in holes. Their longyis were soaking as they stood up to their knees in muddy pools and raised buckets of water and earth and poured them into sluiceboxes which fed the water back into their holes.

'Gold?'

Maung nodded and said they found sufficient gold to make a living but not enough to get rich. 'Taxi much better,' he grinned. He stopped to rest his horse and we began a day of exploring dark temple passages with candles. In one building we came across four Buddhas thirty feet tall, made of gilded teak and with an elegance that resulted in part from the soaring slenderness imposed by each tree's dimensions. But much of the city was in a bad state of disrepair.

'What happened to Pagan to make it like this?'

'Perhaps I am going to tell you we are not sure,' Maung began. Then he recounted the facts and suppositions of Pagan's rise and fall. Its greatness lasted for two hundred years until the reign of King Narathihupate who imprudently executed the emissaries of the Mongol emperor Kublai Khan in 1273 for failing to remove their footwear in his presence. As a result he had to flee the Tartar forces which swept down from the north and is believed to have pulled down half the city before leaving. Kublai Khan occupied the area in 1287 but did not destroy the monuments because he too was a Buddhist. The city was never rebuilt and has remained a ruin for over 650 years.

Late in the afternoon Maung steered the horsecart back to the village, past stalls of lacquer crafts, aluminium pans and mountains of vegetables, and showed me a back-street vendor with a miscellany of bottles and apothecary devices. He pointed out all the aphrodisiacs for sale, though admitting he didn't know if they were all real. By means of his mimes (and some research later) I was able to identify dried rhino blood and powdered horn, velvet from sanbhur antlers, monkey blood and, without doubt, the gall bladder of a python.

(This last had to be researched. It is very hard to mime the gall bladder of a python.) Maung added that tiger urine was believed to cure deafness. He laughed and admitted it wasn't an easy thing to find nowadays. 'Not many tigers left,' he said, and I imagined that there probably weren't that many deaf people left either if following a tiger around with a specimen jar was the prescribed remedy.

We parted here and horsecart driver No. 12 rode off. 'Goodbye!' he shouted. 'Have a good dream tonight.'

There wasn't much time for dreaming as Day Five started at 3.15 a.m. It was to be devoted to the nine-hour journey to the nearest railway station and the twelve-hour train ride to Rangoon. It started well with the discovery of a single bus which avoided the cart-truck-truck-cart-minibus-cart alternative and halved the time of the first stage, but it ended in a major headache. I passed some of the time in the train catching up on my diary and looking out for my first glimpse of jungle but none appeared. This made me wonder if Burma's sacred white elephants had eaten it all. A white elephant (actually closer to pink and having one less toe than normal on each foot) was considered second to a king at one time and was provided with a palace, servants, entertainment and acres of banquets. When my writing was up to date and the view continued to unfold empty fields and dust I began chatting to a group of multi-national travellers. Most of them were fresh out of India and they seemed preoccupied with bowel movements, their quality and quantity. Those of us who had not been to India were unable to contribute much to the conversation so it was an improvement when the topic turned to the other end, so to speak, India's gastronomic delights. It was during this discussion on food that I bought a toffee-coated peanut bar from a passing vendor. My first bite caused a hideous cracking sound and my tongue retrieved a sizeable portion of a broken molar. The tooth's ragged edge made my mouth bleed, and I realised my last day in Burma would have to be spent in a dentist's chair.

I didn't expect the chair to be quite such an antique. I had phoned the British Embassy and a Burmese voice had responded enthusiastically to my enquiry for the name and address of the best dentist. 'All the dentists here are the best,' it had assured me, 'but Dr Prakur is the very best.' Dr Prakur's surgery was to be found through a doorway in a less decrepit street than average and at the top of a filthy flight of stairs. His receptionist showed me into a waiting room where I read in the most recent issue of *Time* magazine that Neil Armstrong had just landed on the moon. Dr Prakur failed to appear for an hour and judging from the lack of patients he didn't appear to be much in demand. Eventually there were footsteps on the stairs and a few minutes later the receptionist led me upstairs to a surgery of high technology from the days of the Raj. It was a comfort to note that at least the drill was electric. And so I found myself lying on a chair like a reclined anglepoise lamp, thinly upholstered and torn, and liberally equipped with thumb-twist clamps. The headrest was designed to accommodate a grapefruit.

Dr Prakur, the very best, was an Indian, polite, friendly and bubbling with bonhomie. He was close to retirement age and wore spotlessly white overalls. 'Good morning, sir. How very-very nice to see you!' he exclaimed.

I tried to reply with equal cheerfulness but talking was difficult as my tongue was cut and slightly swollen. Dr Prakur was understanding and conducted both sides of a conversation for a while before examining my broken tooth.

'Oh dear! Oh my goodness!' he said severely. His expression turned to one of genuine pain. 'What a shame you are leaving Burma tomorrow. I think it is really needing a cap. If only you had come to me three days ago. Even if you had come two days ago. Or yesterday . . . I could have made a perfect cap by now.'

I explained that it had only happened yesterday.

'Yes, quite, sir. I appreciate this but if you had only given me a bit more time, just not even two days but one day, I could have made a lovely cap by now . . . '

Dr Prakur was obsessed with caps and bridges. He described some of the finest ones he had made, his pride making the perfect fit and the joy it brought him to see jaws close with one of his caps looking as if it had grown there. After his gloomy acceptance that there was no time for this remedy he decided the best thing would be to file off the ragged edge and cover the damage with a filling as a temporary measure. He released a clamp which suddenly dropped my head back an inch, and then spent the next few minutes looking for the drill attachment he had dropped. During the next hour he worked away and frequently lent back and talked freely when my mouth was full of instruments. He summarised the fundamental differences between Buddhism and Hinduism, discoursed on meditation – letting your mind empty, concentrating only on the air brushing past the tip of your nose as you breathe in and brushing the base of your nostrils as you breathe out – and saying how he never charged a monk or anyone who would find it hard to pay. 'If one man cannot pay, the next one will,' he smiled, and his tone made me wonder if my bill would be doubled on account of the last customer. It would have been worth it for the relief he brought me.

When at last he finished he was still lamenting. 'If only you'd come two days ago. I could have fitted a cap that would have given you a lifetime's remembrance of me.'

I assured Dr Prakur I would not easily forget him. There were other things I would not easily forget. The little children of Yawng-hwe rushing up with offerings of 'Peas', oxcarts trundling through the lonely majesty of Pagan and Maung's laughter over the scarcity of tiger urine were already secure memories.

Rangoon was quiet at 4.55 a.m. on Day Seven. The Shwe Dagon was radiant and lavished gold on the night. My taxi came at five.

> *Bing, bong, ding, dong*
> *Ping, pong, bing, bong*
> *Dong, ding, ping, 'bop'*
> *'bop', bing, ding, dong*

8 · Calcutta's Flowers

'I am not finding my pen,' the immigration official apologised, patting each of his pockets in turn. He disappeared under his desk for several minutes while the queue behind me increased to fifty hopeful arrivals.

'I am still not finding my pen,' he repeated a few minutes later when he re-emerged. He borrowed one from the immigrant holding out his passport. There was a long wait at the luggage reclaim area because three flights had become mixed up and piles of cases had been dumped all over the place. The vast bulk of them seemed to belong to a group of Muslim pilgrims whose belongings were sewn into identical sacks with a wax seal and the boldly printed words SLIME COMPANY OF THAILAND.

'This is ridiculous,' I said to a fellow passenger.

'No,' he contradicted, 'this is India.'

Take *exactly* ten sets of the British Isles and an extra measure of England, and shape them into a land with a crest of ice-bound mountains in the north and a fringe of tropical beaches running to a point in the south; fill it with a fertile plain in the middle, desert top left, jungle top right and scrub-covered hills at the bottom; be malicious with its ration of rain – none to the desert, just a sprinkle here and there until the earth is desperate, and then pour it all down at once; bless it with warmth and sunshine, curse it with snow, infernal heat, stiffling humidity, drought, flood and famine; furnish it with the world's most beautiful and ornate buildings and surround them with congested cities and squalor (contrast must be the vital ingredient – no one sight or emotion must be allowed to dominate for long); add 687 million people and allow them eighty-seven languages, 845 dialects and a choice of 18,140 newspapers; let them wander near-naked or dress them in drab rags, elegant saris or the simple brilliance of self-coloured cloth; combine them into a restless mass choking an inadequate and antiquated transport system, an uneasy cohabitation of devout spiritualists (five-sixths Hindus) with a hundred gods to support unshakable convictions of social superiority or total acceptance of inferiority; instal a one-rupee (6p) economy

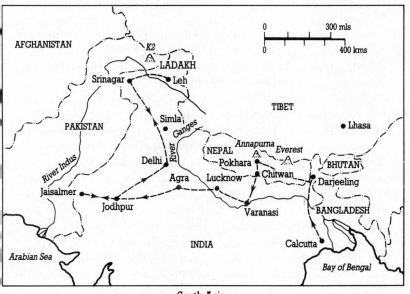

South Asia

but mix in plenty of incongruities, the odd computer amongst the camel-carts and ox-drawn lawnmowers; give the people a dusty nostalgia for extravagance, a refusal to acknowledge obsolescence, a love of cricket, present tenses, fountain pens, large ledgers, rubber stamps and forms in quadruplicate; add wretchedness and flowers and festivals and laughter. The result is not ridiculous, it is complexly India.

Calcutta is the country's largest city and its population rivals that of Greater London. In 1756 Suraj-ud-daula, the Nawab of Murshidabad, attacked the city and captured 146 British inhabitants. He locked them up in a tiny cell, the infamous 'Black Hole', and all but twenty-two were dead by the morning. All traces of the original cell had been eradicated but Calcutta's buses were continuing the policy of Suraj-ud-daula. Bodies bulged out of every gap in the bodywork and more festooned the outside as they hung from every fingerhold. Three Black Holes passed as I waited outside the airport for transport to the city centre but none had any fingerholds free. Eventually I hailed a taxi, a battered 1960 Ambassador that appeared to have cloned every car in sight, with broken seats, flapping bonnet, collapsed windows and a driver who ressembled the Air India motif shown on a nearby billboard, a plump maharaja with pointed toes, turban and up-turned moustache. On the billboard he was depicted playing cricket and having just been bowled. PLEASE KEEP YOUR WICKETS IN AN UPRIGHT POSITION was Air India's winning caption, gently chiding the national team for a recent failure. There were signs everywhere; 'Top people travel by plane for better journey, and use Visakhapatnam or Viziangaram College for better education'. 'J Raj, Tailor. Shirtings and Suitings', and dozens of handpainted cinema adverts in phosphorescent colours – a reminder that this country has the world's most prolific film industry with an output of more than ten full-length features every week.

Calcutta was just as I had imagined it. On foundations of shops with bars protecting their windows, layer upon layer of shabby dwelling units formed blocks which were shedding their outer coats and had been patched with signs. Below them constant flows of motion surrounded the obstructions of parked vehicles, puddles, refuse and vendors squatting over trays of peanuts and other few-paise products. The crowds appeared disorientated and making full use of the narrow pavements, the brightest colours tracing individual gaits among the mass of saris, longyis, jeans, shirtings, suitings and ragged loincloths. Ashok Leyland trucks (very shocked, on the whole) competed for road space with Ambassadors, Black Holes, auto-rickshaws like rowing boats converted into go-karts, bicycles and, to my astonishment, man-pulled rickshaws. They were two-seater chairs on cartwheels and although the passengers would do a backward somersault if the runner let go of the long handles, they must have been masterfully designed for the driver hardly had to control their balance as he ran.

'How far might they run in a single day?' I asked my driver.

'That's a hard one, sir. Maybe some are running forty or fifty miles in one day.'

For a while we stayed level with one of these archaic conveyances, now banned in Red China on account of being inefficient and degrading. The passenger was an obese woman in her early thirties encapsulated in a voluminous purple sari and her expression was cold, as if she resented the jewellery that perforated her nose, cheek and ears. The runner looked an impossibly frail counterweight for the burden that would earn him twenty pence per mile and he had been forced to the extremity of the handles. He was old enough to have been the father of the woman in purple and he trotted on legs of varicose veins, bent forwards, sweating, constantly glancing left and right.

We had to slow down and ease around what, from behind, looked like a low pile of Slime Company sacks lying on the road. A bony creature with horns painted green and pink lay sacredly chewing the cud. There wasn't a square yard of pasture in sight, only a frantic city and the detritus of poverty.

'Where do the cows go to eat?'

The driver shrugged. He didn't see them as cows but as badly parked cars. Later I saw one eating rubbish and the trimmings from a vegetable stall but when it approached the good merchandise it was brusquely chased away. India had 200 million cows at large. Some received scant respect and were worked hard but most were free to wander and allowed to die of old age. Then we came to a traffic island where a woman sat underneath the single tree that grew there. The tree trunk was covered in a rash of brown circles each with a clear hand impression in the middle. The woman sat with a bowl of water and worked cowdung into a sludge, shaped it into pancakes and pressed each against the base of the trunk to dry. Later she would sell them as fuel.

It was February which marked the end of the cool season and the beginning of the hot. Angry horns cut screaming through the sultry air and stirred the dust and fumes until a heavy shower of rain cleared the way. The streets soon became muddy despite the tarred surfaces because great excavations were taking place and hundreds of figures were digging and transporting baskets of earth to distant piles. The driver explained that this was Calcutta's new underground system in the making.

'They're digging an entire underground system *by hand*?'

He nodded proudly. 'It will be ready in 1990.'

We stopped for petrol at a garage where three Sikhs sat cross-legged on a woooden platform above the surrounds of mud, floating oil, litter and general garage debris. They wore immaculately white shirts, trousers and turbans. They looked unconcerned but marooned and ultimately as if they would have to be rescued. Outside the attendant's office a Gandhi-esque figure was meditating in a ragged dhoti. With his eyes closed he sat knotted in the lotus position on top of a fridge advertising Funny Delux Ice Cream.

Calcutta was situated in the east of the roughly diamond-shaped country. My principal destination was the small region of Ladakh adjacent to Kashmir in the northern tip because of its remoteness and its distinct Tibetan culture. To reach there I selected a roundabout route, north by toy railway to Darjeeling, into Nepal and then via the holy city of Varanasi on the Ganges to Jaislemer, a desert town in the west at the far end of Rajasthan. This would still leave me about a thousand miles short of Kashmir but that would be a problem for another day. A special permit was required to visit Darjeeling because the area was a military zone on account of being a slender strip of land between two neighbours and an obvious weakness in any dispute with them. After finding a cheap bed near the centre in the Modern Lodge which, from appearances, had not missed the Indian Mutiny by much, I took a large go-kart to the permit office. It was a journey of around ten minutes and as many near-collisions.

I was hoping to arrive at a building which would stand out from the general impression of decay but I was half a century too late. The headquarters of the Deputy Commissioner, Security Control, had once been yellow and pompously colonial in style but bits had fallen off and the remains were cracked and flaking. Inside was a twilight world of fabled Indian bureaucracy, a dingy cavernous room divided by a wooden and glass panel with speak holes. The far side was a shambles. Wall shelves arched under the weight of ledgers and old wooden desks were laden with highrises of paper whose edges were yellowed, torn and curled. Visible within this maze of documents were the heads of a dozen men. They all wore glasses and were doing little but adding comments to a general conversation, each comment, in true Indian fashion, being delivered with the punch as if it was the final word.

After a while a tall Indian with a dictatorial air and a nose designed for a heavier pair of glasses came striding up to the counter. His sarong flowed out behind. He was curt to the extent of being rude and spoke in short bursts. 'What are you wanting?. . . Wait . . . Fill in this form . . . Not here. Go out to the light.' His manner suggested he had just been deprived of the last word.

When I had completed the form and returned it to him, he disappeared for an hour. Then he came gliding back through the inactivity.

'I am arranging it for you. You can collect it tomorrow at three.' It was this ability of Indians to emerge from chaos with sweeping dignity and offer firm assurances that was to be a constant marvel to me.

That evening the street hustlers, touts and vendors were rife around the cheap hostels of Sudder Street. It was impossible to walk far without being besieged by those asking 'Yes, mister, one rupee baksheesh, yes? Taxi? Hashish? Shoeshine? Anything to sell? Radio? Camera? Baksheesh, yes?' The harassment was constant and it was easy to become exasperated and forget that this was a fiercely competitive land of merchants with a desperate shortage of things to sell and consumers with the means to buy. I managed to slip away from them by turning left at the sign 'Legal and safe – A B O R T I O N S – in just ten minutes, just 100rp' (£6), straight on at 'Sex problems? – Why worry? – Guaranteed cure by International Fame Specialist', and headed across the city centre to the Hooghly River.

Puddles looked as black as plague, a mixture of rain, washing water, oil, faeces, litter and the odd dead rat. The streets were still thronged; pavement barbers wielded cut-throat razors, Calcuttans were stripped to the waist rubbing themselves with soap and cranking a shower from street handpumps, others squatted and talked, played cards, argued before the wares spilling from hole-in-the-wall shops, and beggars hobbled along in gagged steps barely showing enough strength to lift the bamboo staff clasped in both hands, their eyes downcast, shuffling to who knows where. All of Indian life happens on the streets.

Further on the pavement was blocked by a pile of rubbish. A man was urinating against some railings and the liquid flowed back between his feet and into the débris where, within touching distance, barefoot women were sifting through rotten vegetables, street sweepings and offal hoping to find the keepables before stray dogs, crows and a tethered goat rooting in the same pile. The homes of these people were tarpaulins tied to railings and held out with stones. Beyond them was a small stall covered in garlands, thousands of white and orange petals sewn together. The Hooghly River was in flood and this stall was surrounded by thigh-deep water. The vendor sat framed within these laurels waiting for customers to come wading out to him.

My way was then blocked by the notice 'Pedestrian – not allowed over the overpass' but I found a legal way around and confronted the immense Howrah Bridge which crossed the river in a single criss-cross span of steel girders. This was a main artery of Calcutta's clotted traffic flow and was seldom without an unbroken procession of vehicles and walkers in both directions. The inward flow drew me back towards the centre where a street lighter was at work using a pole with a hook on the end. One by one he reached up and flicked a switch to illuminate a household bulb suspended above the pavement. Already the bodies of the street sleepers were stretched out or curled up along the walls and it seemed that for every family with a roof over their heads there had to be one family on the street. The rows of bulging blankets, sacking and plastic sheeting extended as far as the eye could see. I wondered what Red China would have made of India? At least every Indian might have a roof, a meal and a blue sarong.

It was the poverty and decay that turned me against this city and made it ugly but in the half-light I felt a change of heart. The dimness hid the shabbiness and allowed me momentarily to feel a different part of its character, its constant vitality, patience and optimism. *Optimism?* Yes, it was there even though the realisation of this at first felt strange, but on reflection it was no stranger than digging an underground train system by hand or finding a flower stall in the middle of a flooded slum.

Back at the hotel I tried to write my diary but my mind was tired and confused and I had no sooner begun than the city was struck by another of its habitual power cuts – the third that evening. There had only been time to write one word and the next morning I found I had misspelt it. Calclutta.

My permit was not ready at 3 p.m. The staff said they were seeing to it but I suspected it was lost and the office of the Deputy Comissioner, Security Control, was pervaded with an atmosphere of determined apathy. They proved me wrong and the dull piece of paper with its rubber stamp was ready at 4 p.m. Indian bureaucracy actually worked but it took time and was much ado about nothing. The credential required for visiting Darjeeling, it seemed, was the patience to endure a twenty-five-hour delay. I set off for the station, changed some money at a bank guarded by a pathetically fragile man, seemingly dozing and well past retirement age as was the shooting piece with fixed bayonet that lay across his lap, and stopped briefly at the Rat Heap. This was a small corner of the Tram Terminus where dozens of pointed and whiskered faces peeped timidly out of burrows. It was one of Calcutta's little ironies that in this city of starving thousands some people should find entertainment in throwing food to a colony of tame rats.

With time to spare at the station I sat down on my camera case to write my diary from a pocketful of scribbled notes. It took several minutes to locate the one on the Indian Museum which I had visited that morning. Another waiting passenger watched with interest and then approached.

'Excuse me, sir, but may I ask what it is you are doing?'

'Yes, of course. I'm just writing a few lines in my diary.' His expression showed this to be insufficient. 'About the Indian Museum,' I added.

'Ah! The Indian Museum. It is a very beautiful museum, do you not think?'

'Yes, it has a most impressive collection.'

He looked pleased, shook my hand and walked off.

This puzzled me for some time but I decided it was not merely inquisitiveness but as much a display of concern that I should be enjoying his country, an affirmation that it wasn't a bad place to have to call home. Whatever my first answer would have been he would have found some good in it and fished for a compliment about India. This was to be a behavioural trait not confined to Calcutta but common in other areas where flattery was scarce. (The Indian Museum *had* been most impressive, and for much more than my scribbled note gave it credit, but my bias was always towards oddities. 'Nat. Hist. Dept: wonderful collection of casualties, more mothballs than exhibits. One case contained *half* a sting ray, and a handwritten apology, "It has lost its tail in some accident".')

I glanced up, still smiling, to see a young girl of about eighteen passing. She was pretty, or would have been had her face not been consumed by hurt. Her features were twisted into lines of grief. She walked on crutches and my gaze naturally fell to her feet. I could only see a little above the ankles before her legs were hidden by her sari and her nearest leg was grotesquely huge and bulbous with folds of flesh stretched tight to form parallel rings like coils of inflated tubes. She gave me a glance, no more, and then without stopping or trying to beg for sympathy or alms, she continued on her lonely path, her eyes close to tears. I saw her other leg was beginning to show the same crippling disfiguration of elephantiasis. In her face there was no trace of bravery nor of acceptance, simply injustice and hopelessness. The crowd soon absorbed her and she was gone. I wondered where someone like that went for help in a city accustomed to suffering. Was there some International Fame doctor who would treat her even if she couldn't pay, or did the place of her birth condemn her to crutches and shame?

My train arrived and I gathered my luggage quickly, eager to interrupt my thoughts but another deformed woman sat in my way. She held out her arms blindly below a featureless face. She hád no eyebrows and a covering of taut skin grew over each eye and there was no sign of it ever having parted to allow her the use of sight. She had two small breathing holes instead of a nose and severely protruding buck teeth. I thought I had hardened to these sights after more than four years of travelling – and I had, although there was no pride in that – but here were the most pitiful mutations of the human body, here were living carcasses. Like all others before me who have recoiled in horror, thrown down some rupees and fled, I searched for reasons to explain their suffering. The Hindu and Buddhist would see their condition as punishment for the deeds committed in a previous incarnation. And the Muslim and Christian with their omnipotent and forgiving Gods, how would they account for them? The former, as unfortunates on which to exercise his duty of alms-giving? The latter, as evidence of The Fall? I could find no rationale. Gods make convenient but unconvincing scapegoats.

The train moved off and at once I felt cut off from the beggars, the clamouring shoeshines adhering to a Sikh whose shoes they considered dull and a brawny European, whose camera had just been stolen, haranguing a frail man with a frozen smile and a uniform bearing STATION MASTER on a polished badge. The respite was brief because then came ghettos, miles and miles of them. The poorest always live along railway lines; perhaps they draw comfort from a visible threat. My window became a vignette not of India but of the blight on the human conscience, of that state which those who can try to ignore and from which the others pray for salvation. The hues were sombre save for an occasional splash of purple.

Tattooed with povery, mortally stained
The beggars, the sick, the deformed and maimed
Born with misfortune's malignant disease
Third World, Third Class, silent lips, silent pleas
Untouchable, unlikable, whom no one heeds
Helplessly caught on the tide of their needs

Lands that are fashioned by want and neglect
No mirror for beauty, pride nor respect
Ox and sickle and terraced feudal plots
Harvests of sweat for the lucky 'have-nots'
Painstaking, backbreaking, all toils by hand
The hourglass of the poor is rich in sand

Unhealed gutters oozing filth, pus and slime
Septic raw sewage all floating sublime
Quagmires of offal and rubbish piled high
Wet nurse and playground for pest, plague and fly
Here live the hungry, without moral hold
The hunter of mildew hunted by mould

The air hangs tacky with the grime and the dust
A coat that clings with the comfort of rust
Through the wet warmth of the tropical race
The cycles of Life press on with their pace
Rampant procreation, cancerous decay
Share the same bedclothes and share the same day

Some sit and stare as if they are sleeping
Hearts grown hard in the depths beyond weeping
Their children laugh, playing games in the dirt
Calls of the innocent yet to be hurt
Unknowing links in an unbroken chain
Fettered and yolked to a burden of pain . . .

Above them a mantle, bougainvillaea's flowers
Bright clusters of purple in dazzling showers
Defying a wilderness, loving the Least
She smiles on poverty; Beauty and the Beast
Tattooed with poverty, mortally stained
The beggars, the sick, the deformed and maimed
Gasping and choking on a blind world's rope
That mantle of purple, a breath of hope.

9 · Hints of Menace in Nepal

The train travelled north from Calcutta through the night, across a plain which dawn showed to be covered in fields of stubble. New Jalpaiguri station was reached early and here passengers for the former British hill station of Darjeeling transferred to the toy train of the Himalayan Railway. This ran on tracks two feet apart because only a narrow gauge was sufficiently flexible to manage the tortuous route up into the mountains and for a little over a century since its completion in 1881 it has remained one of the marvels of railway history.

The toy train looked just that, as if pulled out of a Victorian play box. The little engine was a boiler with a narrow verandah at the rear designed around two slight Indians, and at the front it carried a funnel, spotlight and a bumper where two other Indians perched as scouts to ensure the track was clear and in the right place. Underneath was the usual confusion of wheels, metal arms, pipes and leaking oil. The locomotive pulled three small carriages with scant headroom to spare for tall passengers and rows of open windows which allowed everyone inside to experience lost pleasure from the eras of slow travel – a wide view, the smells of the countryside, time to appreciate it all – and to receive a generous covering of soot. The toy train, looking even smaller when sunk below the level of a platform which a sign placed at 330 feet above sea-level, was eager to start the journey that would take it fifty miles, round four complete loops and through five sets of switchbacks to a pass at 7400 feet. With a shrill blast of its whistle it dropped a hint, belching great clouds of smoke and making an unnecessary amount of noise as if a century of prestige were not enough.

The station master rang a bell. The driver lent out and looked back along the length of the wagons. Three guards each held out a green flag at the end of a horizontal baton and a stiff arm so that the flag hung without a fold. The signal fell with a heavy chop, the station master blew a silver whistle and the engine answered with a long blast followed by two short as we moved away. Fifty yards further on we passed a diminutive man in a sentry box beside the first points lever. He looked as old as the railway, maybe even older, and had the bored expression as if he had spent his entire life standing there as he did now, holding out his green flag in the prescribed manner. I stared hard but failed to convince myself that he wasn't a figure from a child's story-book that had popped up and got stuck. He lacked only rosy cheeks and a smile, but they had probably faded in 1882.

For an hour the journey was flat but then began the climb that lasted all day, following the twisty sealed road up into the dense tropical greenery of the hills. The valleys soon deepened but the view often stayed the same except that it was seen from a higher perspective. The narrow track balanced between the edge of the single lane road and the steeply falling hillslopes, the gravel from disturbed sleepers trickling onto the tarmac on one side and simply disappearing on the other. The road and the railway were so intertwined that each cut across the other quite freely in 132 unmanned level-crossings, without a single barrier on any regard for blind bends. Vehicles understood that the train had the right of way and listened for the ear-splitting blast of steam that acknowledged each controversial corner. Frequently we rounded a bend to find a waiting lorry confronting us but the track suddenly pulled us to the left or right shortly before a collision seemed unavoidable.

The other passengers were predominantly locals commuting to the next village. Serious Darjeeling travellers went by bus and arrived in three and a half hours against the train's nine. My companion, Mohan Prakhash, was an exception because he liked trains. He was in his early forties, less dark than Calcuttans, with a cheerful disposition and a build similar to mine (on the slim side) which made him look quite stout in my limited view of Indians. He wore a suit and carried a briefcase full of packets of sunflower seeds. His knack of being able to pour quarter of a packet into his mouth and then spit out the shells one by one and swallow the seeds was admirable. The last time I had seen such a skilful display had been in the USA. He noticed me watching.

'Would you like some?' he enquired.

'I was just wondering how you do it.'

He gladly gave a demonstration, explaining how the seeds had to be stored in one cheek and kept as dry as possible while your tongue did this and that, your teeth did something else and Bob was your uncle. 'Here, try some,' he suggested.

I did as instructed and after several failures my cheekful of seeds gradually deflated through the process of crack, spit and swallow. 'Yes! You can do it too,' Mohan praised, 'Bob is your uncle.'

I accepted this compliment but refused any more in case he spotted my incompetence – I was inadvertently swallowing the shells and planting sunflower seeds along the Himalayan Railway.

Mohan worked as a management consultant for Darjeeling's seventy-eight tea gardens. 'Our tea is world famous,' he said with a smile that embraced many statistics and a fear of decline. 'We are producing twenty-three million pounds of tea each year – that's two per cent of India's total, and we are employing almost fifty thousand peoples. But the problem is our bushes are now old and they are getting tired.' He was working on a government project to encourage immediate replanting and assist with the financing of such a policy. He had been born in the mountains and said he wouldn't like to live anywhere else. 'It's so different, it's not really India.' As we rose higher, I understood what he meant. The houses became more solid, turning gradually from mud and matting on stilts to wood and finally to stone. Sarongs and saris disappeared and were replaced by thicker skirts, multiple skirts, trousers, shawls and jerseys. The Indian facial features diminished and were replaced by lighter skin, ruddy mountain cheeks and the rounded Mongol features characteristic of Tibetans.

We passed a covered ox-cart toiling up-hill with six pixie children in red dangling their legs out the back, and rolled through the centre of one-street villages so close to the buildings that passengers could have plucked articles from the vendors' stalls. We stopped frequently to take on water, and women and children came running with fruit, sweetmeats or thermos flasks shouting 'Chai, chai, chayeeeeee', letting the last word drop and scooping it up in a crescendo. A few people gathered by the engine with tongs ready to seize any unconsumed coals when the furnace was raked out. Then we would move on once more, usually with some extra passengers who enjoyed a short free ride. Children waved at us and one gang of tots had a cart whose wheels fitted onto the rails. After we had passed they set off down this hair-raising Cresta Run and frighted a hen which sprinted away in panic. Its neck stretched stiffly in front and its broadly-spaced legs kicked so high and fast I thought it would explode into a puff of feathers.

'Are you going to Darjeeling for the New Year celebrations?'

Mohan asked, his smile now just embracing sunflower seeds. This was February and he saw my puzzled look. 'Now it is the Tibetan New Year and there will be dances at the monasteries.'

'What luck!' I exclaimed. 'No, I hadn't heard about that. I came because I hoped to get a glimpse of Mount Everest. A distant relative of mine left from Darjeeling on an expedition to climb the mountain in the 1920s. I would like to see the town.'

'And will you stay long there?'

'Just a few days. Then I'm heading for Nepal to do some walking and to visit a national park for rhinoceros.'

He nodded and spat, and I could see I wasn't making sense. 'You move very quickly,' he commented.

This hadn't been my intention but the world had proved too big for time-free travel, at least for a traveller who wanted to get home some day. My pace seldom rushed but seldom paused for long in any one area – and four and a half years of this steady pace had taken me only three-quarters of the way round the world. I merely shrugged and smiled at Mohan. The toy train certainly couldn't be described as moving very quickly. Its pace seemed just right.

At about the half-way stage a strange game started. Eight boys in their early teens came running out of one village. They were able to match the train's speed for short bursts and then they rested by leaping against the sides of the coaches and clinging to the window-sills, their bare feet finding a toehold dangerously close to the wheels. Every so often one dropped down and sprinted ahead to gain a few yards on his previous hold and find a new one. When the track looped they all dropped off and scrambled up the banks to meet the train at a higher level and sometimes fought amongst themselves to cause the loser a delay that would test his sprinting ability. They must have been astonishingly fit and have had arms like orang-utans – the game went on for hours. At one of the switchbacks I got out to photograph the train but lingered too long and had to make an alarming dash in order to catch up with the last coach. One of the hangers-on saw me and shook a reprimanding finger. Perhaps this was because my leap had been clumsy or because I had not been invited to play.

The steep slopes continued but became increasingly taken over by Mohan's tired tea bushes. The air had turned cold and passengers were putting on more clothes and shaking carbon and grit from their hair. At one station I went to the engine driver, feeling somewhat schoolboyish, and asked if I could ride for a while on the engine. He hesitated and then ushered me into the cramped compartment.

'But you must leave at the next stop because this is not allowed.'

He said he had been an engine driver for sixteen years and wanted to be one for another sixteen. He looked completely at ease with his charge, covered in its grime of oil and soot, inhaling its hot dusty breath, pulling at its heavy levers, one moment patting a delicate mechanism into place, the next pounding at a stubborn control with a hammer, and constantly glancing suspiciously over the rail at the wheels or checking water and pressure gauges. He exercised his love with a blend of tenderness and brutality and such was the fussing required to steer a middle course between inertia and explosion that he had little time for talking. I stood to one side cautiously mistrustful of every hissing joint and the crude levers that seemed to demand sixteen years of experience to know how hard to assault them and when they were doing their function adequately by just shaking about. Once the driver opened the fire door to throw in a shovel load of coal. His black face flashed orange and a blast of heat forced me against the wall. His assistant spent the entire journey leaning out from the cab and periodically pulled a handle which shot a jet of steam from below his feet and sent it ten feet into the bushes, though doubtless it achieved something useful as well.

'What does that do?' I shouted into his ear.

'It is doing this,' he said. He pulled the handle and a jet of steam shot ten feet into the bushes. I didn't pursue the matter. It looked an essential part of a toy train journey.

When we reached the end of the line Mohan kindly accompanied me for a while through the streets until he was able to give instructions for finding the Youth Hostel. Right, left, right, uphill all the way and Bob should have been my uncle but I must have gone wrong and it was no easy place to find. In terms of ups and downs and ins and outs, Darjeeling is excessive throughout its spread along several miles of high mountain ridge. Its setting appealed to me the next morning as I stood on the balcony of the Youth Hostel, a comfortable and homely building, sipping hot sweet tea in the cold dawn air. British house styles and names were still apparent in the town – Windermere Hotel, Loretto College, Love Buds Nursery School –

but most houses were a haphazard jumble of square shapes set on terraced streets and these fell away steeply so that all I could see was a line of roofs and then clusters of trees growing up from unseen levels below. Smoke from breakfast fires drifted up in lazy curls of royal blue and filtered through the greens and browns of the trees which were just catching the first rays of the sun. Deep in the valley below indistinct ridges of hills were discernible but beyond, in the direction of Everest, was a great mass of cloud. My eyes followed this up, higher than any horizon seemed likely, to glimpse the frozen white crest of Kinchinjunga 19,000 feet above my cup of tea as it poked momentarily through the cloud's ceiling. Perhaps the view had been the same in March 1924 when Andrew Irvine, the second cousin of my paternal grandmother, left Darjeeling for an attempt at Everest.

Irvine was an unusual choice as a member of the climbing party as he was only twenty-two years old and had next to no mountaineering experience. Not long out of Shrewsbury School, he had been on the Oxford Spitsbergen Expedition the previous year and this, along with his strength and fitness, were considered sufficient for selection. The expedition was led by General Bruce, the first to suggest using sherpas as porters, and amongst Irvine's companions were Norton, Odell and Mallory. George Mallory was thirty-nine and this was his third visit to Everest. Two years earlier he had reached the record height of 26,800 feet (29,028 being the summit).

The party were in good condition, acclimatised and had the latest in lightweight oxygen apparatus. It was the best-organised expedition to date but it met with early misfortunes. General Bruce soon collapsed with fever and Norton had to take over as leader, only to be struck by an attack of sciatica at base camp. The party nevertheless began the climb but were twice driven back to base camp by unexpectedly severe weather which brought blizzards and extremely low temperatures. Their tents provided inadequate protection and many of the party were by then suffering from altitude sickness, despite their preparations. Norton had developed double-vision, the first stage of snow-blindness. Undaunted they persevered and by early June a high camp (IV) had been established at 26,500 feet. It was to be Mallory and one other for the final assault and for some reason he chose Irvine instead of the experienced Odell. With the assistance of one porter they pushed on to a point suitable for a final base, Camp VI, and on 8 June the pair set off up the north-east ridge in a

In a Balinese dancer years of discipline and devotion to detail find supreme expression.

Limestone spires above the Gui River, near Yangshuo, China.

Cup Final, Surin, Thailand.
The referee kept well out of the way.

Moonrise and sunset over ruined temples at Pagan, Burma.

Cheroot-smoking, Burma. Her wrinkles expanded and contracted with each puff.

Calcutta reveals the ugliest side of poverty, but also the
indomitable Indian spirit.

Every day thousands of pilgrims crowd the banks of the
revered Ganges at Varanasi.

Kathmandu, Nepal. 'Our new address is . . .'

One of India's 200 million 'sacred' cows, and anachronisms.
Lawnmowers, New Delhi.

Precise eye movements are the
essence of Kathakali dances
in Cochin, India.

Yoked dzomos, a wooden plough and farmers of a Himalayan desert.
Behind is Thiksay village. Ladakh, India.

'Jullay!' An old Tibetan Buddhist with prayer wheel. Chonglamser,
Ladakh.

'... Half sunk, a shattered visage lies, ...' (Shelley).
Colossal heads at Nemrut
Dagi, S.E. Turkey.

Ayros Stephanos Nunnery, Meteora, Greece. A view with a room.

bid for the summit. They wore tweed jackets and cotton windsuits. Their cooker had rolled down the slope and they had forgotten to bring a compass. The day started clear but quickly clouded over and then came intermittent snow showers and a two-hour blizzard which reduced visibility to yards. The two climbers never returned.

There is no conclusive postscript to the tragedy, no proof to say whether they perished *before* or *after* reaching the summit. In 1933 an ice axe made by Willisch of Täsch was found at 27,600 feet but it has not been confirmed that this belonged to either Mallory or Irvine. In May 1960 a Chinese expedition on the first successful ascent via the north slope found a body at around 20,000 feet and buried it. According to a newspaper report at the time 'It had stiffened and shrunk, and the features were beyond identification, but the body had not completely decomposed . . . Its shredded and faded garments were of British make.' If not one of the famous duo then possibly the Chinese found another British climber, Maurice Wilson. He was lost in 1934 though not, purportedly, in this area.

Referring to 1924 in his book *Man of Everest*, Tenzing Norgay wrote, 'This was the year in which the climbers Mallory and Irvine disappeared close to the summit, and when the Solo Khumbu Sherpas came home afterwards I heard their names and never forgot them. Twenty-nine years later when Hillary and I stood on the top, we looked around to see if there was any sign that they too had reached it before they died. But we could find nothing.' In a radio broadcast in 1957 Professor Odell, the last man to see Mallory and Irvine alive, repeated his conviction that they had succeeded. He believed they were so close to the summit they could not have failed to reach it and had died on the descent. (He had received word of the lost cooker from the Camp VI porter and was on his way up with a replacement.) He described how his last glimpse of them on the 'icy-blue' mountain came during a brief gap in the clouds; two small figures far off and near the summit, hours behind schedule, 'going strong for the top'. They were reported lost at 28,239 feet, just 789 feet short of a peak five and a half miles above sea-level.

As Odell concluded, 'Only Everest will ever know.'

Everest (Sagarmartha to the Nepalese, Qomolangma Feng to the Tibetans) remained hidden later that morning when I went to its best viewing point, Tiger Hill, a modest knoll but one which nevertheless allowed the eye to travel 110 miles to Nepal and the great mountain, when the weather permitted. I had brought along a packet of sunflower seeds and was imagining myself at base camp, wallowing in a sense of occasion and practising shelling, when music from the nearby village of Ghoom pulled me back to the present. Of course, it was Tibetan Hogmanay! I hurried back down the track and found the monastery with ease as some children were delighting themselves by blowing amplified raspberries through alpenhorns, eight feet in length, which the monks had left unattended.

Ghoom Monastery was a low square building with a flat roof and was surrounded by similar outhouses whose roofs were already filling up with local spectators. Around the main temple ran a row of prayer wheels fixed into a recess in the outer walls. These were cylinders of brass about one foot high, engraved with Sanskrit prayers and held vertically in a spindle. Devotees walked along the wall from right to left running one hand along the wheels and giving them a clockwise spin as a shortcut method of sending a petition Nirvana-wards. Inside the temple were more ingenious ones like lampshades which turned constantly in the heat of a candle placed underneath. An old monk with a shaved head, dark crimson robes and black shoes that might have come from the court of Charles I with their large silver buckles, beckoned me over to a small hut. It contained an enormous prayer wheel five feet high and three feet in diameter. For a one-rupee fee visitors were allowed to watch as he gave it a slow spin which caused it to rattle and ring a bell.

'This must be your most important prayer?' I suggested.

He nodded and explained that it was a mantra, one of the sacred texts recited as an incantation. 'Om mani padme hum' – 'Oh jewel in the lotus'.

'What is this mantra asking for?'

He hesitated for a moment as if considering how to express the tenets of Buddhism in less than ten words, then shrugged and smiled. He locked the door behind us. 'It is asking for many tourists who will pay one rupee to see it,' he said, and hurried off towards the temple door.

Tibetan Buddhists were a minority in this Hindu area but they supported several monasteries of which this was the largest and oldest. These monks belonged to the Yellow Order, the Reformed Lamaistic Church, which was also found in Tibet and Ladakh. It was the strictest branch and its officials held the highest posts. New Year was a flexible date, similar to our Easter, and a time when old prayer flags were replaced and offerings of butter were brought to the temple. Pomp and decoration were important parts of the festival and dances were performed to symbolise good triumphing over demons and evil. A dance area was being marked out with paint in the temple courtyard. While waiting for the festivities to begin I met a young Belgian traveller.

'Would you like some sunflower seeds?' They were at their best as conversation openers. We got chatting and Alain explained how he had spent the last three months among Buddhists and was very taken with the religion. I asked what he found particularly attractive about it.

He liked above all its peacefulness and tolerance. 'With Buddhism, I feel . . . ,' he unfurled his arms but found the English words wouldn't come, ' . . . I feel,' he repeated and left it at that. It was a perfect summary.

The real alpenhornists appeared and blew a long series of low-pitched growls. They were joined by a band of monks playing percussion and by two distinguished figures in cream-white robes and plumed helmets who puffed their cheeks into Ghoom oboes. It always impressed me the way oriental musicians played by ear and never used sheets of music, but possibly little has been written in the way of orchestral works for alpenhorn, gong, cowbell and cymbal. They made a pleasant jerky sound which suited the dancers' hops. For the next two hours a select troop of monks performed seven traditional masked dances dressed as devils, animals and skeletons. The dances were spectacular more for their costumes than move-ments, and the crowd watched in silence except during the intervals when two boy novices clowned in outsize masks. The highlight was the Black Hat Dance which broke away from the gentle high-kicking and hopping and caused some monks to leap and spin as if possessed. They wore black robes, bright devil masks and black hats two feet high which tapered to a skull and clusters of peacock feathers. As the monks pranced and whirled they revealed a patch-work splash of colours lining their black robes.

'We could be two hundred years back in time,' I said to Alain. 'If the monks weren't wearing digital watches around their elbows.'

The dancing drew to a close and ended with the destruction of effigies representing the Old Year. One monk took a hatchet and sliced a dough figure of a man holding a spear into four pieces and threw one to each point of the compass. Its companion, a winged angel with the face of a skull, was ceremoniously carried to a pile of straw and set on fire. With that, the monks reverted to their usual peaceful, tolerant selves.

I had taken two rolls of film during the dances whereas Alain didn't seem to carry a camera. When I asked him about this he explained that it had been stolen in Kathmandu but now he didn't miss it at all. He was a master of the perfect response.

'Now when I look,' he said, 'eet eze just for zee pleasure of zee eyes.'

Darjeeling was a Land Rover town and the area must have kept the Rover factory busy for years. My journey to Nepal began in a bastardised model but was completed in a relatively comfortable Black Hole with ROCKET painted on its sides. First came the descent along the same road used by the toy train and this time I made a note of the safety signs and moralising messages painted on the rocks. Some took so long to read they must have caused many of the accidents they were aimed at preventing.

THIS IS NOT A RACE NOR A RALLY – DRIVE CAREFULLY AND ENJOY THE VALLEY.
CARELESS DRIVERS KILL AND DIE – LEAVING KITH AND KIN TO CRY.
DO NOT BE RASH AND END IN A CRASH.
IT'S GOOD TO BE LATE, MOTORISTS – AND NOT TO BE LATE MOTORISTS.
IF YOU WANT TO SEE HILLS,　DRIVE SLOWLY. IF YOU WANT TO SEE HELL, DRIVE FAST.
SLOW HAS GOT FOUR LETTERS, SO HAS LIFE. SPEED HAS GOT FIVE LETTERS, SO HAS DEATH.
MIND YOU LEFT YOUR CHILD SMILING AT HOME.
BE LATE THAN NEVER.

Rocket was waiting for passengers just inside the Nepalese border and it took me through the night towards Pokhara. Nepal was a military state and we had to stop at a dozen checkpoints. Army uniforms were prolific and it was obvious how a small country like this could find enough spare soldiers to lend Britain several Gurkha

Regiments. The bus took on an armed guard for the journey across
the plains as bandit attacks had become a problem, and my neighbour pointed to two wrecked buses later on which he said had been
bandit victims. (This was one of the reasons why the reverse of our
tickets stated 'The traveller is responside for his own baggages. If
baggages are lost company not resqonsrble.') I gladly accepted the
odd swig from his bottle of roxy, a sense-mugging concoction from
fermented maize, as we took on an increasing pressure of passengers,
broke down twice and lost six hours. My neighbour assured me this
was good going, but then he had drunk more roxy. *Rocket* referred
to the engine noise.

Delays and discomfort no longer surprised me but I was becoming
more and more disappointed to find my tolerance slipping and
giving way to aggravation. I kept these feelings unexpressed, being
fortunately slow in losing my temper, and reminded myself that a
smile was usually the most powerful weapon in the face of problems.
Getting upset was senseless as ultimately you were the only one to
suffer, and yet this couldn't alter the fact that my patience had grown
thinner. I could only account for this as an early symptom of
excitement at my impending home-coming. My mind was beginning to look beyond the next six to eight months and the many miles
it hoped to fit in and plan a vague schedule for my return to Britain.
But this was still far away in the future. I salvaged a smile for *Rocket*
and tried not to count the hours to Pokhara though the total would
obviously exceed twenty-four. 'Disappointments are diversions to
the next piece of good luck,' had once been said to me, but I wasn't
fond of cast-iron sentiment.

By dawn the bus was stopping frequently to disgorge one crowd
and take on another. In-between the driver drove in a manner that
was exhilarating but highly irresqonsrble. We descended steep sided
valleys with a thousand terraces falling to a river gorge far below and
reached Pokhara in mid-morning. This was Nepal's second largest
town though it was little more than a drowsy village with a wide
scattering of houses. It was situated beside the tranquil Phewa Lake
and in the foothills of the massive Annapurna range which formed its
horizon on clear days. Unfortunately the cloud was low when *Rocket*
parked alongside another pretentious wreck, the SUPER DELUXE
EXPRESS, but Pokhara's delight was immediate. Apart from its
setting and relaxing atmosphere the town was a charm of signs. A

hotel announced 'Running hot and cold showers'; a tailor, 'We await your auspicious arrival *smiling*'; a restaurant, 'Beacon and Eggs', and a souvenir shop, 'Get in here for postcards and rugs'. Most moving, however, was the sign outside a bicycle rental shop. 'Caution – before having a bic. Do not forget to check bic's condition. After when you have bring broke bicycle you must Responsible. So please save your bicycle.'

With the leisurely intention of walking out into the countryside for a few days and staying in wayside houses, I set off in the direction of the cloud covering all 22,956 feet of the sacred mountain, Machapuchare. Ragged children chased hoops with hooked sticks or played keepie-uppie with a round bat and a short pointed stick. Sometimes they came running shouting 'Gimme rupee, gimme, yes, yes,' until one of the women sitting on a doorstep spoke sharply and they dispersed. Pigs rooted in the verges alongside hens scraping and pecking with erratic clockwork movements, and once cows were driven past by a spindly girl made a hunchback by the baby slung from one shoulder. The road was busy with foot traffic and frequent groups of friends greeting friends. Pokhara was a popular trekking centre for foreigners and the odd party of walkers went by, some preceded by a loaded mule train. The mules wore bells and a red pompom on a stalk above their head and each step caused a glassy tinkle.

After a while I caught up with a luminous green backpack sporting a Union Jack and enough buckles to have kept Houdini secure. It was on the back of a Midlander, Tony Sykes, and on first impression I quickly placed him as a thirty-year-old accountant with size ten boots. He also had to be an optimist to be going trekking in white socks. After introducing ourselves we spaced our conversation at intervals suitable for drawing breath. Ahead of us was a party of four foreigners trailing three porters bent under great burdens of luggage. The foreigners carried cameras and light daysacks with a Swedish flag sewn to a rear pocket. Backpackers are an ostentatiously patriotic breed.

'Do you know how much one of those porters gets paid?' I asked.

'The usual rate is twenty rupees per day.'

It took me a moment to convert this and then check my calculation as the result didn't seem credible. 'But that's only one pound . . . per day?'

'Yes, but I suppose you have to see it in relation to the country as a whole. Nepal has so few roads and porters are still the most common means of transporting goods. Foreigners could certainly afford to pay more here but this would upset porters in other areas where there are no trekkers. So twenty rupees is the standard rate.'

He had a point but it was still difficult to imagine how these trekkers found any sense of achievement in strolling behind others who were bent under their crippling amounts of luggage. Apart from anything else, the very sight of them ruined the view.

'Everything is in a delicate state here,' Tony continued. 'Nepal is a small country and yet despite the huge amounts of international aid that have been poured in, the benefits have been minute. Things are in a bad way.' It transpired that Tony was not an accountant but had been working with the Save the Children Fund in Nepal for five years. He blamed corruption in the government for misappropriating much of the lump sum aid and said that charitable organisations now tried to operate with minimum government intervention. Small, low-budget projects were seen as the most efficient means of applying aid in real terms. Erosion was the country's major problem. There was a shortage of fuel, trees were cut down, the top soil was removed by wind, rain and meltwater. 'The problem is now so serious it may be unstoppable. We don't have enough time to teach the people the ways of conversation and repair the damage. It's a sad fact that Nepal is slipping into the Ganges.'

The valley floor was stony and its grass overgrazed. Hills rose up steeply from it and were dotted with houses that appeared to be made of adobe but were brick with an orange-brown coating and roofed with thatch, iron sheeting or tiles. Trees were sporadic enough to have been monuments, as if to stress Tony's argument, but they added touches of green to the brown slopes, and here and there were crops of rape seed in startling bright yellow. To foreigners walking through, the land and its colours could scarcely have been improved.

After a few miles I left Tony and took a steep side track leading up into the hills. The track levelled after an hour and by the time I had walked for several more along a ridge of small farms, the children chanting for rupees had thinned and the distant view had cleared. Far below lay the gravel valley of the Seti River and beyond were the blue outlines of the range that formed its other side, then rising high above all this and forming a skyline that made me cock my head back, the sparkling white icecaps of the High Himalayas; a sugarloaf profile of Annapurna South, the sharp peak of Machapuchare, unconquered (though one party came within 150 feet) and now forbidden to climbers on account of its sanctity, and the tallest, the rounded top of Annapurna III almost touching 25,000 feet. They used their size, ice and wind-blown rock to beguiling effect, at times appearing immense, aloof and unassailably rugged, at others coy, alluring and teasingly available as they let flutter scarves of drifting snow. The thought was inescapable that if one has to find a final resting place on this earth and if beauty plays any part in it, there could be few better choices than among these mountains. I found myself drawn to their serenity but intimidated by their harshness and there was insufficient Andrew Irvine in me to wish for a close relationship. For me it was enough that the Himalayas should remain purely for the pleasure of the eyes.

As evening darkened the sky a youth noticed me still sitting on my rock and looking out over the valley. He approached and unrolled a plastic bag to reveal a ball of brown putty.

'You want hashish?' he asked. I said I didn't smoke. When further persuasion failed he sat down with a heavy sigh and led it into an unhappy story. He needed money to train for a guide's licence, he explained. He had been an unofficial guide for six years but now not many tourists wanted an unofficial one. His family was poor and he had no work. If he could sell the hashish this would help a lot but it was already one month old and he feared it would not be good for much longer. I said I was sorry but everyone asked for money. I didn't have enough to give everyone. So he asked me to write a letter for him as he was unable to write in English. He pulled out the names of foreigners who had given their names and addresses to him after a trek three years earlier. I began the one to the Swiss, 'Dear Hans . . .', and asked what he wanted to say.

'Tell him to send me money.'

I thought for a moment, wondering how one phrased a letter with such a blunt demand and to a complete stranger who had possibly only given his address out of politeness and immediately forgotten about it. I did my best.

'Maybe he only sends a few dollars. Tell him I want three hundred. American dollars.' So I added the line, 'If possible he would like three hundred US dollars,' and wondered if that would seal its fate of a prompt rejection.

'What will you do with three hundred dollars?' I asked.

'First I will get married, then I will sit my guide's licence.'

'Do you think he will send you that much?'

'Yes, he is a good man, and rich. He earns six hundred dollars a month in his country. He has sent money before.' His story may well have been genuine but something in his attitude jarred. He asked for money to post the letter. I offered to post it for him but at that he became irritated and refused, and eventually he walked off muttering abuse. Later he came back to accept.

This was another of the times I felt travelling was corrupting me, hardening me. I still had a basic trust in people but to a lesser degree than before. My trust was not freely given but had to be won, and overcome my initial feeling of suspicion. A defensive attitude was essential as there were plenty of confidence tricksters ready to prey on the gullible, and a need for suspicion was constantly reinforced by the system of haggling. Travelling still enthralled and excited me but I was tired of this one aspect, of always counting the cost, always having to question price and integrity. Long-term travel was very different from being on a three-week holiday when it was possible to shrug off expense in the knowledge that soon one would be back at work and earning again. Travelling for a long time with no income, always paying out and being faced with a choice of many inflated prices and a few good values, forced one to enter the world of haggling, beggars and tricksters with suspicion if funds were to last. Outlook and principles changed. There were times when my sense of proportion disappeared – it was an occupational hazard – and I was appalled by my own meanness and the energy spent on hunting out the best bargain. Moments like these, as with the beggars and hard-luck story-tellers were worrying. They made me wonder how much I had changed and how lasting these changes would be.

Sitting on a rock and staring at Annapurna III did not provide the answer. I left the ridge and walked towards a group of houses in the hope of finding some floor space to rent for the night as this was the common practice in the area. Some women emerged from another path and reached the houses before me, having just walked up from the valley with enormous bundles of sticks and leafy branches bound to their backs and prevented from slipping by a band around their foreheads. From behind it appeared that Great Birnam wood, with a hopeless sense of direction, was on its way to Dunsinane via the Himalayas. A man whose beard had been dyed bright ginger with henna greeted them from his doorway and on seeing me, he came to offer me a place to sleep. It was getting dark and I accepted at once. Baba ushered me into a cramped room whose only light was the glow from a small fire in one corner. It cast a warm sheen over the faces of Baba's teenaged daughter stirring a pot, his wife chopping vegetables and an old man crouched alongside, all huddled up as if confined in a glass dome. Baba squatted beside him and they shared a pipe. It was shaped like a funnel with a wide bowl and a vertical stem. They smoked hashish which was loathe to stay alight and a live ember sat in the bowl for most of the time as each fitted the stem into the hollow of his clasped hands and cocked his head awkwardly to suck the smoke between his thumbs. Baba's wife lit an oil lamp which burnt with a thick trickle of smoke and lit up ten rings spaced around the edge of each of her ears. She set to work grinding millet seeds and I felt the centuries slip away as she turned a handle and fed the grains between two flat stones.

The daughter took out a piece of tube and blew the embers until flames licked up from the few pieces of wood she had placed on top. She seemed an expert at using the bare minimum amount of wood, a skill doubtlessly soon learnt if she had to carry it up from the valley. They said wood was not a problem but water was thirty minutes walk away and there were always long queues. Despite this they were meticulous about washing their right hand before eating and a little boy got a slap for not doing so and had to wash at once. They were a friendly family and we took turns to eat rice, silver beet and dal (lentils) as there wasn't enough plates for everyone to eat together.

One of Baba's sons was learning English and after the meal he came up and asked if I had a cigarette. He was astonished to hear I didn't smoke.

'Why not?' he asked.

'Because it makes me cough.' Baba erupted into a timely coughing fit in the background. 'Do you smoke?' He nodded. He was fourteen. He went to school for four lessons each week because he said he couldn't afford any more.

I went outside for some fresh air. It was a beautiful starry night.

On top of the world. The lights from fires and street lamps flickered down in the valley. A faint murmur of voices and the occasional clamour of children arguing seeped out through the windows and thatched roofs of the nearby houses. A door would open and a silhouette would momentarily appear, bathed in amber. A peaceful mountain hamlet with no radios or televisions – but also no water, fuel or electricity to make these lives easier. I returned to Baba's house and fumbled my way in the dark to the upper room below the thatch. Smoke came up through a hole in the floor and became trapped. The fourteen-year-old son lay on his bed at the far end reading aloud for thirty minutes by the glimmer of an oil lamp. It added more smoke to the murky atmosphere, and he coughed several times. I lay beneath a stiff quilt on a blanket on the floor and reflected on how different the view had appeared from the top of the hill. Vast amounts of international aid were sent to this country but the schoolboy next to me smoked cigarettes and couldn't afford his lessons, his neighbour sold hashish in the hope of gaining a bride and an honourable career, and all the time Nepal, below the unrivalled splendour of her mountains, was slowly slipping into the Ganges.

The mature male Indian rhinoceros is the largest of its kind, weighing two and a half tons and matching a Ford Escort in length. Both he and his consort, the (arguably) fairer sex, are noted for their acute senses of smell and hearing, poor eyesight, quick temper and good acceleration up to 30 mph – which is why it is best to be sitting on top of an elephant when you go looking for them. I have no idea whether a rhinoceros rumbles, squeaks of flaps its ears to signify contentment for it had been a surprise to me even to learn they lived in Nepal. Indian rhinoceroses have no respect for international boundaries and a few were to be found in the south of the country in the Chitwan National Park.

The park was situated four miles off the main road at the end of a dirt track. The land here was flat and covered in sunburnt scrub, though interrupted by frugal farm plots and stands of trees that rose above the tall grass and thorn bushes. I had walked half the distance when the way was blocked by a river which looked at least knee-deep in the best place to ford. While I was contemplating this an ox cart driven by a small boy came along and he offered to take me across.

'How long does it take you to ride from the road to the park' I asked.

He had to think for a while. 'Well, it depends. Old ox he need two hours. Young ox he need one and a half hours.' His English was excellent. He came from a four-ox family.

The warden was a small middle-aged man and he occupied a wooden office beside an elephant compound on the edge of the park. He invited me in and we talked below a picture of a tiger hunt in the heydays of the Raj when up to one thousand elephants were used.

'In this park we have about two hundred rhinoceros, and also some tigers and snow leopards but they are extremely rare. We have to keep a constant vigilance for poachers,' he explained, and handed me the latest list of blackmarket prices for rhinoceros material in Bangkok. He let me make a note of them. The figures were given in US dollars for a pound in weight: Blood, $30; Dried Blood, $34.50; Bone, $2.75; Skin, $5.30; Teeth, $25 (per piece); Horn, $907.

'And all these are regarded as aphrodisiacs?' I asked. He nodded. The demand for rhinoceros mystified me. I failed to see how anyone could regard an animal that was partially blind, overweight, thick-skinned and bad-tempered as a sex symbol.

The park was primarily a refuge for rhinoceros but research was also conducted. Several of the tigers had been caught and fitted with radio collars in order to track their movements. On a typical day the domesticated elephants trampled wide paths through this preserved wilderness and undertook what he called 'conservation work'. In the afternoons they were free to be hired by visitors.

It is difficult to appreciate quite how tall an elephant is and how few footholds it has until you are faced with the prospect of falling off one. An elephant was selected for me and its mahout made it lie down. Using one of its knees as a step and leaping up towards the ridge formed by its backbone, I scrambled aboard. When the elephant began to stand up it lurched first to one side and then to the other so severely that the mahout had to catch one of my ankles to prevent me from tumbling off. After this he decided to fit a saddle of bamboo and matting, and we set off at a comfortable amble. An elephant's gait is pleasant, a slow roll from side to side at one second intervals, and it covers ground at a good walking pace even though its movements always seem unhurried. Elephants have charisma, and a colossal amount of it.

At first it seemed fairly absurd taking one of these mammoths on a safari that would doubtless require a certain degree of stealth and silence, but my reservations were soon squashed. Elephants were perfect vehicles; on open paths they were silent, their footwork was faultless whatever the terrain, they could go anywhere, were considerate and pulled low branches out of the way for the benefit of their passengers when they could have safely passed underneath, provided a superb view and were the first to detect and point out wild game. The mahout sat on the neck. He drummed his heels to make it trot, pulled the appropriate ear to make it turn left or right and tapped its head with a stick when it went wrong. First we had to ford a river and the sound of our splashing sent crocodiles slithering into the water, then we continued along a path through grass as tall as our heads. The mahout smoked a cigarette and I noticed he had two packets tucked in his belt. One bore the picture of a yak and the other a rhino.

'Is there any difference between them?' I asked.

'Yes. Filtered Yak, unfiltered Rhino.'

He pulled the right ear and we turned off the path and into the grass which had lowered to the elephant's forehead. Our mount was just like a tank and the grass opened up as it powered its way leisurely through. Beside a tree it suddenly stopped and let out a hissing noise. The mahout whacked its head to make it quiet and then we saw the grass moving fifty yards in front of us. When the movement reached a clearing, a female rhinoceros – so the guide said; the difference is not at all obvious – walked out with a young calf behind. She stood still for a moment, looking solid, impregnable and ridiculously creased. I saw it as a clothes horse ponderously laden with grey blankets, each covered in tufts and about to slip off. The head was narrow with a square jaw, small ears, swinish eyes and a modest horn swept back. The next moment they had disappeared. Our elephant had plucked a branch from the nearest tree and was standing still, bored, nonchalantly waving it around its face as a fly swat.

'Rhino very dangerous,' said the mahout as we continued, 'very bad bite.' He lit a Yak and described how the horn was really a hard agglomeration of matted hair and that it was rarely used by an aggressive rhinoceros. Teeth were the preferred weapon. Earlier that year a foreigner had evidently disregarded advice and gone out walking on his own. He had been charged by a rhinoceros and was lucky to have survived the attack but one of his legs was so badly bitten that he had spent months in hospital. We saw only one more rhino during the rest of the afternoon and several small spotted deer.

My rhino interest had been aroused, however, and when one of the local farmers came to say he operated an alternative walking tour in the land bordering the park, I agreed to meet him and a fellow guide early the next morning. I slept in a mud-walled lodging house and made my way to the rendezvous point at 4.40 a.m. Patches of fog moved over the ground and it was dark save for the light of a healthy moon. After twenty minutes of walking through fields we came to a former river bed which had been planted with wheat. A voice came from somewhere in the middle and conversed with my guides. It came from a *machan*, a thatched shelter on a platform which was inhabited by a nightwatchman. There was no barrier around the National Park and he was protecting his crops against 200 rhinoceros. One of the guides went off into the murk while we waited at the *machan*. Some time later the guide returned and whispered excitedly to the other two.

'What's happening?' I asked the guide who spoke some English.

'He says the rhinoceros are coming . . . '

'Here comes the cavalry,' ran through my mind but this sounded serious. I wondered how the watchman was going to persuade them not to eat his wheat but when I turned towards him, he had vanished. We retired to the edge of the field and crouched below the banks. The visibility was pathetic and it was only by looking down and using peripheral vision that it was possible to differentiate vague shapes. The guides nudged me and I dimly made out three dark blotches moving along the top of the bank forty yards away. It was impossible to distinguish which end was sharp and which blunt but the bulk was nevertheless impressive. Each figure was like three milk cows squashed into one animal.

They passed with a shuffle and a grunt, and we followed the largest one that took up the rear. The fog thinned and thickened and yet on we went, walking and trotting behind a dark mass on the edge of our visibility. After ten minutes the leading guide stopped.

'Weather is no good,' he said, disappointed.

'No good at all,' I agreed, feeling immensely relieved. The full extent of this folly had been troubling me for some time. Here we were playing follow-my-leader in thick fog with a hint of two and a half tons of highly excitable armour-plated rhinoceros. We turned back. We didn't encounter any more dark masses but we had to tread carefully for there was ample evidence scattered on the track to show that unfiltered rhinos were about.

Chitwan National Park made a return to India seem tame.

10 · Across India from the Ganges to the Desert

The dead man was twenty-four, killed a few days earlier in an accident while constructing a house.

'In other countries doctors might have been able to save him,' said a relative who had seen my camera and come to ask if I would send the family a photograph of the ceremony, 'but here we do not have good doctors.'

The corpse arrived across the back seat of a taxi which was driven slowly with rear doors open. It had been wrapped in a white shroud and parcelled with string in such a manner that the exact shape of the body had been preserved. A group of mourners carried it down to a ghat dedicated to Shiva the Destroyer and Procreator, one of the Hindu trinity, and laid it on a stone slab by the holy Ganges. Two outcaste *chandals* saw to the preparations while relatives grieved in the background and the young widow joined her six sisters in loud crying and wailing.

The *chandals* untied the string and by working their hands under the shroud they rewrapped the body in an orange sheet and tied it as before only leaving the head exposed. This they sprinkled with flour and red powders, and then scattered flowers from end to end. They had already built a stack of acacia wood four feet high with each layer of logs set at right angles to the next, and now they lit a side fire. Women formed a line and went round the body, entering the river up to their ankles and scooping up water which they poured over the head of the dead man before returning to the other mourners. Oil lamps were lit at each end of the deceased, a set of his clothes was laid on his chest but soon removed and several items including a mat were thrown into the river. Four men then came down and carried the corpse for three clockwise circuits around the pyre before laying it on top. More water was poured over the head and when this was done, a cotton wad was placed in the mouth and lit. The pyre was ignited at the base and soon caught. A covering of straw was thrown on and the wailing became louder. A pall of rich blue smoke unwound, suddenly turning an ominous yellow-brown. I was given a·signal and took the photograph. It was the moment they wanted to record. The end of a useless body and the transmigration of its soul. The fire would burn for three or four hours.

Death being the oldest mystery, it is not surprising that it should have become the cause of so many strange rituals. The poor of Bali buried their dead until they could afford an extravagant cremation and then the body would be exhumed and spun round on its way to the pyre, to shake out the spirit, confuse it and prevent it from finding a way back inside. In another part of Bali, beside Lake Trunjun, the dead were laid out in bamboo cages and left to decompose naturally, while in the Celebese Islands they were sealed in niches in a rock face and a wooden balcony was built to hold a lifesize effigy of the deceased. The Tibetan 'sky burial' involved breaking all the corpse's bones, hacking it into little pieces and scattering them for scavengers to devour, but this was less violent than a former practice in Burma. On the death of a Sawbwa ruler it was customary to slaughter 100 men, 100 women, 100 horses and ten elephants to act as a retinue for his last journey. In India the Hindu ritual of *sati* had been prohibited for over a century but had this funeral before me taken place in Nepal just fifty years ago, this young widow might have been expected to throw herself on the pyre. Her husband was dead and with him went her function in life and her reason for living. The thought made my flesh creep. I didn't like funerals. But at least this man was lucky because the sacred Ganges would speed his ashes to where his next incarnation was being planned.

I had arrived in Varanasi late the previous night and taken an auto-rickshaw to the Mint House Motel. It was not at all what the name suggested. The driver left me alone in a dark deserted street outside a length of railings and a formidable gate topped with spikes. I found a dwarf's entrance set in one corner and crawled through into the garden of a dilapidated mansion of a former maharaja. The main door was locked and knocking on windows produced no response but then I came to a side door and entered a large hall. Antlers in various states of collapse adorned the walls as testimony to the front end of a deer herd, and enough shreds of wallpaper dangled round about to give an inkling of what it had looked like from behind. Above a single dim lamp hung a monochrome photograph dated 1926 which showed maharajas sitting in starched rows before the grand building the Mint House Motel had once been. An old wooden desk supported a leather-bound ledger with marbled edges and a bell which I rang repeatedly until grunts and Hindi curses came from behind a closed door. Only when it was obvious that his guest was not going to give up did the elderly manager appear. His mouth and few remaining teeth were stained red from betel nut and this bloodied apparition came floating towards me in a white caftan. The cursing had suddenly stopped and now he assumed an air of official pleasantness, as if he had just been absent for two minutes and not sound asleep. The ability to change from dignity to hysteria and vice versa in an instant was a schizophrenic gift which many Indians possessed. I apologised for disturbing him.

'Not at all, sir,' he replied, 'that's what we're here for. We always welcome you . . . ' He paused briefly. ' . . . for your money.'

I smiled and said he was very honest but he didn't seem to realise what he had said. He pulled on a rope which I feared would bring down the ceiling and a dozen antlers. He had to pull again and shout a name before an equally ghastly figure emerged from the darkness in a tatty white shroud which ran from his head to his knees and had a balaclava slit instead of a face. The Shroud led me along an echoing passage to my room, just fifty yards from where the manager was standing. The service was faultless and the Mint House Motel observed strict job demarcation even if both its staff had to be roused from their beds. The Shroud rummaged around putting on lights and collecting dirty glasses before disappearing. The room was enormous; one and a half squash courts would have fitted into it, and two into its adjoining bathroom where a lavatory, basin and a gnarled piece of pipe for a shower were made to look minuscule in a corner. There was a wardrobe, a teachest affair of a bed, rickety and hard, and a sideboard with a solid marble slab. This, the manager's accent and the rigorous social order even at midnight, were pure and stubborn 1926 in a neglected shell of the Raj. My teachest felt like a four-poster.

The next morning the Shroud served breakfast in a dining room where several sparrows hopped about looking for crumbs and two wild pigeons were fighting in a flowerpot. They were free to come and go through a broken window. The breakfast menu was voiced through the balaclava slit.

'We have vegetable omelette.'

'Would it be possible just to have a plain omelette?'

'We have no eggs.'

'But you have vegetable omelette?'

'Yes, we have vegetable omelette. There are no eggs in vegetable omelette.'

Throughout the whole of the land of eggless omelettes, Varanasi was the holiest Hindu shrine. Here more than anywhere else India's bitter-sweet character was displayed to extreme, here all its vitality, elegance, mysticism and exuberant colours could be seen side by side with their opposites. I was quickly absorbed by the dawn crowds of pilgrims shuffling through the narrow alleys of the old city. They were made narrower by unbroken lines of deformed beggars at the base of one wall. They held out begging bowls and were so closely packed together that sometimes those passing held out a handful of rice and let a trickle of grains fall down. Each bowl received maybe fifty grains – I supposed if enough people did it they would get a meal – and there were scarcely any gaps where a grain might fall between bowls. On and on they went and occasionally a policeman stood watching to prevent foreigners taking photographs. Varanasi had its pride but these pariahs were not a part of it. Small squares often opened out and these were bordered by stalls or temples. Here the air lost its dusty mildewed smell and held pockets of aromas that turned noses towards heaps of spices, the petals of marigolds, sandalwood incense and chapatis. Dye vendors relied on colour to attract their customers and sat surrounded by miniature volcanoes of red, indigo, orange, yellow and purple powders. I felt sure they were going to be disappointed. The crowd already appeared to be saturated with colour.

The babble of voices was intense and it grew stronger when we reached the terraced ghats which, for four miles, formed the banks of the Ganges. Forty-eight minutes before sunrise was the auspicious moment for taking the waters but bathing went on round the clock, as did cremations, on average one every fourteen minutes. A flotilla of overladen boats hugged the edge of the water and the throng of thousands of pilgrims made it hard to tell river from land. Here and there saddhus sat cross-legged in bright red robes, their uncut hair matted into a thick cascade, their eyes closed and painted faces angled slightly up as they caught the rising sun in vacant meditation. Women were standing in the water in full saris while men wore towels, dhotis or scant G-strings. Some were washing, others were ducking three times, others were frozen in the posture of prayer. Obese men touched shoulders with emaciated figures whose ribs could be counted from a distance, and children splashed beside wrinkled crones with withered breasts. India's most polluted river flowed darkly around them, carrying lit candles in boats made of leaves, the ashes of the blessed, the bodies of the destitute, each day's twenty-two million gallons of sewage, and a certain proportion of Nepal besides. Thousands of figures cupped water in their hands and drank, and for many this act registered as a triumph. They tasted privilege, and their faces widened into the smiles of those unaccustomed to fortune's touch.

I had often contemplated whether Hinduism was partly to blame for the suffering of India's poor or whether it was the source of strength that enabled them to endure so much. Hindus were bound by a creed that made no provision whatsoever for forgiveness and demanded total acceptance of misfortune as the penance for past sin. To my mind, making misery appear inescapable in this existence was totally negative and removed any incentive for self-help. But the Ganges, and the faces of those who found in it private moments of tranquillity and justification, caused me to think differently. Hinduism at least gave them a credible explanation for their individual condition and also a moral code to live by in the expectation of a better hereafter. There were so few means for self-help here and hope was little consolation for the harsh reality of being poor and hungry, but perhaps having a religion that had deepened from a simple belief into a way of life tipped the balance in favour of making a burden tolerable.

Pilgrims wandered from one ghat to the next to perform purifying rituals and to visit the temples, some slanting down to the water at worrying angles for Varanasi too was slowly slipping into the rapacious Deliverer. I left the crowds and lost myself in some of the quieter backstreets. At one temple I removed my shoes and leather belt at the entrance, took a firm hold on the top of my trousers and wandered inside. The temple was in the form of a courtyard surrounded by cloisters and alcoves holding statues of the elephant-headed Ganesh (the god of learning) and other many-armed deities.

'Happiness to you, my friend,' said a man whose thin limbs protruded from a knot of green cloth. He was in his later years though his features were hard to see through a prickly beard and a strange mass of hair. All his hair stuck out as long bristles from a small head, and no amount of charity could deny the impression of an imploded porcupine. He stepped out of the shadows and swept me on a tour of the divinities.

'This is Brahma the Creator,' he said, gripping my arm and steering me through the passages, 'this, Vishnu the Preserver, this, Shiva the Destroyer. One God, three aspects of him. These their wives; Sarasvati, Laxmi, Parvati . . . ' Thus far the scheme made sense to me but when he went into the dozen other manifestations each character had, my understanding of the Hindu family tree toppled. Not wishing to appear disrespectful I listened while he entered the mythological carnage of their creation. Ganesh, he explained, lost his human head when his father, Shiva, caught him in bed with his mother, Parvati, and cut it off in anger. Shiva was made to bring their son back to life but to do this he needed a new head and the nearest one he could find belonged to an elephant . . . At this point I noticed a real elephant standing at the far end of the temple and managed to free myself from my guide by paying a rupee.

It was a cow elephant and she stood chained to a stone ring on the ground next to her keeper. An elephant must have stood there for centuries as the stone was hollowed under each of her feet. She rocked from side to side with a movement of the shoulders and gently dipped her head at the end of each swing as if in a storm-bound boat. Her forehead and ears were daubed with a pattern of white markings and I watched in fascination as she gave blessings, but only to those passers-by who paid for the honour. Whenever a ten paise (0.6p) coin was held out, the elephant nimbly took it with her trunk and passed it to the keeper. Then she raised her trunk and lightly tapped the devotee on the forehead.

The keeper and the elephant had an agreement. Anything edible went to the elephant, money went to the keeper. Coins were immediately passed over but fruit, chapatis and even an unopened packet of glucose biscuits, wrappings and all, were thrown into her mouth without any hesitation. Then a woman came with a basket of oranges. She put the basket by her feet and selected seven oranges which she held out. The elephant took three at once in the curl of her trunk and hurled them to the back of her throat. She instantly returned for three more but knocked the remaining one to the ground and it rolled to the far side of the basket. Out went the trunk again. It had to pass over the basket and could easily have selected another three but it showed no sign of temptation and only took the original one that had been offered.

This impressed me immensely. I went to buy a bunch of bananas and returned for my blessing. The keeper looked disapproving of each edible offering but the elephant was audibly pleased. She devoured the bananas. I waited for my blessing but nothing happened. The elephant stopped munching. Still nothing. She had completely forgotten her duty. The keeper noticed, lent forward glowering and prodded the great nose with a cane. The elephant drooped her head, raised her trunk and delicately touched my forehead.

I returned that evening. The keeper had gone and the elephant was alone eating some hay. She swept the hay into a pile, picked up a wad, swished it about in the air, picked up some more, knocked it twice against the stone anchoring the chain, brushed it up and down one leg and finally ate it. She repeated this little ritual for every mouthful as if remembering the exact sequence was the only challenge left for her active mind, until every strand had been eaten. Her huge frame began rocking again. Sometimes she would run her trunk over the stone and feel the chain where it entered the hole. I wondered if she regarded that stone with contempt, if she knew what life could be like not chained to centuries-old footprints and not having to listen to continuous music from the temple loudspeaker. I hoped not. She was only an honorary Hindu, without the conviction, giving blessings without herself being blessed.

There was a long queue at the railway booking office. I settled down for the wait with the day's copy of the *Times of India* and came across the following on page one:

> BALD IS WISE: 'Balder a person, wiser he is.' Making this observation the Karnataka transport minister, Mr P Prakash, said increasing baldness also increased the power of judgement, reports PTI. Mr Prakash was replying in the State Assembly to a question of whether wearing a helmet led to baldness. He said he was not aware of any positive correlation between baldness and helmet wearing.

Much of the paper was taken up with the annual scandal of leaks in the national exam papers. Quite a trade had apparently built up in selling leaked question sheets and even handwritten answers that students could buy and smuggle into the exams. Last year three leaks had been discovered and school children had sat the national exams four times. This year, it was announced, 200,000 chemistry students would be competing for 2000 university places. Also on the nation's mind that day were the usual accounts of 'miscreants' and 'dacoits' shooting, stealing and raping and the more horrific violence that normally placid Indians inflicted when in excited company. A woman in the north was seriously ill after a mob had chopped off her limbs with an axe, villagers in Bengal had formed a hasty court and hanged two teenage lovers who had eloped, and there were several reports of relatives setting fire to a bride or groom who had been deemed unworthy. On a more hopeful note, six Brahmin priests in an arid region of the south were immersing themselves up to the neck in a pond for ten days 'for world peace, brotherhood and rain'.

The queue around me contained many wise men (women had a separate ticket counter which seldom had any queues) and the system certainly encouraged the hair-pulling approach to wisdom. In order to reserve a second-class sleeper I had to go to a different office over a mile from the station. The first queue eventually gave me access to a man who wrote down an extensive list of my family particulars with a fountain pen in a colossal cardboard and paper sandwich, and gave me a form to take to Room 12 in the next building. The man in Room 12 had three phones on his desk and two rang alternately for five minutes and once simultaneously. This wasn't a serious handicap for him, however, and he managed to continue both conversations at once with a receiver to each ear and serve a customer who had barged past me. When down to one phone he scratched my form and returned me to the first counter for a stamp. This provided me with a reservation form which had to be taken back to the station in order to buy the actual ticket. My form reached the first clerk after I had queued for twenty minutes and sat out the hour for lunch when the counters suddenly closed. He stamped my form and passed it to a second clerk. I had to change counter, give this clerk the money and get his stamp. He passed the form back to his colleague. A ten-minute queue had since built up and once this dispersed, I was able to collect the valuable piece of green cardboard. It was job creation at its best.

Sleeper allocation lists were always displayed on a board beside the appropriate train but that evening I was unable to find my name on the sheets pinned alongside the Agra Express. After several attempts I went to find an official.

'I'm looking for "Alastair Scott". I'm afraid I can't see it on any of the lists.'

He came back to the boards with me, looked at my ticket and referred to a code book that looked like pages of logarithms. 'You are here,' he said after a while, 'coach 553758, berth 2U.'

'Sorry. I must have missed it.' It took time to understand a dozen clerks' method of transcribing. I repaired to 2U which was listed against Alstjar Sakhoh.

The compartment had four bunks (just padded benches, but comfortable) and was open to the corridor. The top beds were folded up and the bottom ones were used as seats for general passengers until late evening when they became reserved beds. My ultimate companions were a middle-aged Indian, a young fat Sikh and an American relic of the hippy era. He wore earrings, his hair in a pony tail, a collar of beads, T-shirt ('Grow a greener Goa'), Aladdin baggies and Jesus sandals.

'Hey, what's your name, man?'

'Alstjar,' I replied.

'Alstjar? Say, that's a pretty weird name.'

'Yes. It's half-Scottish, half-Indian.'

His name was Mel. Mel had come from Detroit years ago and now commuted between squattings at the beaches of Goa, the ghats of Varanasi and the mountains of Simla. 'It used to be real cool here, but now it aint no good any more. India's finished.' He explained that resident foreigners were meeting with increasing resentment in small villages. Friends of his had fallen behind 'a little' on their rent and refused to leave when the landlord asked them to do so. One of them had been stabbed to death and the other chased out of town. He felt many Indians were looking for scapegoats on which to vent their daily frustrations and resident foreigners had become their target.

'No kidding. We're India's Jews, man. I aint hangin' around here much longer.'

'Will you go back to the States?'

'*The States*? Shit, no! Alst – it's *violent* there.'

Mel lapsed into a thoughtful slumber and I felt an unwanted gulf between us. He was like a high proportion of Germans I had met who were discontented with their homeland, in the latter's case wanting no part in their country's industrial, military and nuclear excesses. I was travelling for excitement and discovery, they were travelling to escape.

The train rattled and rumbled into the night. The express would take eight hours to Lucknow and a further nine to Agra. It didn't rattle much louder than ordinary trains but there were less intervals of silence for it stopped at fewer stations. It was a disturbed night with passengers trooping past, being wakened by ticket inspectors and the jolts that marked each station. Even during the early hours these were busy. They remained nameless for I regularly seemed to regain consciousness at a platform with no location marked, so the stops could only be identified by the other visible signs. The first place,

TRAINS RUNNING LATE WILL EITHER LOSE OR MAKE UP
TIME

was a substation with only two platforms but the next,

PERSONS WITH INFECTIONS OR CONTAGIOUS DISEASES
WILL NOT BE SERVED HERE

was large enough to have a restaurant. Dawn was beginning to break when we reached

THIS WAITING ROOM IS CLEANED EVERY FRIDAY

though I was unable to decide whether this place was a boast, a warning or an apology.

The first of the beggars appeared early. His ailments were internal and not obvious so he wore them as a framed list which hung from his neck. He was followed by the breakfast attendant who carried a tray stacked with boxes of vegetarian snacks and behind him came the tomato ketchup-wallah holding high his red bottle. Then a shoeshine approached and the Sikh set him to work while he retied his turban, watching as the urchin's head moved from side to side in unison with his brush. Turbans had always fascinated me but this was the end of an era. I had thought they were held together by clever knotting but the secret was less magical. (Pins.)

A series of particularly bad jolts failed to wake Mel but roused the Indian from his bunk and for the next hour he went about his toiletry. He had more wisdom than hair but this little he carefully splashed and wiped with oil from a small bottle, one of many kept in a shortbread tin wrapped in two plastic bags. His luggage seemed to consist entirely of wrapped shortbread tins. From another he extracted the implement of the most obscene Indian sanitary ritual, the tongue scraper. This was like a small pair of ice tongs without any hands. The hinge was a blunt blade and was inserted into the mouth, laid on the back of the tongue and pulled forward. This was repeated again and again and involved a gruelling (for everyone else) amount of hawking, spitting and dribbling. Finally he put everything away and stared at his reflection to practise the extremely common silent head waggle. This was the equivalent of placing the tip of the nose against a window and trying to drill a hole with it, the head swivelling back and forwards on a loose neck. When accompanied by a smile it meant yes, of course, maybe, I don't understand, no problem, no, impossible. When accompanied by a frown it meant exactly the same.

The train rattled across the plains, no gradients, no turns, a flat land of effortless railway engineering. Mud huts stood beside the darker brown patches of poor farmland and helped to distinguish them from the lighter brown sweeps of barren wilds. This area alternated between drought and flood, gales and calm days like this one when farmers had to create their own breeze. Now was the time for winnowing wheat and men were tossing the threshed heads into the air with forks while women waved large fans to blow the chaff aside. It was only their will to succeed that magnified them against the vastness of the plain.

At   *PORTER'S CHARGES*

Up to 37 kg	2rps
Waiting time over 20 minutes	0.5
Carrying injured person	4rps
Carrying dead body	6rps

which was somewhere beyond Lucknow, the train made a long halt. Mel was up by this time and suddenly he shouted 'Look out!' Something flew in the window and burst with a splash above what, a moment earlier, had been a white Sikh. A bag of dyed water had been hurled through the window and now the poor man was a mess of orange. He jumped up cursing and shook his fist at two children running down the platform. I had to turn away to hide my laughter and consequently never noticed the second bag. It came in the other window and hit Mel's shoulder but deposited most of its contents over me.

'What the hell's going on?' I shouted, no longer finding things funny. My best shirt was now half-fawn and half-red, and red stains covered my jeans.

'Today is the festival of Holi,' said the Indian. 'All over India this is happening to mark the start of spring. Don't worry, I think you'll find it washes out.' He tried to maintain his composure but his smile dissolved into a snigger that made his shoulders shake. This set Mel going and then I followed and in no time all four of us were gripped in a helpless fit of laughter. After a while it became painful but none of us could stop. 'Look . . !' said Mel between convulsions, and we looked even though what we saw made things worse. Three children with water bags hidden behind their backs were standing on the platform and looking towards the end where it joined a road. Approaching them was a family of four on a scooter. Father, dressed in white, was driving and remained unaware of the danger until the first bag came along at head height. Instinctively he ducked and his wife, wearing a yellow sari, was hit full in the face and both she and the little girl on her knees turned startling purple. The second bag followed at once and green exploded on the handlebars and drenched both father and the girl in his lap. Indigo was badly aimed and went low, respraying the first child but striking only a narrow trail along the others. The delighted ambushers were already running off when the scooter came to a sudden halt. The father yelled abuse at them and looked furious as he steadied the machine and bent over his daughter. She was shaking her indigo head with an expression of surprise. He turned to his purple wife. She stared at her green husband. They were still huddled in hysterics when our train left five minutes later.

At last we came to HEARTIEST HOLI GREETINGS. Agra.

Three years after Mumtaz Mahal died in 1629 while giving birth to her fourteenth child, work began on a quixotic scale to construct a tomb in proportion to the grief of her husband, the emperor Shah Jahan. He was given to ambitious building schemes but the mausoleum he planned for his favourite wife after their seventeen-year marriage was to surpass them all. He brought in master craftsmen from as far afield as France and Italy and employed 20,000 workers during the twenty-one years it took to complete the tomb. The Taj Mahal stands elevated on a square base at the end of a waterway bordered by marble paths and neatly coiffeured bushes.

Tall tapering minarets rise from each corner and surround the mausoleum whose front consists of a soaring central arch equalled in height by smaller arches upon arches to left and right. The building is close to a cube but slightly flattened by the weight of five onion domes on its roof, chiefly by that of the huge central one which swells up and accounts for half of the Taj Mahal's height. Made entirely of white marble except where semi-precious stones have been inlaid and run wild as flowering creepers, it is a masterpiece unmatched in the world for its perfect symmetry, elegance and artistry. Latterly it became the only object of beauty in its creator's life and also a bitter reminder of his own impotence. For the last seven years of his life Shah Jahan was unable to visit Mumtaz's tomb and could only gaze at it less than a mile away from the window in Agra Fort where he was held prisoner. He had been deposed by his son Aurangzeb, the last effective Mogul emperor, who was impatient for power and resentful of his father squandering fortunes on buildings. Legend asserts that Shah Jahan had planned to build an exact replica of the Taj for his own tomb only in *black* marble, with the same gold-lined vaults and screens cut from single slices of stone and carved into the delicate intricacy of lace. This was not to be for his confinement left him helpless and looking forward only to the day that came in 1666 when he could join Mumtaz in the Taj's lowest chamber, below the false tomb designed to fool grave-robbers.

My first view of the Taj Mahal must have been similar to the last glimpse of it enjoyed by its builder, framed by a window in Agra Fort. If there was any consolation in being locked up perhaps Shah Jahan found it in at least having had the opportunity of building his own prison, albeit unwittingly, for he had also been responsible for the construction of this fortified palace. His influence was evident from the large quantities of marble decorating the rooms, but he hadn't left much else behind. The rooms were almost denuded of furniture. I reached one stately hall during a lull in the jamboree of visitors and was standing gazing at the Taj when I heard the approach of creaking floorboards. I turned and found one of the fort's more senior custodians, a man with a handsome span of moustache, sidling up to me. He stood close, uncomfortably close, smiled and gave the silent head waggle. This puzzled me because the waggle usually followed a question (especially one of some urgency) and seldom came on its own.

'Good afternoon,' I said, in the hope of speeding things up. This stopped the waggle but brought no response. Eventually he spoke in a hushed and cold tone.

'Are you liking beautiful things, sir?'

'Very much,' I replied, wondering what this was leading towards. Then a possibility occurred to me. Perhaps he was referring to my appearance. He found my clothes inappropriate for this palace and was broaching the subject of asking me to leave as politely as possible. 'Sorry about my trousers,' I added. 'Holi, you know . . .?' (My shirt was a spare and clean but the jeans were my only pair and sponging them had brought little improvement.)

He gave a little waggle of understanding. 'Come with me, sir. I have something to show you. He led me across the empty hall to a wooden box and opened the lid. 'These,' he confided, 'are the pride and joy of the fort.' He pulled out some papyrus manuscripts covered in a strange script. 'Not many visitors have the chance to see these, sir.'

'Are they very old?'

'Old? Are these *old*? . . . No, they are only two hundred and fifty years old but *very, very* fine workmanship.' They came from the state of Orissa, he continued, and were extremely rare. They were the most valuable objects in the room, in fact, priceless. He lowered his voice to a whisper and spoke through his moustache. 'How much you give me for them? Yes, sir. How much?'

The ramparts outside this hall were sixty feet high, genuine and apparently still unsold. It was here that I found peace to resume looking across the stony Yamuna River to the Taj, and reflect on the disappearance of Shah Jahan's priceless furniture. My peace was short-lived and shouts could be heard from down in the dry moat where an entertainer was waiting for coins to be thrown his way. Beside him a large Kodiak bear stood on all fours at the end of a lead. When he began beating a drum the bear began to dance. The reaction was instantaneous as if the lead were some remote control that enabled the owner to switch programmes. 'Dance' sent the bear into a trance and it stood erect, waved its paws and bobbed its head while keeping its snout held high. The spectacle appalled me and I turned away, only to witness another bizarre scenario. Two gardeners were cutting the fort's lawns with a simple manual lawnmower. One man was at the rear steering the machine and the other was up front with a stick prodding the bony cow that was pulling it. Together they cut a twentieth-century trail towards a seventeenth-century monument to craftsmanship and style. Not even in China had I encountered a land such as this where so many conflicting elements were to be found side by side and where the common view was a pastiche of beauty, comedy and pathos.

No building deserves its reputation more than the Taj Mahal and its unique splendour was the dominant impression I carried away from Agra. I had forgotten to book my onward passage east to Jaisalmer and the train that pulled up at the station early in the evening was full even by Indian standards. India's railway was the fourth largest in the world and carried nine million passengers every day. This train appeared to hold a good proportion of them both inside and on the roof. After my fourth attempt to get through a door a guard kindly created a spare slot for me. The crowd eased during the night and eventually there was enough room to open out the *Deccan Times*. There was no progress report on how the six Brahmins were faring in their pond, but an unusual account of a wedding:

> After the marriage ceremony, as is customary, the bride and groom played a symbolic game in which the groom has to wrestle free a small object from the bride's hand. She normally gives a token struggle and releases it but this girl, egged on by her friends, refused to let go and the groom was unable to open her hand. His ego and pride hurt, he became so angry he began beating her and the police had to be called. She reported him for assault and wanted a divorce. A court of seniors was hastily assembled. They arranged another husband for the girl, the one she had preferred anyway, and the boy took the hand of another girl he liked equally well. The elders are to be praised for their swift and fair ruling; they found the wife guilty for disobeying her husband and the husband guilty of cruelty.

Later the crowd expanded again and made it impossible for me to get beyond the theatre reviews.

> Othello was played very well by Rajan but Iago's performance was inadequate. The murder scene was executed well. The stage setting was poor and the lighting inadequate. All in all it was a good attempt.

The train was passing through Rajasthan, a state of mountains and deserts, wild peacocks, the brightest costumes in all India, and hill forts whose histories spoke of fearless warriors and mass suicides rather than surrender. For centuries the Rajput warriors fought invaders and each other even when their enemy proved incontestably superior. Under these circumstances the men put on the saffron robes of matrimony and celebration and rode out to be slaughtered on the battlefield while the women committed *jauhau* by walking into a great funeral pyre. (At Chittogarh in 1535 it is said 13,000 women and 32,000 warriors died in these respective ways.)

It took twenty-five hours to reach Jodhpur whose fort was reputed to be held together with mortar made pink by the slave girls who were crushed into the mix. This seemed highly improbable to me as I looked up at the building from outside the railway station, but one could never be quite sure. If newspapers were anything to go by then the improbable was often the norm in India. Beside me stood a statue whose dedication read, ' . . . to the memory of the late Sovereign Lieutenant-General Air Vice Marshal His Highness Raj Rajeshwar Sarmad-I-Raja-I-Hind Maharajah Dhiraja Shri Sir Umaid Singhji Bahadur, GCSI, GCIE, KCVO, LL D', and if his family had built the fort they sounded capable of throwing anything into the mix. My destination, however, was still Jaisalmer. It lay another ten hours away at the very end of the track, and this was one reason for my interest in it. It was the last stop on a line across the full width and character of the land.

Jaisalmer was the odd one out amongst Rajasthani towns despite also being dominated by a fort. As a result of its isolation in the Thar Desert and its strategic position on the camel train route to central Asia it became a prosperous trading post. It suffered an acute decline when camel trains were made obsolete and was all but forgotten until recent times when an important military base was sited here to protect the nearby border with Pakistan. Jaisalmer had retained its medieval appearance and oriental mystique. If carpets could fly, Jaisalmer would be on their route.

The town occupied the only hill in sight, the battlements of its yellowstone fort at the top and a conglomeration of cubist houses in the same material packed around its slopes. The station was outside the town and I covered the distance on a camel-pulled cart with old car tyres. The camel's arrogant grin was made to look modest by the driver's bushy 180-degree moustache which seemed standard for men. He wore earrings and, on his head, a loose heap of coiled cloth in Holi-est orange. Everyone amongst Jaisalmer's 20,000 population was a jolt of colour. A typical woman climbed on in a sarong of bullfighter red and a green sash over her head. I had time to count sixty-four bangles on her arms alone, sixteen above each elbow and sixteen below like sleeves of plastic armour. She had more around her ankles as well as toe rings, finger rings, nose rings, cheek rings, earrings – the last three being connected by silver chains – a forehead band that held a jewel over her eyes and three ponderous necklaces of silver decorated with pendants. She looked dangerously top-heavy but the effect was mesmerising.

I was let out at the bottom of the hill and soon became pleasantly lost in the confusion of narrow twisting streets. They bustled with buyers and sellers haggling over wares spilling out of dingy door-ways; women squatted on the cobblestones beside piles of fruit, vegetables or hundreds of earthenware pots; camels could be heard snorting while their loads were being prepared and everywhere were colours, jewellery and moustaches. Some of the alleys were only one cow-length wide and plenty of cows were proving it. With difficulty I passed around them and continued to lose myself among the houses of former wealthy merchants who had only stopped adding carvings to the exteriors when they had run out of space.

I was looking for a fitting conclusion to this stage of the journey from Calcutta. It wasn't to be found in a Jain temple where rats and all living things were allowed sanctuary among its sculptures. A sadhu, a man who had renounced his possessions and then lived by begging as he wandered in search of enlightenment, was sitting meditating in one corner. He wore only a loincloth and a bundle of hair which was matted into a clump and fell down his back. Had he stood up it would have hung below his knees. I adopted a similar cross-legged posture near the entrance and tried to let my mind go blank. The words of Dr Prakur – God bless his fillings – came back to me, ' . . . concentrating only on the air brushing past the tip of your nose as you breathe in and brushing the base of your nostrils as you breathe out'. After twenty minutes of this my mind was clear and focused solely on the agonising cramp in my knees. To cap it all I discovered that during my incapacitated state a cow had crept up (and sacred cows can certainly creep), found my luggage just inside the doorway and made off with a bag of oranges. By the time I caught up with her she was chewing the bag and the fruit had disappeared down a drain. This was the only incident to occur in Jaisalmer so I had to go further afield for my conclusion.

Evening found me preparing to spend the night in some desert ruins about a mile from the town. Pillars supporting domes, arches, stone slabs and graves half-covered in sand were grouped on a low ridge with a view of the fort and houses. The silence and the gracefully shaped stones being consumed by the desert made me feel as if I were the first person to come here and had stumbled on the remains of a lost city. No other people were about, only camels lying amongst the pillars and the occasional one walking by and making the sand squeak under its feet. Silence. It was so unusual to experience it in India. I began to feel more at peace with the country. It had taken time to come to terms with its ways because they were overwhelming in their impact, all extremes and little placid medium. Life's dimensions were exaggerated to their greatest in this sub-continent and it was not possible to travel through India without being constantly thrown off balance by its trinity of poverty, beauty and mysticism. Here, it seemed, was where perfection and chaos were inexorably intertwined.

The sun was almost down. The Thar Desert had darkened to a yellow shadow but the fort caught the last rays and looked on fire. My thoughts turned to my next goal of Ladakh, one thousand miles to the north, but it seemed too distant, an eternity away by train. My mind could only remain on the present and my lost city. If the flying carpets had come, I would have let them go without me.

11 · Among the Tibetans of Ladakh

The state of Kashmir and Jammu in the extreme north of India is well known for the wool of its soft-haired goats, the houseboats on Dal Lake that the British built as summer homes when they were denied land, its temperate climate and less so for cricket bats. Trees are not apparent for most of the night and day journey from Delhi to the state capital of Srinagar until the end of a long tunnel which opens into the Kashmir Valley. Then pines and cricket bat willows become denser, and government signs campaign against the traditional view that a tree is a one-off source of firewood and a waste of potential farmland.

WOOD IS GOOD BUT TREE IS BETTER.
WE HAD BETTER BE WITHOUT GOLD THAN TREES.
A TREE PLANTED BY A BELIEVER IS A SOURCE OF BLESSING TO HIM AND AN EVERLASTING CHARITY.
TREES PROVIDE HARMONY THROUGH AESTHETIC AND RE-CREATIONARY BENEFITS.
THE FOREST IS A PECULIAR ORGANISM OF UNLIMITED KINDNESS AND BENEVOLENCE THAT MAKES NO DEMANDS FOR SUSTENANCE AND EXTENDS GENEROUSLY THE PRODUCTS OF ITS LIFE ACTIVITY. IT AFFORDS PROTECTION TO ALL BEINGS, OFFERING SHADE EVEN TO THE AXEMEN WHO DESTROY IT.

The originality of India's educational campaigns was invigorating but the messages themselves conveyed a sense of epic verse that died early, as if the captions editor had hastily cut and paraphrased because the signs had already consumed too many trees.

It was early May but spring had not yet come to the remote region of Ladakh, a corner of the Himalayas, and the road to its principal town of Leh was still blocked by snow. A plane flew there every other day but for a week my attempts to find a seat were thwarted by full bookings, bad weather upsetting the schedule and Indian Airlines' gift for muddle. At last I managed to get a stand-by place. The couple sitting next to me also considered themselves lucky to be aboard the plane until a chance remark caused them to leave hurriedly just as the pilot was exercising his flaps. They had passed through four Indian Airlines checkpoints on an over-subscribed flight to Leh with tickets to New Delhi.

The flight lasted thirty minutes, too short for refreshments and too steep for a table to hold them. It was an uphill flight ending at 11,500 feet in a place that has been called medieval, more Tibetan that Tibet, 'moonland' and the last Shangri-La. The other passengers were soldiers except for a small group of Ladakhis and amongst them was a woman in her late forties. She appeared ordinary in her manner and dress but when the others came close to her or caught her eye, they bowed their heads. She was the Queen of Ladakh.

Ladakh is a high-altitude desert, deprived of rain by the mighty Himalayas to the south-east and watered only by their snowmelt and a youthful River Indus. Geographically the area belongs to the Tibetan plateau and today, despite a high Muslim population, it is the only remaining place where Tibetan Buddhism exists in its original form. Politically it belongs to India but China vehemently refutes this and believes Ladakh is hers, and Ladakh's sensitive position is exacerbated by Pakistan's similar contention over Kashmir. Leh was once an important stop on the old silk route but once the traffic declined, the community had little contact with the outside world. Monks were in regular communication with Lhasa even during winter when the more distinguished travellers were provided with Tibetan snowploughs, a herd of yaks sent ahead to trample a path. The Indian government closed Ladakh to visitors in 1950 when China invaded Tibet and began the thirty-year regime of terror that was as brutal as anything this century has witnessed. Ladakh was ignored even as the first of 100,000 Tibetan refugees fled the purge and came into India, including the Dalai Lama – the reincarnate Buddha and God King – in 1959. It was not until three years after this that India realised China had annexed a disputed part of Ladakh, and launched a counter-offensive. The enemy's military strength in the region was badly underestimated, forty-three army posts were captured and Indian resistance was quashed. Since then the new Sino-Indian border has been morosely acknowledged, military camps have been installed and the first road to Leh has been constructed. Ladakh's royal family still holds property and commands respect here but its role is more titular and the individual members live most of the year in Delhi. (The king died in 1974 and his son is expected to succeed when the auspices are favourable.) The ban on visitors to this region was lifted in 1975 but large areas still remain out of civilian bounds.

The plane spent most of the journey rummaging through cloud and most of the passengers were waiting for the common apology to say we were heading back, but suddenly the cloud parted and we looked down on mountain ranges, harsh ridges of black rock running in parallel lines, one side covered in snow, the other bare rock cleared by the winds. The world's second highest peak, K2 (Karakorum Range, the second peak to be measured) was said to be visible in good weather but it remained hidden as we began the short descent. The snow disappeared except on the tops and we dropped into a valley of utter desolation; sandy-grey hillsides scarred by cliffs, and trails of scree and a floor of sand dunes that at first appeared smooth, then rutted like the furrows left on a beach at low tide, and finally as a bed of shattered rocks. A single-track road moved in zigzags through this valley and occasionally touched a small adobe house and a field bordering a stream. The tiny patches of green looked harassed by the expanse of desert. We turned into a side valley where the fields increased to form a green puddle on the land and descended onto a runway among nissen huts, tin roofs and barbed-wire tornados that had collapsed. The pilot applied the brakes so fiercely that my neighbour's fieldglasses swung out from his khaki chest and reached the height of his nose. Had seat belts not been provided for the pilot's protection, most of us would have ended up in the cockpit. We had arrived. Moonland.

'Jullay!' 'Jullay!' 'Jullay!' The Ladakhis' general-purpose word rang out constantly in the streets of Leh. It conveyed everything positive and had none of the silent head waggle's doubts. It meant hello, goodbye, thanks, see you later and anything else that was considered either friendly or polite. Leh was a town of 10,000 Jullayers living in a hotch-potch of adobe buildings, some white-washed but all featuring many windows, an ill-fitting door and a flat roof. They were connected by narrow alleys that turned right angles every twenty paces and had a thin trail of litter where a pavement might have been expected. The town ran uphill to the base of a ruined palace which was a monstrous building with the brooding austerity of a prison. A wall of window holes and balconies presented a front nine storeys high but such was the angle of the hill that there were only four storeys at the back. Above this at the top of the hill was a small gompa (monastery). Buddhist symbols always occupied the highest places in Ladakh, if not gompas then prayer flags in their five colours and the hills surrounding Leh were spiked with lines of flagpoles like remnants of ski slaloms.

The dominant feature of the town was its large grassless polo ground. When I arrived an archery contest was in progress at one end and a game of cricket at the other, each trying not to overlap. Some of the cricketers wore whites and the hessian mat laid on the ground made their high-altitude wicket fast enough for one batsman to consider a head guard necessary. The bowlers worked at a furious pace but the batsmen were equal and kept twenty-three fielders on their toes. The off-side seemed to include a main thoroughfare and each time a lorry chugged past in mid-play, all the down-wind fielders disappeared in its wake of dust. At one point a good drive sent the ball towards two laden donkeys being herded through the outfield. The leader panicked and ran off, the other followed and play had to be halted while some fielders helped recover the beasts. A cow wandered aimlessly around square-leg and at times the bowlers seemed disturbed by two labourers with pick and shovel who were laying a drain at deep mid-on.

'I think the score is seventy-two for twelve and they're chasing one hundred and twenty,' called a stranger's voice from higher up the slope. A white girl, broadly built and with short fair hair was leaning against a rock and had seen me take an interest in the game.

'For twelve? How many are in a team?'

'There aren't really any fixed limits in local matches like this one. It depends on how many want to play. They take it seriously but it's not exactly the MCC here.'

We talked through a four and the partial disappearance of the game as a result of lorries before either of us thought of introducing ourselves. Name swapping often came as an after-thought between foreigners abroad as there were more interesting whats, where-froms and how-was-its to discover first. She was Lorna Ellis, about thirty years old and a volunteer doctor from Australia working a few miles away at a Tibetan SOS village. Her year's contract had almost ended and she was anxiously hoping it would be renewed. 'And you?' she asked, 'what do you do?'

It was a question that always defeated me. There was no precise category which fitted me or to which I could authentically lay claim. 'At the moment I travel, exercise a camera and take any work going when my money gets low. I don't know what I'll be when it's time to retire.' She murmured in the way that doctors do murmur on hearing symptoms and asked where I was heading for next. This was a better question for me. 'Egypt.'

'Jesus! And how are you going to get from Ladakh to Egypt. . . ?'

It was back to the tricky ones. I had yet to work that one out. 'Look, I've only just got here . . !' I protested. We agreed not to talk about the end of her contract and the obstacles between Leh and Egypt. 'Maybe you can advise me on where to go in the area? I'd like to stay in one of the monasteries.'

'Most of them take visitors for a small fee. Perhaps Rizong would be a good one. It's about forty miles from here and said to be one of the strictest. If you'd like to visit the SOS Village you should go to the school and ask for Llamo. She's a lovely friendly person and speaks fluent English.'

We talked on until Lorna had to leave for her afternoon surgery. We arranged to meet for a meal that evening in the Gaytime Restaurant. 'Honestly, that's it's name!' she said with a laugh and began walking off. 'Oh! Tell me who wins the cricket . . . '

At that particular moment it looked as if the hazards were winning. Play had been stopped by the cow and spectators were drifting towards the archery contest where about thirty men were competing. They only had three bows to share around and these were not fancy ones with sights and stabilisers but basic Robin Hood models. Each man fired one arrow in turn at a target until there were no more arrows left and they had to go and retrieve them. The crowd cheered each time the target was hit but although the arrows flew forcefully, they didn't give much cause for cheering.

Ladakhis carried considerable weights of ornamental gold, coral and turquoise and wore their hair in long pigtails. Many men wore trousers and pullovers but the traditional heavy dressing gowns tied with a sash came a close second, and were standard for women who draped bright shawls over the dark material. The most distinctive feature, however, was the astonishing hat worn by married women and elderly men. It resembled a top hat with the front split up the middle as if it had been rammed onto a head too large for it and the entire lower edge, including the split, was lined with fur. The hats were made of stiff felt, sometimes embroidered with a silver fern, and came in as many colours as prayer flags only deeper, more subdued shades. They sat, unhappily I felt, on the very back of the head.

The drain at deep mid-on had made little progress (the workers preferred the excitement of a test match) when a short ceremonial dance ended all the afternoon's sporting events. As the crowd dispersed distant robed figures cut haunting silhouettes against the sandy wilderness which encroached on the town. I made my way into the centre and found a room in a simple guesthouse. The afternoon had slipped quickly by – the way time seemed to give half-measure in this region was one of the few faults I discovered – and I set off for the Gaytime Restaurant. Leh only had one principal street which was busy in a lazy mountain sort of way with pedestrians, some army jeeps and several goats which were so fluffy they might have just been tumble-dried. The overriding impressions were nevertheless of those magnificent hats, Ladakhis failing to exhaust their humour despite emptying copious amounts of laughter over whatever they were doing, and an unusual amount of sharing.

The Gaytime Restaurant sounded a wild seedy joint but it was a quiet café far removed from frolic and innuendo. Lorna was already waiting and looking disarmingly large as a shadow projected by the light of a hurricane lamp. I added my shadow to the opposite wall and explained about the hazards winning the cricket while she chose Gaytime Chicken. I avoided this in case it had suffered a Chinese execution and went for Gaytime Curry and Kashmiri tea (which, after the curry, could be described only as pink).

'Did you have an interesting afternoon?' I asked.

'Nothing special. One suspected tuberculosis, which is not uncommon, and the usual numbers with bronchitis. That's the major problem here. Apart from those it was minor things. Colds, scabies, fleas and lice.'

'Hmmm,' I murmured, as non-doctors do when they ask regretted questions and prod their curry. 'You said this afternoon you were hoping to stay here another year, so you obviously like it. Aside from bronchitis and fleas, is Ladakh Shangri-La?'

'Life is very hard here but, in a sense, I think it is. The people are poor and work long hours but they are still a very caring, integrated society, kept together by their religion and traditions. You won't find a warmer or friendlier people, and they seem content with little. Certainly they laugh a lot. Sometimes I think they must put something in their butter tea.' She had been surprised to find that adults lived long lives, into their seventies, and one woman who had died recently was believed to have been over one hundred, but the infant mortality rate was very high. The normal practice at funerals was for the body to be tied into a cross-legged sitting position and placed in a compact square coffin which was then cremated. 'But there's been an interesting new development. They're still very superstitious and now the coffins of those who die of cancer are not cremated in case the disease enters the air and spreads quickly. Instead the coffins are buried and apparently this doesn't affect the deceased's hereafter in any way.'

'Hmm.' My curry tended to look better when the topic changed to superstition. Lorna lived in a hospital quarter that was modern and luxurious by Ladakhi standards but the local nurses refused to inhabit the building at first because they believed the spirit of a woman who had died there three years earlier was haunting it. A lama was summoned to exorcise the rooms and he placed a spirit trap outside. Traps were cones of woven straw with the skull of a sheep, goat or dog placed on the top. This had reassured the staff and they had returned but on portentous days they had to observe certain rituals.

Her own experiences during the year had convinced her that there were people here who had supernatural powers. When reports reached Leh of disastrous bushfires sweeping Lorna's home area on the edge of Melbourne, she became desperately worried. Her parents' house stood in sixty acres of bush. She was unable to contact Australia or even Delhi by phone. One day the husband of a friend came to her and told her to be calm. Her family and home were safe. 'He was a *rintzen*, a reincarnated lama of a less strict sect which allows marriage, tobacco and alcohol. When I did eventually get through to my parents they said their house was the only one in the district to have survived. The flames had come within ten feet of the wooden walls and they had been forced to fight the fire with wet blankets for fourteen hours.' She shrugged. 'I don't believe it was a lucky guess. Somehow he *knew*. And later the same *rintzen* correctly predicted that my sister-in-law's baby would be a boy and that there would be a minor complication. There was because it was a premature birth.'

'I believe these powers exist too,' I agreed, 'and in the power of spiritual healing. Are there any healers in the area?'

'In the village of Sabu there is a family who do this and they also give prophecies. The ability is passed from mother to daughter and the girl is said to throw a fit during adolescence when the spirit enters her. After some training she is ready to hold meetings. The family is rich because they charge five rupees for a consultation. I went along once and there were sixty people there.' Lorna had watched the mother go into a trance though it had been hard to tell how genuine this was as the woman's face was mostly hidden behind scarves. The sick pointed to their afflicted parts and the woman either bit their skin or sucked at it through a tube and spat out dark bile which she proclaimed was the cause of the problem. The performance looked impressive but Lorna suspected it could easily have been trickery. But she accepted that cures were undoubtedly brought about even if the chief medicine was applied psychology.

'To use her power as an oracle, certain rules have to be observed. You aren't allowed to ask open questions such as "What should I do today?" but only ones that provide alternatives. "Should I do A, B or C?" An Australian friend came to visit me once and he wanted to go to Sabu as he had a list of girlfriends and wanted to ask which one he should marry!'

'How did he get on?'

She laughed. 'It rather ruined the rest of his stay. He kept on muttering, "Damn! I wish she'd chosen one of the others." I haven't heard which one he went for in the end.'

We talked on over Gaytime coffee and then walked through Leh's dark street.

'It's colds and bugs for me as usual tomorrow. How about you?'

'I'm going to join a monastery.'

We parted, Lorna carrying an unpaid doctor's love of Ladakh into a crowded bus and leaving me feeling light with only curiosity.

The owner of the guesthouse was sitting in the kitchen below shelves of copper pans when I entered. He was absorbed in the timeless chore of agitating milk in a slender wooden churn. I sat nearby and asked if I could share the light of his paraffin lamp to write my diary.

'Jullay, jullay!' (of course, of course) he affirmed cheerfully. 'Here, electricity at night, seven to ten. O-cha! Today Tuesday. Tuesday, no electricity.'

'Jullay!' (no problem), I replied, and scribbled down 'O-cha' as an addition to my list of new expressions. It went well with 'gompa'. Hanging on the wall between us was his wife's most precious heirloom, a long mantle of turquoise stones stitched together so as to leave no gaps. It was shaped like a wig with ear flaps and the layer of turquoise stretched from the forehead to the small of the back. It was only worn on special occasions by those with strong neck muscles as it weighed over fourteen pounds.

When my diary was up to date I studied a map to see how best to reach Rizong Gompa. O-cha! It was only a few miles walk from a main road which had to be served by buses. Then the butter was ready and my host got up. We exchanged another 'jullay' (goodnight). I went to bed hoping it would snow that night, and that I would be marooned here for months.

The bus heading towards Rizong was as full of cargo as it was of people and it was as much the social event of the day as a means of transport. The driver stopped frequently to chat but drove with gusto in-between, throwing the vehicle around corners and displaying great faith in the small sign above his head, 'God Save Us And The Bus'. At the third stop the roof was loaded to capacity with bags of potatoes and bundles of wood and the aisle was filled with bales of straw. Fearfully unbalanced we set off once more with two hundred sideless hairpins ahead of us. God Save Us, never mind the bus.

I disembarked at Ullay Tokpo, a hamlet at the junction of the path to the monastery, and was immediately called over to an army checkpoint. While the soldier was noting details from my passport I looked around his hut. The walls were papered with the centrefolds from Indian girlie magazines. The models were all fully clothed and the most revealing showed her breasts hazily though a thin sari. Among these pictures was a memo in English from HQ complaining how lax the vigilance at checkpoints had been and threatening strict disciplinary action if standards did not improve. He copied the details faithfully. If a copy of *Playboy* ever fell into Indian army hands, Ladakh would be defenceless.

The path had once been a gravel road but it had been partly washed away and could only be negotiated on foot or hoof. From its edges crumbling mountains of shale and schist rose steeply and formed a valley that in places narrowed to a ravine. Spurs of solid rock jutted out from the rubble every so often but otherwise the slopes were made of rockfalls and banks of scree in striking bands of purple, yellows, greys and dark blues. It seemed that a breath of wind might upset this equilibrium and make the mountains come crashing down. Then apricot trees holding canopies of white and pink blossom began appearing in straggling numbers. One of these was singing.

It was only after walking around its trunk that I realised the voice was coming from its roots. A goatherd inhabited a shelter burrowed into the bank beneath the tree and when he heard my footsteps he came out and beckoned me down for butter tea. His hair would not have been out of place on a sadhu of thirty years sitting. It hung down his back in a single pigtail and had been tucked through the sash around his gown before being allowed to continue its descent for another foot. His face had thick eyebrows, a dense beard and a breaker of dark locks poised above his forehead. If the Himalayan yeti does not actually exist then a photograph of this man would readily explain how the myth arose. He expressed great interest in a biro protruding from one of my pockets and so I gave it to him. His companion was an old woman who sat spinning in a dark corner. A kitten nestled in her lap and made swipes at the hanging spindle of wool. The woman smiled but never broke her rhythm, for seventy years of experience was not easily distracted. Butter tea was salty and tasted unpleasant until I forced myself to think of it as soup and almost at once it became enjoyable. We drank in silence without a common language, and we had no need of one as the novelty of unexpected encounter was sufficient. In these simple acts of kindness and unspoken friendships I found travel's richest sentiment. The apricot tree was singing again when I left.

The track continued to follow a stream for a mile and then a pocket of green fields and a dense grove of fruit trees interrupted the shingle landscape. This wilderness garden belonged to Julichen nunnery, a mud and stone building with a walled courtyard where three nuns were sitting spinning. They wore the same deep crimson robes as monks but did not shave their heads. They smiled and brought a bowl of *tsampa*, toasted barley mixed in porridge with butter soup, but I politely refused in order to reach the monastery in good time.

Nuns were respected but less reverently than monks and lamas – their higher reincarnations and the equivalent of priests. Buddha accepted that women could achieve Nirvana on their own but in general women were considered inferior and would have to be born again as men and then progress along the normal spiritual path.

Rizong Gompa was situated three-quarters of a mile further on at the end of a sharp climb. It was built into a hillside of grey scree and filled the end of the valley as a massive agglomeration of rooms stuck together and white-washed. There was little evidence of planning in its construction and expansion had simply involved adding on another room in any direction. The result was intriguing. Before reaching it I came to a wall which seemed to serve no purpose despite the huge effort that must have gone into its construction. It was fifteen feet wide, three feet high and four hundred yards long. Then I saw that *every* stone was carved with an inscription.

'It's a *mani* wall,' said a monk who had appeared on the track and was also heading to Rizong. 'The stones are carved with the mantra *Om Mani Padme Hum*. When you walk around one of these walls, always keep it on your right. This is the good side, the side for spiritual expansion.'

'It must have taken years and years to build,' I observed. I kept my good side to the wall and walked down backwards to rejoin the path. We continued together.

'Do you think it will be possile for me to stay the night in the monastery,' I asked.

'Yes, visitors may stay. There is no bed for you but you can sleep on a mat.' He fumbled in his robes for a while and produced a pancake-sized piece of *nan* bread. I wasn't sure if he had just been keeping it warm next to his body or if this was the baking method, but it was delicious. Between mouthfuls he said his name was Lobsang. He was thirty-two years old and had chosen to be a monk at the age of ten. An English Buddhist had spent one year at this monastery not long ago and he had learnt English then and still studied. Lobsang seemed to be a walking bakery and he brought out more *nan* before we reached the monastery. He led the way through narrow doorways and along labyrinthine passages until we reached the entrance to the temple. Lobsang went straight in but I stopped to take off my boots. The stone step felt like ice to my bare foot.

Lobsang reappeared a moment later. He pointed at my bare foot and shook his head.

'Too cold,' he said. I replaced my boot and entered. Buddhism had its softer side.

The room was dimly lit by oil lamps and ran back deep into the building. Monks sat cross-legged on cushions in four rows which were in pairs so that each monk sat facing another. There were about forty people in the room including two rows of boy monks on one side under the watchful gaze of an elderly fat monk in a bundle of frilly pleats. Everyone else appeared to have shrunk into his robes and most were muttering while staring at the empty food bowls before them. At the far end were three senior lamas on wooden seats and an empty throne, highest of all, reserved for the Dalai Lama's rare visits. Tankas hung from the ceiling like flags but the main shrine was at the back beyond the senior lamas; a jumble of statues, pictures, pots, drapes and other things one might expect to see heaped in the props room of a theatre. The shrine seemed to play no part in the service.

The frilly monk gave a shout and four little monks hauled around two copper jugs almost as big as themselves and poured butter tea in every bowl. Monks began chanting and the boys joined in, some high-spirited ones each trying to out-shout the others until the frilly monk killed the contest with a cold glare. More butter tea was served and then followed one and a half hours of singing, meditation, reading, bell-ringing, drum-beating, chanting and several more gallons of tea being served. The service allowed for individuals to go at their own speed and opt out of certain parts, and the casual atmosphere was heightened by the head lama who seemed to have forgotten his book and lent over the shoulder of his junior to share a copy. I felt relaxed and at ease with Buddhists. They could not have received someone who was a foreigner in every sense with greater courtesy and tolerance. A bowl was brought to me and filled along with all the others.

'We pray twice each day,' Lobsang explained after they had finished, 'first at six in the morning and then late in the afternoon. In the middle we work and do studies. Every twentieth day we pray from early morning to night.' We went to the library which contained the Kangyur, the Tibetan Bible, in 108 volumes and 200 companion volumes of commentaries. The books were loose-leaf pages pressed between wafers of wood and bound with a sash, each one about the size of an elongated brick. A teenaged monk sat in one corner turning over pages and reciting the words as fast as his tongue could manage and every so often he hit a drum once with a sickle-shaped drumstick, and sometimes even managed to simultaneously shake cymbals without losing a word. Beside him I was astonished to see the very same biro I had given to the goatherd. I asked Lobsang how it could have got there.

'The goatherd will not be able to write and he would have accepted it in order to give it to a monk. He will acquire merit by this act.'

'But it got here almost as fast as if I had brought it myself.'

'He must have come shortly after you left. It is not so fast. The hills are easier when you know them. This is in our tradition. In Tibet they used to have *lung gompa* – trance runners. They could run sixty miles in a day without food or water.'

We made our way to the kitchen, passing many doors with padlocks that must have required ponderous keys to open them. In earlier times there had been little need for them but now, he said, the increase in visitors put the monastery's valuable artefacts at risk. We entered a dungeon kitchen with two large pots sunk into a stone oven with a fire burning inside. The larger of the two could have bathed an adult and permitted an underwater somersault. Another fat monk stirred the shallow layer of *thukpa* – noodles and a vegetable like silver beet – and served the monks who then took their bowl and slurped noisily while crouching against the wall. The scene might have been cut from a canvas of Pieter Bruegel, with the cook doling out the portion to a line of thickly wrapped figures, his bald head visible above the steam rising from his enormous two-handed ladle.

After the meal Lobsang led me to a mat on an open balcony where he said I could sleep. 'We live quietly and go to bed early. Some visitors are disappointed with monastery life,' he said, and went to fetch a blanket. Disappointment could not have been further from my mind. The balcony offered the finest view of any bed in the kingdom. The valley lay in cold shadow now that the sun was low on someone else's horizon, for it had long since sunk below ours, and the immediate land was uniform grey with only dark crags and chedi like white tombstones standing out as details. The hill shoulders fell down from left and right and formed receding Vs to a distant mountain which blocked the way, its strata layers suggesting a gigantic skier had herring-boned an ascent and left his tracks in the rock. The highest peaks above Rizong were crusted in snow and tinted to the pinkness of Kashmiri tea. It was not a view of brazen charm but one of gentle superiority. I thought I saw an eagle slipping over the skyline but it was possibly just my imagination, over-excited because everything seemed to be here and in the right proportion.

The night chill reached me. No blanket had appeared so I unrolled some prayer mats at the end of my sleeping patch and pulled three of them over me. It struck me then what a unique moment this was, being in a remote Tibetan gompa, under the stars and bedded in a pile of Buddhist prayer mats. But the overwhelming sensation was one of being slowly crushed. Each mat was extremely solid. Lobsang suddenly arrived with the blanket. He looked at me, nodded, then peeled off each of the mats, spread his blanket over me and replaced the covers. He lifted them in turn high above me, pulled them until the end was in line with my chin and casually dropped them into place. The blows struck my chest and sent a century of dust rolling over my face. And each layer compressed me to yet another stage beyond the uncomfortable. I exhaled 'Jullay. Good-night,' more forcefully than intended and it was only with consider-able effort that I managed to reinflate my lungs again. Thus pinned down I listened to the odd monk shuffle past and then I fell asleep.

I dreamt that the wind had blown, Ladakh had caved in and I was underneath.

In a valley beyond Leh, on the opposite side to Rizong, villages were all built on individual hills and rose in a pyramid to a white gompa which always crowned the top. Life revolved around the monastery and there were few families without a son who had served as a novice. Aside from their daily devotions the villagers worked the land, labouring in small fields which bordered the Indus River as emerald marquetry. These were divided by dry-stone walls, irriga-tion ditches and terraces and extended to the edge of the valley floor where they immediately disintegrated into sand and then stones piled in to 20,000 foot mountains. Against this barren and snow-capped background the new crop was being sewn with the help of yaks (males), dris' (females) and dzomos (yak/domestic cow cross).

They were dark shaggy animals and worked in pairs as they pulled wooden ploughs through the soil. A single ploughman steered the implement around the stones, and behind him came a biblical sewer scattering barley with a sweep of his arm. Then followed teams of women with rakes chanting songs and working in perfect unison, out-in, out-in, as they covered the seed. Some were barefoot, others wore sandals cut from car tyres. The ploughman too sang catchy jingles and any misbehaviour from one of his animals did not stop his singing but jarred the pitch and tempo as he strained to keep the single furrow straight.

The method was so primitive and yet there was enviable spirit and camaraderie in their joint effort. Nevertheless I doubted that anyone who called Ladakh a Shangri-La had spent ten hours raking the soil or had worked on the hydro-electric project being constructed higher up the valley. Here a canal to feed water to huge turbines was being excavated with picks and shovels. Men and women had been paired off and issued with one shovel. The former worked behind the handle while the latter stood opposite with gauze wrapped around their faces as protection against dust, pulling on a rope tied to the top of the shovel blade and timing their efforts with the men's strokes. And these people would succeed in the end because they had a proven record, having already lifted a million rocks, engraved them and built them into *mani* walls.

It began to spit with rain, some of the region's annual four inches, and I hurried on to the Tibetan SOS Village of Chonglamser. It was one of several enclaves established by the Dalai Lama to perpetuate the Tibetan culture and help his exiled people come to terms with the new world they were suddenly forced to enter. The village was small and compact, comprising adobe houses, weaving and craft work-shops, Lorna's hospital and the school where Llamo was a teacher. The sounds of children playing drew me to this stone building with its modern wood and glass extension, and by chance Llamo was the first person to appear. She was in her late thirties, short and stocky, and pitched slightly forwards with the weight of the baby carried in a backsling. Her face was round and happy, and I noticed later that when she laughed her eyes all but closed. Before I could explain that Lorna had given me her name she had invited me in for tea.

'If you're tired of butter tea we can give you Chinese green, Kashmiri pink or Darjeeling black,' she beamed. Llamo's eyes were often eclipsed.

'No, butter tea would be terrific. Whatever's easiest.' Butter tea was easiest. There were at least five gallons ready for the morning break. She took me to the common room where we joined six other teachers sitting on the floor. In terms of cheerfulness these people ranked equal to the Balinese and Burmese. There is a hint of frustration expressed in a Tibetan smile, as if it finds the human face too small.

Llamo was the only one who spoke English and she acted as interpreter. Her colleagues wanted to know where my wife was. I explained that I wasn't married, and this surprised them. The baby also took umbrage at the situation and began crying. Llamo withdrew a breast and began feeding her child. 'How old are you?' she asked.

'Twenty-nine.'

'O-cha! Then you still have plenty of time.' The others nodded in agreement but continued to look a little worried. My cup was topped up even though there was barely a mouthful missing. Conversation seemed so easy, as if we had been life-long friends. It turned from marriage to work and I asked about the workers in the fields. Llamo explained that many belonged to cooperatives and the produce was shared in proportion to each member's labour. Others worked for wages, about twenty rupees (£1.20) per day, for richer families who owned the land. It wasn't a high wage, she admitted, but the land wasn't very productive. 'It's still better than they would earn under the Chinese in modern Tibet.'

Conversation always returned to China's invasion. It had torn their nation apart and, understandably, the bitterness was undiminished. On a wall above us hung a bilingual quote:

> Tibet will not die because there is no death for the human spirit. Communism will not succeed because man will not be a slave forever.
> Tyrannies have come and gone and so have Caesars, Czars and dictators.
> But the spirit of man goes on forever.
>
> Jayaprakash Narayan

'Most of us here had to flee from Tibet, so we escaped what happened later. We've heard of the terrible time and the destruction that those who were left had to face. They say out of nearly four thousand of our monasteries, less than fifteen now survive. The Red Guards killed, raped and stole. Every few months houses would be stripped of food, bedding and clothes, even in winter. The animals, vital to Tibet, were slaughtered and useless crops were introduced and there was no food when they failed. Some mothers cut themselves to put their own blood in soup so it would contain a little nutrition for their children. Many people were killed. Parents were forced to applaud while their children were executed.' Llamo managed a weak smile. 'And sometimes we think we are suffering here when we have a power cut . . . '

Butter tea did the round again. It was impossible to lower the level in my cup half an inch without it being refilled. Polite refusals made no difference and the moment my attention was distracted, the bottomless cup would have replenished itself. It was a relief when a bell sounded and the school's 103 children lined up with their bowls and the remaining butter tea from a vat in the kitchen was exhausted on them. When classes resumed I watched some of the younger children play word games. One girl fitted a puzzle of animals and their English names together in no time and without any help from the shapes. Another wrote and sang, *bring, sing, ring, sting, thing*, and the youngest ones had chalk and blackboards and copied *a b c d*.

'They have to learn a completely new alphabet. Do they find this hard?' I asked.

'They have to learn *three* alphabets,' Llamo replied. 'Ladakhi, which is almost identical to Tibetan, Hindi and English. But they learn so fast, it is not hard for them.'

Later she asked the children to practise some dances. They skipped and clapped through traditional folk dances and several foreign ones which included a touch-and-name game of parts of the body in English. They danced and sang with great energy. One of the dances, however, stood out from the others. The children, even the youngest tots, chanted and made aggressive movements, stamping angrily and punching the air. I commented on this after the performance was over and said it looked as if the children were fighting.

'Yes, they were,' Llamo answered. 'This is a dance and song we made up ourselves. Its meaning is that one day these children will fight the Chinese and then . . . then we can go back to our home in Tibet.' The sadness in her voice made it falter. I asked what her village in Tibet had been like.

'It was similar to here, only much nicer. Grass was plentiful because more rain fell and lots of things grew there. Our houses here are better but our families are scattered – and our hearts are in Tibet.'

The people of Ladakh had a love of laughter, their friendship was voracious, their mountain landscape arrestingly beautiful. But Ladakh was not Shangri-La. It was an exile's reminder of what had been left behind and lost, an outsider's fascination for stone-age simplicity in a twentieth-century world. The Ladakhis had managed to retain their identity and trust. Their strength was in their spirit. They would need it all because isolation was no longer an immunity to the culture-corrosive times.

The five-mile walk back to Leh felt longer than it had been that morning. The town's normal population of 10,000 was now matched one to one by visitors in the summer season. Kashmiri vendors came up to cash in on the trade. The young were being wooed by an expanding number of video cinemas. Monasteries *were* benefiting by using their increased revenues for overdue repairs but some were changing centuries-old festivals to more lucrative summer dates and there was rumour of more lax standards. If there was a magic formula for survival, one that would lead forward and heal the old wound, then it had to be lying gathering dust in one of Ladakh's hilltop gompas or somewhere among the million stones of its *mani* walls. The teachers at the SOS school didn't know it. I thought back to the faces of the adorable Tibetan children, their straight black hair, large brown eyes and restricted smiles.

'One day these children will fight the Chinese . . . '

12 · Moscow –
A Statement of Forgotten Things

Destination: Egypt. Problem: land crossings difficult as a result of Afghanistan's border being closed and Iran, still trembling under Ayatollah fanaticism and the war against Iraq, requiring six weeks to consider an uncertain visa. Solution: fly Aeroflot, the cheapest airline even though it doubles the distance by going via Moscow and even though tickets cannot officially be bought in India. Such is the world we live in. It says a lot for owning a yak in Ladakh.

Aeroflot has an office in Delhi but its staff will not sell tickets. They explain that it is illegal for them to do so and direct would-be passengers to one of several small travel agencies nearby. In exchange for the correct amount of cash the agent will go to the back door of Aeroflot's office and buy the ticket. It is a red ticket bearing a commercial white lie for it states it was issued outside India, and this makes it valid for use at an Indian airport.

Shortly before three on the morning of departure, the passengers for my flight were driven by bus from the terminal to a plane waiting on an outlying runway. On the way an Air India plane came taxying towards us from one side. The bus driver considered he had right of way and didn't stop until the plane was almost upon us. Then he braked suddenly as if a cyclist had cut in front of him without warning, and slammed his fist down on the horn. For ten seconds he honked his horn in angry protest at the 747 as it rumbled past with its engines roaring. I admired his spirit.

An engine fault delayed the flight for three hours and during this time the Russian air hostesses went about their duties with the minimum of fuss and politeness. 'Sit down there,' they said, 'take your books off the chair,' and 'here' as they thrust red cans of Coca-Cola at us and then partook themselves of this unlikely communion. I put their attitude down to fatigue after a long day and tried to like their blonde and red hair but after recently meeting 687 million Indians, their hair looked false and their white faces sickly – an impression no doubt enhanced by the omission of a mirror in my luggage.

Aeroflot, affectionately known as 'Chicken Airlines' in the trade, had to postpone the flight for nine hours and then we lifted off successfully. During the eighteen hour journey we were served a pleasant meal, chicken, and reached Moskva that evening. The airport was vast and scores of identical planes littered the ground, each being white with a blue stripe to offset the airline's name. Aeroflot is four times larger than any other airline and half the fleet could have been accommodated in the terminal building, an ultra-modern and futuristic design. Everything was made of either glass or a highly polished material and as a result the number of men in green helmets and green uniforms who stood around as guards was doubled through reflection. These were conscripts, unarmed, and the chubbier of them looked gnome-like despite their serious expressions. They would remain green in appearance throughout their three-year mandatory service in the Soviet army.

My onward flight to Cairo was not for three days and I was driven by bus to be locked inside a transit hotel with a stroganoff of other temporarily stalled travellers. There were Japanese, Fins, Ethiopians, a team of gymnasts from China, a New Zealand geologist obsessed by UFOs and a Canadian anthropologist working in Papua New Guinea ('The average household in New Guinea has Mother, Father, 2.5 children and an anthropologist.') There was a laughing black girl who had a cockney accent, her hair in braids and a ticket to Ghana. And there was a Peruvian on his way to Denmark; his route was Lima → Cuba → Shannon – (Denmark) → Moscow → (3000 bonus miles later) Copenhagen. Aeroflot flies the world by boomeranging around Moscow. This involves a fearsome number of chickens.

At the hotel we waited patiently for our luggage to arrive but it never appeared, only more assorted passengers. Two guards unlocked the door to let them in and locked it again after them.

'I'll go and ask at reception,' I said to the anthropologist.

'No, no. Let me go,' he volunteered and I was glad to step down as the receptionists were Amazonian in build, mugwumpish in attitude. One of them told him he should have waited for it at the airport.

'But we were told to get on the bus and our luggage would be sent here.'

'You should have waited for your case. Now you will get it when you leave.'

'But I'm here for three days.'

'You should have waited for your case.'

'I have no clothes, no toothbrush, no books . . . nothing.'

'I will look into it tomorrow.'

The hotel was a bleak lesson in rouble-effective architecture. A ten-storey cube subdivided into miniature cubes – severely functional but far in excess of my usual level of comfort – with a no-nonsense matron guarding keys on each floor. One could be forgiven for thinking it was a matriarchal society. My room window could only be opened with a special key which was not provided, and looked out on the airport fence and a wood of pine trees mixed with the lyrical silver birch. Moscow was out of sight twelve miles away. I watched a man follow a path alongside the wood until he suddenly turned off and disappeared into the trees. To an on-looker prejudiced by his confinement, it looked a risky thing to be doing.

The bed's top sheet was so starched it stuck out flat for several inches on either side of my body and then fell down at a forty-five degree angle, creating a feeling of having been badly boxed. Above the bed was an Orwellian sign which reminded me that the freezer vaults of a Faeroese fish factory are held at minus 22° Centigrade:

> In winter during the heating season, the room temperature must not fall below minus 18° Centigrade.
>
> For visitors who stay a long time, bed linen will be changed at least once per week, towels at least twice per week.
>
> If forgotten things are discovered every effort will be made to return them to the owner. If the owner is not found forgotten things are registered in the Statement of Forgotten Things and left in the Checkroom of Forgotten Things.

Breakfast consisted of water in champagne glasses, unlimited bread, sour cream, buns, salami, spam and two boiled eggs. White coffee was free but black coffee, tea and mineral water had to be paid for with foreign currency only. The waiter collected foreign coins and ran a private enterprise of exchanging roubles for foreign notes at the blackmarket rate, twice the official rate. He said the staff were rotated about the hotel daily to avoid over-friendliness. He earned the average wage of 168 roubles (£14.80) a month but said that this was supposed to rise to 180 roubles soon. This explained how Aeroflot could undercut other airlines even when it deviated thousands of miles and included several days in a hotel at no extra cost. All one could reasonably expect on top of this was some fresh air and one's luggage.

I went to reception to inquire about it. The manageress was there. Her rank was in proportion to her physical size and she wore her hair in a massive bun. It looked as if a wad of black dough had been dropped on her from above.

'Oh no, no, no, no, no,' (at least five), she said. 'You should have waited at the airport for it.'

I accepted this as it wasn't her fault. She was simply in a pigeon-hole of authority, a large one, but I wished she could have delivered her excuses sympathetically, even if a Statement of Counter-Arguments governed the exact wording. Then she relented and said my pack would arrive in the evening. In the meantime there was to be a free tour around Moscow. The bus was about to leave. Outside the sweet smell of pine needles pervaded the air. A Japanese man looked skywards and held out his arms as if floating. We all felt a sense of escape.

A dual carriage-way with flyovers and branch loops took us to Moscow. We passed two hitchhikers standing by a sign to Leningrad and a racing cyclist gliding along with his nose to the handlebars. Forest gave way to slightly undulating farmland; fields of wheat and pasture, no fences, and farms sparsely sited in copses of trees; a meandering river with picnickers and sunbathers on its banks; a pond where a man was fishing and beyond which three hikers were walking across a meadow. There was a certain toy-town compression of activity but we could have been anywhere in the western world.

Then the suburbs began, neutral blocks of modern dwelling places but in pleasantly spacious areas of grass and trees. Moscow, when seen from an official bus, was attractive with its clean, wide thoroughfares, one-tenth of the traffic to be expected in a city of nine million people, and a river, the Moscow River, which was clean enough for bathing to be popular. The main difference to other developed cities of the world, apart from the abundance of Herculean buildings, the outstanding statuary, the city centre ski-jump and billboards appealing to national pride with barrel-chested and fist-clenching youths, was the absence of pets, outlandish fashions and unusual hairstyles – nothing exotic or freaky. The young wore jeans and T-shirts while the others wore suits or skirts that varied from maxi to long in proportion to the wearer's years. Clumps of soldiers in green boots were scattered liberally about, Tolstoy sat hugely in a chair growing out of a boulder and the ubiquitous wayside benches had scarcely a seat unoccupied. It came as a relief to see the odd pair of lovers arm in arm.

The bus guide gave a running commentary and let cameras be pressed to the windows but quintuplicately refused to allow the door to be opened even a lens-width. 'I'm sure you will agree,' she announced as a change of subject, 'that it is better to see our beautiful city once than to hear about it a hundred times.' She glowed and then proceeded to tell us about it a hundred times.

Russia had no unemployment, she informed. My inquiry as to whether the situation was similar to that of China where there was also 'no unemployment' but considerable numbers of people 'waiting for employment' was ignored. She pointed out this church and that church, only she called them 'choyches' in a way that made me want to reach out and adjust her vowels. She refused to discuss religion but said Moscow had forty choyches. They looked immaculate – as if a fingermark would show – but as memorials to, rather than centres of, their religious faiths. She was strongest on statistics and the people's love of culture. We heard that Moscow has twenty-six professional theatres, thirteen million volumes in its Lenin Library, three Nobel prize-winners lecturing at its university, 103,000 seats in its Olympic stadium, 196 new flats constructed daily, 6000 beds in its Russia Hotel, gives its babies four health checks free each year and printed its first book in 1564. She didn't talk about the queues at shops but commented at length on those before the tomb of the Unknown Soldier.

'Every day people come to place flowers on that grave. We, the Soviet peoples, want peace. We lost twenty million men, women and children in the last war – we want no more war, no more the evils of war.'

I believed her. I believed the Russian people wanted peace just as those of Europe and America wanted peace. She and I were just the same but such a revelation would scarcely put the fear of death into our leaders.

No country should be judged solely on its capital and certainly not when viewed through state-owned glass, but transit passengers have no alternative. When our onward flights resumed we had to carry our luggage (which had eventually been returned to us) across the airport terminal. The black cockney girl on her way to Ghana was boomeranging there on my flight to Cairo. She had more than twice the normal amount of luggage and bulged with suitcases, boxes, parcels and carrier bags. The airport was quiet and many green gnomes stood around looking bored. As the girl was passing one of them a parcel slipped and fell at his feet. She stopped and asked if he would kindly replace it in the gap under her arm. Through gesture alone, her request was obvious but he turned and walked away. For a moment she stared in disbelief and then let everything drop. Suitcases, boxes, parcels and bags, everything crashed to the floor. She put her hands to her hips and glared at the retreating figure, her braids hanging to one side.

'Oh yeah, just you'se ignore me, mate,' she shouted. 'Mustn't overwork ourselves, must we then?' By this time he was some distance away so she raised her voice to a yell that was heard all over the central foyer of Moscow's Sheremet'yevo 2 Airport. 'Tell ye what, lov'. If you'se ever makes it to Ghana . . . I'll boil yer 'ead 'n' eat it.'

At approximately the same time, presumably, in another part of Moscow, my yellow toothbrush was being registered in a Statement of Forgotten Things.

13 · By Metered Camel
to Mount Sinai

With the exceptions of the Suez Canal, completed in 1869, and the upper Aswan Dam, 1972, there have been few constructive changes in Egypt since its civilisation peaked 3500 years ago. In those days the Egyptians worshipped the sun, regarded cats as sacred, played bagpipes and threw larger boomerangs than the average missile of Australian Aboriginals. Their scribes were crafty but suspicious by nature, some to the extent of mutilating the animal hieroglyphs they painted on the tombs of their masters. They painted monkeys and dogs with broken limbs, and owls and falcons with injured wings because they feared the creatures might hop off or flap away and ruin the text. The texts survive and tell of victorious wars and the massive numbers of slaves that enabled Egypt's great monuments to be built. Today these monuments are still spectacular, even in ruin, and many are wired up with electronic wizardry so that at night they flaunt in coloured lights and tell their own stories in French, German, English or Arabic, depending on who's listening. Egypt's modern monuments serve more practical ends but are equally sensational in scale. The Aswan Dam has not yet learnt to speak so it relies on others to relate how its concrete mass, equivalent to seventeen Great Pyramids of Cheops, has increased the country's cultivatable land by twenty per cent. But the voice of the Suez Canal would have the last word. In terms of construction effort it equals thirty-four Great Pyramids and a couple of Sphinxes thrown in as well.

One evening in the town of Suez, two hours to the east of Cairo along a desert highway, I stood beside a very different monument. Three Israeli tanks had been elevated side by side on a concrete plinth. They were relics from the Six-Day War and now performed the function of damaged hieroglyphs testifying less to victories but to the fact that war will not go away. I was waiting for that day's convoy of southbound ships to pass and the first of them was already approaching. Each morning ships set out from their respective ends of the 100-mile canal and travelled in convoy, two long lines with

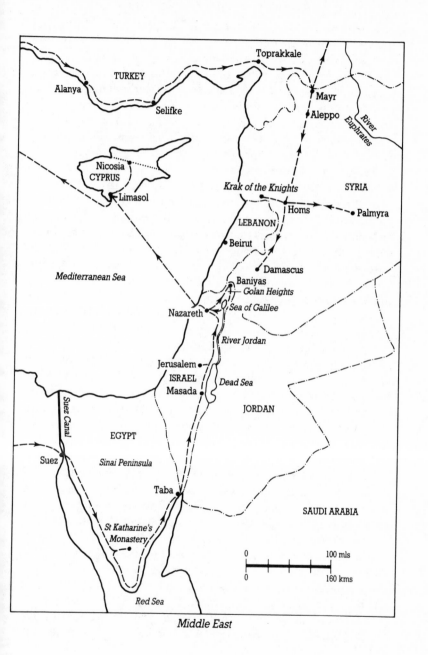

Middle East

each participant at half-mile intervals. They completed the journey without interruption for there were no locks between the Mediterranean and the Red Sea. By standing back from the deep blue canal, behind the chalky-yellow sand dunes that formed its banks, it was possible to catch these leviathans from an enthralling angle. No water in sight, just the bright colours of the world's largest ocean tramps slipping through the sand and leaving a dark bent finger of smoke against the sky. The flags of Panama, China, USA, Russia, Singapore and dozens more paraded by as a tidy summary of my journey, and – Holland, Greece – a timely reminder that it had almost come full circle. The lure of home was growing stronger with the proximity of Europe, and I estimated that three more months might be enough to complete the rest of the route. My intention was to cross over into Sinai to visit St Katharine's Monastery and then travel to Europe via Israel, Syria and Turkey. Middle-East politics made this impossible by a direct route but I hoped to find a way round the obstacles, and the hostilities. They were very much in evidence. Masses of trenches and dug-outs, gun posts, miles of communication lines, a burnt-out tank, barbed wire corridors and land mine warnings formed an ominous foreground to the desert ships and the Sinai Peninsula beyond.

'LA'ILAHA 'ILLA 'LLAH, MUHAMMADUN RASULU 'LLAH.' The muezzin's words sang out, droned and crackled from a mosque in Suez, and were repeated by millions of Mecca-aligned devotees: 'THERE IS NO GOD BUT THE ONE GOD, MUHAMMAD IS THE APOSTLE OF GOD.' Islam, which broke away from Judaism after the time of Solomon *c.* 1000 BC recognises Noah, Abraham, Moses and Jesus amongst its prophets, and is very much a man's opium. Women do not prostrate themselves in public five times daily, possibly because they have less to look forward to in heaven. Each man, however, who reaches the celestial garden has the promised companionship of 8000 attractive divorcees and 4000 'bashful virgins as fair as corals and rubies'.

It was the start of Ramadan, a notoriously grumpy period in the Islamic calendar when complete abstinence from food, drink and earthly pleasures must be observed from one month to the next during the hours between sunrise and sunset. Transport became erratic from Suez down the gulf coast to Wadi Feirân, the turn-off for St Katharine's, and then petered out in a town of mud huts growing out of barren hills. The ground reflected the sun's brutal glare and helped to raise the air temperature to above 120°F. On days such as this I had to drink an extra one and a half gallons of water to stop myself from evaporating. The heat made walking a last alternative and with ten miles still to go I hit on the idea of hiring another type of desert ship. A few were ambling around the huts and an inquiry soon led me to Asfran, a young man in a pyjama-striped galabiya.

''allo fine moustache,' he said. He had once worked at the pyramids of Giza and so he spoke salesman English and German, and had the Arab's natural talent for flattery. His moustache was much finer than mine.

'Das hisst voondershön, mein Freud,' he replied in response to my idea of hiring one of his camels. He agreed to come as a guide and we settled on a price of E£10 (£5.50 sterling) for the three-hour journey. He went off and soon returned leading two camels by halters attached to nostril rings. The first looked down on me disdainfully, its arrogant expression enhanced by its tufted eyebrows, bristling face and thick smiling lips. Then it bent down and bit a hole in my pack.

'Heeeeeeech!' Asfran shouted and pulled the head away. 'This, California. This, Mickey Mouse.' Having introduced us he made California lie down and I climbed onto the rounded platform covering her single hump. Asfran grinned as she tossed me through the slow contortions of a bucking-bronco rider, first forwards, then backwards. California was twenty-five years old, elderly by camel standards but she matched the younger M. Mouse's pace though the taste of my pack (now tied on above her tail) had whetted her appetite. Once she stoped to nibble at some yellow foxgloves and a stand of Scottish thistles. 'Heeeeeeech!' I cried and tugged on the halter but this had no effect whatsoever. It took a prod from Asfran who was following to move her. My feelings of high adventure were only tempered by the absurd Disneyesque names of the camels. California's feet fascinated me. They seemed quite small in mid-stride but on the ground they spread out and doubled in size. A light tap with my legs made her accelerate into a brisk trot and she would throw up her heels like a startled hen and make me bob around like a startled blancmange. Camels are not designed for speed. They are happiest when their feet are at their widest.

During the ride Asfran took the opportunity of visiting all his friends who might have something that I wanted to buy. Arabs have a remarkable ability to emerge from an empty desert and we came across vendors of soup, goat skins and textiles. Asfran's character slowly began to change and his friendly chatter became colder and more business-like. The cost of the trip began to go up as if California's feet were metered and each step clicked up another few piastres on the payscale. Our original destination became the optional extra at an inflated price! By the time we reached the hamlet of ten stone buildings and twenty mud huts, still one mile short of the monastery itself, Asfran had become bad-tempered. The price had to be reassessed, he demanded. Lots of new factors had arisen. I hadn't paid baksheesh to the headman of his village and, most importantly, the journey had been uphill. This now came as a surprise to my guide and meant his camels would be hungrier. He would have to pay more for food.

'But we agreed ten pounds,' I protested.

'Yes . . . five pounds for California, five pounds for Mickey Mouse. But what about five pounds for Asfran, your number one friend?' Ten pounds, he argued, was the downhill rate. Then he became heated and shouted at me. I shouted back and we shouted for several minutes before coming to a compromise. Twelve Egyptian pounds. Asfran returned to his former charming self. He shook my hand vigorously. 'Thank you. Dank shön. Goodbye fine moustache.' My number one friend departed downhill at a trot, California and Mickey Mouse sending up puffs of sand from each foot.

Oh Allah! What a way to do business.

The plant Bladder Senna, *Colutea arborescens*, displays yellowish pods and grows into a tall bushy clump like a creeping bamboo that climbs itself. It was said that an experiment to plant the Sinai Peninsula with this species had inexplicably failed and there was only one example to be found on the whole of the peninsula. This was growing in an alley in St Katharine's monastery and was even acclaimed as being the same Burning Bush that Moses beheld. The monastery is believed to be the oldest in continuous use, founded in A D 530 by a work party sent from Constantinople by Justinian I, and until 1489 its name honoured the Virgin Mary. In that year it was re-dedicated to Saint Katharine, the daughter of a fourth-century ruler, who converted to Christianity and was executed as a result. The spiked wheel intended to impale her (the likes of which now bear her name) fortuitously collapsed before reaching her but she was be-headed instead, and then, legend asserts, milk not blood flowed from her body. During the Middle Ages she became widely cele-brated for her visitation to Joan of Arc and her rumoured marriage to Christ, but historically there is no mention of her existence until 400 years after her supposed death. Her intact body was miraculously transported to one of the nearby hills where it was discovered and taken to be enshrined in the monastery.

Also housed here is what hearsay ranks as the world's second greatest library of theological books and ancient manuscripts, second to the Vatican's collection. The library is not open to visitors, understandably ever since a Russian emissary, Constantin von Tis-chendorf, borrowed a fourth-century biblical manuscript in 1859 and never returned it. The circumstances are obscure but it was Tischen-dorf's second visit to the monastery and his second acquisition of unique writings. He believed he had been given the texts outright in exchange for a guarantee for non-aggression by the Tsar – and that he had actually saved them from being burnt – but the monastery professes to hold an agreement signed by Tischendorf which speci-fies the exact terms of the loan. The monastery is still waiting for the return of the manuscript, the Codex Sinaiticus, even though in 1933 it was sold to Britain by the Soviet authorities for £100,000 and is now resting in the British Museum.

The monastery is situated in isolation in a valley of boulders below the 7500 foot high Jabal Musa (Mount Moses), a conglomeration of crags otherwise known as Mount Sinai. It had been designed as a fortress in justified expectation of a troubled history, being Christian in a Muslim land, and had an outer wall of granite thirty feet tall. A wooden hut clung to the top of the wall on one side and contained a windlass to haul up provisions and visitors. Until last century the main gate remained closed and access was exclusively by invitation and rope. Inside was an area less than one hundred yards square crammed with buildings forming a warren of doors, arches and dark narrow alleys. About twenty reclusive Greek Orthodox monks lived here but they slipped through the shadows and rarely let one glimpse their long black robes, black beards and black, round, flat-topped hats. My knock on the warproof gate was answered by an Arab attendant in soiled white. His turban was tied on with a white sling which gave the impression that he had mumps or toothache. He eyed me up and down as part of his duties for his orders were to refuse admission to anyone wearing a sleeveless shirt, short pair of trousers or less than full-length skirt.

A young monk appeared and offered to lead me to the visitors' dormitory but on hearing that I intended to climb Mount Sinai before dark and sleep at the top, he excused himself and quickly disappeared. The monastery fell silent except for the periodic sound of doors opening and shutting, but always around a corner. I chased noises in the hope of seeing human life but the view never showed more than a row of closed doors. The elusive activities drew me deeper into the maze and eventually to a tall burst of green and an English label pinned to its base: 'Burning Bush'.

It looked strong and virulent though unassuming in its shady spot by a wall. Lichens are considered capable of living for 10,000 years and if Moses is accepted as having lived around 1300 B C then it is scientifically possible that plant life could have flamed before him and survived to this day. Only this wasn't a lichen. I stared doubtfully at *Colutea arborescens* until I caught a faint whiff of smouldering. My gaze became more critical and after an expectant pause during which there was no appreciable change in the bush's state, I recognised the smell as incense and followed it round to a small dark chapel. It was also deserted. A partially concealed mosaic of St Katharine brightened the gloom created by dwarf windows, high-backed chairs and a hallelujah of cobwebs among the hanging tangle of oil lamp chandeliers and incense swingers. I crept out. Creak, shuffle, bang. All other doors were closed. I had not been invited here and the atmosphere was one of trespass and claustrophobia, and I quickly tried to lose myself back to the main gate. This time the Arab appeared to me as the guardian of the underworld though I could no longer tell if I were leaving it or about to enter it. He seemed to understand my uncertainty and beckoned me to follow. We went into another chapel and he pointed through some chicken mesh into a dingy chamber. The bones of 3000 monks all neatly aligned and piled up to the height of my chest filled the room with the smell of mould. He tapped me on the shoulder. Behind us the skulls that had once been connected to the bones were stacked up and a multitude of sightless sockets leered at us. I nodded respectfully to Charon and fled outside to the path up Mount Sinai.

The light was already fading as I began the two-hour ascent but the path was clearly defined despite the abundance of rocks and rubble through which it zigzagged. The mountains had the same splendid desolation of Ladakh, a splendour that failed when it became a race to reach the top before darkness made the path indistinguishable from the precipices which increasingly bordered it. My skull would not have been deemed worthy of becoming number 3001 on the stack but I had no intention of letting the possibility come into question. I stopped to rest once and lit a match to check a rock for scorpions before sitting on it, wondering if Moses had thought about these things when he came up here to collect the Ten Commandment slabs.

On a distant horizon a square building was just visible. It was said to be – the Sinai is a delightful oasis of allegation – an unfinished palace intended for the asthmatic Egyptian ruler (1849–54), Khedive Abbas I. The story goes that he sent some men to scour the country for the spot with the purest and lightest air. After a long search they were unable to decide between several places and so they slaughtered a dog in each and left the carcasses to see which would stay fresh for the longest. The dead dog on the mountain opposite won and the palace was started but the reclusive Abbas never lived to occupy it. According to one account he was strangled by two servants, according to another he was killed in a fight with one of his ministers whom he had caught in bed with his wife. Feeling tired and cold on a dark, scorpion-infested mountain, I went along with the second version.

There were two modest buildings on the summit but by then it was too dark to recognise them and I lit a candle. The first was a chapel to St Katharine. Some paintings were visible through a window but it looked neglected and its door was locked. The other building was a hut built beside a hole in the ground – Moses's grotto. It was a dismal-looking hole, even as holes go, but if Moses had spent forty days fasting in it I assumed there would be enough space to sleep. I climbed down into it, a matter of six feet, and was alarmed to hear voices. I froze and listened intently, hoping to convince myself it had been my imagination. But no. Voices were coming from the rock. It was only after cautiously emerging from the grotto that I realised the sounds were coming from inside the hut, a tiny mosque, and their direction had been distorted by the acoustics of the grotto. I knocked on the door and waited for a response.

It opened and by the light of candles and camping stoves I made out a crushed circle of foreigners sitting on the carpeted floor. The mutual surprise dissolved into smiles and soon I found myself throwing in a few of my tins of food into the general goulash steaming in the middle, and sitting amongst eleven others who had come up earlier that afternoon. We represented seven nations.

'I can't believe it,' said a German girl. (English was the common language.) 'Two days ago I was in Frankfurt.'

'Two days?' queried an Aussie. 'Gee. Reckon ya name must be Kath'ran.'

We had plenty to talk and laugh about. We were seven girls, four from Germany and three from Australia, a Frenchman, Dutchman, Spaniard, Egyptian and a Scotsman all in a mosque at the top of Mount Sinai. We knew we were the makings of another good story.

We got up at 4 a.m. to see the sunrise. It began as a faint colouring that grew brighter until it filled the sky as a blaze of yellow. The hills around us stood out in jet black profile until the sun appeared and stroked its way down from the chapel and the mosque and gently fingered among the bumps and boulders of the lower slopes. Then the sun seemed not so much to touch the surface from above but to enter the hills from below and radiate outwards so that ridges and crags beneath us became infused with gold and lay glowing fiercely amid coal-black shadows. Nothing seemed improbable in this region. Fact and fiction merged and a distinction was rendered unnecessary by the land's natural sense of drama. Even after thousands of years Mount Sinai still knew a trick or two.

14 · Lines Drawn Around Israel

'Six Israelis together,' Daveed explained with a wry grin, 'means twelve opinions and an argument. But if the argument is over our homeland, they are like twelve men with one opinion.'

The day after the state was proclaimed in May 1948, Israel was simultaneously attacked by five Arab nations including all four neighbours. Within eight months the attackers had been repulsed, one million Arabs had become refugees and Israel had expanded by half. As a result of the Six-Day War in 1967 Israel extended her boundaries again, taking Sinai and the Gaza Strip from Egypt, Jerusalem's Arab sector and the West Bank from Jordan and the Golan Heights from Syria. The birthplace of three of the greatest and oldest religions (Judaism, Islam and Christianity) now spent one-third of its national budget on defence and armaments, was the world's fourth strongest military power and a major exporter of munitions. Its citizens were used to being frisked at shop entrances and stood unconcerned in supermarket queues with an automatic rifle pointing at their ankles as it hung from the shoulder of a fellow shopper, a war-ready boy or girl in casual army dress. They were three million Jews (six million opinions but all Zionists) and a few others come together from 120 different nations to occupy a country the size of Holland. It was, and still is, Palestine to the 1½ million Arabs who also live there and to the hostile neighbours on all landward sides. Life in Israel is lived intensely, expensively and with the borrow-and-spend attitude that an annual inflation rate of 140 per cent encourages. People hope today will be like yesterday, forget about tomorrow and plan ahead for the next generation. Construction, industry and agriculture push down roots as if trying to recoup 2000 years of lost growth within half a century. The hotel at Taba and the ruined fortress of Masada are symbols of the stubborn determination and self-sacrifice that have shaped the land and characterised the Jewish people from the old times of Goliath to the modern ones of Daveed.

The luxury Sonesta Hotel, Taba, was sited in half a mile of no-man's land between the Egyptian and Israeli borders. The Israelis allowed it to be built by an Elat businessman after capturing the Sinai Peninsula, in full knowledge that the hotel would lie just outside their negotiated border. It was their policy to maintain an outward pressure on their limits and although the Egyptians were still angered by this flagrant act of squatting, the hotel remained and prospered. I passed through the Egyptian border control and left two armed soldiers gazing over their empty section of beach to the Taba crowd of Israelis who were lying between coils of barbed wire and sunbathing in a minimum of string and triangles. The sight must have made the last days of Ramadan harder to bear.

The Israeli border post was staffed by women who were efficient and strict, and pretty despite being swaddled in battledress. They made a list of my camera equipment, noted that my destination was Masada and let me pass. Masada was positioned in the Judean Desert 130 miles to the north and was also at sea level but because the surrounding land fell down to the lowest point on the earth's surface, minus 1300 feet, it crowned a yellow mountain overlooking the Dead Sea. My arrival in Israel was on a Saturday, the Sabbath, when everything except the hotels and the defence system shut down and my journey was stalled through lack of transport.

It resumed on the Sunday, passing through an area of canyons as white as desert snow which extended to the Dead Sea, and here a large processing plant (potassium and salt) was capitalising on what remains of Sodom, Gomorrah and Lot's unfortunate wife (Gen. 19). After this the canyons turned brimstone yellow, fizzled out and reappeared near the base of Masada. The elements had eaten into the sides of this flat-topped hill and separated it from the ridge behind. Two-thirds of its height was covered in scree and then the final third rose in near vertical crags. The fortress walls were extensions of these cliffs and must have made an adamantine stronghold when intact. The chairlift that marred the view on one side was closed when I arrived and so was the historical site itself but I disregarded the signs 'No entry after 3 p.m.', 'Staying overnight on Masada is an illegal offence', and took a steeply twisting path to the top. Two guards watched my progress and then ignored me. It would have been a different story in AD 66.

In that year a party of Zealots, an extreme Jewish sect, made a surprise attack on the fort which had long been occupied by the

Romans. They massacred the inhabitants and for seven years, one thousand, men, women and children repulsed all attempts by the Romans to retake the fort. Their defence was an inspiration to the rest of their people and a shaming irritation to Rome. Masada fell in AD 73 to Rome's Tenth Legion under General Silva. When 15,000 soldiers eventually stormed the walls after a siege lasting almost two years, they met with no resistance. Only two women and five children remained alive. The other defenders, 960 in all, had died by their own swords in a suicide pact when defeat was seen to be inevitable. Today Masada is held as an Israeli shrine, a symbol of courage, freedom and death before surrender.

Little remained of Herod's Hanging Palace (built on a precipitous spur at one end), the storehouses, baths and other buildings except some foundations, walls and mosaics. At dawn parties of Jewish families with thirteen-year-old sons wearing shorts, best shirt, skullcap and a phylactery wrapped around one forearm came up to perform the Bar Mitzvah, the ceremony marking their coming of age. It was while gazing at these devotions among the cold ruins and at the spectacular view beyond that I met Daveed. His Bar Mitzvah must have taken place about twenty-five years earlier and now, having just completed his military service, he was taking a break to tour the country in a battered van. He had a head of shaggy black curls and was an American Jew recently immigrated, an artist, one who let no disagreement go unargued, was proud to a degree of arrogance and, despite his small stature, must have been the sort of figure General Silva complained about in his reports to Rome for two years. Daveed was going to visit a kibbutz near Nazareth for a few days and then drive to the Golan Heights, and was looking for a companion to share the petrol costs. We shook hands on the deal before I had laid eyes on the vehicle. It was certainly no bargain and seemed an unusual choice. A van that gargled and swallowed a gallon of oil every ten miles had to be on the side of the Arabs.

'All men and women have to do three years' military service here. After that we must do four to six weeks each year up to the age of fifty.'

'Do employers automatically give you leave and hold your job?'

'Yes, and they have to go sometime as well. Only Hassidic Jews are exempt military service on religious grounds . . . but they say they pray for us.'

We stopped to float in the Dead Sea with what looked like icebergs but were really lumps of crystallised salt. The beach of white, yellow, grey and pink sand left around the lake by the receding water evidenced serious fears that the Dead Sea was itself slowly dying. The water looked greasy and to the touch it was an acid test for cuts or broken skin. We barely dented the surface and bobbed like polystyrene flotsam as we watched figures coated in black therapeutic mud tiptoe down to the water on rocks frosted with salt. Then, thoroughly pickled, we steered our van north for fifteen gallons to Nazareth. After the vast distances of India and China, Israel seemed delightfully compact and easy to travel even though the van protested the whole way and converted half its energy into noise. We gargled up out of the rock desert. The hills became sparsely covered in grass and there were occasional herds of goats and the tents of their keepers. *While shepherds watched their flocks by night . . .* The association was irresistible and the map brought back names and images with a thrill that had previously been denied me on my quest for Ordinary-level Divinity. Jericho fell by as an unassuming township, but the name was enough, and then we were running close to the River Jordan, a large stream that was hard to make out through twin Y-shaped fences of barbed wire. The Middle East was an insatiable consumer of the stuff and it kept snagging the text of my Bible.

We reached Jesus's hometown late in the afternoon. Nazareth had more television aerials than I had imagined as a child. It was built on steep hills and its maze of alleys contained many churches and markets. Among the latter were 'Holyland Souvenirs', 'Nazareth Carvings' and 'Nativity Enterprises' which sold T-shirts reading 'My Dad went to Nazareth and all he brought me back was this lousy T-shirt'. You could substitute 'Dad' for 'friend' or one of a dozen relatives and choose from a wide range of colours and sizes. I wasn't tempted by these or by the postcards bearing 'Greetings from Israel' beneath a picture of the cast of *Dallas* looking bored and obstructing a view of the Holy Sepulchre, and walked up to the Church of Jesus the Adolescent. At the foot of pillars and arches supporting a magnificent vaulted roof I sat down and enjoyed a moment's peace before Bible Land Pilgrimages Ltd arrived with a tour. Two American boys (about the same age as Jesus, I supposed, when he lived here) trailed at the back of the group. 'Like this,' exclaimed one pilgrim as he let fly a kung-fu kick and aimed a chop at his companion's head. His companion didn't agree and gave his version of the movement, and then they discussed the body's weakpoints and the appropriate blows that would administer instant death by collapsing lungs, crushing temples or severing vital nerves.

'How was Nazareth, then?' asked Daveed when we met back at the van.

'Not quite how I expected. I would have preferred less jumble sales, an odd donkey or two or some feeling of other-worldliness. I didn't expect to come away with a yellow belt in karate.'

We repaired to Ginnegar, to the kibbutz where Daveed had once worked. This kibbutz, he explained, was one of the largest and oldest, dating back to the 1920s. Kibbutzes varied in ideology from those encouraging individual ownership and profit (moshés) to those giving priority to religious worship, but most had retained the original outline of being communal farms where everyone would have food, work and a place to stay. A small wage was paid but otherwise income was ploughed back into the community. Children lived together under a guardian and thus parents were free to serve the community. All members had one vote and equal status at the weekly meetings where decisions were made democratically. Ginnegar was a prosperous kibbutz. It had 600 members, owned 1000 acres of land, 300 milk cows, 40,000 battery hens and a plastic sheeting factory. We drove past orchards and fields of wheat and vegetables, and into the landscaped grounds of the kibbutz buildings. At the base of a wooded hill were lawns and flowering shrubs among modern buildings fitted to a high degree of comfort; members' houses, all furnished with colour televisions as a result of the previous year's profits, recreation rooms with partitions that lowered from the ceilings at the push of a button, volunteer workers' quarters, school, stores and communal dining room.

'Can anyone just arrive and stay in a kibbutz?' I asked.

'Only if you've got contacts there. Guests can stay free for a few days. We can crash with some of my friends. Wait till you see the food!' Daveed grinned and raised his eyebrows until they disappeared into his fringe.

My eyes widened. The serving trays were laden with soup, meats, vegetables, salads, sauces, yoghurt, cheese, sweets, fruit, bread, milk and honey. It was one of my recurring dreams, merciless gluttony, and I set out to fulfil it with Israeli determination. We sat with Daveed's friends, Amos and his English girlfriend Julie.

'Would you like to work here?' Amos asked as we finished eating. 'We normally have fifty volunteers but we're twelve short at the moment.'

I paused to consider the proposition but it seemed less attractive after a sudden increase of a pound in weight. 'I think I'm too close to home to feel like settling down for a while. Besides, you'd have to make me work too hard to pay for the food I'd eat.'

Julie smiled. She had been here as a volunteer for a year. 'We all eat too much when we first come. It's an easy life. In fact it's so easy and sheltered that most volunteers get nervous about the thought of leaving.' She said she had felt unsettled to begin with as the kibbutzniks were used to a high turnover of volunteers and it took several months to win their confidence. Volunteers worked six hours a day and received free accommodation, meals and four packets of cigarettes each weak, and a monthly wage of 490 shekels (£10) which doubled after a minimum period of service. 'The kibbutz arranges sightseeing tours for us, weekly films, discos, and we can use the television rooms, tennis courts and swimming pool. But we work hard as well. The jobs are rotated every so often but volunteers tend to get the worst ones, mainly cleaning. I milk the cows which is one of the better ones. You can come along if you want. I think 514 is about to give birth soon which might interest you.'

It did interest me as the only time I had seen this happening was on continuous video with an entourage of candy floss-eaters at the Calgary Stampede.

The next morning, on my way to the cowsheds to meet Julie, I passed the school and stopped to take a photograph of the mini-kibbutzniks who were playing outside. They were all aged between four and six. A teacher was supervising them and it seemed courteous to first seek her permission.

'Wait a moment,' she replied. 'I shall ask the children if they want to be photographed.' She went off and shouted something in Hebrew. About half said it was 'O.K.' and half ignored her so I presumed it wasn't O.K. with them.

'It really is a very democratic system they've got here,' I commented to Julie some time later, recounting the incident as we wiped, plugged in and activated rows of udders.

'Yes! I find the life for children a bit strange. They see so little of their parents they get quite excited when they happen to meet. Family bonds are naturally weak but the children grow up very open and suffer no hang-ups about mixing socially. They are given responsible work at a young age and this makes some become bloody cocky, but you get used to it. Kibbutzniks never lack self-confidence and I think that's an important achievement of the system.'

I found milking extremely soothing and gratifying. The simple act of applying an octopus of cups and thereby bringing immediate relief to a fellow creature brought me a strong sense of being useful and benevolent. If my years were filled with endless rows of quadruple teats then the pleasure would doubtless diminish but that morning I was sorry to be disturbed when Julie came to say Cow 514 was in labour and experiencing a tricky delivery. As we walked over to the maternity barn I asked about farming methods here.

'The community is geared towards intensive farming and a policy of no grazing. New born calves are taken away shortly after their birth and bottlefed, and never see their mothers again. It's all very business-like. Cows are merely shekels on legs. Their high-protein diets cost two-thirds of the milk yield but enable milking to take place three times daily and the yields are very good.'

The Friesians here were certainly the largest I had ever seen and Cow 514 was larger still. By this time the cowman had arrived and had managed to tie a rope around the legs of the calf still in its mother's womb. He winched the calf out into the world using a ratchet and a special T-bar brace that fitted against the rear of the cow. The calf lay on the ground covered in membrane. The cowman cleared its throat and it gulped air. Mother 514 licked it clean, knocking the fragile head with each rasp of her powerful tongue and causing the calf to blink in surprise at the harshness of nativity. For a while it lay there, dwarfed by its huge mother and then it gingerly struggled to its feet, fell over several times and eventually took a few tentative steps on its trembling legs.

'Sweet, isn't it?' Julie said. I nodded. 'Pity it's a bull calf. It'll be slaughtered in a month. They only keep the cows.'

Shekels on legs; this one was a low denomination, too low to keep.

I thought I would fit in a quick visit to the 40,000 hens before continuing my relief work among the rest of the herd, and went to the hen houses which were inside a barbed wire enclosure. A middle-aged kibbutznik came out of the first building as I approached. I asked her about the possibility of going inside, and facetiously wondered if she would say, 'Hang on a minute, I'll just go and ask them.'

Instead she waggled a forbidding finger. 'There is a danger of your infection.'

'I don't mind. I'm prepared to risk it.'

She glared at me. 'It's the hens I'm worried about.'

Of course. Shekels in feathers. I was too sentimental to take to the farming methods of a small country.

Daveed and I were allowed to stay three days as guests at Ginnegar and then we drove north for a morning, rounded a corner of Israel's precious fresh water reservoir, the Sea of Galilee, and headed towards the hills of the Golan Heights. Conversation with Daveed was becoming increasingly harder. He hated any criticism of his country and was suspicious of compliments. He stated his opinions dogmatically but frequently contradicted these with his actions. I began to see him as a temperamental artist who had not quite settled into a consistent level of eccentricity. The journey had not got off to a good start for when we had stopped to visit the Church of the Beatitudes which overlooked the Sea, a nun had refused to let Daveed enter in shorts. He could have changed but he just smouldered. 'The House of God is always open, huh? Except when you aren't covering enough of the skin God gave you.'

He cheered up a bit when we came close to the Lebanese border of Qiryat Shemona in an area of ripe wheat fields being harvested and pine plantations. He had seen six months' active service in Lebanon.

'You ever been in a war?' he asked. I shook my head. 'You learn to fight in training but it's different when you've got live bullets flying around and coming from someone who wants to kill you. I was shit-scared. Smoke, flames, the noise of bombs, and your friends falling beside you – then you know what it's all about. It's bloody terrifying, and yet you get sort of used to the fighting. It's the waiting I hated. The only bit of fortune we have in being surrounded by enemies is that they're Arabs. They're not good fighters. Usually they are young, untrained, undisciplined and poorly equipped. Many times we've found Syrians chained to their gun posts to stop them deserting. But the Syrians are the worst if they capture an

Israeli. They torture and humiliate their prisoners before killing them.'

'You talk about war the way we discuss the weather.'

'War is a reality for us. It's never far away. Life is never *normal* in Israel. We've got war and we've got inflation.'

We stopped at a waterfall amongst trees near Baniyas and swam in a green-black pool. Then we drove higher into the hills and again war came to mind but this time it was the Holy Crusades, when we came to the imposing ruins of Nimrod Castle. Daveed made some watercolours while I went exploring. It was strange to think that English Knights had come so far from their homeland to build this fortress, and that this site was still of strategic importance and a scene of battle 800 years later. We returned to Baniyas and slept beside a rock-cut swimming pool once used by Syrian officers. Other campers were there too and someone played guitar. The notes seemed to linger in the cold mountain air long after the haunting melodies stopped, as if they and the bubbling water had always been the only sounds here.

The following day we drove to some Druze villages. One family invited us into their home for coffee spiced with cardamom, and sheets of pitta bread two feet in diameter folded around hunks of goat cheese. These people were neither Christians nor Muslims but practised a largely unknown and secret religion which incorporated elements of both faiths and was passed down from one generation to the next. Their homes were simple, their villages looked poor and many Druzes were goatherds but an uncommon number of Mercedes-Benz cars travelled their roads. Then we drove on to Mount Hermon which divides itself fairly between Syria, Lebanon and Israel – Syria owning the highest of its three peaks at 9232 feet and Israel holding the one 2000 feet lower. Since 1967 it has been the highest point of Israeli-administered territory but this is subject to qualification (the temporary custodianship of the higher Mount Sinai in 1973), as are most definitive statements about a land which lacks *normal* consistency. Under Syrian control the area had been barren and one vast minefield. The Israelis had cleared the ground foot by foot, lifting even the plastic mines that defied metal detectors, and established orchards that ran for miles across the hillsides. They were part of the Israeli miracle, the transformation of deserts into gardens, the planting of 100 million trees in thirty years.

Beyond were 100 billion barbed wire spikes. A brace of helicopters patrolled the lines, coveys of fighters passed overhead.

'I hate it,' Daveed said suddenly. 'There's land over there, and there's land over here. Why can't we wander freely over there? Why can't they wander freely over here? I want peace. Israel wants peace, but the rest of the world thinks we are warmongers.' His features hardened. 'I don't know why the world hates us Jews but as long as they do, we will have to fight to defend our homeland.' He sighed and shrugged. 'We have no choice.'

I pictured someone else sighing too. Had I been an artist I would have sketched him; an old man with a long flowing beard and a pained expression looking down on the birthplace of three great religions and seeing it surrounded by bitterness and barbed wire. I would rather have drawn it otherwise, as a happy scene, a peaceful cohabitation of Israelis and Palestinians, the old man chuckling, his beard parting to reveal a lousy white T-shirt, large size. 'My Son went to Nazareth . . . '

15 · In the Antique Land of Syria

Syria had been a handful of miles away from my route around the Golan Heights but in order to get a visa to enter the most hard-line of Arab states, I had to take a boat to Cyprus. Syria had severed diplomatic relations with Egypt and so it had been impossible to get the visa in Cairo. The political paperchase then became more complex. Ferries from Israel only went to the Greek half of Cyprus. Ferries from Cyprus to a port close to Syria only went from the Turkish half, and Cyprus's internal border could only be crossed by day-visitors without luggage. All this meant a 1500 mile detour via Cyprus, Rhodes and the south coast of Turkey in order to stand on the Syrian side of the fence. Assuming, that is, I could conceal my visit to Israel from the Syrian consul. Any evidence of association with 'the enemy' would result in no visa and a prompt ejection.

Before entering the Consulate in the Greek half of Nicosia I checked my pockets to ensure there were no leftover Israeli coins or Hebrew wrappings. The last stamp in my passport showed my entry into Egypt and fortunately all other stamps which showed my movements at the Israeli border had been put on a separate piece of paper which I had subsequently thrown away. There were still several embarrassing questions the consul could ask, and while waiting to be seen, I rehearsed some of my answers.

. . . What is the last country you visited? (Egypt.) . . . Your passport shows you entered Cyprus at Limasol but that port has no links with Egypt. So how did you get here? (Hitched on a private yacht.) . . . Why have you no exit stamp from Egypt? (I can't read Arabic. I thought emigration had stamped this page.) . . . If you say you have been in Egypt for the last two months, why was your visa only valid for one month? (Sorry to have bothered you. I can find my own way out.)

A secretary led me into the consul's office and I sat before a man in army uniform who had a finer moustache that Asfran. He carefully worked his way through forty-four pages of stamps in my passport.

'Where is Trinidad?' he asked. I explained. He moved on to an inky giant tortoise. 'And Galapagos?'

'They're islands off South America. The animals there have no fear of man. I like taking photographs and it's wonderful when the animals don't run away.' I immediately regretted bringing up the touchy subject of cameras. Fortunately he merely smiled.

'Have you been to Israel?' His tone was pleasantly curious.

'No.'

'Why not?' Now he spoke drily. 'You'll like the Israelis. *They* don't run away from cameras.'

My visa was ready the next day and I made my way slowly over the remaining thousand miles to Syria, following the footsteps of the Crusaders. Their castles marked the route at regular intervals; Kolossi, Palace of the Masters (Rhodes), Bodrun, Mamure, Softa, Liman, Selifke, Kizkalesi, Koryos, Yilanlikale, Toprakkale . . . on and on they went. There never had been an easy way to visit the Middle-East. You needed either a visa or a string of castles. Most of the latter dated from the great era of castle-building which began in the early twelfth century, shortly before the Second Crusade, and now stood as ruined reminders of their stonemasons' skill and the huge scale of the folly that repeatedly lured Christian armies along a trail of defeat. Amongst the pride of Crusader castles and one to send a shiver down a Saracen's breastplate, was Krak of the Knights (*Crac des Chevaliers*), and it was to see this castle that I wanted to visit Syria. It was situated halfway down the country in the west, near the Lebanese border.

Covering the first Syrian mile was a delicate business but the first of many instances of Arab kindness. I crossed the border at a small country post and began walking south as there was no traffic. After a short while a young Arab cyclist approached from behind and stopped. He nodded and pointed at the slender rack above the rear wheel of his pushbike. I smiled and pointed at my luggage; a large kitbag fitted with shoulder straps, a heavy camera case and a three-pint water bottle. He seemed undeterred so I climbed on. Balancing was difficult as my pack threatened to pull me off backwards, both my hands were full and there was nowhere to rest my feet. We set off hesitantly and began wobbling to an alarming degree until he had pedalled up enough speed to make gravity feel less menacing. After half a mile my stomach muscles were aching and the bike was groaning. After one mile my situation had become untenable and I volunteered to be put down before I fell down. I thanked the driver and watched him quietly roll away into a flat landscape thinly clad in wheatfields.

I walked for several miles until the village of Mayr, a collection of beehive huts made of adobe, and sat down to rest. In no time an old woman brought me a glass of water and her hospitality was repeated by another who appeared with sweet tea and celery. Beyond the houses men were scything wheat and simultaneously gathering by sandwiching the fallen stalks between their left foot and the flat of the blade. On their left foot they wore a contraption like a snowshoe made of shrub branches. As they pulled the scythe blade inwards on the cutting sweep, they stepped down on the falling corn with this enormous foot, sandwiched the stalks and lifted them forwards enough to deposit them on the next patch of corn to be cut. In this way the load built up under their foot. Every ten paces they left a pile for women to collect. They took the wheat to a threshing area where it was strewn in a circle on the ground. A horse pulled two women who sat on a sledge to put weight on the four cutting discs that served as wheels. Round and round they rode all day until the wheat had been chopped to a state suitable for winnowing. Mayr's lack of a press-button dining room and combine harvesters was all that distinguished it from my last kibbutz.

Syria's poorness, an abundance of soldiers and hilly farmland that needed a drench of rain dominated the view from a bus which took me south to Homs, the turn-off for Krak of the Knights. It was dark by the time I changed buses and I was tired. I tucked myself around my luggage as a precaution against theft and went to sleep, unaware that I had been directed onto the wrong bus. Instead of going west towards the coast this bus was going east into the Syrian desert.

The bus jolted me awake in the early hours of the morning when it stopped among some buildings. I realised something was amiss from the time the journey had taken. 'Palmyra,' the driver shouted, and he began collecting the fares from those leaving. My map marked Palmyra with a symbol for archaeological ruins and showed it to be 100 miles off my intended route. The bus was continuing east and so I got out. It was too late to hunt for a hotel room and I set off to look for a place to sleep rough. The streets soon came to an end and opened into the emptiness of desert. I lit a candle to check the ground but the first likely spot was occupied by a dead snake. The second appeared fine until a spider with a three-inch span walked up to my bare feet. I leapt blindly out into the darkness and waited for it to disappear. My reaction was probably unnecessary as the smallest species are usually the most poisonous but I judge a spider's ferocity by the length of its stride. I moved to a third spot, scratched a groove in the sand and stones, and wriggled into my blanket. Dogs began to howl and for a long time they kept me awake, along with thoughts of long-striding spiders, snakes and being lost.

Dawn came early and roused me to an astonishing sight. My scratched bed lay before the monumental ruins of a Greek city; streets, temples, houses, arches and pillars stretched from left to right and into the background until they dissolved into a scattering of funeral towers and a solitary Arabic castle atop a desert hill. The castle's bucket-and-spade architecture appeared crude in comparison to the Classical shapes it looked down upon, sculptured sandstone forming two square miles of yellow skeletons on the fawn desert and hinting at buildings of staggering proportions. One row of over fifty columns supported lintels but no roof, arches soared as entrances to walls that had disappeared, and generous rows of tiered seating surrounded the stages of a theatre and meeting place. Fallen stones lay littered about. A breath of wind stirred sand and whirled the particles against worn carvings and cracked cinctures. A sense of dignity pervaded the ruins, and injustice that such great works had been allowed to crumble. Now a graveyard of splendour, Palmyra had been given over to the wilderness and stray dogs that fell silent by day and howled by night. A bedouin woman in black and with small crosses tattooed on her face slipped quietly through the streets, her herd of goats clambering over the stones as if they were any outcrop of desert crags. They were in fact the remains of the Temple of Baal (the God of Rain) of which only eight of its 390 columns remained standing, but it wasn't until later that I discovered the details and the history that makes travel meaningful. At that moment I felt only the breathlessness of having stumbled across the kingdom of Ozymandias.

Palmyra, or Tadmor as it was known one thousand years before Christ, is reputed to have been founded by Solomon and became important as an Assyrian trading post on the camel caravan route between Damascus and the Euphrates. Around 100 B C it was taken over by the Greeks and used as an outstation of their empire for one century until the insatiable Romans marched in and annexed the region. Then began Palmyra's illustrious period, first as a 'free city' and later as a *colonia* which allowed it exemption from taxes. At its peak in the third century the Palmyrenes' trading influence extended from Rome to India, and their leader, Septimus Odaenathus (partly of Arabic extraction), was appointed 'Governor of all the East' for having saved this corner of the Roman Empire from the powerful Sasanian forces of Iran. Palmyra's fall came within five years as a result of Odaenathus's second wife, Zenobia, whom Arab history records as az-Zabba, 'the murderous Queen'. In 268 she allegedly poisoned her husband and step-son, gave the now vacant titles of 'Governor of all the East' and '*King of Kings*' to her son, and led an army in defiance of Rome to claim the East and everything else besides. She captured Egypt and most of Asia Minor before her rampage was cut short. In 272 Zenobia was captured by the Romans, in 274 she was the showpiece in Aurelian's triumphal procession of captives, then she married a senator and became a housewife. Meanwhile Palmyra had been destroyed by the Romans. The city was restored but it remained relatively insignificant for a thousand years until sacked by Tamerlane, after which its ruins lay forgotten for the next 300 years. And they are still largely forgotten.

A luxury hotel stood empty in the shadow of the old city it had been built to serve, shunned by international tourists who preferred other destinations to the troubled Middle-East. Also in the shadow were a modern museum and a drab village of square buildings which had reverted to the role of Tadmor – the name it still bears in Arabic – as a depot on the road to the Euphrates. But the modern Tadmorians had clearly retained their old character and their small market was a glorious parade ground of the Arab wardrobe. Baggy trousers with crotches hanging down to the ankles, striped galabiyas, flowing caftans, and slippers tapering to curlicue points were prolific menswear. For protection against the sun men wore the traditional white headcloth held on with a heavy black band, what looked like a pile of washing their wives had dumped on their heads out of spite, or a crimson fez as sold by the local fez-maker who was moulding one hat in a hot press and cutting the next from a roll of fabric 'Made in Czechoslovakia'. Women moved about apparently blindly but with a pin-pricked window in the black chador that enveloped them from toe to crown and rendered them shapeless. A minority wore brighter colours but were still de-sexed and only recognisable as human by the eyes staring out from the chink in their yashmaks.

I saw everyone as Sinbads, Aladdins, genies, sheiks or Scheherazades until one woman appeared who didn't fit my portfolio. She wore an ankle-length gown of velvet, bright purple, and a black shawl which covered her head but left her face open and a few shocks of red hair exposed. Her features were Arabic despite her unusual colour of hair, and beautifully proportioned. A heavy gold chain hung from her neck down to her chest and she walked with a proud bearing. The effect was entrancing and I stood and stared until she disappeared. Then a man on a donkey almost knocked me over and I went to look for a hotel, passing a café of men smoking hookahs. They held a tube between their lips and sucked, creating bubbles four feet away in what resembled a Victorian lampstand adapted by Heath Robinson. Smoking, like praying, was man's work and seemingly a full-time occupation.

At the first down-market hostelry a man wearing Sinbad baggies led me upstairs to a dormitory. He found the door was locked from the inside and gave a heavy knock. He had to repeat this three times before the door was flung open. A youth of Asian appearance stood there bleary-eyed and half-dressed and began shouting in his own language. Then he changed to English.

'You hit my door like that again,' he snarled, 'and I will kill you.'

The manager seemed to have been expecting trouble and patted the air in a calming gesture. 'Please do not shout. There is no need to be angry. I have another guest. I am your friend.' He held out his hand. The Asian made a spitting gesture and held up clenched fists.

'You treat me like some animal . . . I'm just like you. You hit my door like that and I will kill you.'

I turned to go. The manager restrained me and the Asian grabbed one arm and said he was happy to have me. I said the atmosphere wasn't very welcoming and that I'd prefer not to interfere. The manager led me away and smiled weakly. 'I do not know the problem. He is a very angry man.' The next room had a spare bed amongst three Arab men my own age. One of them spoke fluent English and said they were students in Damascus.

'Are you originally from Damascus?' I asked.

'No, we are from Tiberius.'

'Tiberius in Is . . .' I caught myself just in time. ' . . . in Palestine?'

He smiled kindly. 'That's right. Those bastard Israelis have taken our homeland.'

'They would say they've only taken back what was theirs two thousand years ago.'

'And who owned it for two thousand years before that?'

'Can't you share it?'

'*Share* it?' It was only the absurdity of my suggestion that stopped him from raging. 'Impossible. How can you divide Palestine equally? You'd have to cut every desert, town and field into halves. And why should we give them anything? How would you feel if I came along to the house your family had owned for centuries, threw you out and killed some of your brothers? Would you want to make friends and settle for just a few rooms? No. Palestine will be ours again. One day . . . soon . . . we'll . . .' He left the threat unfinished.

My choice of roommates was between a murdering Mongol and three war-hungry Palestinians. I chose the Palestinians for fear that a third choice might prove worse. It was the sort of hostel that doubtless kept a few Greeks, Romans and Saracens on the boil too.

Hitching from Palmyra back to Homs proved easy and a truck driver gave me a lift the following morning. He spoke no English and I understood only one word during the three-hour journey. This was when we passed the largest military airfield in the country. Its radar scanner looked flimsy, like a clockwork decoration. He muttered in Arabic and then slammed his fist down on the dashboard. The word 'Israel' was unmistakable. The army made its presence felt in Syria – soldiers, convoys or camps were never far away. The heat made me drowsy as we followed an oil pipeline connecting Iraq to the Mediterranean but counting whirlwinds kept me awake. Eight of them once vacuumed the horizon simultaneously, sucking spiralling columns of dust and sand high into the sky like Indian rope tricks. Gradually sporadic salt bushes merged into scrubland and then flat plains of impoverished grazing flocks of brown sheep.

From Homs another lift took me downhill for forty miles and then uphill for the last stretch to the village at the base of Krak of the Knights. The driver, Husni al-Hourani, was on his way to visit his

parents who ran the village bakery and he invited me to stay the
night with them. Husni was short, stocky, meticulously groomed
with a pin-pointed moustache, and wore jeans and a casual shirt. He
had spent five years in Russia studying engineering at Leningrad
University, and considered Leningrad to be the most beautiful city
in the world. He had married a Russian girl and brought her back to
Syria along with their two-year-old son but then he had decided to
join the army and because it was forbidden for army personnel to be
married to foreigners, his wife and son had been forced to return to
Russia. He didn't seem to be upset by this ruling but had other
regrets.

'Syrian girls are no good,' he lamented. 'All short and fat. I like tall
blonde girls.' Customised Swedish girls seemed to be a central
fantasy of Arab men.

'Don't you miss your wife and son?'

'Of course, but it's not the end of the world. My career and
country come first.'

He told me his son had learnt to say the word 'boogie' and had
liked to dance to American disco music. His dashboard was lined
with such cassettes. In the same breath he said how much he hated
the United States because they gave money and arms to Israel.

'But you drive a Dodge,' I pointed out, 'and all other cars in Syria
are Pontiacs or Chevrolets if they aren't Mercedes'. You teach your
son American words, listen to American music and wear jeans . . . '

'That's only because these things are better than the other makes
we can buy here. I like Syrian music too.' He rummaged around in
another assortment of cassettes which all showed a late middle-aged
female singer of a typical Syrian build caught in full cry, clutching a
handkerchief and wearing dark glasses. I didn't want to take sides
because I couldn't understand the lyrics and was trying to bridge a
cultural gap that had me at full stretch, but I couldn't help feeling that
the woman whose voice we heard would have been better employed
within earshot of the Israeli trenches.

Husni called in at several houses on the way to visit friends. He
made me feel uncomfortable, as if a coldness was being suppressed
just below the surface and his kindness stemmed merely from my
novelty value. This feeling vanished when we met his parents and
the extended family that shared their house. They took me on a tour
of the bakery in the adjacent building to see a new machine which

rolled dough into pancakes the size of deflated beachballs. The Qal'at al Husn bakery employed one man and five boys not yet in their teens who were never stationary and broke sweat as they loaded gas-fired dome ovens. The dough-roller must have shown 'Jackpot' on its gauges from the generous way it spat out its goods and it had no idea of the stress it was causing on either side. We stood admiring it until it had created a pillar of pancakes up to the ceiling, and then moved on to the house. Only Husni spoke good English but the rest of the family had fluent smiles. They sat me on the living-room carpet, pulled a tablecloth over my knees and served a can of beer with a silver platter of cheese, olives, beachball slices of bread and salad. For a while they all gathered round and stared while I ate. Their scrutiny stemmed from the hope that twenty eyes might better spot any flaw in their hospitality, but there was none.

The house had looked typically drab from the outside but inside it was carpeted, furnished with armchairs, crafted cabinets displaying silverware and ornamental china, and beside some family photographs were a Canon SLR camera and a Sony colour television with video-recorder. I ate modestly and went out to a courtyard to sit in the sun. The family had disappeared except for a small boy tottering about and an old grandmother who sat in a chair. She grabbed the boy when he wandered within reach and began playing with him, bumping him up and down on her knees. A walking stick was propped against her chair. The wrinkles of her skin matched the grain of the wood and her bony wrists and arms were every bit as gnarled and knotted. She crooned baby noises and when he got bored and climbed down she caught him and hauled him back. Her face brightened as she played with her own longing, loving youth with the envy of age. The boy escaped. She smiled at his fading image. Then she sat morosely in her chair and seemed to grow older by the minute.

Husni's family sent me on my way the next morning with an invitation to return and an armful of bread. The streets slanted upwards to the edge of the village and then a road continued to wind upwards to Krak of the Knights. The castle seemed to grow more immense with every step. In its time it was the foremost bastion of the land and for one and a half centuries, as one Muslim chronicler wrote, 'it stuck like a bone in the very throat of the Saracens'. Its defences were formidable and cunning, its base was of solid rock which prevented the walls from being undermined – the greatest technical danger to a castle under attack – and with its own water supply, immense oil storage facility and granary, and even a windmill on its battlements for grinding corn, the castle was equipped to outlast years of siege. Krak of the Knights remains the finest and most remarkable example of military architecture of the twelfth and thirteenth centuries.

As a result of its solid construction, good fortune and careful restoration by the French, Krak looked as though it could still enjoy a good siege. It stood on one spur of a horseshoe-shaped summit with steep slopes falling away on three sides, and its concentric design, incorporating a tall outer wall and a much taller inner wall, meant that in effect it was a castle within a castle. Even if an assailant chose the side with the weakest natural defences he would still have to cross the moat that ran around the whole construction. He would then face the great outer wall with its regular towers and arrow slits permitting flanking fire from the defenders and its parapets for their convenience in administering hot oil. Once over this he would find a second moat, wider and deeper than the first, and rising out of its far side, the acutely sloping talus of the inner walls, *eighty* feet thick at their base and towering sixty feet above the surface of the water. After this he would have reached the inner ward, the main living area, and would be home though scarcely dry. This approach was possibly easier than by way of the main entrance; two long tunnels sloping uphill, perforated with holes for arrows and oil and amply furnished with barriers, sharp bends and posterns where equally sharp knights gathered for surprise attacks. Either way, wet or dry, the inner ward contained a final test for the so-far successful invader – a redoubt of such strength it was a third castle in addition to the two he had just penetrated.

Armed only with a newly-acquired booklet on Syria's archaeological heritage, I reached the main entrance and found the gates open and Krak deserted. Not a soul was there, just the suspense of unsprung ambushes round dark corners and the silence of 700 years. Krak's origin lay in a more modest fortress which the Kurds had built on this spot. By 1100 the fortress was in Frankish hands and in 1142 it was transferred to the charge of the prominent knights of the Crusades, the Order of Hospital. They converted the fortress into its present form, made it their headquarters and remained in occupation for the rest of its undefeated history. The Hospitallers withstood at least twelve full-scale sieges, survived severe earthquake damage in 1170 and, eighteen years later, thwarted the ambition of the mighty Saladin who briefly assessed the castle's strength and went away without attempting an assault.

After 1250 Frankish power in the Holy Lands began to decline, all around castles fell to the army of Sultan Baibars and by early 1271 only Krak and Margat remained of the great northern castles, but both were crucially undermanned. Baibars, known at the time as the 'Panther', was an efficient general but, unlike Saladin whose character won wide respect among Christian historians, he was noted for his brutality and fondness for torture. He began his siege of Krak on 3 March 1271, and by the end of the month his men had penetrated the inner ward. The knights and fighting monks withdrew to the redoubt and held out for a further ten days. It is believed Baibars wanted to take the castle intact and brought about the final surrender by delivering a letter in which the Franks' commander at Tripoli instructed them to yield. The letter was a forgery but on 10 April the Hospitallers laid down their arms and for the first time in 161 years, Krak of the Knights was conquered.

My footsteps echoed in rooms with arched doorways, three-leafed clover windows and beautifully vaulted ceilings as I tried to recognise 'box-machicoulis' and 'merlons' from a guidebook that was a mixture of medieval construction terms and propaganda. (For an archaeological report it made good mileage out of Krak's demise; ' . . . even this great Crusader castle had eventually fallen to the superiority of the Syrian Arabs who liberated their land from the invading forces, just as we will always fight to defend our homeland.') The castle's inner ward covered seven acres and consisted of a courtyard from which staircases spiralled up, sometimes for six storeys, into the surrounding buildings. One staircase led me to the Chamber of the Grand Master, still decorated with a frieze of flowers. In 1268 the Grand Master was one Hughes Revel and in this room he penned a letter home bemoaning the castle's inadequate resources and lack of manpower. In 1200 the castle had maintained a garrison of around 2000 knights but in 1268 Krak and Margat *together* could only muster 300. These men had been quartered in the castle's largest room, a great curved hall 400 feet long. I wondered how many roasted oxen 2000 Crusaders would consume after a hard day's battle. It was fascinating to speculate. A nearby room had been tastefully restored and contained some of the large earthenware pots once used for storing olive oil. Then came the two kitchens, one for making the oil and the other for preparing food. A vast bread oven was to be found there as well as the castle well which provided no barrier and no dark mirror to distort my face – just a five second drop and a splash for a small stone or, for that matter, a careless visitor. As was common in the castles of the day, the kitchen was near the twin-level dungeon so that the banquet aromas would tantalise those who more often than not were left to starve to death. The Crusaders were punitive forces out for their own glory, and not the first to use the name of religion as a suppository for their own nastiness.

Finally I reached the top of the redoubt and while gazing down from this vantage point, as every Grand Master must have done with a degree of arrogance, I noticed a taxi drive up to the castle entrance and deposit two tourists. In 1240, say, we would have been ready for them. The oil would be simmering. Under a hail of arrows they would have to swim the moat, batter through the raised drawbridge and enter the first tunnel. Through loopholes with bell-shaped bases we would be pumping them full of arrows as they tried to break down four sets of gates and one portcullis, negotiate three elbow bends and hack a way through ambushers sallying out from the posterns. Soldiers would be running with jars of scalding oil to replenish the gallons already descending on the couple through the machicoulis (holes in the roof for this very purpose). My mind interrupted the attack to consider the implications of this in more detail. Even if the oil had been cold, how could anyone find the enthusiasm to fight with a greasy liquid trickling down chest and back, slurping through breeches and filling up boots? The tourists were still advancing. They entered the gap between the two tunnels, exposing themselves to the heavy rocks we sent crashing down. They would find another portcullis in the next tunnel, another shower of arrows and still plenty hot oil. But they appeared in the courtyard having strolled through unscathed, their straight black hair still smoothed down and cameras gently rubbing against their stomachs. Apart from withdrawing to our final refuge there was nothing left to us but the futile gesture of dropping a half-eaten cow on them.

I went down to meet the invaders on my way out of the castle. To my surprise they were Japanese. We nodded on passing and then I stopped to examine a piece of stonework. They stopped before a pile of rusting cannonballs from a later period. I can't imagine why they spoke in English, but they did.

She said, 'They certainly had so many of those ballbearing things in those days.'

He replied, 'They aren't ballbearings, they're bombs.'

How very odd. Did Japan miss out on the real cannon?

16 · Quietly, Heavily, Through Gallipoli and the Somme

In 1915 my grandfather on my mother's side was in Western Turkey. He was twenty-six years old, newly qualified as a doctor and, like 160,000 other volunteers, one of the 'lions led by donkeys' (according to one contemporary description) trying to gain access to Constantinople by taking the Gallipoli Peninsula. The 600-year-old Ottoman Empire had declined and was ailing but Turkey still comprised a vast territory in 1915, including Syria, Palestine, Arabia and Iraq. The disastrous Gallipoli campaign lasted eight and a half months and was a tragic case of misjudgement, of a blundering delay that lost the advantage of surprise and enabled 'Johnnie Turk' to complete his defences, of insufficient forces thrown gloriously at impregnable positions, of stalemate and ultimate success only in evacuation. Before the campaign was called off an estimated 265,000 British, ANZAC and allied soldiers had been killed, one-sixth of these while advancing on the steep open hills where 40,000 Turks and Germans were securely entrenched, and uncounted numbers freezing to death during a winter storm which hit the coast unexpectedly early. The outcome of Gallipoli might have been different if Lieutenant-Colonel Mustafa Kemal ('maturity and perfection') had not been the Turkish commander and if the bullet that smashed the watch in his breast pocket and was deflected as he stood on the Heights of Sari Bair had been aimed fractionally to one side. Three years earlier he had been put in charge of the Peninsula's defence and had made a thorough strategic survey. He knew the region intimately and his policies proved decisive in the resulting victory, and marked the advent of his rise to power. The 'saviour of Constantinople' and 'father of modern Turkey', Atatürk, as he later became known, restored pride in the Turkish people after their eventual defeat and prevented their country from being shared out as booty.

My grandfather was a gentle and quiet man. He served with the RAMC and was attached to the 6th Battalion North Lancs, but his time in Gallipoli was shortened by sickness, endemic on the fly-infested

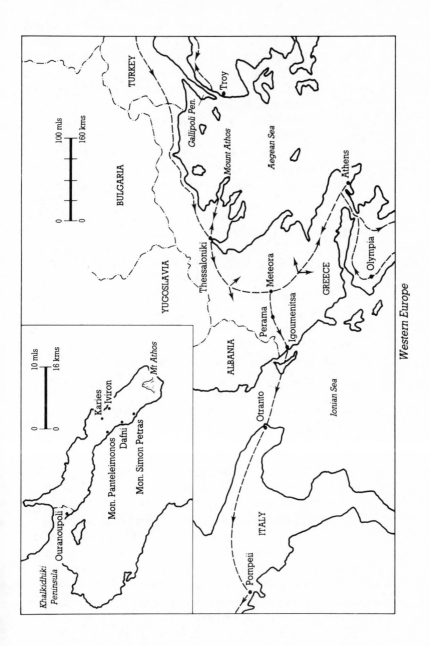

Western Europe

Peninsula. After his recovery he was sent to France, and later decorated for his work in gassed trenches. He survived the war but I never heard him talk about his ordeal because he died when I was too young to think of asking and besides, it was evidently a subject he never discussed. Years later I came across a diary of his early war experiences but, to my disappointment, the entries ended shortly after his arrival at Gallipoli. My interest was roused, however, and I sought out other diaries from the campaign in order to see what my grandfather's blank pages might have said, and found those of 2/Lieutenant (later Lt-Colonel) Malcolm Hancock and Captain (later Major) Raymond Lane. From then on I felt a strong compulsion to visit Gallipoli to see the shape of the land they and my grandfather had looked out on seventy years earlier and to place myself at the scene of something I couldn't begin to comprehend.

Laying a piece of string against the map and measuring a route from the Syrian border through the centre of Turkey to Gallipoli gave a familiar result – about one thousand miles. Over the next eleven days hitching produced several periods of doldrums but allowed me to cover the distance on a par with the bus schedule. (Many of my lifts were in British Leyland trucks – the company had made quite a killing in Turkey with a model called 'Crusader'.) The journey was mountainous for most of its length. At first dry and rugged the terrain became more productive for a spell with wheat fields filling valleys from wall to wall with gold, and then turned to the high stony plateau in the centre of the country which was given over to small farms and grazing. Turkey is the largest wool producer in Europe and grows more hazel nuts than any other country in the world. The hazel trees preferred the area around the Black Sea but the sheep were abundant in the centre. One flock blocked the street of a small town in Cappadocia and the dye marks on their fleeces were so colourful it was like watching a Persian carpet walk past. The houses of Cappadocia all had flat roofs where apricots were laid out to dry and when seen from above they formed startling patterns in bright orange, but the area's most unusual feature was its bizarre gnomeland scenery. Countless pinnacles rose up as twisted cones of white, red, yellow and grey rock and many were patterned by dark rectangles of doorways and windows. A thousand years ago Christians had hollowed out troglodyte homes and even entire underground cities in the soft rock to escape persecution. Further to the west on the approach to the Dardanelles, Turkey rounded off its varied character with Alpine meadows, woods and white houses with red roofs.

The Dardanelles, a strait forty miles long and one mile wide at its narrowest, has medieval castles on both sides and Troy at one end to show that it has long been regarded as a military prize. Here Asia and Europe almost touch but in failing they allow ships access to what is now Istanbul, the Black Sea and Russia. The scars had healed well and to me it seemed unlikely that the small fishing villages along the strait had witnessed anything more violent than frail boats of anglers being rocked in the wakes of Russian freighters that passed at frequent intervals. I crossed onto the European side, the Gallipoli Peninsula, hitched a short lift and walked the remaining twelve miles to the first war cemeteries of Anzac and Suvla on the far side. The countryside was sparsely inhabited but some of the western beaches were popular with local day-trippers. The road wound through hills which were now thickly covered in pine forest and brush. Every so often there were acres of orchards and irrigated fields where corn, vegetables and vines were growing handsomely. It was a quiet August afternoon. The air was warm under a cloudless sky and sweet with pollen from the wild flowers that lined the way:

> The land was rough and uninviting, with scrubby thorn bushes growing up to four or five feet high. And it wasn't very green but dreary-looking country, a dull misty grey . . .

wrote 2/Lieutenant Hancock in the summer of 1915. The sudden snowstorm had not yet come and the days were oppressively hot. Water was always scarce, the sounds of shelling and gunfire allowed no peace and the air around Hill 60 carried no fragrance of pollen, just the smells of cordite's greeny-yellow flash, and worse, as he described to his parents in a letter dated 26 September:

> . . . the enemy must have suffered pretty heavy losses for the dead were lying in and around the trenches in heaps. A fortnight later, when we first went up there we found these heaps lying outside the trenches and left half exposed. In the heat they had reached most appalling stages of decomposition, and even the very sight of them made one feel sick. In one particular spot so many had been killed that a part of the trench, some thirty or forty yards long, was

filled with bodies four or five deep and practically no attempt had
been made to cover them in. We have just had to dig another
trench round this one and a more revolting job could scarcely be
imagined. . . . we lived here [under these conditions] for about
ten or twelve days, and had I not seen these things for myself I
could hardly have given credit to them.

Now can you wonder that soldiers want cigarettes? It is not for
the sake of smoking them, but in order to as far as possible
counteract the revolting smells which pervaded, and still do in one
or two places, the whole network of the trenches. No, we smoke
them in self-defence . . .

Hill 60, sloping gradually up to a crest that was low in comparison
to the neighbouring ranges, was three miles north of the point where
my road reached the Aegean Sea after traversing the Peninsula. Here
the road forked, one branch running along the coast in the direction
of Hill 60 and the other turning into the woods. Two Turkish
families camping on a beach waved to me and I went over to ask
them which road would take me to some white monuments on a
distant hilltop that had been visible earlier. We spoke in German as
this was Turkey's second language. Many Turks had worked in
Germany as *Gastarbeiter* and these families were no exceptions.
Within minutes they had opened a bottle of wine, set a plate of
chicken before me and surrounded it with bowls of vegetables, fruit,
bread and cakes.

This was typical of my treatment in Turkey. If Syrian hospitality
had been remarkable, that of Turkey was overwhelming. The Turks
seemed to look for opportunities to offload kindness onto me. On
occasions soldiers had helped me hitchhike by stopping cars and
asking the driver to give me a lift. Some drivers had gone miles out
of their way to deliver me to my destination, and some who were
stopping short had dropped me off at a bus station and secretly paid
my fare. Shopkeepers had frequently scorned money or else given
twice the value of goods in exchange. Families had given me a bed
for the night even when we hadn't a single word in common, and a
woman had once stopped her horse and cart, while riding *downhill*,
and filled my arms with apricots. She had refused all my efforts at
payment. 'Well what can I do with these?' I had asked, holding out a
rich handful of lirasi. 'I'm never allowed to spend them.' She had
replied, 'In Turkey you are our guest. Please, just accept.' Here at

Gallipoli it was the same. Hostility has nothing to do with nationality, place or instinct – it is as transient and irrational as the whims of
fashion.

After my meal we went swimming in the blue-green waters of
Anzac Cove and the two families tried to persuade me to stay the
night. One of the wives held up a large white rabbit that was
intended for the pot and her husband broke into a sort of Highland
Fling to indicate the festivities in store. It was hard to refuse but
when they saw that I really wanted to find the monuments before
sunset, they prepared a large bag of food and one of the men, Salih
Göklan, said he would drive me to the place. His son came too and
we set off up through the woods. The irony of the situation did not
escape me – speaking German with Turks and being driven in a
Volkswagen towards the lines where, seventy years earlier, my
grandfather had been confronted with 'bullets from Turkish rifles
spattering on the ground like hail', and Captain Lane had met with a
similar reception:

> [the guns] . . . opened up with a shattering concentrated burst of
> fire. In response to this timed reverberating crash, great chunks of
> the Peninsula shot up into the air in a mighty flurry of dust, smoke
> and confusion. . . . in the split second that sometimes seems to be
> given in moments of crisis, I received a fearful shock of astonish-
> ment that these men, whom I had known and loved so well, and
> who, but a few brief seconds before were so full of life and eager
> excitement, could be flung into such grotesque shapes at the touch
> of a small fragment of flying metal no larger than one of the joints
> of my little finger.
>
> . . . Masses of stricken bodies were still lying there, just as they
> had fallen. It seemed as if the whole Battalion was there but
> petrified into uncouth shapes that had no meaning. The sea
> presented an even grimmer spectacle, the little red wavelets
> frothing up around and over the closely-packed bodies, some face
> downwards as if hiding from the light of day – whilst the grey
> dead faces of those who stared sightlessly through the crimson
> water will remain forever in my mind as a grim reminder of the
> stupidity of war.
>
> . . . Men could be seen to crumple up quietly, as if tired of the
> whole proceedings. Many of the boats began to drift, helplessly
> and sideways onto the shore. Still more boatloads came into view

to suffer the same devastating annihilation – a few temporary survivors threw themselves into the sea and clung to the trailing ropes until, in this unprotected state, they were shot one by one – and quietly letting go, became one with the red water . . . Each boat, as it came into sight, had its Midshipman in the stern – bolt upright, and with never a blench at the butchery that was all around.

'Just look at those Midshipmen,' I said to Henderson. 'They're only kids.'

He just nodded, and I noticed that his eyes were filled with tears.

Our Volkswagen stopped at a rusty gun still in position but now deep in fir trees. Its barrel, broken at the tip, remained elevated and aimed towards the beaches. Even now relics could be found all over the Peninsula. A few days previously Salih had come across a .303 cartridge and two bones, human finger bones. He described two lead bullets that had collided in mid-air and had been discovered years ago. One had penetrated the other from the side and they had fallen to the ground interlocked in a perfect X. It was a chance in a million but, of course, millions of bullets had flown. When it rained, he said, you could smell the battle.

'Are any of your family buried here?' Salih's ten-year-old son asked. I shook my head and explained about my grandfather. 'And what about your family?'

'My grandfather's brother was killed here,' he said.

Salih gazed along the line of the barrel and sighed. 'Nobody won at Gallipoli. Everyone lost.'

We drove past signposts to some of the forty cemeteries on the Peninsula: Lone Pine, Brown's Dip, Shrapnel Valley, Parade Ground, Johnston's Jolly, Baby 700 . . . 36,000 Allies were buried here, 27,000 in nameless graves. Salih explained that for many years the Turks had felt sad that all the cemeteries belonged to foreigners and their 300,000 dead had none. According to custom they had been buried where they fell and their graves were now lost. But the government had recently erected a circle of five elegant slabs twenty feet high and tapering at their base as a memorial to the Turks who died, and these were the white stones on the Heights of Sari Bair that I had seen from the road.

We entered Lone Pine cemetery, by chance on the exact

anniversary (6th August) of its creation. The single pine was still on the hilltop at one end of ranks of carefully-tended graves. Mainly Australians were buried here as a result of the Anzac's heroic but costly seizure of the ridge. Of the nine Victoria Crosses awarded on the Peninsula during August, seven were won that afternoon on this spot. I walked along reading ages that made me feel old; 18, 21, 26, 20, 22, 20 . . . The names of familiar Australian towns transported my mind back to that country, to a hill in the south-west near Albany, to the ANZAC memorial overlooking the bay from which the troop ships sailed to take these young men to the battlefields of Europe. That hill I was remembering had once been in the minds of those that lay beneath my feet as their last view of their homeland. My journey around the world was not so disjointed. There were many links and one of them ran from that hill in SW Australia to this almost identical hill on a remote peninsula in Turkey. No logic, nothing but the whims of fashion.

'Their name liveth for evermore,' read the stones, 'Their glory shall not be blotted out . . . Lord thou knowest best . . . To the memory of my dear husband . . . Reached the fartherest objective till the dawn break, and shadows flee . . . He died for God, Right and Liberty, and such a death is immortality . . . Could I just clasp your hand once more and say, Well Done . . . He has changed his faded coat of brown for one of glorious white . . . A mother's thoughts often wander to this sad and lonely grave . . .' The sentiments vacillated from the emotional to the virtuous, expressions of grief and shreds of comfort to take the place of reason. 565,000 dead sons. How many must mourn 565,000?

Five weeks later I visited the battlefield of the Somme, my last stop before returning to Britain. Its graveyards intensified the emotions I had felt at Gallipoli. 1,200,000 lives were taken here during four months of 1916, half of them Allied soldiers who died for a gain of a thousand yards of mud. 19,240 died on the very first day and the majority in the first hour. The scale of death was meaningless until it became tangible, beautifully landscaped into gardens and symmetrical patterns which occupied great tracts of French farmland.

In a Newfoundlanders' cemetery at Beaumont-Hamel, beneath the bronze statue of a caribou with its head thrown back in full bellow, I met a fifty-year-old Canadian who was working with the

NATO forces in Germany. We looked out at the trenches and bomb craters which were now covered in grass and neatly mown. Rain added a fitting sense of gloom to the scene.

'The worst is that we haven't learnt anything from it,' I commented.

'No,' he answered. 'We should have listened to General Paton at the end of the last war. He said then that seeing as all our army and war machinery were over here, we ought to just carry on and finish off the Communists.'

'Do you honestly believe another twenty million dead Russians would have solved today's problems?' His answer angered and depressed me. 'That's exactly the bigoted attitude that caused all this. Why must everyone always think "fight" and "kill" instead of looking for ways of trying to work together?'

He called me a dreamer, an idealist. We argued for some time until eventually I turned and walked away while he was expounding on the *Soviet Threat*. Employees of the war business always stressed it big. I had no will to fight.

My generation had never known war. We had never experienced its power to unite towards a common goal nor its camaraderie, but we had been spared its destruction and horrors. There had to be a turning point, when the world actively worked towards the ideal of peace rather than hoping to achieve it by threatening war.

Yes, I was a dreamer. It was a modest dream . . . that all the world's leaders might be brought here once every year – for our memories are short – to wander alone through the Somme. They would see tens of thousands of white crosses and roses that bloom red and sway in the breeze, knocking against the inscriptions 'A Soldier of the Great War' and at the bottom, 'Known unto God'. Perhaps they would be able to feel the solitude, the sadness, the folly. Perhaps in this panorama of white tombstones a united sense of responsibility would emerge.

Concluding his *History of the Great War*, John Buchan wrote (in 1921–2),

Again, the ground had been cleared for a better ordering of the world, much of the débris of past ages was now estimated at its true worthlessness, ancient inequitable frontiers could be adjusted, old wrongs could be righted. Again, the magnitude and the horrors of the contest had gone far to sicken mankind of strife and predispose them to find a more rational way of settling differences. Already the conception of a true internationalism was dawning which should add to the patriotism of races and nations a patriotism of humanity.

I left Beaumont-Hamel and carried my dream northwards. The cemeteries of the Somme seemed to go on forever, stretching insignificantly towards the patriotism of humanity.

17 · Under the Holy Shadow of Mount Athos

The Khalkidhiki Peninsula juts out from the north-east coast of Greece like a three-clawed footprint. At the point of the right-hand claw is Mount Athos, a sharp 6670-foot-high peak which gives its name to a state that is unique in the world. It is an autonomous monastic state, independent from the Greek government, with dimensions twenty-five miles long and five to seven miles wide that are occupied largely by a steep range of hills. This leaves little level ground for its one village situated in the centre, its hundreds of cells and hermitages scattered throughout, and its twenty gigantic monasteries which, for the most part, hold their irreplaceable Byzantine treasures close to the sea. Mount Athos is a restricted area. Its land border is closed to traffic, no woman or female animal is allowed to enter the community and access for male visitors is strictly controlled by a limited number of permits. In order to acquire one of these permits I became the personal message-bearer of the British Consulate. It was a distinction that cost me 840 drachmas (£6).

ΖΑΧΑΡΟΠΛΑΣΤΕΙΟΝ ΛΟΚΜΑΔΕΣ

Shortly after entering the country I stared at this sign and admired the magnificent Greek alphabet. A smaller sign beneath it said 'Do'nuts for sale'. Everything looks much more important in Greek and judging from their love of words ten feet long, the Greeks know it. I travelled from Konstantinoupoli to Alexandroupoli, Eleftheroupoli and Thessaloniki, and bought two extra biros for writing my diary. My application for a permit to visit Mount Athos had to be accompanied by a letter of recommendation from the British Consulate. One morning I was waiting outside the Consul's door when he arrived for work. He ushered me into his office for a short interview.

'Of course Mount Athos is not a place for tourists . . .' he began.

'I don't consider myself a tourist, sir.'

This was the right answer. Without delving any deeper into my character he signed a form and passed it to his secretary. She typed out the date and four words from my passport on a machine that needed a new ribbon. I felt they could have afforded one out of the fee, but I was delighted to have the bit of paper. It was nothing special, not even headed paper but a skeleton photocopy of diplomatic claptrap with my details filling the blanks, and only distinguished by a rubber stamp:

> The British Consulate present their compliments to the Ministry of Northern Greece and have the honour to request them to be so good as to grant a permit to visit Mount Athos to the undermentioned British subject. The British Consulate avail themselves of this opportunity to renew to the Ministry of Northern Greece the assurance of their highest consideration.

Written in Greek, the message would have looked devastating.

Clutching this bit of paper I went to the office of the Ministry to pass on the request and renew the Consulate's assurances. The Ministry took the news calmly and one of its officials explained that all permits were booked for the next week. A permit was valid for a five-day visit and only ten such permits were issued each day. I booked the first available place, paid another fee and took the permit to a police station to be stamped. All that remained was to be at the small harbour town of Ouranoupoli, just under 100 miles away, in time for the morning ferry to Mount Athos on the day my permit specified.

Before leaving Thessaloniki (Salonika) I sent a message home asking for my kilt and sporran to be sent out to me. They had travelled with me, around me, for most of the miles between Iceland and Australia and it seemed fitting that we should end the journey together. The impulse to dash for home was growing ever stronger and there were times when it seemed I could smell the damp heather of the Highlands (I had been away too long and hackneyed images were all that were left, but they held an irresistible attraction all the same). I had decided not to rush Greece but once in Italy to cover the remaining distance to Britain without delay.

The Khalkidhiki footprint was a dry mountainous peninsula where tobacco and grapes were grown, Aristotle once lived and hitching was slow. My first lift was at 10 mph with three old men who laughed often enough for me to see they had twelve teeth between them. They wore large cloth caps and off-the-peg jackets, off the wrong peg mostly. On hearing I came from Scotland they nodded and frowned sympathetically. Their destination was a village church in the hills where a festival was taking place in honour of the Virgin Mary and they invited me to come along. There would be all-night folk dancing, said the one with three of the teeth, adding that dancing must surely be scarce in Scotland under the present circumstances.

This remark puzzled me. 'Are you familiar with Scotland?' I asked.

No, he admitted, but they had all heard about it and its war with El Salvador. The others agreed. I suggested there had to be a misunderstanding. The two countries were thousands of miles apart and had nothing to quarrel over. They remained adamant. It had been in the news recently. Either they were wrong, I reflected, or else it was high time I was back at home. Or maybe it was best to give home a miss and keep travelling? It was the first time the thought had occurred to me.

The church was outside the village on a forested hillside and was thronged with hundreds of people. On a stage set before the main door a chain of schoolchildren were demonstrating dances to the accompaniment of an electric bouzouki. The musician seesawed and bounced his bow over the strings and occasionally *pizzicatoed* to produce scintillating limb-jerking melodies, but the dancers were restrained compared to what a crowd of Trinidadians would have made of the music. Girls in gypsy frocks seemed most concerned with poise and timing while their dark uniformed partners endeavoured to keep control of a yellow pompom at the end of their long drooping nightcaps, and some clearly wished they were in Trinidad.

Beyond them a shantytown of stalls offered religious souvenirs, hydrogen balloons depicting ΜΙΚU ΜΑΟUS, ΤΑρΖΑΝ swinging through jungle and Superman escaping from green ΚρуπΤσΝΙΤΗΣ; hot dogs, teddy bears and books, amongst which was one in English on the Loch Ness Monster.

'This is in Scotland!' I exclaimed, holding out one of the photographs to the three old men, but they showed no sign of interest as if it were something banal like a Scottish submarine off San Salvador.

Informal dances sprang up in the crowd who, fortified by ouzo, carried on all night. Greek dances were ideal social events as they absorbed everyone, were simple enough for strangers in boots to cope with and supported the shoulders of those unaccustomed to ouzo. The old men danced away their age and were still dancing when I went to get a few hours sleep in the cemetery which doubled as a campsite. By morning the atmosphere was sober in preparation for the day of religious ceremonies.

These culminated in a procession led by four bishops, resplendent in red, white, yellow and purple dalmatics, gold chains and black hats trailing black veils. They all possessed luxuriously bushy Moses beards and a solemn dignity that inspired rather than conveyed God-fearingness. The one leading flicked an incense ball on a chain in a hypnotic motion that made a regular *chink* and emitted a puff of blue vapour. Behind them came an icon of the Virgin in a ponderous sedan chair carried by four men. The effort was visible in their faces and yet they looked proud and unquestioning as to why a small lightweight picture had to be set in half a ton of baroque woodwork.

I was looking at the icon while its bearers rested before reaching the main crowd when I noticed that policemen had roped the other spectators back and formed a tight cordon around this section of the procession and I was caught in the middle. The crowd suddenly swelled around us, the police tightened their circle to prevent anyone breaking through and the procession set off once more amid shouts and wild gesticulations. My position among the dignitaries was acutely embarrassing but at that moment it appeared less disruptive to try and slip submissively along than to struggle out, and the advancing icon forced me to keep a close step behind the bishops. Rows of adoring faces were smiling at us, hundreds of arms were waving and handkerchiefs were fluttered in abundance. My embarrassment was replaced by surprise. The air was charged with emotion and it was impossible not to respond. The mass of smiling faces was inexhaustible. I smiled back and once I got carried away and gave a little wave. Arms flailed the air. Someone threw a cup of scented water at us. A bishop and I had to duck but we still got wet. He was forced to steady his hat and I tried to catch his eye so we could share a laugh. The crowd was growing hysterical and there was a carnival atmosphere. Then I went cold.

People were bowing, kneeling, holding out clasped hands and crossing themselves. Before the bishops? The icon? – suddenly it didn't seem to matter which. Such was fervour to worship that the

objects of worship became confused and assumed fanatical importance. I merely happened to be caught between an excited crowd and
intermediaries of their faith, and the effect was frightening. People
struggled and fought their way through the densely packed bodies,
broke the police line and threw themselves on the ground before the
bishops and the icon. They waited until the holy image had passed
over them, and those who couldn't reach it threw articles of clothing
into the path of its shadow. I found a way out as the bedlam grew
worse. The procession still held together and disappeared into the
church. The police regained control and formed a chain behind the
tail to stop the throng from following. They pushed and jostled and
clamoured around the blockade. I saw an aged woman who was
pitifully frail. She was down on her hands and knees trying to crawl
between the policemen's legs, and getting nowhere. She had missed
the icon's shadow and was crying.

It was the start of a very unusual day. With one of my tent's
guy-ropes tied to a notice that said 'Camping strictly forbidden' in
four languages, I could hardly tell the policeman who woke me early
in the morning that I hadn't seen it. I apologised and explained that I
preferred these sorts of places as they tended to attract the dedicated
camper and keep away the noisy element, and besides, my campsites
were always left in immaculate condition. Fortunately he accepted
this and didn't delay me as it was the day my Mount Athos permit
became valid and I was still twenty miles short of the ferry at
Ouronoupoli. It was a bus full of workmen that took me there. They
all sat on the left-hand side of the bus for the first half of the journey
and then changed to the right-hand side when we crossed an
isthmus, always keeping as close to the sea as possible. Camping by
the road to the holy Mount was usually frowned upon but topless
sunbathing was often admired.

A group of around fifty men were waiting for the ferry and most
were Greeks who apparently did not require a permit. We set off and
the boat kicked up a powerful wake alongside the wooded peninsula
that rose steeply to its central ridge. Occasionally valleys cut through
the ridge as deep clefts but there were no roads, monasteries or signs
of life to be seen, just dolphins knitting patterns before our bow and
flying fish gliding on transparent fins that glinted in the sun. Small
hermitages began to appear along the coast and then the storehouses

of monasteries reared up as castellated towers, each with its own jetty. These were impressive enough but the monasteries, when they first came into view, were awesome. They were immense constructions, strikingly similar to the monasteries and palaces of Ladakh, rising to five or six storeys but then doubling their height by sitting on massive fortress walls. The upper sections were of wood and too large for their foundations so that they spilled out and were held over long drops by angled supports. Balconies, rooms and even entire annexes had been tacked on and left precariously attached to the solid core. The buildings had towers, spires, hundreds of windows, red, green or yellow walls and red roofs, and yet each monastery had fitted these ingredients into a unique design. Above all, it was their sheer magnitude that made the most forceful impression.

The majority of monasteries on Mount Athos are one thousand years old, the notable exceptions being the oldest with fifth-century foundations and the two youngest dating from the fourteenth century. All have been either partially or totally rebuilt as a result of accidental fire or damage caused by pirates who repeatedly attacked and preyed on the peninsula. At its peak in the fifteenth century there were 40,000 monks to be found here and forty monasteries, of which only half have survived. They are all Eastern Orthodox, and all are Greek except one Serbian, one Bulgarian and one Russian, the largest, Agiou Panteleimonos. We passed it shortly before reaching the main jetty at Dafni. Beneath its onion domes it was still a vast edifice and said to count 3000 cells within its walls. In 1903 there were 1446 monks using its thirty-five chapels, but now its outer buildings were burnt-out shells and each of the thirty resident monks of Panteleimonos could have had a chapel to himself.

A bus met the boat and took us five miles up multiple bends to the top of the hill and then down a few more to Karies, the state capital. It was a strange place, nestling at the foot of another monastery which dwarfed the few streets. The buildings all had an ecclesiastical appearance except the police-administration office which was Corinthian, a straggle of houses which were tumble-down and a few faceless shops where monks sold crucifixes, maps and a narrow range of wares. The monks walking around were equalled in number by plain-clothed workmen. There wasn't a single woman in Mount Athos. A few dogs strolled the streets, large healthy-looking dogs, all wearing a bell. They were wonderfully friendly and responded to attention by lowering their heads, looking up from the tops of their eyes and wagging their tails feverishly. Except for the tail-wagging it was a pious gesture. They didn't seem to mind that there wasn't a single bitch in Mount Athos.

At the police station my permit was stamped and an additional fee of 500 drachmas was charged to cover hospitality and accommodation. No more money changed hands during a visitor's stay and he was free to visit any monastery where an evening meal and a bed would be provided if available. From Karies I set off downhill towards the east coast on a gravel road. Little hermitages appeared all over the wooded hillsides. Many looked derelict but inhabited; shoes stood on a doorstep, tinned catfood rested on a window ledge and a mule grazed in a garden below a laden fig tree. When the road came to a fork the choice of routes was marked on the arms of a cross, and a cautionary message was given on a square board alongside. 'A forest is a place of calming and God smiling – protect it from fire.' The only person to pass was a monk driving a Ferrari tractor. Even this was done with great dignity though his tall cylindrical hat looked slightly out of place. Then Iviron Monastery loomed up out of the trees ahead with a sense of unblinking permanence.

A monk leaving on a mule directed me to the entrance in the lofty walls, a passage which led between marble pillars, past golden icons and into a courtyard monopolised by a large church in the middle and a chapel in each corner. The walls of the courtyard were lined with corbelled balconies on different levels, the lowest overgrown with vines that threatened their collapse through the weight of red grapes. There were no more than five monks shuffling about on their own. They each looked 110 years old, small bent figures in black, straggly unkempt beards in white. Their manner was one of being tired and dazed but I supposed that was only to be expected at such an age. None spoke English but one led me upstairs to a dormitory at the end of a long corridor and we were followed by the echo of his lugubrious plod. It was a simple room with a bare wooden floor, cracks in the whitewashed walls, a cupboard with one door missing and the other reduced to a riddle by woodworm, four beds and a small window. Through the window the outer gardens were visible. A monk was working there beside a scarecrow, a black cassock draped over a cross, and for most of the time it was impossible to tell which was which. Another direction showed a wall of the monastery, a sagging roof, broken slates and windows, drooping balconies and chairs holding one leg in the air over warped floorboards. On this side Iviron's permanence was blinking. It was like a visual puzzle that distorted perspective.

Only three monks came for supper that evening and I sat with them at one end of a marble table with a surface area of thirty square feet. There were twenty-eight of these tables in the dining room, all of them empty except ours. We ate in silence; one portion of white rice, a spoonful of tomato sauce, bread, olives and a glass of water. After the meal it became dark quickly. A monk gave me a kerosene lamp and then he disappeared with the others. Shadows from the lamp danced around me as I made my way back to the dormitory, the air smelt of dust, cobwebs wavered from the ceiling and floorboards squeaked. One of the passage doors swung with such an evocative multi-toned groan that I gave it an extra push just for the pleasure of listening to it. Never has a building appeared more animate.

I woke in the night to the sound of a door banging in the dark with a regularity that suggested someone was doing it on purpose. It was just the wind. No electricity, no switch for magic light. I fumbled for matches but before I could find them the room suddenly lit up for a fraction of a second. I was still bewildered by all these happenings when a crash of thunder sounded close to the roof and made the whole building shake. I went to the window. A fork of lightning stabbed the darkness and cut a bright scar across the night, throwing the tower of the church into silhouette and an eerie silvery glow over the monastery wall and grounds. The image of the monk standing stiffly in the garden was retained for an instant in my mind and it made my spine shiver. I stood in the dark expecting at any moment to hear a banshee wail, but it never came. Banshees were female. There wasn't a single banshee in the whole of Mount Athos.

It was still dark when I left Iviron the next morning at about six, though time was hard to tell as all of the monastery's clocks were wrong. My destination was the Monastery of Simon Petras, ten miles away over the mountain and on the other coast, where the ferryman had said there was a resident English monk. The walk took most of the day because the peacefulness, crops of wild blackberries and the splendid views made destinations seem unimportant. This changed, however, when Simon Petras came into view. It had the most dramatic setting of all the monasteries and the furthest to fall. The building was six storeys high, painted a dull white and it perched half on a crag and half off, its foundations on three sides dropping 200 feet to the base of the rock. A typical assortment of balconies ran around the upper reaches and on a few of these some monks were visible gazing at the void below their feet. Judging from the angle of their habits, a breeze at sea level was gale force six in the heights of Simon Petras. Below the monastery terraced fields and gardens fell away steeply to the sea.

The community of monks here seemed younger and friendlier, even though I had no right to expect friendliness when I must have been interrupting their spiritual pursuits. A glass of ouzo, a cup of coffee and a piece of Turkish Delight were placed on a table before me, and a few minutes later a tall thin man in his late twenties approached. He was dressed in customary black but his wild beard was unusual for being ginger. He spoke in Greek but quickly switched to English.

'Father Isaiah,' he said, and added with a smile, 'as in the prophet.' We shook hands and he invited me over to some chairs on a parapet. He had joined the Order many years earlier but had only recently given up his job as an underwriter with Lloyds and come to Mount Athos, having applied from his home in the Midlands and been accepted after a probational period. From where we were sitting a monk was visible as a speck far below through a gap in the floorboards.

'Do you feel safe up here?' I asked.

'It does take a little getting used to especially when earth tremors are not uncommon in these parts. We had one lasting twelve seconds a few weeks back, but it is written that earthquakes will never damage us. Fire is our biggest worry. Twice in our history we have been burnt down.' He related that the last fire had occurred in 1821 when the Abbot was in Russia collecting alms. The news reached him while he was returning so he ordered the ship about and went straight back. He collected money for four more years and raised four times the amount needed to rebuild the monastery. Some of the excess had been invested in property in Athens and this was still an important source of revenue. 'Simon Petras is relatively prosperous compared to others on Mount Athos but we are still desperately short of money to do all the necessary repairs.'

He explained that the European Economic Community had immediately recognised the state as a unique cultural and spiritual centre when Greece became a member and had given considerable financial support. As a result of Greek politics and internal wrangling the distribution of the EEC grant had been unequal and this had caused much ill-feeling. Since then a central body had been set up to administer future grants fairly and to allocate the revenue from visitors to the monasteries that incur costs by receiving them. The monasteries were otherwise self-supporting. The Greek government had seldom shown any concern for Mount Athos and what offers of assistance had been given imposed the obligation to open up for tourism.

Tourism had driven the monks away from Meteora, another region of imposing monasteries in central Greece, and Mount Athos was anxious to avoid the same fate. And yet the ease with which he talked and anticipated questions indicated he was used to visitors. I asked if their (really meaning *my*) intrusion was currently a problem.

'Every year we grit our teeth and bear the onslaught as best we can. So far this summer we've had over one thousand visitors to Simon Petras and often our thirty beds have been full. We like receiving those who come for spiritual guidance and who are genuinely interested in our buildings and history, but many use us for a cheap holiday. Some even complain about the service!'

There were 1500 monks on Mount Athos and about 1000 others. Most lived in the monasteries, some in sketes – holy villages – several hundred in hermitages and a few in 'hollow trees and caves'. Father Isaiah said he could live in a tree if he wanted to but he would have to convince his Abbot that it was necessary for his spiritual development. Simon Petras had sixty monks but some were associates and lived abroad. Many monasteries were having trouble finding recruits and an average of only two or three monks entered Mount Athos each year.

I inquired about the 110 year-old monks at Iviron.

'Yes, they are all very old there. Iviron is one of several that are idiorythmic. They don't have an Abbot and all monks have an equal share in running the monastery. They are allocated their own money and jobs, and work independently of each other. The idea is to give an individual greater freedom to find a routine that suits his own particular spiritual needs. We are cenobitic which is the traditional

system and the most common. We have an Abbot and a hierarchy of
elders to govern the monastery. It is the better system as we work
together and create a closer community. When I go to Iviron I notice
at once that their independence makes them colder and no one takes
on responsibility for looking after visitors. It's true that everything
works but I feel it is a shell without a soul. And young monks are just
not attracted to the idiorythmic system. I don't know what will
happen with Iviron.'

'Does your routine follow the clock? I haven't seen one yet that
shows the correct time.'

His tone was charitable. 'That's because we work on Byzantine
time, not that of mainland Greece. We are four hours ahead of the
Greek clock.' His day began at midnight (4 a.m. Byzantine) which
was regarded as sunset. He got up and spent some time praying and
resting. At 3 a.m. (7 a.m. Byz) he went to the main service which
lasted four hours. He returned to his cell and continued praying and
resting until the first meal at 10.30 a.m. After that he went to work.
His job was attending to visitors' accommodation and he would do
this for a year until jobs were reallocated by rotation. Some monks
kept their jobs if they had a special skill. Monks originally from the
country usually made better gardeners and fishermen while city
monks tended towards administrative work. At 5 p.m. he attended
Vespers for an hour and then came the second and last meal of the
day. For the rest of the evening he was free (no talking permitted
after 10 p.m.) until 11.30 when there was a final short service.

'But when do you sleep?

'We get about six hours, interrupted and at different times, but it is
enough. You get used to it.'

'Can you change to another monastery or leave altogether?'

'Yes, the option is available but generally when you join a
monastery, you stay for life.'

'You make it sound like a sentence . . . does it ever seem that
way?'

'No, of course not. We see it as our vocation. We all have had the
chance to think about ourselves and our lives before coming here.
We are all here by choice. Come, I'll show you where I'll end up.'
From the balcony he pointed to a small chapel and shed on the slope
down to the sea. He explained that they had a small cemetery there
with five graves. Because Simon Petras had a high proportion of

young monks there was concern about how they would cope with the expected burial problem in forty or fifty years time when many would be dying. As a result of this pragmatic foresight they were about to extend the cemetery. 'We bury bodies for three years then dig up the bones and lay them in the charnel-house beside the chapel. We don't have much room for graves and besides, we believe this way shows more respect. When the soul leaves the body we have no more use for that body but because it has carried the soul for so long, we believe it deserves respect. So we place the bones together with those of our past brothers. If the soul ever wants to, it can find its own bones amongst them. That's where I'll be put one day.'

'I can't think of a more beautiful place to end up,' I said. 'The view is stunning.

A smile parted his beard. 'Yes, but it's a bit late for views when you've passed on.'

We were interrupted by a monk hammering on a symendra, a wooden plank which he balanced on one shoulder. It was the call to Vespers. Father Isaiah begged to be excused and calmly vanished into the hinterland of stairs and passages.

In common with St Katharine's Monastery in the Sinai, this building was a labyrinth but by chance I came to the chapel just before the service began. An English visitor, who I later learnt was called Harold, was at the doorway talking to a monk. Harold was in his fifties and a devout Anglican.

'Orthodox?' the monk asked.

'Anglican,' Harold replied. The monk frowned and hmmmmed. '*High* Anglican,' Harold added decisively. The monk continued to frown and hmmmmmmmmmed for longer. Then he ushered us into a back room with a view through the main door. Harold was obviously affronted but he said nothing and we sat down. The Great Schism in the Church that split Roman Catholicism from Eastern Orthodoxy in 1054 and resulted in both excommunicating the other for 911 years, had not healed. Catholicism was nevertheless tolerated but Protestantism was regarded as degenerate. We could see monks kissing the icons on the walls as they entered the chapel and then sitting down, never crossing their legs at the knees as this was in some way of sacrilegious through association with the posture of crucifixion. Above me were frescos that mixed Tolkien's dragons with the hell of Hieronymus Bosch. Close to my nose was a flying

maiden whose lower half was a scorpion's tail. There was much I
didn't understand.

Vespers was followed by the evening meal. Simon Petras enjoyed
richer fare than Iviron and delicious vegetable soup, bread, olives,
fruit and a glass of red wine were consumed silently while a monk
read from the Scriptures. The atmosphere was less solemn the next
morning when breakfast was provided for guests at a separate
sitting. Harold hadn't appeared and there were only three Greeks
talking quietly when I took my place. A fourth Greek entered, an
extrovert character who spoke some German-English, and sat down
beside me. I was sipping some herbal tea when he turned to me.

'Orthodox?' he asked.

'Non-aligned,' I replied. He took this to mean Protestant.

'Ach!' he scorned. 'Protestants is *nichts. Nichts, nichts, nichts.*' He
took out a piece of paper, drew a circle and wrote 'Orthodox' in the
centre. Then he drew four arrows like compass points and labelled
them Catholics, Protestants and two undecipherables. 'Orthodox is
. . .' He raised his hands and eyes to the ceiling and adored. After this
he stubbed his finger hard on the other names and repeated '*nichts*'. I
took his bit of paper, drew a straight line with Orthodox, Catholics,
Protestants and two undecipherables on the level underneath and
then ran a line up from each to the single word 'God'. But he waved
the paper away. He wasn't interested in discussing, just in preaching
– and he'd finished. He leant forward with a smile on his face to attack
the food. Soon he was tearing in with both hands. I passed him the
water jug and he stopped gorging himself for a moment to accept it.
Having breakfast with a bigot makes you feel very holy.

I was sorry when my time on Mount Athos came to an end.
The scenery and extraordinary buildings were only a part of this
peninsula's powerful charm. More mysterious, and more alluring,
was the profound sanctity that made me feel an unwilling outsider.
Even for a non-Orthodox it was a place of calming. As Mount Athos
faded from view I caught a glimpse of two black figures standing
high above their fortress wall on a wilting balcony. Dolphins and
flying fish led the boat back to the outer world, and for the first time
in five days I thought of home.

18 · Home: A View with a Room

Things were looking black, one of those rare moments when there was a possibility I might not make it after all. At first there seemed little danger, just the discomfort of the cold but as the minutes went by my doubts increased. What a way to end a journey. 191,000 miles down, almost home, only to end up being slowly calcified into a stalagmite. The *drip, drip, drip* on my head was constant no matter which way I leant and each splash redefined the shape of my skull with its seeping coldness. I began to sing but only timidly. An echo would have been entertaining, even reassuring, but the unseen depths of the cavern absorbed my voice into the darkness and this shrank me further into my isolation. My camera case provided an adequate seat but sitting meant that my kilt failed to cover the ends of my knees and the cold drips found them too. My only consolation was the thought that at least I would make an unusual stalagmite.

The cave was only two hours from the Greek port of Igoumenitsa on the west coast, and from there daily ferries left for Italy. My kilt had been waiting poste restante on my return from Mount Athos and had been an invaluable aid for three weeks of hitching around the country. It had taken several days for me to adjust to wearing a kilt again and to lose my initial feelings of self-consciousness (as well as the smell of mothballs). It was back to the standard reactions; nudges, whispered alerts, conversations choked, long stares, be-wilderment, embarrassment, scorn, or friendly smiles, waves and calls of "'allo Scotia!' which made all the others bearable. Psychologically humans have suffered a messy evolution but I had forgotten how additionally intriguing and unpredictable they are when seen from inside a kilt. Wearing a kilt abroad certainly prevents one from taking life too seriously for it comes needing a pinch of salt and good humour, whether or not one feels like salting and humouring.

My experiences in the region of Olympia were cases in point. A group of redundant men sitting outside a café had greeted my appearance with a roar of derision. This had hurt me at the time but the only sensible recourse was to nod in a courteous, orthodox way while walking by and imagine the whole group on pedestals at a coconut shy. Then later the same afternoon a similar incident had happened only it was a woman who shouted the derogatory remarks and raised a laugh from her neighbours. On this occasion a man emerging from a gate in a high wall had come to my defence and spoken to her so sharply that she had blushed and hurried away.

'You must excuse her,' he had said in fluent English. 'She was making fun of you and saying you were wearing a woman's skirt. It is simply ignorance.'

'Thank you for your support. But what did you say to her? She turned bright red.'

'I reminded her that the Greek national costume is almost identical. Had she forgotten that her father had also worn a "skirt"? Had she laughed at him? . . . '

And it was true. I had seen Greek kilts worn by guards outside the Tomb of the Unknown Soldier in Athens. They were pleated all the way round and worn over woolly white tights with black garters criss-crossed up to the knees. The kilts were a little on the brief side and rather plain in self-coloured fawn (and the accompanying red shoes with a huge black pompom over the toes would not have been my choice) but I had nevertheless felt the affinity of our respective costumes and the shared blue and white of our national flags.

'Your hitching is not going too well, is it?' this man had commented after we had been talking on the roadside for thirty minutes.

'No. At least not at the moment.' In this respect *his* appearance had not helped my chances for he was a doctor in white overalls and stood holding a tray of syringes and a full specimen bottle. But my choice of a place to wait had also been at fault, unwittingly, because behind us was the establishment where he worked. Prisons make notoriously poor sites for hitching. Apart from on this one afternoon the reaction to my kilt had generally been very favourable and hitching had run smoothly as far as my present predicament in the cave at Perama.

It was to have been a quick visit. I entered the cave behind a flock of nuns on a guided tour. They made a noisy procession; off-duty nuns show appreciation even for the smallest things of creation, and Perama Cave is enormous. The guide led us into an underground passage half a mile long which periodically expanded into caverns and was a maze of paths winding through floodlit stalagmites. His discourse was in Greek and not being able to understand, I soon got bored and wandered on alone. Twenty minutes later I was ambling along admiring the weird multitude of limestone daggers held above my head and feeling secure in the knowledge that I was ahead of the group, when all the lights went out. I didn't dare move. The darkness was absolute. The path had no handrail and twisted and turned illogically amongst hunks of rocks, pools of water and chasms. The nuns had disappeared and there was silence except for the *drip, drip, drip* that I had barely noticed before. Now it seemed very loud. Was it a power cut? What if they had closed for the weekend? I would have to spend thirty-six hours down here. I had felt cold right from the start and soon the drips had wet my hair, my knees and were saturating my thin jersey. My pack was hidden in some bushes outside so that wouldn't help to raise the alarm. I began to shiver intentionally to generate some warmth, and sang to raise my spirits but I didn't like the sound of my voice, nor what happened to it.

Alone, lost and made helpless by five useless senses, I tried to count my blessings but couldn't get beyond three: being alive, uninjured and of reasonably sound mind. My reasonably sound mind turned to other things that had become wearisome or objects of longing after five years as an orphan of the road. Some were absurdly trivial but had assumed disproportionate importance. I was looking forward to morning mail, out-of-the-blue visits from friends, a visible product resulting from my daily output of energy, a choice of clothes that would enable me to look my best, just for a while, and I was longing to write my first personal cheque because the thought of satisfying payment with a scrawled signature seemed a remarkable privilege. These were all related in some way to a diminished sense of identity, no easy factor to maintain on a long journey. At times I had to think hard to remember my name. It was of no more use to me than letters on a passport. No one ever called it across a room or a street, though 'Alstjar' had come close, because I lived in a world of anonymous people. Frequent casual acquaintances helped to compensate for the scarcity of deep friendships but there were still periods when my social life appeared overwhelmingly monastic. I was tiring of leading a scrimping existence attached to a backpack, hunting for hostel beds or dry patches of ground, grappling with the basics of languages too numerous to learn and being confined to the framework of my mother-tongue, stripped of colour and vitality. Lone travel could seem a selfish world of more opportunities to take than give, an abdication of responsibility and diaries excessively filled with first-person pronouns. My travelling had never been intended as an escape but at that moment it seemed to have become one, a bad one, and I wanted to regain the self and security that had been left behind.

And yet things weren't so bad when compared to the alternatives. Most of my longings could be dismissed either because they were of no more substance than novelty value or because they resulted from being jaded and were nothing that a week of change would not cure. Grass-root travel was often both mentally and physically demanding but it had undoubtedly provided me with my deepest insights and most memorable adventures. There was no more representative level for sampling a country and its people. Missing family and friends was an unavoidable part of journeying but absence in itself did not sever the bonds of special relationships, and travel brought many new ones. Travel was not all take, it was constantly giving though not always in physical terms. It was an exchange of views and trust, a widening of vision for all parties and in these respects it entailed responsibility. And gradually, deep in my cave, my perspective reverted to the attitude that had sustained me for five years. I didn't see this period as a block of weeks and months as others would but as a capricious ramble which had crossed six continents and put 1¼ million words in my diary and 17,000 photographs through my camera. The road had not orphaned me, but adopted me. Its frustrations were trivial and no more than those found at fixed addresses. I was happy in this lifestyle. Suddenly it seemed easier to go on travelling. I needed very little. My earnings from jobs along the way had always been sufficient to cover my costs, so why not continue in the same way? I could take a plane and start a new journey in Indonesia tomorrow. The realisation that one didn't have to travel for four years to reach Indonesia at first seemed unfair but then it opened up all sorts of fabulous travel plans . . . I was having cold feet about returning home.

I was cold all over now and shivering involuntarily. It had been at least forty minutes since the cave had been plunged into darkness and I got to my feet to stamp up some warmth. Suddenly the lights went on. I hurried along the paths in case it was only a temporary measure, through cavern after cavern until a series of arrows guided me to the exit. The nuns must have taken a shorter route and left the cave before the lights had gone out. A side door led me out into the warm sunlight and railings channelled me back to the main entrance where the custodian was surprised to see me. I asked what had happened. He pointed at some notices. I had already read the first two – 'Breaking the stalagmites is Panished', 'Please don't walk out the path' – but the third was in Greek.

He translated it for me. 'Visitors may only enter Perama Cave with a guide. Between guided tours the lights will be turned off.'

I had never come across Italians in such quantities before as on the ferry from Igoumenitsa to Otranto, a loose tack in Italy's heel. Like the Chinese, their preferred elements are noise and bustle. I had thought the wild gesticulations accredited to them as a national characteristic were exaggerated but it transpired they were understated. Theirs is the only language to be simultaneously spoken and mimed, and in the ship's canteen it looked a pointless exercise asking for the salt-cellar to be passed along a table-length of talking Italians. No people are more vivacious and the intensity with which they live can only be admired, unsalted tagliatelle notwithstanding.

The next two weeks passed quickly and I covered the remaining 3071 miles to Calais in exactly eighty lifts. One of the longest was with a New Zealand couple originally from Scotland and it lasted several days as our destinations were the same. First came Pompeii and seeing this old town which Vesuvius had suddenly buried in A D 79 fulfilled a modest ambition of mine, but replaced it with disappointment. Half the ruins were fenced off and the weeds grew chest high. The last earthquake to shake Pompeii (1980) had left an attitude worse than apathy, that of intended neglect, and the impression that in twenty years archaeologists would have to be sent in to rediscover its houses, erotic signs and paved streets rutted by Roman chariots.

Jim put me in charge of map-reading from Pompeii to the capital because Marge, his wife, tended to confuse lefts and rights, but I found it almost impossible to cope with a tagliatelle road system.

'Did you see which way to go?' I asked at one particularly bad tangle.

'Listen, Jimmy,' replied Jim, reverting to his native Glaswegian and its simplified nomenclature of the species, 'there's nae need tae worry. A' roads lead tae Rome.'

There seemed to be a lot of truth in this. The choice was the length of auto-tagliatelle that took you there and we managed to find a fairly short one although it increased its loops near the end. Rome soon convinced me it was the most beautiful and fascinating city I had seen, and a ruthlessly efficient jay-walkers' abattoir.

It was a marble city. Marble was everywhere, sandwiching the River Tiber and encasing the seven hills. Marble ran throughout the interior of St Peter's, from its necropolis where an empty sarcophagus had already been inscribed with the name of the current Pope and the first of his dates, to the dome but excluding four public lavatories of a man-made material which stood tall like sentry boxes on the roof. (If you peeped through the minute windows in these toelette you could look down on the streets of Rome, their names carved in polished marble, and on the predatory traffic amongst which even the smallest Fiats, reduced by distance to a scale of motorised rice crispies, were rounding corners on two wheels as they hunted for pedestrians.)

Jim hadn't been allowed into St Peter's for wearing shorts and so Marge and I met him outside the Vatican where he was trying to photograph some Swiss guards. A baggy beret sat severely askew on their heads and they wore knickerbockers made of red, blue and yellow ribbons loosely attached top and bottom so that they bulged and contracted each time the guards moved. The risk of indecency seemed sufficient to keep them motionless until their reliefs arrived, and to ensure a quick change-over. They were touchy about having their uniforms photographed and Jim was rudely ordered to go away. I understood how they felt but thought they would have realised how futile it is getting annoyed when you're wearing something unusual, particularly red, blue and yellow striped knickerbockers.

Vatican City (108.7 acres) was similar to most independent states in having its own citizenship, currency, stamps, newspaper, railway station and radio transmitter (Pius XI asked Marconi to instal the first one) but its art galleries were almighty. Outside the state walls we passed street confessionals, nuns with a million plastic crucifixes to sell and lines of beggars whose outstretched arms tried to reach the constant coming and going of the clergy. Everyone wanted a share in the Vatican's wealth. Along with at least 20,000 others that day we paid our 1750 lira (£1) entry fee and chose a self-guided tour from markers offering from one to five hours, when five days would have been more realistic to appreciate this art collection. The world's richest treasure house held miles of palatial corridors that were in themselves exhibitions of inlaid marble, stucco-work and murals by the thousand. Here were to be found statues by the most celebrated sculptors sometimes rising six rows high along both walls, countless tapestries and paintings of incomparable expertise, artefacts of genius in gold, silver, ivory and everything else that can be studded with percious stones. Such was the concentration of objects that the display had the crush of an overloaded attic and every second step served as a layman's guide to masterpiece. It was overwhelming, and marvellous to find such a wealth of possessions in one place. It just struck me as odd that it should be in the Vatican.

Near the end of our tour we would have fallen into a deep pit had it not been for a grid. We peered down into the hole and watched a priest wading through a pile of lira as he swept up the donations with a broom. Then we paused by a plaque underneath a tapestry which explained that each square meter represented three years labour for four pairs of hands. Jim was suffering from a surfeit of magnificence by this stage. He didn't even look at the tapestry but reread the plaque out aloud.

'Hear that, Jimmy? Jist like the roads back hame, eh?'

Jim and Marge took me to Assisi where our routes diverged, and let me out beside its cathedral which reared up like a three-dimensional zebra crossing. I hitched on by way of Florence and Venice and vowed in each that I had found the world's most beautiful city. Hitching became erratic in a corner of Yugoslavia where the people could be forgiven for not knowing who they were for they had been Austrian up to the First World War and Italian until the Second. The Austrian border also seemed to have cut through a mode of life and my eagerness to speak German with the people south of Klagenfurt was confounded by some Slavonic tongue. It rained during my night in Vienna woods, Munich was under siege by festival-goers who regarded beer-swilling as a holy mission . . . and so soon I found myself at Calais, tired, excited, anxious, slightly stained with Somme battlefield mud and clutching a ferry ticket to the fifty-third country of the trip.

It was a stormy crossing and spray lashed the ship's windows. The White Cliffs were not visible until we docked. I was first to disembark and place my feet in an English puddle being dimpled by rain. The immigration officer examined my passport briefly, smiled and let me pass. My patched and mistreated kilt caught the eye of a customs officer, John De . . . (the rest was hidden under his lapel), on the fringe of the green zone. He beckoned me over.

'Have you anything to declare?' he asked.

'Only that I'm back.'

John De . . . sighed and rephrased the question with painful exactness. He was obviously used to such tedious little quips. ('I have nothing to declare but my genius.' Oscar Wilde.) He gave a quick rummage through my pack.

'Don't you have any duty-free at all?'

'No.' I had got out of the habit of carrying unnecessary luggage except for a universal bathplug which had acquired sentimental value because of its uselessness.

He too let me pass. I was surrounded by English-speakers. The subtleties of speech were open to me again, notices were comprehensible and billboards advertised familiar products. I left the terminal and wanted to dance, to celebrate no longer being an absent person, to mark the end of a self-imposed exile that had lasted exactly one week short of five years. Elation seized my body but my legs refused to dance because they were weighed down with the rest of me, sixty pounds of essentials and one universal bathplug. The pavement tapered into a grass verge and ended abruptly at NO PEDESTRIANS. I ignored the order. No sign was going to ruin my return by telling me I couldn't walk on my own homeland. Quarter of a mile later I paused to jot a few thoughts down on a scrap of paper when an empty bus pulled up beside me.

'Whereyeforemate?'

'London.'

''op in, then.' It was lift number 3154, and I hadn't even been hitching. We drove on the wrong side of the motorway the whole way. The fields were the greenest I had seen since New Zealand. What would a Mexican bull bound for the arena or an Indian cow bound to a lawn-mower give to be an indolent Friesian munching a trail through Britain? Many of the cars looked new and there was no shortage of them at petrol stations now asking £1.65 for the gallon that had last cost me seventy-four pence. I asked the driver how much a pint of beer cost now.

'Varies. 'bout sixty-eight.'

At the start of my trip one pound would have bought four and half pints and left one penny change.

On the approach to London it came as a surprise to see so many individual houses instead of the blocks of flats that introduce most of the world's cities. My knowledge of London had been gleaned from postcards, Monopoly boards and one day of sole-splitting sight-seeing and so it should have appeared as just another large strange city. Yet I felt a strong sense of belonging in London. I suddenly found myself noticing things not because they were different but because they were indirectly familiar. It was a new sensation to be constantly reminded of my own background. There were all the things I wanted to find, from institutions to eccentricity; red double-decker buses, red letter boxes and phone booths, runaway dog-walkers, Pig and Whistle pubs with a veneer of the past over everything except their prices, the honesty of milk bottles on doorsteps, the *clink* of the milkman putting them there and the curiosity of passersby using them as indicators of who was lying in, an old woman in a park scolding individual ducks for being greedy and upsetting the fair distribution of a crust among the flock, unarmed policemen, orderly bus queues, the stiff upper locks of punks in shrieking colours and the stiff upper lips of those sufficient-ly aghast to give a sideways glance, one-and-a-half-window shops with their trivial but soul-stroking chitchat; every second pace revealed something homely or masterfully British.

Simply being back provided hours of entertainment and it was late at night when I decided to sleep rough somewhere and hitch up north the following day. At the back of the Grosvenor Hotel there was a suitable spot but it was already occupied by another dosser. I stepped over him and went up some steps to sleep on a landing. A notice by my head read 'Single Rooms £38'. It probably would have read '£10' if this had been the first night of my trip.

On the way north I was enchanted by hedges, winding lanes, village cricket greens, gardens still fussy with colours even though it was autumn and trees were yellowing, and miles of drystane dykes. Nothing could spoil my delight, not even the factory-scapes aban-doned as the detritus of revolution, the abundance of litter, the madder stampede of traffic and service stations where 'medium' had been reclassified as 'gigantic'. Gradually the countryside became more familiar as distance fell away in the company of a long-haul truck driver.

'You can always tell when you're in Scotland,' he observed, 'as the houses are smaller and neater, made of real stone and have a nice solid look about them.'

'I hadn't noticed that before. Towns had grown a bit bigger and some had been bypassed by roads that now ran straighter. Otherwise it was only the different prices that made me feel a stranger.

My pack had never felt lighter than during my walk through the centre of Edinburgh. I hurried round corners merely for the joy of confirming that I knew what lay beyond them. The back street shop that had made my kilt was still in business but it was closed. Just as well. The aged kiltmaker would have been horrified to have seen what had happened to his handiwork. Opposite was a bakery with trays of irresistible pastries and dainties, and I went in before broaching the final 150 miles that would take my journey full circle to the Spey Valley.

Behind the counter was a cheerful and endearing old lady, of the type to scold ducks for the good of others. Her tongs duplicated my finger movements behind the glass showcase and skimmed over chocolate éclairs, coconut snowballs and sickly cubes of pink and green cake. She noticed I was slightly tanned and asked if I had been abroad. I explained briefly. She raised her eyebrows momentarily but was preoccupied with the vanilla slices which were proving elusive. I could picture her in Greenland selling whale, or in Costa Rica over a pile of pineapples, or dressed her in a Mao blue uniform and she would have fitted into China. Guidebooks to the world take hundreds of pages to tell us how each part is different and in what way its culture is unique, which it may be, but behind the disguises its people are none other than ourselves.

'Well, well! Five years!' she mused, grasping a vanilla slice in triumph. 'And have you had a nice time?'

My kilt hangs undisturbed in a cupboard worrying only about moths, and my boots, the same second-hand pair from Australia, stand underneath and slant away from each other at peculiar angles. And I sit at a desk frequently looking up from my writing to gaze at the mountains that fill the view from my window. Now we are on the west coast, opposite Skye, and my universal bathplug is as valuable as ever because my current abode has no bath. If we travelled hopefully, we were fortunate to arrive content. The Highlands of Scotland and their constantly changing moods can hold someone accustomed to a constantly changing view.

In summer the mountains were mellowed by the greenness that clamours around the dull sweeps of heather. In autumn they pouted their richest and subtlest hues, the heather blooming purple, bracken faltering between green and gold, moorland grasses adding fawn and rowan trees splashing forebodings in red. Now, in winter, the mountains look lean and austere, their colours have darkened and rocks protrude from their sides like ribs. Soon the snows will come and deer will gather on their south-facing slopes to scratch at the less frozen ground.

The surface of the sea changes hourly and its edges never tire of conjuring up rocks, sand banks and islands and making them disappear again, clouds rise and fall as if toying with the idea of creating a new horizon, mist sometimes lingers thoughtfully but seldom for long, and the intensity of light is never the same but varies from the soft glow of evening to the strong beams that interrupt storms and move mysteriously across the land selecting features to spotlight. The vegetation and climate lend my view its inconsistent and abstracting quality but what makes it so alluring to me are its wildness, emptiness and grandeur.

Yes, we are wholly content. My boots and kilt may nevertheless like to know what my atlas is doing on the windowsill. It lies open at page fifty-seven, a place none of us has yet visited.